SUBJECT SIXTY-SEVEN

JASON ANDREWS

For Brian and Alex.

"A brother is a gift to the heart, a friend to the spirit" ~ Unknown

Produced by Aurodonnan Media

ISBN: 978-1-7321214-3-0

PART ONE

A FEW OLD THREADS

A GODDESS AMONG US
A Hero Is Born From Poseidon's Wrath

By May Patsiavas, Metro Inquirer Opinion Columnist

The world as we knew it is gone forever.

It was less than a week ago that the National Oceanic and Atmospheric Administration (NOAA) issued its first warning that the Storm of the Century, perhaps of the Millennium, would make landfall in southern Virginia and travel deep into the Carolinas. Evacuation orders were issued. Emergency plans were put into motion.

But then, to stand a turn of phrase on its head, everything went *north*.

Hurricane Clarice threaded the needle of the Chesapeake Bay as a Category Three, picking up speed and ferocity before she invaded our nation's capital as a Category Five. Later, a NOAA spokesperson said, "Category Five doesn't accurately describe this monstrosity. This one was off the charts. We're in the process of re-evaluating our hurricane threat levels as global climate change continues to worsen."

It was the mighty breath of Clarice that extinguished the cap of the Washington Monument like a toddler blowing out a birthday candle. The top third of the old sandstone structure withered before her, cracking and crumbling in her wake. The destruction was unprecedented in the history of our sacred monument, in the history of our young nation.

Yet there was no worldly precedent for what came next. Or rather, *who* came next.

"She flew out of nowhere and started tossing around huge chunks of the monument like they were nothing but plastic toys," said Lieutenant Bertram, a D.C. Metro Police officer who was called to the National Mall that night. "And when I say she flew, I mean she was flying. On my word as a police officer, she was flying."

Office Bertram later retracted his comments ahead of the release of an official statement from D.C. Metro Police. But there were other witnesses.

Hayward Browers, an elevator technician who was working in the monument that night, had this to say:

"I knew I wasn't supposed to be in there during the storm, but our team was behind schedule and they said it was going to hit far to the south anyway. I could feel the entire monument swaying. Then the lightning hit. Before I knew it, I got buried by falling debris. Crushed ribs and everything. Couldn't breathe. I thought I was a goner, and then the rubble just lost its weight. It dispersed and I was looking up at this dark [silhouette]. A girl. A young woman, I mean. Long, wet hair blowing around like crazy. She grabbed me and Jensen, who I didn't even know had been buried with me, like we weighed nothing and lifted us out of there. I mean to say that she *flew* us out of there, down to the ground. Down to safety. Then she went back up to rescue Gales and Delgado. I'm telling you, there were no cables, no ropes, no nothing holding her up. No tricks. I've never seen anything like it except in movies and comic books when I was a kid."

Hayward's account matches that of a dozen other workers, officers, and bystanders that happened to be caught near the Washington Monument when Hurricane Clarice altered course and blew into town. There are other stories making the rounds as well, all equally miraculous. A family's story of their minivan being plucked from the churning waters of the Potomac, for example.

But we'll save those yarns for when I spin a later column.

There is such a thing as a shared delusion, an event that grows in grandeur as it is repeated. Sometimes people simply want a good story to tell, to be a part of something larger than themselves. They begin to believe their own tales in the retelling. Video was taken of the event and broadcast on news networks and social media channels, but video can be manipulated. It is up to us to make up our own minds in this day and age. To interpret truth from fiction.

I will say this, however. I was stuck in traffic on the 14th Street bridge that fateful evening. I saw a figure streak across the sky against the backdrop of sequential flashes of lightning. It was too small for an aircraft yet too large for a bird.

Am I caught up in this mass hysteria as well? Am I risking my journalistic integrity by perpetuating it? Time will tell.

Daughter of Poseidon, if you're out there, if you're real, know that you've changed the course of human history forever. The world as we knew it is gone.

But I, for one, welcome the new one.

Chapter One

HE HAD DAVID'S EYES. The conclusion couldn't be contested.

"I'll be damned," David whispered to himself, backing his head away from the rifle scope for another wide-angle view of the situation that hadn't changed in the last ten minutes.

An ideal search and rescue operation would allow for a thorough reconnaissance that would shape the plan and dictate the terms of the mission's execution. There was no time for that now. Ten minutes had already been too long, despite the fact that he had made the trip from Washington D.C. to Charlottesville in record time, the heavy panic in his gut oozing into his right foot to weigh down the accelerator pedal with relentless desperation. If the Virginia State Trooper he had passed had been going in the same direction, David's mission would have ended in Culpeper.

He poked a finger into his shirt and drew the tip across the Steyr's scope lens to wipe away the condensation that gathered there, then put his eye to it once more.

There were two of them. One inside the house with Elyse and another in the backyard with Duncan. Tony's agents waited for instructions that would never come, unless the shattered skull of their deceased supervisor somehow reassembled itself and breathed life back into the still lungs of its corpse long enough to find a phone and make the call that would put a horrifying end to David's estranged family.

But were they his family? Could he—should he—call them that? Or was David's family hiding in an Alexandria hotel room, waiting for confirmation that his plan had succeeded. Waiting for him to tell them what to do next.

Or was his family soaring through the skies over D.C., using her supernatural gifts to convince the military that she wasn't a menace, that she had a place in this world just as much as they did?

His hand moved to the bolt mechanism for a third time, but a round was already chambered and had been for a while. Indecision ate away at time he didn't have. David saw several avenues of approach, but none of them ended without Elyse dead or his son scarred for life—or the inverse of that scenario. Post traumatic stress was a tenacious companion that David had never fully accepted into his life, despite the wishes of therapists and fellow veterans whom had begged him to do so. It was something that he would never inflict upon Duncan or Elyse if he could help it. Elyse would have a hard enough time trying to come to terms with the fact that she and her son had been taken captive in their own home. That is, of course, if she lived long enough to have a chance to cope with the fallout of her situation.

David's jaw clenched. He was determined to give her that chance. Her and Duncan both.

It appeared that the agent watching over David's son was a comedian, as evidenced by Duncan's fits of laughter. They sat at a kid-sized picnic table of blue and yellow plastic, Duncan eating an ice cream cone despite the chill of the November night. The porch light mounted above the back door of the house fell over the frozen treat—mint chocolate chip, from the looks of it—and highlighted the drippings that ran in sugary rivulets over the child's small fingers. Tony's man had no doubt been introduced as "Mommy's friend" or "Mommy's cousin" or some other nonsense, and had ingratiated himself with David's son while he awaited further orders. David wondered if the agent was keeping it clean or was reciting the filthy nursery rhymes of Andrew Dice Clay. He resisted the urge to deprive the joker of his punch line with a simple squeeze of the trigger. But no, to see Mommy's old high school chum's head explode from a .243 Winchester round at three hundred and thirty-eight yards would put a serious roadblock in Duncan's developmental journey into healthy adulthood.

A narrow slit in the window curtains allowed only momentary glimpses of Elyse's slender form as she moved about the kitchen, no doubt struggling to maintain a calm demeanor while checking on her son as often as possible. A husky man walked through David's field of vision, retrieving something from the pocket of his khaki blazer. He paced back and forth, crossing David's line of sight several times before slipping the object back into his pocket. Chalky, blue smoke drifted past the window. Then Elyse was there, pointing to the front door.

David drew back from the rifle scope and blinked in amazement. Was a seasoned intelligence agent trained in combat, espionage, counter-terrorism and who knows what else really going to be shamed into taking his cigarette outside at the insistence of the very person he had been ordered to keep captive?

David could hardly wait to find out. This could be his chance.

He scrambled from his rooftop sniper's nest, not caring about stealth in his haste to descend to the earth. He had eyeballed the house from the online map, selecting it for its strategic proximity to Elyse's home rather than its current occupancy. He was pretty sure no one was home, but couldn't be certain. It didn't matter. David intended to end this before any cop could respond to a suburban family's concern about noises on their roof.

David skirted the broad circumference of the street light as he made his way around the corner of the house and into the hedges of another property. He crouched in the darkness and pressed his eye to the scope, maneuvering the sniper rifle's tip into position with calm efficiency. The front door of Elyse's modest, ranch-style home was cracked open less than a foot to emit plumes of cigarette smoke. It would seem that Tony's goon had managed to obey the homeowner's directive while maintaining the upper hand. He wasn't outside, but at least had the decency to aim his exhales in that direction.

Unfortunately for David, there was no clear shot. Urgency blossomed anew.

"To hell with this," he muttered, sliding the Steyr into a makeshift cradle of juniper branches and emerging from the bushes in a full sprint.

He reached the front door in the span of seven heartbeats and maintained his momentum through the completion of his front snap kick. Smoker had just flicked the butt of his cigarette onto the decorative lava rocks that served as the beds for Elyse's low-maintenance landscaping efforts when David's heel connected with the door just below the tarnished brass knob. The inertia blasted the door into the man's jowled face even as he exhaled his last lungful of tar-laden vapor. The crunch of nasal cartilage and bone was dampened by the surprised yelp from Elyse, but David heard it. He felt it too. He growled as he used Smoker's momentary disorientation to seize the man's ears and jerk downward while bringing his knee to bear with a ferocity that finished the impromptu nasal surgery with fatal result.

David had moved past his stunned ex-fiancé before the body hit the floor.

"Get out."

His voice was cool, centered. Elyse didn't move.

David dropped to a knee, ducking below the tiled countertop to the right of the kitchen access door that led to the back yard.

"Circle around and get the boy," he said.

Elyse didn't move. The doorknob turned with a click. There was no time for further instruction.

Comedian entered the house with focused intent, a semi-automatic pistol gripped in his left hand. David didn't linger on the fact that fate had gifted him a southpaw, that the weapon was held on the side of the man's body nearest to David, when there was an eighty-seven percent chance that this should not be so according to the latest scientific study on handedness. David read pretty much anything he could get his hands on while sipping his morning coffee. Had it been otherwise, David would have had to contend with a defensive free hand to disarm his target.

Comedian was well trained, it appeared, in addition to being the life of the ice cream party. He didn't stop moving as he assessed the situation; the woman he had been ordered to detain, to kill if necessary, standing motionless with saucer eyes and quivering, parted lips, the grotesque ruins of his partner's face, now a concave mass of gore. The truth of the situation was revealed to him in an instant.

David watched his quarry survey the scene while drawing the Ka-Bar from his waistband. The blade flashed in the incandescent ceiling light as it made its way toward the agent's wrist with practiced fluidity. Adrenaline retarded the process in David's perception, slowing the knife as though it were connected to an elastic band. Comedian's weapon arm flinched in unconscious reflex at the sudden threat, tendons tightening the fingers. The slide retracted and snapped back into position. The report transformed David's hearing into a high-pitched whine.

The Ka-Bar's razor edge found flesh, severing the skin and muscle of its victim's wrist. David followed through with the strike, tracing a bloody line up the man's face from jaw to temple. His opposite hand seized an elbow while the knife hand snaked around the agent's weapon arm. The tip of the combat knife found the armpit and kept going. The firearm clattered to the floor. A cry of agony degenerated into a horrible, gurgling grunt as Comedian's lung filled with blood. David let the man drop and kicked the gun away.

Light footsteps approached the door from the backyard.

"Mom?"

David pushed the door closed and locked it, then raised his eyes to Elyse. She knelt on the floor, having lost all strength in her legs, her fingers pawing at the length of dark hair she had pulled over her right shoulder. David thought he saw wisps of smoke there.

"He...he shot my hair," she said.

A second call came from outside, accompanied by frenzied attempts to open the door.

"Go around and get your boy, Elyse, " David said. "I'll clean this up."

Elyse didn't move.

"Elyse! Get! Duncan!"

Tears filled her eyes at the terse, barked order. David hauled Elyse to her feet by the upper arm and gave her a shove toward the front door. She stutter stepped away from him and disappeared from sight. David closed front door after her and took a deep, shuddering breath before setting about his grim task.

"Why are there blankets on the floor, Mom? Are we building a fort?"

David hadn't had much time to make the house presentable to a five-year old with such an inquisitive, perceptive nature. Duncan had been enjoying his ice cream one moment and reacting to a gunshot inside his house the next. "Mommy's friends" had to leave in a hurry, as far as the boy knew, and both David and Elyse thought it best that Duncan remain unaware of the fact that "Mommy's friends" were undergoing the early stages of rigor mortis in the garage. A bucket of hot water and a dish towel could only do so much to hide what had really transpired. Blankets would have to do for now.

Elyse shifted Duncan on her lap and pulled him close, resting her chin on his glossy, chestnut hair as she answered. Her eyes never left David's.

"I'm just drying them out, honey. Come on, it's time for bed."

The explanation made little sense considering that there was a perfectly good dryer in the laundry room, but adult logic had not yet seen fit to make its presence known to the boy. He didn't pursue the perfectly legitimate line of questioning, and instead let his mother lead him into his bedroom. The ringing in David's ears had subsided, allowing him to hear Duncan's final question before being tucked in for the night.

"Who is that man, mom?"

The door closed before Elyse answered.

David used the momentary respite to search Elyse's refrigerator for something to wash away the fatigue that had replaced the surge of cortisol released during the encounter. He settled on a bottle of Moscato and bit the cork free while pulling a glass tumbler from a cupboard. He paused, then took a second glass from the shelf and filled both of them. The wine was sweet and fruity, not that David lingered on the flavor. He drained his glass in two gulps before refilling it.

His gaze traveled across the living room as soft, muted murmurs drifted down the hallway from behind Duncan's bedroom door. The round that had spared Elyse's life was now embedded in the mortar between two ruddy bricks on the front of the fireplace. An easy fix, much easier than scrubbing blood and brain matter from the baked clay and mortar. David took a seat at the kitchen table, a sheet of thick glass atop a stainless steel frame. He ran his fingers across the clear surface. Elyse had always like modern decor. The simple painting of abstract geometric shapes hung above the wounded fireplace. Elyse had texted David a picture of it from the auction, worrying that it was too expensive. He had urged her to bid on it. The piece of art had hung over their mantle as well.

"Well?"

David found Elyse standing in the hallway just outside of the kitchen, as though afraid to come any further. Her arms were crossed over her chest, shoulders hunched. The tiniest hint of light crept out from beneath Duncan's bedroom door at the end of the corridor, a night light to ward away his frightened confusion. Better frightened confusion than the terrifying images that would have paid him a visit that night in his sleep had the situation gone another way.

David's fingertips pressed into the glass tabletop.

"Hi Elyse," David said, pushing the glass of wine he had poured for her towards an empty chair next to him.

The staring contest that followed came to a conclusion when Elyse strode to the table and took a seat opposite him instead of the chair he had indicated. Her elbows found the tabletop, her hands clasping the back of her neck as her head drooped forward. Her voice was just above a whisper.

"Almost six years, David."

David swished the pink liquid in circles, making a game of not letting any slip over the rim.

"Not a single, motherfucking word," she said. "Not a single call returned. Not a single letter or Email or text answered. Nothing."

The last word was an expectoration as her face rose to meet his, and was repeated with a scowl.

"Nothing!"

Several drops of Moscato found their way over the edge of the glass. David was determined to do better with his next try.

"Say something!"

David raised the tumbler and filled his mouth with the aromatic beverage. He refused to return her stare.

"Jesus Christ, David," said Elyse, letting her hands drop to the table and spreading her fingers to absorb the coolness of the surface. "Please."

"Those men had orders to kill you and your—our—son."

He let that gestate before continuing.

"Otherwise you never would have heard from me again."

"Look at me, David."

Her hands slid towards him, flipping to present her palms. David didn't accept them. He cleared his throat and stood, angling his body away from her and running his hand through his hair.

"I'm not him anymore, Elyse. I'm not that guy you knew. I'm so much worse. The things that happened during that second tour...the things I saw...the things I..."

Elyse picked up her glass before leaning back in her chair.

"I know," she said. "I can see it, sense it."

"I can't believe that *this* is what you want to talk about. I just murdered two men right in front of you. Men that were going to hurt Duncan. Hurt you."

There it was, a crack in his voice. A tremble in that last syllable. Elyse's wine paused halfway to her lips when she detected it. David realized that this was the first time she had heard him break. In their happiest moments, during their shared disappointments and sadness, his stoic veneer had always remained intact. He had been her protector. Her caretaker. He had been in control.

Not anymore.

"We have all night to talk about who those men were and what they were going to do," she said. "But right now I just want to know if you're okay. Sit."

David studied her face for the first time since their conversation had begun. Her eyes were red and puffy, but no less piercing. Her dark hair was disheveled and mussed. He spotted a hint of gray and decided that it suited her. He slumped back into the chair and rubbed his palms into his eyes.

"I don't know what to tell you, Elyse. I've never been okay."

A vibrating pulse sounded from the kitchen counter. David had found Elyse's phone in Smoker's pocket and had placed it where she could easily find it. If Elyse had heard the muted notification, she didn't reveal it to David.

"You going to get that?" he said.

"I didn't wait around for you, you know," she said, sidestepping his trivial question. "I tried to move on. I really did. But I have an unfortunate habit of choosing men with psychological baggage. And Duncan doesn't deserve that."

"He seems like a good kid. Takes after his mother."

Elyse drained the glass and returned it to the glass tabletop with more force than was necessary. Her eyes narrowed.

"I see you every time I look at that boy, David. Every fucking day. Always. I'm always reminded of you and how you left without so much as a 'fuck off'."

David didn't look away this time. Elyse's phone lurched into a series of vibrations for the second time. The device was again ignored.

"Elyse, listen," he said. "There was a period of time when I thought about reaching out to you. I was finished with the military and starting my own consulting business. Starting a new life. I wanted to contact you, but I kept putting it off. Every time I held my phone in my hand, ready to call you, another reason would arise that prevented it."

Elyse bit her bottom lip. Her eyes moistened and dropped to the empty glass cupped in her hands.

"Then the biggest reason of all manifested itself and changed my life forever, " said David.

David's ex-fiancé didn't miss a beat.

"What's her name?"

David sighed, his shoulders sinking under the weight of the events that had transpired over the past twenty-four hours. Tony's demands. Samantha. Betrayal.

"Mom? Can I have a drink of water?"

The gravity of their conversation had masked the presence of the sock-footed five year-old emerging from his bedroom with sleepy eyes. Elyse rose and made her way to the kitchen sink.

"You can have a little bit, but then right back to bed."

Water splashed into the stainless steel basin. A cupboard door opened with a creak. Duncan stared at David.

"I heard you like superheroes," David said, forcing his mouth into a tired smile.

Duncan returned the smile, his bashful gaze dropping to the floor. He accepted the shallow cup from his mother and brought it to his lips with both hands. David's eyes stared back at him from over the rim. Elyse squeezed Duncan's shoulder and scooped up her phone.

"Alright, young man. Now off to—"

Her hand froze on her son's shoulder. The backlight from her phone screen illuminated a face transfixed with confused surprise.

"This can't be real," she said.

"What?"

Elyse's thumb moved across the screen with increasing urgency.

"What is it?" David pressed.

"I, uh, no way. I don't believe it."

David stood. His hackles rose like a gazelle picking up a threatening scent in the African savannah breeze.

Elyse looked up at him, the hand holding her phone dropping to her side.

"That masked woman. The...um, you know, the...Kinetic Star?" she said.

David held his breath.

"She...oh my god...she attacked the National Guard, and—"

"And what?"

"She's dead."

David steadied himself with the back of a kitchen chair as the lance penetrated his heart. Elyse continued, unaware that his legs had weakened almost to the point of failure.

"That's a real shame," she said. "I kind of liked her."

Chapter Two

IT HAD BEEN THREE WEEKS since the catastrophe on the National Mall. Since Samantha had been blown to bits in the Museum of Natural History. Three weeks since the disappearance of Samantha's mother—or the woman who claimed to be Samantha's mother. Three weeks of growing tension among the world's most powerful nations that had now become a test of wills, a game in which the first to blink would be annihilated. Three weeks since David had returned from Charlottesville only to sequester himself in the solitude of his Dupont Circle apartment, refusing to answer calls, texts, or even his front door.

It had been three weeks of hell.

Despite all of this, Marissa sat in the corner booth of McGuffy's Diner wondering when someone would finally notice her and take her order. The faux leather booth seat groaned and creaked as she shifted her weight, as though mocking the persistent anxiety that had eaten away at her for much longer than three weeks. Probably since she had been shot by a sniper in David's cottage out in Montgomery county. No, since the hurricane. Everything had changed after that. The unsettling, urgent sense of doom was now compounded by a grief more powerful than she thought possible. Maybe an herbal tea would calm her nerves. Now if only she could manage to order one.

She resisted the urge to check her phone. The device that had once been an entertaining way to ward off boredom had become a constant reminder of her sorrow. The never-ending speculation and analysis of the events on the mall by both military officials, news media and unqualified commentators—most of whom belong in the former category—was more prevalent than when Samantha had first revealed herself to the world. Even her friends on social media wouldn't give it a rest. If you owned a smartphone and could access the internet, you were an instant expert. Marissa was sick of it.

The Starchildren Facebook page, created and maintained by Brie as the online home for the Kinetic Star fan club, had replaced its profile graphic, formerly an action photo of Samantha in full costume soaring overhead, with single blue tear drop on a field of black. Marissa had asked Brie to change it back, or at the very least choose a more hopeful image that reflected Samantha's heroic actions in her short time on this earth, but her plea had fallen on deaf ears. The social media community would rather wallow in their misery. It aided them in their virtue signaling, after all.

Brie had also kept her distance during the past several weeks, citing that she hadn't signed up for being traumatized by terrifying illusions forced upon her by a creepy, unconscious woman, nor had she sanctioned running for her life from government intelligence agencies. Marissa didn't hold Brie's reaction against her. How could she? But their "time out", as Brie now called it, had stolen yet another load-bearing support from the quickly-destabilizing structure of Marissa's world.

"Cheer up, honey. It's the holiday season."

A heavy set older woman with bright orange curls beamed positive energy down to Marissa from rows of teeth too white to be natural. Bright eyes twinkled beneath painted eyebrows as she let her directive hang between them. Marissa tried her best to return the smile, but the muscles around her mouth wouldn't cooperate.

"Chamomile tea, please," said Marissa, setting her elbows on the table then removing them as a silent voice from her childhood admonished her.

"You need a menu?"

Marissa nodded and adjusted her thick frames higher on her nose, noting a small, plastic placard pinned below the server's collar. It read: **Darla**.

"Yes. Two, please."

Darla nodded at Marissa's raised pair of fingers and was gone.

Marissa's gaze followed her behind the breakfast counter where a flat screen television broadcast a cable news channel. A chyron of red and blue displayed its message in bold white across the bottom third of the display.

STRANGE MINERAL FOUND IN POTOMAC

A pair of boats were anchored on the wide river above the chyron, one small and unadorned, the other large and marked with the seal of the Potomac River Fisheries Commission. Men and women in uniform stood with hands on hips, staring at a dark mass that hung suspended from a heavy fishing net off the port side of the smaller vessel. Captions appeared over the chyron, black bars with white, blocky text that rolled onto the screen as the news anchor explained that the unexpected discovery had occurred during a routine survey of the riverbed and that the geological identification process would begin soon. Whatever it was, it had been dumped into the Potomac, and authorities say that a criminal investigation was to follow.

Marissa tried to avert her eyes before the newscast switched to the next story, the sexy story, the one that would generate the most ad revenue. She knew it was coming. It was inevitable.

PRESIDENT DIETRICH ENDS MARTIAL LAW IN DC

The news was almost a week old, but the network was milking it for all it was worth. It was yet another avenue through which they could retell the story of the city's once-beloved masked protector turning on America's brave men and women in uniform. The narrative changed depending on which news network one watched. Marissa felt the familiar tightening in her stomach.

A steaming cup resting on a glossy white saucer broke Marissa's line of sight. China clinked together as Darla set the tea before her, accompanied by two laminated menus boasting McGuffy's eclectic fare.

"Do you want to order something while you wait, dear?"

Marissa opened her mouth to reply, but was cut off as a familiar shape entered her peripheral vision. A mouth lined with the wear of late middle age creased into a smile as dark eyes found Marissa.

"Sorry I'm late," Alan said, skirting around Darla. "Coffee, please. Black."

"You got it."

Marissa waited for Darla to turn away before rising to plant herself between Alan's outstretched arms that folded around her. No words were spoken, only a gentle rocking as though the pair were locked into a static, mournful dance. They sat across from each other, Alan settling into a practiced, rigid posture, Marissa reaching for the handle of her teacup but changing her mind and hunching over her clasped hands in nervous indecision.

"Traffic was backed up on 495," Alan said, shrugging off his coat and tossing it to the bench beside him.

"It's been that way since last Tuesday," Marissa said, "since they started letting people back into the city."

"I couldn't get a flight out of Columbus, Dayton or Cincinnati until today. Not even to Bethesda. Incoming air traffic has been cancelled for weeks."

Marissa nodded and let the small talk play out. It was a necessary precursor to what was to come.

"I'm sure your sister was glad to see you. How long had it been?"

"Since last Christmas. Almost a year," said Alan, choosing that moment to peruse the menu with an empty stare that read nothing. "Lizzie took it hard. First her nephew, and now her only niece. Lizzie kept referring to her as 'that sweet, sweet girl.' She never had any kids of her own, so Cole and Sammy were like her...well...I, um... Yeah."

Marissa noticed Alan's mouth tightening, his eyes darting left and right over the menu as they glazed over with moisture. The daily special might as well have been written in ancient Aramaic. She sipped at her tea while the carrot-curled server delivered Alan's coffee. The decision not to eat was unanimous, and the menus were scooped up on the condition that they let Darla know if they changed their minds. Apparently the tortilla chicken soup was delightful.

Marissa had no idea how much Samantha's Aunt Lizzie knew about her niece's heroic alter ego. Did she even know that Samantha had died in that horrible battle on the National Mall? Marissa couldn't help but wonder how much Alan had told her, but decided not to pursue it. It wasn't Marissa's business anyway. They were family.

"I don't know if 'sweet' is the word I'd use," Marissa said. "Your daughter had a mouth like a sewage basin."

Alan's shock at Marissa's blunt observation melted into amusement, culminating in a laugh that came from his belly.

"She did," he said, wiping at an eye. "She certainly did. You'd think she was raised by longshoremen."

"Oh, I'd say you did a pretty damn good job, Mr. McAllister. Especially since you raised them all by yourself."

Alan pursed his lips and blew into his coffee before testing it.

"Enough with the 'mister' nonsense. It's Alan. Now tell me, Miss Sanchez. Tell me what you couldn't tell me over the phone."

Marissa leaned back and pulled the sleeve of her sweater further down her wrist. Alan's eyes followed the motion then darted back to her face as she reset her glasses onto her ears.

"There's so much to tell you," she started, lowering her voice and casting an exploratory glance around the diner. "I just...I don't know. It's just that I feel like I'm still being monitored, even though David told me that I'm safe now. Before he stopped calling me back, that is."

"I'm going to assume he didn't elaborate," Alan said. "And you're not being paranoid. I think your prudence is justified. Considering what you've been put through, I mean. That doesn't just go away. It will take time. David knows the game, and wouldn't say that unless he meant it. How did he get back into the city when it was locked down, anyway?"

"Knowing him, he probably found the most heavily-guarded roadblock and ramped over the barricade while blaring *Dixie* from his car horn. I can almost hear the 'Yee-haw!'"

Alan chuckled at that. Marissa shook her head.

"I'm not sure, really," she said. "He didn't elaborate on that either."

"And his family?"

It took a moment for Marissa to infer his meaning, even though it should have been obvious whom Alan meant. The events of the past year had forged friendships and acquaintances into a new family, one crafted from hardship and necessity. She doubted that David considered his ex-fiancé family, but the discovery of his son may have changed everything. Marissa felt a pang of uncertainty. What would this revelation mean for she and David? How would the death of Samantha affect their familial bond?

"Safe and sound," she said. "He put them up in a hotel. That's all he said."

Alan nodded. Marissa peered into the brown depths of her tea.

"He hasn't said much more than that since he got back, Mister Mc—Alan, sorry. He hasn't been the same since he joined Brie and I at the hotel in Alexandria. Before he went to Charlottesville, I mean. I think something happened just before that, when he met with his intelligence contact. You know, the one who—"

"Tony Aldridge," said Alan. "The man they found murdered in front of that bar uptown. Gruesome way to die."

"I could see it in David's eyes. There is something off. Maybe I'm just imagining things," Marissa said, "but there was something he wasn't telling me. I tried to press him while Brie was hacking into Aldridge's phone, but he shut me down."

Alan covered her hand with his.

"That man carries a lot of weight, Marissa. He's pursued by demons, one might say. War changes a person."

Marissa decided not to share her doubts about Alan's supposition with him. David had carried the trauma of his war experience with grace, having accepted it as part of who he was long before she had met him. No, this was different.

This was new.

"Maybe," she said, patting his hand before taking up her tea cup.

Alan watched her sip, waiting as she replaced the cup on the saucer.

"Oh right," she said, twisting her torso to rummage through her bag. "I brought this for you."

He accepted a flat, rectangular object wrapped in a floral-patterned pillowcase. Marissa concentrated on his face as he unwrapped the picture frame and studied it. The pain withered his features, aging him beyond his years as he took in the moment frozen in time.

"I remember this day," he said.

"She told me it was her favorite photo," said Marissa. "She kept it by her bed. She said it was the only object left untouched when her room got trashed by her telekinetic nightmares way back when."

Alan continued to stare at the photo without comment. Marissa followed his eyes as they traveled over the image of his smiling children, a son and daughter trapped in eternal youth. He rewrapped the frame after a time and set it on the booth bench beside him. A sip of his coffee let Marissa know that the moment had passed. Still, his voice was unsteady when he spoke, thick with emotion.

"Thank you, Marissa."

Marissa didn't reply right away. She thought she had planned this meeting well, that presenting Alan with the photo would somehow lessen the burden she was about to drop on him. She considered changing the subject to a lighter tone, to tell him that Mal the Siamese was okay and enjoying his new life with Marissa's Maine coon Brownie, and that she had a key to Samantha's apartment for him so he could put her affairs in order when he was ready, but the real reason Marissa had asked to meet loomed over the booth like a storm cloud casting a shadow over these trivial topics and her impotent efforts to soften the impending blow. Marissa's exhale was heavy.

She didn't want to say it. Didn't know how to say it. So she just said it.

"Alan, your wife. She's alive. Samantha's mother. She—"

The cloud burst over Alan, saturating his countenance with disbelief. His jaw went slack, his eyes wild and accusatory. Thick eyebrows rippled and quivered in sheer anguish. Why would a close friend of his deceased daughter say such a cruel thing at a time like this? The reaction had stopped Marissa mid-sentence.

"What did you just say?"

Marissa found herself leaning away from him, pressing herself into seat back. The cheap upholstery chided her again with a taunting squeak. She forced herself relax and sat forward as she explained, hoping that the words she chose would penetrate his initial shock and register with him for the long term.

"I know how this sounds, but it's true. Sam rescued her mom from a secret government facility in Alaska. She was taking care of her, nursing her back to health, when everything...well, when the shit hit the fan."

Marissa had decided to omit the horrifying details of Alan's wife's convalescence long before walking into the diner. She had no idea how he would react, and the multi-lingual babbling followed by the telepathic attacks might be too much for the grieving father to bear. Does he even know what she is capable of?

"Madelyn..." Alan whispered, his face as pale as the china. "How can you be sure?"

"I met her. Samantha is a spitting image of her mother, Alan. It's obvious. Sam's hair is more blonde, but the resemblance is unmistakable. Was, I mean. Was more blonde. But aside from that, just the eyes alone..."

Marissa's voice quieted and trailed off as she looked down at the teaspoon rolling between her fingertips.

"Dammit. I'm sorry," she said. "Maybe this wasn't the right time."

Alan tented his fingers and rested his elbows on the table, his eyes far away.

"Oh my god," he said. "I didn't hear from Sammy for a while. That must have been why. She was probably trying to figure out how to tell me."

Marissa let him work it out on his own.

"Maddie's alive. Oh my god. Oh my *god*."

"Please understand that Sam had a lot going on in her final days," said Marissa. "In addition to the stress of trying to keep me safe and the sudden appearance of her dead mother, she had to deal with a super powered maniac that came out of nowhere."

"Yes, I remember," Alan said, managing a sly grin directed at Marissa. "You were all over the news with your pepper spray heroics. Well done."

Marissa felt her face grow hot. Her return grin didn't come easily.

"You seem different after taking down the monster that tried to hurt my little girl."

Marissa flipped a lock of jet black hair from her shoulder.

"Dyed my hair. New glasses, too," she explained with a tap to the frames. "I'm like Clark Kent. Nobody recognizes me."

Alan's stare lingered on her.

"No, it's more than that. You've changed, young lady."

Marissa's eyes revisited the spoon. Alan took his time finishing his coffee and nodded at Darla who appeared to refill it. When she had gone, Alan cleared his throat and straightened in his seat.

"Now. Tell me about Samantha's mother, Marissa," he said. "Tell me everything that happened."

Marissa swallowed hard, her eyes locked onto the utensil.

"Everything?"

"Everything."

Chapter Three

THIS WASN'T THE FIRST TIME that David had been in Samantha's home when she had gone missing, but he knew it would be the last. He stood in the middle of the living room, unsure of where he should begin his search. Unsure of what he was searching for. Investigations that started with nothing to go on were rare for David. He had a natural talent for discovering useful clues where none were apparent, but this time his knack for detecting relevant minutiae was clouded by...what?

Love? Guilt? Grief?

He had become reacquainted with these three emotions in recent days. Newfound love for Duncan, the son he never knew he had. Guilt over abandoning Elyse to raise the boy on her own. Grief over a marriage with her that had failed before it could begin. He had left those feelings with Duncan and Elyse in a hotel outside of Charlottesville, along with a promise to let them know when it was safe for them to return home. Duncan's excited expression lingered like the afterimage of a flashbulb as David closed the hotel room door behind him. Elyse had led him to believe that they were on a surprise vacation, and the boy was ready jump into the hotel's indoor pool. David had paused just outside the door to let Duncan's face burn into his memory. He had no idea when—or if—he'd see his son again.

Love. Guilt. Grief.

David had to admit that throwing himself back into his work was the only way he could cope. He had to keep moving or he would drown. The last thing he expected was a renewed cycle of those emotions when he picked the lock to Samantha's townhouse and stepped through the door. The scent of candles and freshly-cleaned carpets washed over him. He sensed spectral images of Samantha moving throughout the space, busy with whatever chore or past time she had decided to occupy herself with that day. David stood in the open doorway and absorbed these impressions with a deep, shuddering breath.

Love didn't quite cover it. He and Samantha had shared a bond unlike any two in human history. Before romantic love had blossomed, they had been hunter and prey. Mentor and student. Custodians of a strange and frightening power that had brought incredible danger down upon them. Love was there, yes, but the word was insufficient.

Guilt was another matter.

There was no way to escape the massive boulder of regret that David had carried on his shoulders since that day in Tapio's Tavern. The day Tony Aldridge had wrested Kinetic Star's real name from David's lips.

The day Tony had won.

David had analyzed the memory thousands of times since then, approaching it from every possible angle, even to the point of holding silent, imaginary conversations with objective phantoms in an attempt to explain himself. Some of those incorporeal counselors said he had made the right choice in electing to save his son's life. Others praised him for owning up to the fact that he was just a man, a normal human being placed in an impossible position. But one hadn't been so objective. He could see this dissident in his mind's eye; a strong, intelligent young woman with pretty green eyes and the power to pulverize his boulder of guilt into dust with three simple words:

"I forgive you."

But that would never happen now. Samantha was gone.

David found himself standing in her living room with clenched fists. The silence was oppressive.

He collapsed into her sofa and let the grief come.

David decided to start at the top of the townhouse and work his way down. He mounted the last step and paused there, expecting Mal to emerge from Samantha's bedroom and greet him with curious, throaty purrs. When he had finally reached out to Marissa after his return to D.C. she informed him that she had adopted the blue-eyed Siamese. David was greeted with more silence as he stepped through the door.

It turned out that Marissa knew little more than David about what had transpired on the mall that day. While it was true that she and Brie had met the woman who called herself Samantha's mother, the stranger had been incoherent at first. Fleeting, disjointed consciousness had become focused aggression against Marissa, Brie and Samantha, a malevolent invasion of their minds. Even now, a month later, Marissa still hadn't told David the specifics of the ethereal terrors that had been visited upon her, but she informed him that the aftermath had not been good for Marissa and Brie. It was hard for David to believe that the weak, lifeless woman with the matted red hair and filthy hospitable gown that he and Samantha had found in the military bunker was capable of such a thing. Yet Marissa's and Brie's accounts of the events that had transpired in this very room were undeniable. He believed Marissa, ruling out the possibility that she had suffered a stress-related mental break. After all, Brie had experienced the very same thing at the very same time. David had seen the haunted looks in their eyes firsthand as they recounted their stories. The resulting rift in their relationship lent even more credence. Post traumatic stress can strain the love that people share. David knew this well.

The photo of Samantha and her family was gone. David wouldn't miss it. He had, more often than not, repositioned it face down on the bedside nightstand during their lovemaking. Alan was a good man, but his smiling eyes transformed into a disapproving stare during David's intimacy with his daughter. Worse, the frozen image of Cole in that picture frame summoned images of the young man's burnt and bleeding body in David's mind, a snapshot memory that David would never forget. Perhaps Marissa or Alan had taken the frame. The latter made the most sense.

David turned away from the night table and slid the closet doors aside. The upper shelf was laden with a variety of folded sweaters and athletic wear, organized by color and assigned their place according to function and season. Dozens of hangers clung to the rod just below the shelf, draped in blouses, jeans, dresses, slacks and other garments which David recognized but couldn't label with his limited knowledge of women's apparel. He thought one of them might be called a chemise. Or was it a slip? David shook his head and moved on.

The bottom of the closet was littered with shoe boxes and plastic bins, some with lids akimbo or missing entirely. It occurred to David that Samantha's sense of order didn't make it to the ground floor of her closet. He dropped to a knee to push aside several shoe boxes, but paused as a memory struck him. The last time David had rummaged through the bottom of Samantha's closet he'd almost had his head blown off by his old Navy buddy.

"Hmph," he muttered, resisting the urge to glance over his shoulder.

He found the motorcycle suit buried beneath two thick, woolen blankets in the bottom bin. His palms chilled with immediate perspiration. A glint of reflective amber caught his eye as he pulled the garments free. He carried the suit and cowl to the bed and laid them out on Samantha's downy comforter. He suppressed his emotion with a stoic shove as he took in the red and black leathers, yet couldn't stop his fingertips from exploring the hasty stitch work that she had performed on the suit after her near-disastrous clash with Harkins at the Capitol. The garish mask glared up at him, accusing him, reminding him of his treachery. Samantha hadn't found time to replace the mismatched lens before she died.

David seized the cowl and launched it against the wall. It flattened for a moment with a leathery slap, then sank to the carpet like a lifeless bat.

"You're a fucking asshole," he whispered as he picked up the cowl and replaced it on the bed. "You didn't deserve her."

It was the David of the past that spoke to him. The David that had held her close on his cottage porch on that summer night in Montgomery county. The David that stood in awe the first time he had laid eyes upon her, hovering over the Potomac while pulling a two-ton minivan from the river with a thought. The David that had existed just seconds prior to revealing her identity to the government operative who hunted her. The rationalization leading up to that final moment had been exquisite, had given agency to his betrayal. It had defeated him. Tony was dead and no one else knew what David had done, but he knew.

David knew. That was the moment the old David was snuffed out forever.

He cleared his throat and shook his head, blinking moisture away from reddened eyes. He had work to do.

He fished through the multitude of pockets in the leather jacket and pants, and let the smile come when he withdrew a tiny sphere from the front right pants pocket. The discovery was a welcome reprieve from his dark train of thought. How the white marble hadn't been crushed during the beating Samantha had taken at the hands of Harkins's constructs David would never understand. Maybe some small, subconscious part of her had protected it. He pinched the orb between thumb and forefinger and held it up to the overhead light. A reflection manifested in the pale, unmarred surface, a memory of David wishing Samantha luck as he handed the marble to her on the patio of the Occidental just before she raced off to save the day. Before her first encounter with Harkins. Before the series of events were set into motion that had led him to this very moment. The orb found a new home in the pocket of his blazer, a keepsake from a happier time. A reminder of the David from before.

David decided to take the suit and cowl with him as well, not as another memento, but as evidence that had to be destroyed. Now that martial law had been lifted, Alan would eventually be coming to get Samantha's affairs in order. It had been a month already, and the fact that her home had been left untouched thus far was proof that Alan was not handling this well. David couldn't blame him. Going through her belongings would be difficult enough for the grieving father, especially considering that it wouldn't the first time he'd had to perform such a grim task for one of his children, and David surmised that Alan didn't need such a brazen reminder of his daughter's alter ego. No, the suit represented the partnership she and David had formed. It belonged with him. He would make sure it could never be traced back to her.

He replaced the leathers and cowl in the blanket bin and set it at the top of the stairs, then placed his hands on his hips as he considered his next move. The stabbing heartache he had experienced upon entering Samantha's townhouse had dulled to a throbbing ache, one that he doubted would ever go away, but immersing himself in the grief had alleviated the pain somewhat. Now he could focus. He flipped an imaginary, internal switch from the emotional setting to the analytical one. David was good at that. He'd had years of practice at shoving his feelings into a lockbox and tossing the key.

He moved to the bedroom doorway, took a deep breath, and exhaled while turning to take in the room with a new perspective.

"Okay," he whispered, "let's see."

The woman who claimed to be Samantha's mother was still out there. According to Marissa, who was his best witness in this impromptu and unwarranted investigation, Samantha had last been seen with her so-called mother in this very bedroom just before Marissa had chased after Brie following their harrowing experience with the terrifying visions. That meant David's best chance of learning what had really driven Samantha to take on the National Guard in the heart of the nation's capital lay with this mysterious woman.

Doubt crept into his resolve from the hazy edges of his consciousness. That damned woman. What is she capable of? What powers does she possess? More importantly, what the hell does she want?

David rubbed his eyes and blinked away his apprehension. Horrifying hallucinations be damned. He had a job to do.

A persistent notion nagged at him, one that had been born weeks ago, the moment he'd heard the news of Samantha's demise. It had matured since then, piercing the sorrow that had also sprung to life in the awful moment when Elyse had read the text from a friend who had been watching the news. The notion evolved into a memory from his very recent past, when he lay atop the roof of his Montgomery county cottage peering through the scope of a sniper rifle, body in agony from an array of broken ribs. Samantha had been blindsided by an AIM-92 Stinger missile launched from an Apache attack helicopter. Months later, as they sat sipping water after a brisk workout session, David had asked about that moment. He let the conversation come back to him.

"I thought you were gone, disintegrated into fiery atoms."

"Me too, for a second," Samantha said.

"Then how...?"

"What did Evan call it? A 'reflex response'? He theorized that my abilities can protect me from threats I don't even know exist."

"Why the hell did he assume that?"

"Because the asshole shot me in the back of the head."

David recalled her shifting uncomfortably in the silence that followed, and had decided not to pursue the topic any further. Somehow, she still missed the piece of shit that had betrayed her. David let the irony sink in. Samantha seemed to attract traitorous men.

That model of Stinger missile carried a three-kilogram, high-explosive blast fragmentation warhead propelled from a dual thrust, solid fuel rocket motor, and all it had done was ring her bell? How the hell had a couple of shoulder-mounted, rocket propelled grenades blasted her into oblivion, leaving no trace of her remains? Well, almost no trace. The official word from military investigators was that burnt hair fibers had been found on the fringes of the blast radius. The news networks had taken this as confirmation that Kinetic Star was dead. The government had as well—as far as the public knew—although they had waited to rescind the order of martial law just to be sure. David had a hard time refuting the unanimous conclusion, but it still didn't make sense.

David let the facts speak for themselves, free from bias or prejudice. Video footage from that day showed Samantha attacking the National Guard in downtown D.C. He was sure it was her.

After all, David didn't know anyone else that could fly.

But the emergence of Roger Harkins, a second Enhanced Individual, proved that others were out there. Others like her. Perhaps others that could mimic her powers. But one brave camera operator had dared to try for a close shot. David recognized the scarf that Samantha had used to cover her face and head. He had bought it for her on a whim while making a quick run to Tyson's Corner, a woolen blend the shade of charcoal. The odds of an impostor wearing that same scarf were microscopic.

David gathered his fractured thoughts and laid them out in systematic fashion, arranging them on an imaginary, wall-mounted logic board like a conspiracy theorist attempting to link clues together with lengths of red yarn.

Samantha had engaged the U.S. military. Fact.

Samantha had been blasted into the Natural History Museum by air-to-air missiles. Fact.

Rocket-propelled grenades had followed her inside. Fact.

She had not come back out.

"Fuck." David muttered, combing back his hair with clawed fingers.

He found himself standing in Samantha's kitchen with no memory of descending the staircase or placing the plastic bin on the kitchen table. He opened one of the cabinets on whim; a futile, nostalgic attempt to find a valuable clue in the exact spot where he had found one in the past. The voluminous serving bowl he had plucked from the cupboard of her Clarendon apartment had been decorated with black and red magic marker, lines and numbers spaced symmetrically to resemble a roulette wheel. They had never really discussed the bowl— or the disastrous trip to Las Vegas that had followed—in great detail. There had only been a passing reference from David that she laughed off as if to say "None of your damn business." No gaming table replicas greeted him this time, just mundane stacks of ceramic dinnerware.

He kept going through her cupboards, however, at a loss for any solid reason as to why. What did he hope to find? There was nothing in these pre-fabricated, wood-paneled cabinets that would bring him any closer to an answer. Nothing that would bring her back to him. Not that he was worthy of her. Not anymore.

The search moved from the cupboards to the kitchen drawers, then to the refrigerator and freezer before moving on to the living room. He found nothing useful there, either. Not even a lost dime or popcorn kernel sentenced to a solitary existence beneath the sofa cushions. The coat closet near the front door was perhaps the most difficult to search. The charcoal scarf was conspicuously absent, as was the brown leather jacket she often wore. Both garments were now reduced to ash. David's hand tightened around the brass knob as he closed the door.

He returned to the kitchen and went to the sink, bending at the waist to cup his hands below the faucet. He brought the cool water to his face in an attempt to counteract the burning frustration that had risen there.

Chg! Chg! Chng!

David closed the spigot and shook his hands several times before drying them on a checkered dish towel. Probably just a loose pipe joint. Easy enough to fix.

He knelt and swung open the doors of the cabinet beneath the sink, revisiting the boxes of aluminum foil and plastic wrap he had discovered during his initial search of the kitchen. He kept his eyes on the plumbing while stretching an arm over the sink to twist the spigot knob.

Chng! Chng! Chgl chgl chgl...

David spotted the culprit and twisted a threaded joint fitting back into place. The job would need to be completed with a pipe wrench, but it was doubtful that Samantha kept such a tool in her junk drawer. He began to rise, but stopped in a half crouch. His shadow passed over the contents of the sink cupboard, revealing a flash of pale manila. It seemed out of place behind the bottles of cleaner and dish soap and dried husks of mildewed sponges that Samantha had never thrown in the garbage. It might have been missed by the casual observer, or passed over as yet another banal kitchen implement that lived in the cabinet beneath the sink. But David was in full investigative mode, and had trained himself to leave no stone unturned.

Pushing the blanket bin aside, David laid the flaxen-hued envelope on the kitchen table and examined it before touching it further. A New York postmark had been imprinted over the double-stamped postage. Samantha's name stood out, written above a Bethesda mailing address in black, felt-tip pen. The script was graceful, almost artistic, the characters reminiscent of pictograms yet well within confines of the conventional alphabet. David had a passing familiarity with the science of graphology, or pseudoscience, as some might say, and detected certain characteristics in the bold, angular strokes. The capital **S** and **M** in Samantha's name were quite tall, signaling an assertive personality, or at least an assertive disposition at the time the letters had been put to paper. The name and address lines were neat and level, indicating that the author of this missive probably exhibited good control. The bleeding ink suggested heavy pen pressure, a trait associated with decisiveness. David wiped his hands across his pants before opening the envelope.

He was careful not to contaminate the stack of cardstock within as he slid it from the envelope to the tabletop. He might be able to lift some prints if this turned out to be a worthwhile find. The stack appeared to be four inches by six, a standard size for photos. The cover card was an arctic grey with flowing black script written with the same idiosyncrasies as the name and address on the envelope, though the writing was embossed there and not imprinted by a felt-tip pen. The language was not English.

Far from it.

وتعويض الشر هو عقاب مثله.

"Arabic."

The revelation escaped David's parted lips before he knew he had spoken aloud. It was not a question. It was the last thing he expected to see.

Sand-scorched road signs flashed through his mind, faded and shimmering in the desert heat. Shouts for mercy rang in his ears, bargains and denials, as he dragged people from their beds at the end of an assault rifle in the middle of the night. David had never truly learned Modern Arabic, but he knew it well enough. Acevedo had been fluent. David swallowed, banishing the lump that had begun to form in his throat at the memory of his brother-in-arms.

He narrowed his eyes as he perused the script, as though staring would somehow help translate the nonsensical characters. One word stood out, however, taunting him from behind its cloak of mystery. It wasn't one he'd seen on a road sign or printed on a store front window. It was very similar to a word included on the business-card sized handouts that he and his squad had carried with them in Iraq to allay the fears of the citizens:

We are Americans. We are here to help you. We mean you no harm.

David almost chuckled at the irony. They had been outfitted for war carrying promises of peace.

Harm

That was the word that clicked as he studied the Arabic script. One of the words closely resembled the term. Perhaps it was interchangeable with a similar word; hurt or punish or abuse. David couldn't be certain until he had the phrase translated into English, but his suspicion was that the familiar word carried with it a negative connotation. And it had been included in a phrase written at the top of a stack of cardstock in a parcel addressed to Samantha. Interesting.

He flipped the gray card over to reveal the first photo.

David's skin flushed with heat even as icy spikes penetrated his spine. The sensation grew more intense as each image was revealed, compounding his confusion and horror with the simple flip of a photo. His heart was pounding in his ears by the time he came to the final layer in the stack, another piece of gray, medium-weight cardstock. This time, the words appeared in thick, red marker, but were no doubt written by the same assertive, controlled, decisive person.

Find Me

and on the flip side:

Tell <u>No</u> <u>One</u>

David fought to stabilize his reeling mind enough to control his motor functions. He stuffed the stack back into the envelope and deposited it into the bin before seizing the plastic container and exiting Samantha's home, perhaps for the last time.

Chapter Four

HARKINS' TREASURES WAS AN EYESORE, its facade an ostentatious patchwork of stained glass that captured the ambient light of the New Orleans Arts District and reflected it back in a brilliant display of over-inflated ego. It was an insult to Ana, who had wiled away many hours watching the construction of the cathedral at Chartres during one of her longer stints in France.

Now *that* was stained glass.

The hours had grown into days, and the days into months. Before she knew it, several years had passed and the cathedral was nearing its completion. She hadn't lingered about for its grand unveiling, however, as much as it pained her to leave. Ana was careful not to outstay her welcome. Her five years were up. That was the rule, and had been for centuries. Survivors followed the rules.

A creak returned her to the twenty-first century as Talbot opened the door and stepped aside, the multi-hued glow from the storefront illuminating his bald pate like a Christmas tree ornament. It reminded her of the holidays in the 1950's, painted string bulbs hot to the touch.

A voice met Ana at the threshold, traveling across the large showroom to reach her ears. The southern twang was barely perceptible, having been trained out of his dialect, and the timbre was much deeper than she remembered. Of course it was. This was no longer the voice of a child.

"We're closing in ten minutes."

Ana moved from sculpture to sculpture in silence, admiring the exquisite craftsmanship. These works of copper, iron and glass would have taken a normal artist years to perfect; humanoid shapes formed from stone and marble, silver and granite, and even lead. Every piece had been fashioned with an uncanny realism, as though any one of them would step down from its pedestal and start a conversation. Ana wondered what they might say, whether they would share the secret of their creation. Michelangelo had created perhaps thirty sculptures in his lifetime, Ana mused, but here she counted at least fifty and their creator hadn't yet reached his fiftieth birthday. They were masterpieces, and she doubted that this was the extent of the artist's portfolio.

A man materialized in her peripheral vision.

"See anything that tickles your—"

Ana didn't need to scan his surface thoughts to understand why he hadn't completed his sentence. It was written across his suddenly peaked face. She saw her reflection projected onto his dark eyes.

Recognition.

A typical person with average powers of observation might have first locked his or her attention onto the hulking presence of the seven-foot man with the shaven head and piercing gray eyes, but the proprietor of Harkins' Treasures couldn't tear his eyes away from the petite woman with the crimson mane and emerald gaze.

"Indeed I do," said Ana. "You tickle my fancy, Roger."

Roger Harkins stood dumbfounded. Ana projected her awareness into those wide, dark eyes and traveled far beyond.

The mental images were blurry at first, as they always were during times of heightened emotion, faraway objects in sluggish motion through a snowstorm. Ana cleared a path with practiced precision, pushing aside useless snippets of conscious thought such as finalizing the online orders from the past week and preparing them for shipment. Deciding whether or not to take something for the heartburn he had contracted from a spicy breakfast and vowing to lay off the Tabasco. Wondering if he should text Helen or Dakota for his evening entertainment. Helen was a good conversationalist, but Dakota did that thing with her tongue.

It was in there somewhere, obscured by useless, mundane thoughts and memories. Yes. A face revealed from beneath a cowl of red and black leather.

Her face.

It was all Ana could do to maintain the connection as her stomach tightened into knots.

"Hi, I'm Samantha," said Roger's memory. "I'm your little sister."

Ana's control faltered. She tasted processed potato snacks, felt them roiling in her belly. Patches of black shot through her vision. She experienced Roger's physical reaction to meeting his sister in the woods of Fairfax County that day, and it almost made her sick.

Ana forced the sensation away and concentrated. She was no novice, and refused to let the personal nature of Roger's thoughts affect her ability to seize what she wanted from him. She probed further, and heard a memory of Samantha's voice—her dear Little Star—penetrate Roger's ears.

"She says she's your mother too..."

Roger's fingers went to his temples.

"... she told me what you can do..."

He squinted against an unseen irritation.

"...and her name is Ana."

45

Ana raised her eyes to Roger's.

You know who I am.

Roger flinched. The motion was echoed by every single statue in the room, like ripples escaping a pebble dropped into a still pond. Ana sensed Talbot's weight shifting behind her, heard a low rumble in his barrel chest. Roger's finger extended to the door.

"Get the fuck out of here!"

"Let's talk," said Ana.

Calm down and show me respect, boy.

Roger backed away, eyes widening for a moment before narrowing under a furrowed brow.

"Stay out of my head, you fucking freak! Leave! Now!"

Ana's sizable escort stepped in front of her, his expression grim. Fifty sculpted heads turned to follow the motion.

"What, Kojak? You got something to say?" Roger said, halting his retreat and throwing his arms out wide.

"You'll listen first. Then we leave."

Talbot's voice was earth shifting on bedrock, preternatural in its depth. Roger leaned in despite the unnerving tone, his own voice softening.

"Do you know the tensile strength of martensitic-grade iron, Roid Rage?"

A pair of sculptures dropped to the floor and moved to flank Ana and Talbot, one a magnificent study of the human male made from solid iron, the other an intricate tapestry of thin, iron rods bent and woven into the shape of a woman. Their impressive mass was confirmed by the cracks that followed them across the polished cement floor of the showroom. The others monitored the situation from their pedestals, silent sentinels awaiting their master's command.

"Over ninety thousand pounds per square inch," said Roger. "That means they can rip those tree trunk arms from your torso and use them to beat you into a quivering lump of gym rat."

Talbot bared his white teeth into a dangerous smile. Ana placed a slim hand on Talbot's shoulder and stepped forward.

"I am impressed, Roger," she said, eyes twinkling as she ran her fingers along the jawline of the male sculpture. "Very impressed. But I can see that you refuse to agree to a simple conversation without a reason to believe that I am worth listening to. After all, your time is precious and Dakota does that special thing with her tongue."

Roger's face flushed.

"Your tart can wait," said Ana.

Roger drew in a breath to speak, no doubt to repeat his directive that they leave his establishment or face the consequences, but Ana continued before he could begin.

"Let me give you that reason, my long lost son."

Twenty years of languishing in a psychotropic haze had dulled Ana sharp memory, but she managed to conjure the sights, sounds and smells of the colonial plantation home with near-perfect accuracy. Towering live oaks dripping with musty Spanish moss. Insects buzzing past multi-paned windows with instinctual urgency. Creaks and groans of the old wooden framework as it protested against the Gulf wind. The scent of boiled herbs that preceded Miss June up the staircase as she delivered the afternoon tea. Ana packaged these sensations and hurled them into Roger's brain with unerring cruelty. Ana's will followed close behind.

She chose a specific location to hold their conversation, one that would take the edge from Roger's bravado and give her the advantage. Roger's bedroom was as she remembered it just before she had left. Roger had been five years old. The decor of the room reflected the seventies, down to the pea green shag carpet and the wood-paneled walls. The tiny bed was fitted with sheets covered in various types of train cars, the frame crafted to resemble an 1800s-era locomotive, complete with a toy box shaped like a cowcatcher at the foot of the bed. Ana's son sat on the edge of the bed, nostalgic recognition painted across his features.

"What the fuck is this?" he said, lips tight and spine rigid.

Ana crossed her legs and rested her palms on the curved arms of the rocker. This detail of her past was flawless, the rails and stretchers and legs gleaming from Miss June's polish and customary elbow grease. Ana had spent many hours in this chair watching Roger sleep, waiting for his father to stumble through the front door in a drunken stupor, reeking of gin, perfume and cigar smoke. She had stopped trying to censor his behavior after Roger was born. After that, she simply didn't care about her husband's adolescent indulgences. She had given birth. The five-year countdown had begun.

She sent the rocker into motion and waited for Roger to come to terms with his new situation. It took most people a while to realize that their cerebrum had been hijacked. Ana could wait.

Roger lurched to his feet and rushed to the door, pausing long enough to throw it open before charging through. He emerged from the closet door on the opposite side of the room. Ana rolled her eyes at his second and third attempts to flee, both efforts resulting in him staring back at the closet door in disbelief.

"Sit down, Roger," she said with calm patience.

Roger bolted through the door a fourth time, his brain unable to register the fact that universal laws of physics had decided to abandon him. He glanced over his shoulder at the neat row of small hangers draped in little boy-sized garments that hung inside the closet. He paled and clutched at the sides of his head.

Sit. Down.

Ana watched his jaw set. His eyes hardened as he scanned the room, fists clenching and relaxing.

"You won't find anything useful in here, Roger. I removed all inorganic material from your bedroom when your gift first revealed itself," said Ana. "Call it Mother's Intuition if you like. It just wouldn't do to have a child crafting sharp knives or pointy spikes out of his Tonka trucks or Matchbox cars. That's how eyes get poked out, you see."

"What is this?" Roger repeated, this time with quiet reservation.

Ana motioned toward the bed.

"This is a mother convincing her son that she deserves respect," she said. "This is me urging you to take a seat before your legs fail you. As I said, I just want to talk."

Roger ran a shaky hand over his face before he returned to the tiny bed. Box springs protested as they took his weight.

"Good," said Ana, uncrossing her legs and leaning forward. "Now, have you been following the news, or has your time been spent at the bottom of a bottle of booze or between the legs of your floozies? That is, when you're not exploiting your formidable talents to fatten your pocketbook, I mean."

She scanned his thoughts as he prepared an answer. The first one she detected was the observation that her vocabulary was outdated and made her sound silly. The second image was explicitly pornographic, and the third was a memory of sizable numbers from multiple banking and investment accounts displayed on various computer monitors.

"How much do I have to pay you to get the fuck out of my life, lady?" said Roger.

But his thoughts turned to headlines painted across television screens and short bursts of information scrolling past his phone display with the flick of a thumb. Ana picked out certain key words as they flashed by and set them aside, gathering them into an exclusive collection and discarding the rest.

Kinetic Star. Martial Law. World War Three. President Dietrich.

Ana went deeper, digging past the initial digital input and descending into the trenches of his comprehension where she found more collectibles.

Green eyes. Sister. Samantha. Family. Dead. Mother. Why?

Ana relaxed her expression when she discovered that her mouth had stiffened into a thin line. She found Roger watching her, waiting.

"Well?" she said.

"Fine, let's get this over with," said Roger. "I catch a news headline here and there. Why?"

"Then you know that the world is broken. It is a fact. One that is out there for all to see. It is written about and broadcast in an endless loop, twenty-four hours a day. Murder. Genocide. Oppression. Drought. Famine. *Hate.*"

"What does that have to do with me?" said Roger, running his fingertips over a cartoonish caboose printed onto the cotton material beside him. "I have a mansion. More money than I could possibly spend in my lifetime. I have a servant, for Christ's sake."

"Apathy is not a trait I possess. You must have gotten that from your father," Ana said, smoothing the tartan skirt over her ankle. "And I'm sure you have sports cars and boats and vacation houses, too."

Roger nodded along as if she were confirming a favorable weather forecast or telling him the time of day.

"Is that enough for you?" said Ana.

"So far, so good. Can't complain, and other clichés. Or are those turns of phrase? Who cares. Pick whichever one answers your question and get me the hell out of this nightmare."

Ana watched him peruse the crayon drawings and macaroni artwork that she had hung on the walls after his first week of pre-school. She removed a stray strand of hair from her alabaster cheek with a flick of her pinky.

"The world is broken, Roger."

"Yeah, you said that."

"Listen to me, son. The slate must be wiped clean. It must get worse before it gets better."

The flippant retort that was perched on Roger's tongue lost its balance and toppled away.

"Better for who?" he said.

"Better for us."

Roger shook his head, not following at first. Then he squinted at her as realization dawned.

"You're talking about war," he said. "A fucking apocalypse! A...a...a goddamn holocaust!"

Her silence confirmed it.

"How is mutually-assured destruction going to be 'better' for a population of eight billion people?" said Roger, hooking his fingers into quotation marks.

Ana leaned back and gripped the armrests, again folding one knee over the other.

"No, son," she said. "Not better for them. Better for *us*."

The rocker rocked. Roger stared.

"You have all of these material things, but that is all they are. Things. Objects without meaning or substance. Possessions that provide momentary entertainment or fleeting satisfaction until one day you realize they don't fill the void, don't give you purpose. And so you use your power to craft more works of art, and you sell that art to purchase more intangible fulfillment. In reality, Roger, there is only one thing that matters: your gift. The gift that your mother gave you."

Ana could tell that Roger was an intelligent man, albeit narcissistic and stubborn. She watched his expression as the pieces fell into place.

"My mother left me when I was five," he said.

"Your mother sits before you now."

The rocker rocked.

"What do you want from me?" Roger said, head shaking as his chin dropped.

"I want to guide you," Ana said. "I want you to come with me and join your brothers. We will rebuild the world together and—"

Roger snapped his gaze back to hers.

"Samantha said no. You killed her for it."

The rocker stopped.

"Didn't you?" Roger said.

Ana found herself standing, fingers curled into claws and skin a bright, burning pink. Roger sat motionless, the corner of his mouth curling into a grin.

"Miss June raised me—after you abandoned me, of course—with a down-home, southern brand of common sense. You know the kind. Or maybe you don't," he said. "In simple terms, it means that I can see the pile of shit without being distracted by the pretty flowers and butterflies surrounding it. So sit down, Ana. My turn to talk."

Ana hesitated. Perhaps this had been a mistake. It would be so easy to crush him, to leave him slobbering in his own insanity atop a memory of his childhood bed. The New Orleans police department would receive the call the next day, shortly after business hours had begun, a report of the owner of Harkins' Treasures laying comatose on the floor of his own showroom. How dare he conjure the memory of her only daughter? How dare this insolent boy use Samantha's name as a shield?

"...she put me in a hole in the ground. Hell, I probably deserved it."

Ana realized Roger was speaking.

"She was so damn powerful. Looked silly in that mask but still intimidating, especially after I knew what she was capable of. But when she took the stupid thing off, I just saw a young woman barely into her twenties with reddish-blonde hair and big, green eyes just like yours. She told me about you. Told me your name and what you can do. She told me she was my sister and tried to convince me to come with her. To come see you."

Ana reclaimed her seat. The rocker creaked but remained stationary.

"So it isn't hard to figure out, Ana. It isn't hard to part the flowers and wave away the butterflies to see the steaming pile of crap. You show up out of nowhere, and shortly after that my sister goes ballistic on a battalion of National Guardsmen. You show up and my sister gets blown to pieces. You show up and the only person on this shit hole of a planet that I'd even remotely consider calling family is gone. Just like that. Convenient, huh?"

Ana said nothing. Her concentration was focused on the blood boiling in her veins. Even with centuries of practice in maintaining her composure, it was all she could do not to launch herself from the chair and pluck out his eyeballs with her fingernails, powers be damned.

"I don't think it's coincidence. Not one bit. You had this little talk with her, too," Roger said. "What mind tricks did you play on her to try and get her on your side, Ana? What did her childhood bedroom look like in your addled memory? Or did you take a more sinister strategy with her?"

Ana's heart thrummed in her ears, threatening to drown out his insolent tirade.

"And my 'brothers'? Join my 'brothers'? How many freakish kids do you have, anyway? Is that walking bicep you brought with you one of them? What's his so-called gift? Can he flex so hard that his tiny, testosterone-ridden balls—"

SILENCE, BOY!

She made sure to issue the command with a dose of pain that would ensure compliance. Roger winced and fell silent. Ana's voice was quiet and measured.

"You are a simpleton. An infantile man with no regard for the wider world outside of his own pitiful selfishness."

The plantation house bedroom slid away like strong rain against a resilient storm window and was replaced by the sprawling showroom of Harkins' Treasures.

Roger staggered, hands raised to ward off the unnerving experience of being thrust back into the real world.

"Holy shit," he said.

Ana looked up at her escort.

"Come, Talbot. He isn't the first of my sons to refuse our generous offer, but there are others. There is nothing for us here."

Talbot's thick arm extended to open the door for Ana. They passed through it without looking back. Roger's shout echoed throughout the large room, following her into the night.

"I didn't have a train bed, Ana! It was a spaceship!"

The door closed, leaving Roger alone with his thoughts. His voice dropped to a whisper.

"An X-wing fighter, actually."

PART TWO

GIVE ME MYSELF AGAIN

IN LOVING MEMORY OF KINETIC STAR
Eulogy For a Hero

By May Patsiavas, Metro Inquirer Opinion Columnist

I mourned over my coffee this morning when the final leaf fell from the dogwood tree outside of my office. It had long since browned and withered, yet still clung to the branch with stubborn resilience, a superb strength of will that had outlasted all of its brethren. I don't usually shed a tear over such trivial things, but this leaf's perseverance bordered on heroic. Yet it was destined to fall. As all things are.

I'll chalk my heightened emotional state up to the death of Kinetic Star.

We never knew her real name, and perhaps never will. All that remains of D.C.'s mysterious, super-powered benefactor are traces of DNA extracted from a few strands of singed hair collected at the scene, according to investigators. I'd wager that to be insufficient for a DNA match. If the hair even belongs to her, that is.

Who attacked first, the National Guard or Kinetic Star, cannot be determined until the full investigation is complete. What cannot be contested, however, are the fourteen deaths of innocent bystanders caused by National Guard firearms.

Let's not dwell on the controversy. Instead, let's reflect.

Let's remember my exclusive interview with Rhea Fine, the Rosslyn-based small-business owner who lost her child to leukemia a month before deciding to end her agony at the ledge of a high-rise building.

"She took off her mask to show me her face," said Rhea. "I was stunned. I forgot all about jumping. She was so...normal. Just a pretty girl. Just a regular young woman. The police—and then the FBI—tried to coerce me into working with a sketch artist, but I refused. That young lady saved my life. I owe her a debt I can never repay."

But Kinetic Star was anything but normal or regular, as D.C. Metro bus driver Lenora Cheeves attested in the aftermath of the H Street catastrophe.

"I didn't see him [un]til the last second. He was covered in this black, tar-like stuff, and had a bunch of extra limbs like a spider. Real creepy. I thought for sure I was going to run him over, but then everything went upside-down and the next thing I knew the bus was on its side. I heard screaming from the passengers and I smelled burning fuel. There was a thumping sound on the top of the bus, and by top I mean side, I suppose, since we had flipped over and all, and then the windows burst up and out. All at once. Then the passengers floated through the open windows like they were pushing off real hard from the bottom of a pool. She saved me last. That sweet girl. I got to see my grandchildren again because of her."

Lenora and her passengers escaped with minor scrapes and bruises instead of being immolated in a fiery deathtrap.

Yet it was fire that killed Kinetic Star. Fire accompanied by explosive force of grenades launched from shoulder-mounted weapons of war. She was the fifteenth casualty on that day.

Today let's remember Kinetic Star, not just through the memories of those she saved and whose lives she touched with miraculous deeds we'll never know, but also through the immortalized words of Homer's *The Iliad:*

"Let me not then die ingloriously and without a struggle, but let me first do some great thing that shall be told among men hereafter."

Chapter Five

CONSCIOUSNESS CAME AND WENT, flowing through faulty elevator doors that opened and closed in convulsive fits and starts. Sometimes the gap in those doors would admit sounds of gunfire or the beat of helicopter rotors from a field of black pitch, other times there was only pain. Scorching, white-hot pain. The little girl was there every now and then, standing in a far away door frame or hovering close and staring with large, cinnamon eyes that she would one day grow into. Consciousness lingered when the girl was present, the elevator doors holding fast as though she was the herald of its coming, as though she was the anchor to the waking world. The Watcher.

Samantha longed for these moments, but they were fleeting.

She wondered if she was in Hell, if her nearly non-existent religious beliefs had been wrong after all. Maybe centuries of Christianity had been right and Hell did exist. Perhaps Samantha was being punished. For what, she couldn't remember.

The elevator doors slammed home.

Consciousness fled.

Beep...beep...beep...

The sensation was demonic in its perseverance. It covered a massive area of her body, though Samantha couldn't tell exactly where it existed. She couldn't determine left from right or up from down. Dead people didn't have a sense of direction, and she had been blown apart by rocket-propelled grenades. It had begun as a mild irritation that crept along the edges of her blistering agony with tentative, probing exploration, but it might as well have been a fire extinguisher against a volcano.

That was how the sensation first greeted her.

Now it had spread like a virus, quenching as it went until the pain finally surrendered. But the burning torment was replaced by something far more sinister, something that confirmed the theory that her soul had indeed been damned to some sort of hellish underworld.

Samantha's entire being had become a maddening, unscratchable itch.

Beep...beep...beep...

The Watcher was back. Her raven hair was gathered into a topknot that followed her like a jet black cobra, weaving about her shoulders as she passed through the doorway. Time skipped ahead, and now the Watcher's face loomed close, her dusky face smooth and unblemished in its youth. Her bottom lip disappeared beneath her upper teeth as consternation darkened her features. She stole a quick glance over her shoulder, checking the door. Satisfied, she turned back to Samantha. A small index finger materialized, growing larger until it blurred and disappeared. Samantha would have felt the bony tip press into her nose, but dead people didn't feel such things.

Beep...beep...beep...

The chorus of voices far above accompanied the incessant beeping. They weren't new. They descended upon Samantha like clockwork, their repetitive mantra bleeding into her ears from an unknown origin. She made a game of matching their rhythm to that of the digital beeps that were much closer to her, but it was a losing battle. The sounds were discordant, a beat and a melody never to be married in synchronicity.

The voices were male, she could discern that much. Deep and resonant. The arrangement was non-musical yet on key and in step. Much like a group prayer, perhaps. Yes, that was it. Samantha had heard this before—

Beep...beep...beep...

—in the frigid bowels of a deserted power station. Broadcast from a flat screen television. Masses of people on bent knees, foreheads to the floor and hands pressed to the earth. Samantha had been forced to watch with eyes full of sand, barely aware of the images playing out before her yet riveted to them nonetheless. They had been presented to her in chronological fashion, beginning with the worst terrorist attack in American history and ending with a ceaseless war in the Middle East. The prayers were interspersed among the broadcasts. She remembered them well. And—

Beep...beep...beep...

—the power station. Galina. The escape. The rain. That sweet, cleansing rain. The powerful winds of a hurricane whispering in her ear.

"Go to sleep."

I can't, Daddy. Not yet.

Samantha sat up.

Beep-beep-beep-beep-beep-beep-beep—

The Watcher was there.

"Look what I can do!"

She couldn't have been older than eight, but performed a standing back flip with flawless precision. Her face was solemn as she completed the maneuver, hands held high as she awaited feedback from an imaginary panel of judges.

Samantha blinked.

"Well?"

The Watcher waited for her approval.

What the fuck?

The chorus of prayers continued, filtering through a slatted vent set into a nondescript wall near a nondescript ceiling.

What is this? Where...

The room was unremarkable as well, small and musty. It was illuminated by a single globe lamp suspended from a chain in the center of the ceiling, positioned directly over a hospital bed whereupon Samantha sat in confused bewilderment. An array of medical equipment surrounded her, and she was tethered to it by tubes and wires connected to her arms, her temples, her fingertips. More tubes and wires disappeared beneath a powder blue hospital gown and tugged at her when she moved.

Beep-beep-beep-beep-beep-beep-beep—

A memory dropped onto Samantha with a weight that forced her head back to the pillows. A medical bay in a top secret military bunker. A slight woman with crimson, matted hair. Tubes and wires sticking out from beneath a stained, white medical gown. Voices uttered in urgency.

"Can you pull that shit out of her but keep her under?"

63

"I'm just a combat medic, Footlong, but I can try."

The memory ushered in more mental images, waking nightmares and gunfire. People screaming as they died. Bodies falling to reveal national monuments on the skyline behind them. The screams of missiles and the bursts of exhaust from grenade launchers.

Ana.

Goodbye, Little Star.

Samantha dug her palms into her eyes, rubbing at them before dropping her hands to take a second inventory of her situation through bleary vision. Nothing had changed. The Watcher still watched her, having retreated several steps toward the single door in the corner near the vent, her expression pensive. Samantha sat up again, this time swooning from the effort. More echoes followed the motion.

"Only you and I have what it takes to reshape civilization."

Ana.

We are givers of life, Little Star.

Mother. Oh my god...

Samantha's hands flew to her lower abdomen. Her fingers spread wide over the cotton material, pressing and exploring, searching her belly for signs of a life that was too premature for detection under such crude examination. Her palms became clammy, moistening the gown as they clutched at it. She couldn't feel anything there, couldn't find it. The explosions must have—

So much fire. Agony. Hair. I smelled burning hair.

A terrible wail drowned out the prayers. It was her own, and heard only by her. Another echo from the past.

Have to get out of here. Have to stop her.

Samantha winced as she yanked a set of tubes from the crook of her elbow, ignoring the droplets of blood that followed.

"I-I-I don't think you're supposed to... Hey, y-you're not supposed to do that!"

The voice belonged to the Watcher, who was now at the door with her little hands wrapped around the handle. Samantha reached beneath the gown to tear at the leads that clung to her chest and belly like hungry leeches. The finger cuff followed, and then the wires at her temples.

Beep-beep-beeeeeeeeee...

Samantha ignored the annoying, constant digital note and slid from the bed, unsure if her legs would support her. Bare toes stretched and connected with a cold, tile floor.

Okay, I got this.

She pushed herself from the bed. A sharp, stabbing pain erupted in her groin, doubling her over. She gnashed her teeth together, catching a bit of her cheek in the process. She tasted copper as she clutched at the bed for support. Her vision swam and darkened.

Catheter. Of course. Fuck.

Elevator doors chimed and closed.

Beep...beep...beep...

Someone was close. Looming. Standing over the hospital bed. Leaning over Samantha. This wasn't the Watcher. It was a shimmering disturbance in the air, a shape that defied definition and substance. It was a ghost. No, not a ghost. Ghosts were incorporeal, lingering spirits without mass. Buttons scattered across medical monitoring machines couldn't depress without the application of mass and weight, dials couldn't turn without a solid, applied force manipulating them. Samantha shouldn't have been able to feel a ghost's fingers press against her neck just below the left ear, or reattach adhesive leads to her temples, chest and stomach where she had torn them away in her delirium. She tried to move, tried to push the non-ghost away from her, but she was caught in that terrifying moment between sleep and wakefulness. She was paralyzed, watching through eyelid slits as the blurry wraith went about its business.

It left after a time, as evidenced by the light footfalls across the tile floor and punctuated by the soft click of the door latch.

Beep...beep...beep...

Samantha descended back into sleep, reasoning that the completion of the REM cycle would release her from the protective paralysis that prevented her from acting out her dreams. And she hoped that this was indeed all a dream. Maybe she would wake up in her Clarendon apartment and hop on the Orange line to grab dinner and do some people watching before her shift at the Bibbing Plot.

Maybe none of this really happened.

She couldn't wait to tell Evan about her weird dream. He was going to get a real kick out of it. That geek was obsessed with superheroes and other such nonsense, and never shut up about it. Yes, she would be sure to blame it on him.

It was the absence of all sound that woke her up. The incessant beeping had stopped. The ensemble of deep, male voices united in prayer was nowhere to be found. The vent awaited the next furnace cycle in silence.

Samantha rose to an elbow and twisted her head. The medical monitors were dark and lifeless. The only readings on their screens were the reflections of the spherical lamp overhead that had been dimmed to a soft glow. She raised her hand to find no sign of the finger cuff. Her eyes traveled to her elbow, where she discovered the intravenous tubes missing. Even the bandage had been removed from the crook of her elbow, the droplets of blood wiped clean.

Maybe...

She sent her hand beneath the powder blue gown. The leads had been removed, as had the accursed catheter. Her hand flew to her head as she let loose with a relieved exhale, and found that her temples had been released from the wires as well.

I'm free of all that shit.

She ran her fingers through her hair as she sat up.

Thank God—wait a minute.

Trembling fingers explored her scalp and found velvety stubble where her luxurious mane of reddish-gold hair should have been.

Beepbeepbeepbeepbeepbeepbeep—

The heart rate monitor was shut down, but pulsed in her ears with imagined urgency.

Her other hand joined the first, exploring her skull in a frantic search for a second opinion. The diagnosis was confirmed. Her thick locks had been shorn into a soft pelt.

Hey, Demi pulled it off. So did Britney. Well, sort of, I guess. Why can't I?

She swung her legs to the side and let them hang from the bed, welcoming the prickly sensation as blood recirculated to accommodate the new position. She counted ten breaths, all while by wiggling her toes to pump life back into them, before pushing herself from the bed. The floor was cold against the soles of her feet, and she held onto the bed railing for support as she was reacquainted with the balance required to stand upright. Her body felt heavy, her weight more of a burden than she remembered, as if she had woken up on an alien planet where the pull of gravity was many times that of Earth.

What is this place?

She spotted a low bench at the end of the bed, carved from walnut with exquisite craftsmanship. An antique, from the looks of it, and quite out of place in the sparsely-furnished room. A folded pile of black clothes had been set on the bench. A matching pair of laceless slippers rested beside it. Samantha made her way to the bench in shuffling steps.

I'm going to go ahead and assume these are for me.

She held up the first garment and let the folds drop away. It was a dress of some sort, adorned only by the embroidery that decorated it from neck to navel. There was no discernable cut to it, no style, giving Samantha the impression that it was more of a robe than a dress. She set it aside and reached for the next piece. Loose, billowy pants of the same shimmering, black silk. Beneath that she discovered a roomy cloak of cotton, this garment's tone matching that of its predecessors. The final piece was a rectangular length of black silk, not quite large enough for a shawl.

What's this supposed to be?

She held it at arm's length and twirled it about before dropping it over the slippers. Her eyes fell over the outfit, scrutinizing each garment as an image of a completed puzzle began to form in her mind. It solidified and was followed by other images, still frames plucked from movies and news broadcasts she had seen. Women crying over the lifeless bodies of their loved ones, cursing soldiers as they paraded past.

The formless dress. The cloak. She retrieved the rectangular swatch of silk.

This is a hijāb. Okay...

She perused the rest of the outfit, hesitating in indecision. The ventilation system kicked on, startling her. The air was disturbed, sending a chilly draft through the open back of the hospitable gown. Her attention fell over the door then flickered back to the outfit.

Well I can't go sashaying through—wherever this is—with my junk hanging out.

Samantha cast another cautious glance at the door before doffing the gown. She threw the dress over her head and shimmied into it while reaching for the pants. She was swimming in silk by the time she was done, unused to the roomy fit of the clothes. The cloak rested on her shoulders, providing a weight to the outfit that gave her a sense of security. The slippers came next, a perfect fit. She let the hijāb lay where she had dropped it and moved to the exit.

The metal door was cool against her ear. She held her breath and listened. A tiny reflection caught her eye, perched in the ceiling corner across the room from the vent. It was a darkness within the darkness, small and boxy, a more substantial blackness settled into the corner. Something had reflected the lamp light, had caught her attention. Perhaps metal or glass. Maybe a camera lens.

Hope you enjoyed the peep show, creep.

She almost laughed at the absurdity of the thought. Whoever was on the other end of that camera had probably put her in the hospital gown in the first place. Had most likely saved her life. The ghost.

Not a ghost, Sammy. Now focus.

She tried the door handle. It gave with ease. Samantha sucked in a breath and held it, listening again. Nothing. Satisfied, she exhaled quietly and opened the door.

A corridor lay beyond, lit by a single, red bulb at the far end. Cinder blocks formed the left wall and a waist high metal handrail ran along the right side, interspersed by thick concrete pillars that were wide enough to support a large building. Blackness lay beyond the railing and Samantha sensed a broad, open space there, an expanse confirmed when her voice took its time in bouncing back from the gloom.

"Hello?"

There was no answer.

She found a utility door beneath the red light at the end of the hall, which opened as readily as the first one, and then stairs leading up to a third door. Through that door were more stairs and then another corridor, this one perpendicular to the staircase upon which she stood and leading to a door at each end.

For fuck's sake, just let me out of here.

69

Silk swished around her ankles as she chose the left door. It didn't budge. Turning on a slippered heel, Samantha tried the opposite door. A blast of warm air passed over her when it opened, carrying with it the scents of cedar and incense. A shallow stairwell led up to a blank wall. This wall was made up of solid, dark wood, unlike the cinder block walls she has encountered thus far. Despite the change of scenery, it was a dead end.

Then where is that air coming from?

She mounted the steps and ran her fingertips over the wood, searching for a niche or an irregularity, something to grab onto. She reached up and stood on her toes to explore the top, dropped to a knee to search along the floor. There it was, a tiny opening carved into the jamb near the threshold. Just big enough to admit two fingers. Hidden hinges creaked when she pulled, their protests filling the corridors and stairwells behind her. There was more warm air, more cedar and incense, but also absolute darkness. Samantha heard the trickling of water somewhere nearby.

Okay, well I'm not sleeping in that hospital bed for the rest of my life, so onward and upward.

She plunged into the void, hands outstretched before her. The floor was different beneath her feet, no longer tile or concrete. It was warmer and had a different sound as her soles scuffed against it. Perhaps wooden planking. She kept moving, sliding one foot in front of the other, one arm scouting for a point of reference while the other stayed firmly in front of her face to avoid a blind collision. Something solid butted against her hip bone. Her hands came down to identify the obstruction. Objects clattered about. There was a soft *bong!* She spread her fingers wide and grasped at whatever they were, and found a pair of candlesticks laying on their side. She had knocked them against a metal bowl in her clumsy exploration. The surface of the table was smooth and soft, covered by cloth. Samantha let her hands guide her around the edge of the table and beyond. She discovered the opposite wall, and followed it until she found the exit.

Samantha blinked as she opened the door. A warm, orange glow from dozens of candles penetrated a freestanding wall of wooden lattice work. The light made its way throughout the large chamber, touching a high, domed ceiling inlaid with intricate mosaics in solemn hues. A shining floor of polished oak stretched beyond the lattice wall, disappearing into shadowy nooks. She made her way to the center of the expanse, forgetting for the moment her urge to flee this place as she marveled at the architecture and craftsmanship of the dome overhead.

This is a mosque. I'm in a mosque.

The candlelight flickered, causing Samantha's gigantic shadow to dance across the mosaics. She felt a sudden and immediate presence.

"Who's there?"

No answer.

She spun a full circle, squinting her eyes at the lattice wall. Something moved there. Behind it. She felt her breath quicken.

"Come out!" she said.

The candlelight was disturbed again, mocking her command with its flicker.

"You refuse to wear the hijāb in this holy place, girl."

The voice was synthetic and strange, over-modulated. It came from behind her.

Samantha spun to find a shimmering disturbance, several inches taller than her and vaguely humanoid in shape. It didn't move.

"You disrespect me," said the ghost.

Samantha planted her heels and brought her hands up before her. She reached out with her will to lift the shape from the floor and hold it immobile. It was time to put an end to this game of hide-and-seek.

Time for some answers.

71

The shape didn't move. Samantha blinked and tried again. Nothing.

She turned her palms inward to study them, to blame them even though they had nothing at all to do with her abilities and never had.

"My...my powers..."

A man materialized before her, clad in a dark bodysuit covered with thin, intersecting channels and decorated sporadically with tiny, circular nodules that glowed with a cold, alien light. His entire head was covered in a faceless, form-fitting mask which sprouted more of the strange nodules. The same modulated voice came through the mask.

"Perhaps trauma has clouded your memory, Samantha McAllister," he said. "Kinetic Star is dead."

Chapter Six

REMEMBER.

A deafening blast, then hellfire and brimstone.

Smoke, acrid and pungent, filled her lungs, stung her eyes. There was a heavy weight, ponderous and suffocating.

No, before that.

There was a massive hole in a solid, stone wall, beyond which stood a dozen men in uniform, all eyes fixed on her. Half of them steadied grenade launchers on their shoulders. One of the men had his arm raised high, fingers pointed to the sky. Samantha heard her own voice, shaking and desperate.

"WAIT!"

The soldier dropped his arm, signaling her doom.

No, Sammy. Before that. Go back further.

Movie night. Jurassic Park, to be specific. She and Cole were fighting over who would sit next to Daddy on the couch.

No, too broad.

A Tyrannosaurus Rex.

Getting warmer.

The dinosaur skull, it had been that of a Tyrannosaurus Rex. The impact of the air-to-air missiles had knocked her from the sky and into the Natural History Museum. Her joints and muscles throbbed with pulsating aches. Her senses were trapped in a gyroscope, fumbling over each other for dominance yet providing no clarity. Someone was speaking to her, but not through verbal means. It was a voice in her head. A woman. But who could possibly—

Remember, dammit!

The prominent memory returned with sharp force, a sudden snap as though someone had crawled into her ear canal and sundered the synapses in her brain.

Yes, the voice! But go back to just before that. What did she say?

It wasn't so much what the woman had said, but the emotions that she had imparted on Samantha just before the sundering. There was sadness and disappointment. But also love.

What did she say, Sammy?

You know what she said. Feel it. Remember it.

Goodbye, Little Star.

Samantha tilted her head to look into the featureless face of the masked man. She had fallen to her knees without realizing it, sunken lower with each unveiled memory.

"And then..." she said, "and then I died."

My powers are gone. Ana—my mother—took them from me.

She couldn't ignore the seedling of hope that struggled to reach daylight beneath the weight of her sorrow and confusion.

Am I normal again?

A black-gloved hand extended to her.

"Come, Samantha McAllister," came the cold, sterile voice. "Dead people don't need to eat, but you do. Intravenous nutrients are no substitute for solid food."

Samantha scrutinized the stranger as she ignored the hand and rose to her feet.

"Who are you? Where am I?"

"I am who I need to be right now," he said. "In this moment. As are you. And we are in the Mosque of the Calm Redemption. New York City. Harlem."

Samantha felt her resolve returning. The recovered memories had carried a sense of catharsis with them. And with it, a renewed urgency.

"Who you need to be?" she said, taking a step back. "Do you think this is a game? There is a psychopath out there, right now, who wants to burn this world to the ground."

She could feel the stare boring into her from behind the opaque mask.

"I have some broccoli and cheddar soup that will heat up quite nicely," said the stranger.

Samantha threw her arms wide.

"You've got to be fucking kidding me!"

The stranger's posture changed. It was barely perceptible.

"We do not use that kind of language in this place of worship."

She turned away from him, feeling heat rise at the back of her neck.

I have to get out of here. Have to stop her. Now.

Samantha spun in a circle, eyes scanning the dark places beyond the candlelight.

"Which way is the door?"

She picked a direction at random and started walking, not waiting for answer.

"You can't leave this place, Samantha. It's not safe for you."

She paused in the center of the large room.

"I can take care of myself. Powers or no powers."

The man appeared in her field of vision, moving with a swiftness that surprised her.

"No," he said. "You cannot."

She attempted to brush past him but was blocked.

Okay, so this is happening. Fine.

"How about you take your silly motion-capture suit and your silly mosque, and shove them straight up—*urk!*"

She was on her stomach now, left wrist in a vise and twisted into her upper back. A lean, muscular arm was wrapped around her throat, squeezing like a python. She couldn't breathe. Spots danced in her vision. The man's voice was quiet next to her ear.

"You have disrespected this place twice now. There won't be a third time."

The pressure relented. Samantha heard him step away as she rolled to her back and gasped for air. Her left shoulder throbbed in time with her rapid heartbeat. The shadowy gloom overhead mocked her as she stared into its depths.

Well, shit.

"Get up, Samantha."

She rose and faced him. Her hands closed into fists and drew inward, thumbs just touching her jaw line. She tucked her elbows in and shifted her stance, sixty percent to the rear foot, forty to the front.

"No, Samantha. You're not thinking clearly," he said. "You've suffered major physical trauma and you're still—"

"Save your breath. I'm leaving," she said. "And apparently I have to go through you to do it."

Her right jab was all but ignored, acknowledged only by the slightest movement of his head out of its intended path. Her knuckles even brushed the black material that covered his cheek bone as it went by. Her rear cross—the true, committed attack—was entangled in his arms before it had completed its full motion. Her fist was now trapped in his armpit, his right hand snaking under her extended elbow to clasp his left arm which had braced itself against her shoulder. All he had to do now was flex his arms and lean away from her which, of course, he did. Samantha's elbow became a white hot furnace of agony.

She bit her lip to keep from screaming.

Hours of sparring with David had taught her to respect his skill. At first, she knew her minor victories had been given to her, a fortunate leg sweep here or a conveniently successful arm drag there, but as her skills had improved she understood that her victories were earned. She had obtained them through pain and sweat and perseverance. David was a natural fighter, fast and strong, experienced and brilliant. But this mysterious man moved with preternatural finesse.

"You are going to need this arm in the coming weeks," he said. "Shall we renew your convalescence, or would you like to sit down for a nice meal and talk? There are things you need to know before you leave here."

Her free hand pulled and clawed at his arms, but there was no escaping the lock. He could snap her elbow anytime he wanted.

"Okay!" she heard herself say. "Okay."

Fuck.

She was careful not to let the curse escape her lips.

"Very well," he said.

The pain in her joint subsided the instant she was released. The man stood his ground, inches from her. Samantha took several wary steps away from him, bending her elbow and rolling her shoulder to soothe the aches.

"This way, please."

He guided her back to the chamber through which she had discovered the expansive prayer room. The flick of a light switch revealed an office of rich, dark wood. The candles she had overturned in her blind exploration still lay splayed about a red-clothed table where other religious implements had been disturbed by her passing. One wall was lined with bookshelves, and a small armoire rested against the opposite wall. A modest, antique desk sat askew on the far wall, with a simple desk chair behind and two matching chairs in front of it. The hidden door that Samantha had found was still cracked open, leading back to the series of staircases and eventually the room in which she had awoken. The man pushed the hidden door closed. Samantha watched in fascination as it disappeared, the seams in the wall all but vanishing. Questions swirled and multiplied in her mind, each one branching out to spawn several more, but they were overshadowed by the most important query of all.

Um, who the hell are you?

"Have a seat," he said, motioning to one of the nondescript desk chairs.

Are you the caretaker of this mosque? Just some regular dude with a penchant for wearing weird costumes during the night shift?

"I'll return shortly," said the masked man.

No, not the night caretaker. I don't know of any regular dudes who can move like he can. Is he the...what do they call it? Imam. Yeah, pretty sure that's it.

The man paused next to the lattice-work wall and turned to face her.

"If you are thinking of making your exit while I am gone, know that she will find you the moment you set foot outside these walls."

Samantha's internal sleuthing was put on hold. Her eyes widened at the blunt statement. There was no question in her mind about who he was referring to.

"And she will finish what she started," he said.

And just like that, he gets more mysterious.

The masked man backed into the darkness and was gone. Samantha resisted the urge to leap from the chair and follow him.

How? How could he possibly know about Ana?

Only a handful of people knew about her existence. At least, as far as Samantha was aware. David, Marissa, Brie, her father, Lange and Gonzales. Roger knew, too.

Okay, more than a handful. Maybe this—whoever he is—got to one of them. Maybe he's playing games with me. Did Ana send him? A last ditch effort to trick me? To recruit me to her cause?

None of it made sense. Why take away her abilities and leave her to die only to send someone to rescue her?

Because she wants me to feel safe. Wants me pliable. She sends someone to gain my trust and plant the seeds of doubt, forcing me to test my convictions.

Samantha had to admit that the underhanded brilliance certainly seemed like something from Ana's sinister playbook.

I should never have taken her out of the townhouse that day. This is my fault. Innocent people died because of me.

Again.

Samantha rose from the chair, unable to sit still. A letter opener rested on a stack of unopened envelopes neatly arranged on top of the desk. The handle was carved into the likeness of a sword hilt, the cross guard a pair of feline paws, the pommel a roaring lion's head. She picked it up and tapped the flat of the blade against her open palm as she wandered to the bookshelves. Not all of the texts were religious or philosophical as she would expect, she also spotted *Heart of Darkness* and *The Brothers Karamazov*—both of which she had read in college— along with other great works of literature that she'd had no interest in reading. One entire shelf was devoted to practical endeavors, boasting titles such as *Fluid Mechanics* and *Probability and Statistics*. She skipped over those, wondering why a night watchman or an Imam would have any interest in such things. Marcy had once joked to her that everything you'd want to know about a man you can learn by looking at his Netflix watch list. Samantha smiled at the memory.

And I seriously doubt this guy has a Netflix account.

The assumption was reinforced when she ran her finger over the spine of *Popular Media and the Decline of Human Interaction*.

She drifted to the table and returned the toppled candlesticks to their original positions one by one. She passed her hand over one of the blackened, shriveled wicks, imagining the sting of a nonexistent flame. The motion reminded her of something, but she couldn't quite put her finger on it.

Straight pins? Why did I just get an image of straight pins?

It had something to do with inflicting pain on herself. Frustration and pity accompanied the elusive memory.

Self pity, to put a finer point on it.

Her old apartment in Clarendon. She had been in denial about her revelation, about her powers. Samantha held on to the resurfaced impressions and attempted to narrow them down. It hadn't been about the discovery of her powers. What was it then?

I couldn't turn them off. I tried and tried. Straight pins from my sewing kit bent and broke against the back of my hand. And then...

Her body heat seeped into the cool steel handle of the letter opener in her grasp. Her eyes traveled down find the warm light of the table lamps reflected along the blade.

And then I ruined a filleting knife trying to skewer my hand.

The table cloth was soft against her palm, a well-worn blend of cotton and polyester. The fair skin of her hand was a pale counterpoint to the deep red material. She flipped the letter opener into a reverse grip and raised it high, preparing to stab the point home. Her fingers spread out like a starfish, their tips whitened in anticipation.

Am I finally free of the responsibility? Am I truly normal again?

She readjusted the letter opener for a better grip and sucked in a breath.

Let's find out.

"Ahem!"

A man stood at the entrance. Steam rose in twin wisps from a wide, shallow bowl and a white teacup, both balanced upon a serving tray in his hands. Above the tray, a thick, black eyebrow arched over a dark eye set into a chiseled face the dusky hue of desert sand. He appeared to be on the precipice of middle age.

"My suturing skills are rusty so I can't guarantee a proper stitching, but by all means, plunge the opener into your hand if you think it will prove something."

The voice was unfiltered, free of modulation.

"Just try to avoid nerve or tendon damage, if you please. You're going to need that hand if we're going to stop your mother."

The letter opener dropped, caught the edge of the table, and clattered to the floor. Samantha let it lay there.

The man entered the office and set the tray on the desk. Samantha's stomach gurgled at the rich smell of creamy soup, but her eyes never left the man.

"Are...are you...?"

"For the most part, yes. Well, this is one of my faces. This is who I need to be in this moment. I apologize for the earlier theatrics," he said, pulling out a chair for her and motioning to it, "but I needed you to understand that you can't leave. Not yet. Now come. Eat."

Samantha's hunger won out over her dissatisfaction with his answer. She attacked the soup with ravenous disregard for its temperature, ignoring the pain then swallowing a gulp of bitter tea that was just as hot. She paused for a moment to tighten her lips into an O, inhaling cool air over her tongue to alleviate the sting before digging back in.

"Come downstairs when you're finished," said the man. "Leave the tray and close the door behind you."

He moved through the hidden door and disappeared from sight.

Samantha wiped her mouth with the sleeve of her robe as she rose from her meal several minutes later. She passed through the secret portal, making sure to close the door behind her as instructed. The staircases and corridors were now lit with a strange, purplish-green hue that glowed from cable lighting nestled into the ceiling corners. She retraced her steps from the recovery room, now descending staircases she had climbed before emerging into the mosque. The door that had previously denied her entry was now cracked open. Beyond it she mounted a spiral staircase set into the corner of a vast chamber hewn from the bedrock upon which the city was built. She had to pause halfway down, her journey interrupted by the breadth of sensory input that overwhelmed her.

Holy. Shit.

There was too much to take in at once, but her immediate attention was drawn to the massive projection plastered against an empty, sprawling wall. The steady beams of light from the ceiling-mounted projector resolved into a computer desktop screen, the digital display littered with too many files and folders for Samantha to take in before her gaze was hijacked and reoriented onto the chamber's centerpiece.

It was a large vessel enameled in glossy black, roughly the size of a Volkswagen and shaped like an egg with a flat bottom. The rounded contours reflected the eerie light that filtered from above to give it the appearance of a prop from a high-budget science fiction film. A symbol had been etched in white across the top, an alien rune consisting of bold, sinuous curves and terse, sharp accents. It made Samantha's nape hairs prickle.

He hired Darth Vader's interior decorator.

She resumed her descent, letting the banister guide her while her eyes continued their exploration. She noted the handrails and the thick, rounded pillars high above, and deduced that the door to the room where she had awoken lay in the darkness beyond them.

The man stood atop a wide platform that extended from the wall below the projection, his fingers skittering across the keys of an expansive console in front of him.

"I see you have a Batcave," she called, running a finger along the arm of a kung fu training dummy as she approached the platform. "Very, um, charming?"

He motioned to the access ramp that formed the edges of the dais.

"And I see that proper sustenance has restored your sarcastic wit," he said.

How do you know about my sarcastic wit?

He pushed a wheeled desk chair towards her as she joined him on the platform. Samantha stopped it with her foot but didn't sit.

"I suggest you sit down, Samantha."

She remained standing and indicated the shiny black vessel in the center of the chamber with a nod of her head.

"Can we talk about that?"

"No."

"What does that creepy symbol mean?"

"Sit down, Samantha."

"Did that thing carry you here from the planet Gotham when you were a baby?"

The man dismissed her quip with a shake of his head and turned back to the console. His fingers resumed their keyboard cadence.

"I have something to show you, and it's going to be hard to watch," he said. "So sit."

A video player window leapt onto the massive screen. A click from the console increased it to span the entire projection area. He looked

83

over his shoulder, first to her and then the chair. He waited. Samantha didn't move.

He shrugged and set the video into motion.

"Just letting you know that I don't do the sidekick thing," said Samantha. "And I'm definitely not wearing a leotar—"

The screen split into four quadrants, their perspectives of the National Mall originating from surveillance cameras mounted on faraway rooftops or from hand-held devices at street level. The former provided a wide-angled retelling of the events from that day. The latter was an intimate, guerilla-style documentary on the demise of Kinetic Star.

Samantha was already airborne and in motion, the tails of the charcoal scarf that concealed her identity fluttering like pennants behind her.

"Weapons free!"

A chorus of automatic weapon fire erupted from the company of National Guard soldiers.

"They're people! Stop!"

It was Samantha's voice, distant and garbled among the terrified screams of the crowd, but no less urgent. But the Guardsmen hadn't been firing at the people.

They had been firing at her.

Magazines ejected from their rifles as one, dozens of them cracking open to release a useless bounty of unspent cartridges.

"Run, damn it!" came Samantha's distant command.

But there was no one there. All civilians were already well on their way out of the hot zone, already clear of the danger.

Samantha searched the fleeing crowd below, pausing as though in search of something or someone. Her head tilted back as her body shot upward, the hand held cameras losing her for a moment while the surveillance cameras kept her rapid ascension in frame. Again she paused, surveying the scene below. More gunfire followed, impotent rounds ricocheting from her body or missing her altogether. She burst into motion, moving so fast that she disappeared from the close cameras as though she had blinked out of existence. The wide angles, however, caught a blurry figure that reached out to touch every soldier in the immediate vicinity like a laser activated in a hall of mirrors, leaving empty weapons and human-shaped tracers in its wake.

She reappeared high above the Mall, rotating a full three hundred and sixty degrees with arms outstretched and face skyward. The weapons fire slowed, then grew sporadic before it ceased altogether. The nearest points of view recorded disturbances in the air emanating from her in waves, distortions in the atmosphere like the smoldering summer sun on a desert highway at noon. The surveillance cameras told a different story. Military vehicles and mobile machinery anywhere near the National Mall levitated from the ground and were either ripped apart or crushed into uselessness, drivers and operators abandoning ship in desperate leaps. Companies of infantry followed suit, rising as though gravity no longer had any hold over them. They clutched at each other, at empty air, faces frozen in horror.

A keening wail found the microphones of the hand held devices. Three dots appeared on the horizon, captured by the surveillance cameras and growing larger by the second. Smaller dots ejected from them, approaching much faster and drawing black contrails across the clear blue sky in their wake. Men, women and machines fell in unison, gravity's cruel jest completed as it reclaimed them with bone fracturing force. Their cries of agony were muted by the screams of the approaching missiles. Samantha twisted about. Her hands flew up in an instinctual, reflexive motion. The impact shook all four quadrants of the video, jolted cameras near and far. The video darkened, resolving into a field of black.

Samantha sat on her rear end beside the chair. The screen blurred and doubled as her eyes burned and moistened. Her lips parted and closed, trying to form words that were too elusive to explain what she had just seen. The man turned to her and waited, his expression sympathetic.

After a time, Samantha reached out to steady herself with the chair and used it to assist herself to her feet. She smoothed out the loose dress over her chest and belly, putting her hands to work in an attempt to stop their tremors.

"She... none of it...none of it was....real."

Oh my god.

The man took a step toward her.

"Ana asked you to join her, didn't she? Gave you an ultimatum," he said.

Samantha collapsed into the chair. Her head fell into her hands.

"She made me believe that I was saving people, that those soldiers were shooting innocent... Oh my god."

"You refused her," said the man. "Refused to be part of her plan. She entered your mind and twisted your perception."

Her eyes found him as the color drained from her face, twin emeralds set into a sheet of white.

"I would never attack anyone without a reason, especially not the National Guard! This can't be real! That video footage is bullsh—"

"But you did."

Samantha dropped her head and shook it. Tears carved tributaries down her cheeks as she slammed her eyes shut. The man watched her shoulders tremble but made no move to comfort his guest.

"And now President Dietrich has the excuse he needs to bring the full might of the United States military against you. He might have other concerns at the moment, given the terrifying state of affairs with rival nations, but I don't have to tell you about his stance on people like you and your mother."

My dream. The armies of the world uniting against me. It's coming true.

"However," he continued, "the world thinks you are dead. So you must remain dead."

Again Samantha's gaze locked with his. She sniffled and cleared her throat.

"But they couldn't have found a body. There is no proof."

"The payload from the shoulder-mounted ordinance reduced what was left of the museum wall to rubble. Follow up investigations found enough DNA to confirm that a human female had been vaporized in the explosions."

Another memory presented itself to Samantha. A collision of bone and muscle. The wind being knocked from her. The searing pain of her next inhale. The scent of burning hair.

"You."

She stood up with a swift motion. The chair rolled away from her in protest.

"Y-you tackled me. Knocked me clear of the explosions."

He held her stare but said nothing.

"I think I...."

Yes. Someone was in the museum with me. Creeping in the shadows just before it all went to hell.

"I think I remember now."

Samantha's hand flew to her fuzzy scalp.

"I'm afraid the fire claimed your hair," he said. "A small price to pay, considering the alternative. It will grow back."

"What were you doing there?" she said. "I find it hard to believe that you were just a Good Samaritan who happened to be passing by. "

He pivoted and returned to the console. The video player shrunk and disappeared. Samantha's eyes were drawn to the plethora of files and folders once more. Then they, too, disappeared as the projector deactivated. One of the folder titles captured her attention however, lingering in negative exposure after the screen had gone dark.

Regenesis? What's that? Who the hell is this guy?

"It is time for you to rest, Samantha," he said, motioning to the spiral staircase across the vast room. "More will be made clear to you in the coming days. You've endured a trauma that has created holes in your memory. Those rifts will close in time, and you will regain clarity."

"I'm not tired," she said. "I don't need rest."

The tone of his reply reminded her of the agony of his arm lock.

"Then sit on your bed and stare at the wall. It makes no difference to me. We begin at dawn."

Begin?

"Begin what?"

The man's sigh was audible as he made his way down the ramp.

"Tomorrow we take the first steps that will save this world. Your mother must pay for what she has done. And for what she will do."

Samantha couldn't reply at first. He drew farther away from her.

Wait a minute...

"What do you mean 'we'? Why would you help me take Ana down?"

He was at the staircase now. His answer boomed back at her in rebounding echoes.

"Because, Samantha McAllister, I am the last of many men and women throughout history whom have dedicated their lives to doing just that."

Chapter Seven

SAMANTHA DIDN'T REMEMBER THE WALK back to her room. Her mind reeled from the video images and the dispassionate manner in which her host had presented them. Questions buzzed around her in a swarm, dive-bombing into her brain one after the other. She had no answers to ward them off.

Someone had placed a stack of freshly-washed sheets on the bench at the foot of the hospital bed while Samantha was learning about her unprovoked attack on the United States military. She marveled at the precise neatness of the fitted sheet fold. She had never been able to do that, even with telekinesis. That particular item of linen had been rolled into a ball and stuffed into the closet more often than not. It had been a long time since she had changed bed sheets using her hands instead of her powers, but she became reacquainted with the process. A large wash basin had been set beside the sheets, and a fluffy towel the color of ocean water lay next to it. A bar of soap lay atop the towel, its effervescent package matching the hue of the towel and promising all-day freshness and long-lasting moisturizing agents.

Maybe this is a not-so-subtle hint.

Samantha hooked a finger into the neckline of the silken dress and dipped her nose below. Two quick, exploratory sniffs had her lips pursed and her nostrils flared. The odor was worse than the time she had worked a double shift at the Bibbing Plot on thirty-cent wing night then had gone for a three-mile run. She took the hint and doffed her clothing before unwrapping the bar of soap and going to work.

She toweled off and dressed, then crept onto the small bed. The firm, utilitarian mattress was nowhere near as comfortable as her queen-sized pillow-top back home.

Home. Mal.

She was sure that the Siamese was okay. David or Marissa had no doubt taken care of him after her disappearance. She secretly hoped it was Marissa.

Cat people know cats, after all.

David. Marissa.

Daddy.

What were they going through right now? Had they seen the news coverage from the mall? The horrifying death of Samantha McAllister?

Of Sammy.

Of course they had. Such an event would have been consumed by the news media and regurgitated onto their broadcasts with great zeal and aplomb, filling the twenty-four-hour news cycle on repeat. Talking heads had no doubt welcomed unqualified analysts to pick apart the events frame by frame.

David. Marissa. Daddy.

Samantha felt a lump form in her throat. She wanted to take their grief as her own or, better yet, to show up out of nowhere and wrap them in a great, group bear hug. Tell them that she was alive. That she was okay.

But am I okay?

She brought her hands up and pressed a sharp thumbnail into her opposite palm. The sting was a salient reminder of her mortality. Pain had never left her once her abilities had manifested, it just didn't seem to matter. Her brain had issued the warning signals that something wasn't right, that she *should* be experiencing pain, but her body simply didn't seem to care. She had been all but invulnerable.

But now I'm normal again.

It was all she had wanted in those early days that, according to the conventional calendar, weren't so far in the past. But her night terrors, the video camera on her bookshelf, her confession to Evan, the junkyard tests, her abduction, the choppers, Cole...

It all seems so long ago.

She had wanted it all to go away. And now it had.

Samantha raised her head from the pillow and spied the crumpled, wet towel perched on the edge of the bench where she had left it. It lay motionless, daring her. Taunting her.

Why not?

Her hand came up, fingers extended.

Rise.

She focused her will, picturing the plush terrycloth obeying her command. A memory punctured the hazy membrane of her consciousness, black underwear swinging from the bedroom ceiling fan in her Clarendon apartment after she had unwittingly placed it there during a telekinesis-fueled nightmare.

 Nothing happened.

It used to be effortless. Her powers had developed to the point where they had become extensions of her, a multitude of invisible arms with the reach of anything she could see, anything she was aware of, ready for her commands. Menial tasks such as cooking and cleaning were done while she dozed on the couch, allowing her to rise to a fresh townhouse and a hot meal. Litter she passed during her morning runs had found its way into the nearest trash receptacle with no one ever touching it.

Samantha sharpened her focus, blocking out the bed, the room, the end table. Only the teal-hued towel existed now, and she ordered it to come to her.

The obstinate piece of linen refused to comply.

Samantha lay back, issuing a sound that was somewhere between an expletive and an exhale. She stared at the single overhead light until it hurt her eyes then followed its afterimage across the blank ceiling, blinking every now and then to create a negative exposure behind her eyelids. The image was replaced by injured military personnel and three missiles streaking across the sky over the Mall.

She rolled to her side and began counting, but lost track at three thousand eight hundred and seventy-three. Sleep would not come.

I wonder if Daddy and my friends will speak to me when they find out I was alive and didn't tell them about it.

She flipped to her opposite side and adjusted the pillow beneath her head.

But if Ana wins they won't be alive to find out. I can't let that happen.

Samantha pulled the covers to her chin.

But what can I do? What does Mystery Man think I can do against her now that I'm useless.

His disembodied words found her in the silence of her room.

"Tomorrow we take the first steps that will save this world. Your mother must pay for what she has done. And for what she will do."

She rolled to her stomach and pressed her face into the pillow.

Maybe this is for the best. Maybe this is the way it's supposed to be. I wanted to be normal so bad, and then I got it in my head to wear a mask and fly around the city helping people and fighting bad guys. What the fuck was I thinking? That's not a real life. A real life is—

Another memory nudged against an ethereal membrane, forceful and insistent.

—is what? It's what I want it to be. When this is all over, I'll make it official with David. I'll tell him what I want and hopefully we'll start a life together—

The memory pushed, trying to break through. It was more urgent than those that had transcended her trauma thus far.

—a life without violence and superpowers and suffering. It will be so nice. Grocery shopping and house hunting. Vacations. Arguments about money and laundry and other stupid shit. Make-up sex.

The memory charged and thrashed, caught in the net which her psyche had put in place to protect her.

Samantha smiled and closed her eyes. The persistent memory was subjugated into stillness as sleep finally found her, retreating to gather its strength in anticipation of another attempt at freedom.

The towel slipped to the floor.

Samantha's eyes opened. Someone had scooped out her eyeballs during the night and filled the empty sockets with burning sand. It took a while to focus her vision and come to terms with the discomfort. Her sleep had been fitful, filled with disconnected images that fled with consciousness. Something had pulled her from her slumber. A presence.

She rolled over and found a young girl standing beside the bed.

The Watcher. She's real. Or am I still asleep?

The girl stared at Samantha, who in turn stared back without bothering to move from the warmth of the bed. Samantha stuck out her tongue. The girl scrunched up her nose. Samantha crossed her eyes. The girl giggled and turned her head away, revealing a small patch of missing hair over her right ear.

"What happened there?" said Samantha, indicating the bald patch with a nod.

The girl ran her fingers over the spot, her gaze dropping to the floor.

"It's okay. You can tell me."

"Papa said I can't have my hair like yours."

Samantha rose to an elbow and pushed back the covers.

"Oh? What else did he say?"

"He said that your hair was an accident and that it's not proper for little girls."

"I see," said Samantha, swinging her legs over the edge of the bed and sitting up. "Well I think it looks cool."

The girl's face brightened.

"You do?" she said.

"Papas don't always know what's cool," Samantha said with a shrug.

The girl bit her lip as she pondered that fact.

"Do you want to feel it?"

Samantha lowered the top of her head toward her visitor. A small hand ran over the reddish pelt then quickly retreated. The girl giggled again. Samantha joined her.

"I'm Samantha, by the way, but my friends call me Sam. You can call me Sam if you want to, okay?"

The girl nodded. Samantha noticed that a folded piece of black cloth rested in her hands.

"Papa told me to fetch you because—"

"And what's your name?"

"I'm Isra, but we have to go because—"

"Pleased to meet you, Isra. And what does your Papa do here at the Mosque of the Calm Redemption?"

Isra's nose scrunched up again. Her dark eyes were accusatory, as though Samantha were teasing her.

"He's the Imam, silly!"

Samantha let that sink in. It made sense. He obviously had free run of the place, knew every nook and cranny, and managed to keep the underground levels hidden from prying eyes.

So Batdude is a holy man.

Samantha stood up and stretched.

"Tell me, Isra, where does a little girl go tinkle around here?"

Isra smiled, revealing a double crown of obsolete baby teeth clinging to pink gums among their adult successors.

"I'll show you, but first you need to put on your hijāb."

Samantha held up her hands, palms out.

"Oh I don't think that's necess—"

"And this, too."

She presented the folded piece of cloth she had been holding.

"What is that?"

"It's a niqāb," explained Isra as if it were obvious. "There are men in the mosque today, and you have to wear this because you're a grown up."

Samantha had never been student of Muslim culture, and knew very little of it beyond a brief mention or two in her architecture classes or its biased portrayal in American popular culture. Something nagged at her, another cloudy recollection, this one more of a sense memory than a visual one. She was hungry and freezing. Her wrists supported her weight. There was water. Too much water. Emotions were there, too. Anxiety and resentment. An image superceded the sensations. Women dressed in hijābs and veils holding anti-American placards and chanting threats in a foreign language. But this wasn't a firsthand memory. It had been presented to her on a television screen. A television screen in a cold, dank chamber beneath an abandoned power station outside of D.C.

Isra took a step back, her expression revealing sudden uncertainty as she studied Samantha's face. Samantha dismissed the memory and relaxed.

"What makes you think I'd wear such a thing, Isra? Even if your dad is the Imam?"

The girl's face lost some of its youthful innocence. There was a mischief there, glimpsed by Samantha during the brief, feverish waking moments of her recovery.

"I guess it depends on how bad you have to pee," Isra said, tossing the niqāb to Samantha.

The veil was surprisingly roomy and not at all restrictive. Only Samantha's sense of pride was suffocated. Once she had finished her business, Isra led her upstairs and across the prayer hall. The girl weaved through several corridors, then guided her into a storeroom filled with stacks of boxes and lined with industrial shelving. Isra stopped in front of a janitorial closet at the opposite end of the room and pushed the door open.

"This morning you'll do the main prayer hall," Isra said. "Sweep first, then scrub. You'll find everything you need in here."

The tone was very authoritarian for such a young voice, and Samantha had a feeling that the instructions were being recited from memory, passed down from on high.

"You...you want me to scrub the floors?"

"Papa does. I don't really care."

"What if I don't want to?"

Samantha noted that the niqāb moved slightly with the exhalation of her words, like sheer drapery in front of an open window on a lazy summer afternoon.

Well that's distracting.

"Papa said you might say that," Isra said. "He said to tell you that it's part of your training."

Samantha's sarcastic grin was hidden from Isra's eyes.

"Wax on, wax off, Samantha-san," said Samantha. "I get it."

Isra cocked her head in confusion. Samantha let it go.

"Also, Papa said to keep your eyes downcast when men are present."

The headwear became stifling for the first time. Samantha felt her blood stir.

How the hell would they even see my eyes behind this thing?

"Oh, did he now?"

Isra nodded as though she had just informed Samantha that the sky was blue. Samantha didn't want to burden the little girl with adult matters, but couldn't help herself. Maybe she would learn something.

"Is that because he wants us women to know our place?"

Isra cocked her head to the side, her brow furrowed.

"No, it's because your eyes are big and green and pretty, and you need to keep up the disguise."

"Listen, I'm wearing this get up out of respect for what your father did for me, but—"

"And he said he doesn't want take any chances with your...um...iden...id...your ident—"

"Identity."

"Yeah, that's what I said. Ideninny. Okay, so have fun scrubbing!"

She turned and cartwheeled away.

"Wait! What about you?"

Isra's voice reached Samantha from the other end of the store room.

"I have to go to school! Bye!"

Brat.

Samantha's scrubbing endeavors hadn't reached the halfway point of the prayer hall floor when she found herself reconsidering the notion that the loss of her powers had afforded her any sense of freedom. Her knees ached from crawling across the hardwood and her fingers were shriveled prunes from prolonged exposure to the soapy water. Blisters had formed across her palms, threatening to burst at any moment.

Wax on, wax off. Wax on, wax off.

The fact that no actual wax was involved in the process didn't stop her from repeating the mantra. Another fact that didn't escape her was the notion that if she still had her abilities she could have finished scrubbing every floor in the mosque before she had finished a snack-sized bag of Funyuns. Her stomach echoed the sentiment.

Shit. I didn't eat breakfast, did I?

People passed by from time to time, dark men with dark whiskers, some clad in Western garb and others in Middle Eastern attire. Her mysterious host chatted with them in a foreign tongue as he led them across the prayer hall and into his office—treading across her freshly-scrubbed hardwood more often than not. Not so much as a sidelong glance was cast Samantha's way. She had lost track of time when she finally finished the prayer hall, and plunked the flat brush into the plastic bucket before toppling onto her back and issuing a sigh of relief, not caring about the dampness that seeped through the silken garments from the spot she had just scrubbed. She was enjoying the lethargy that came from studying the intricate mosaics on the ceiling when a familiar face appeared in her field of vision.

"Up," said the man.

"Really?"

"Up, up."

He snapped his fingers with each "up" and backed away. Samantha rolled her head to regard him upside down.

"But I'm very comfortable here."

"You may remove the niqāb."

She couldn't pull it from her head fast enough.

"I have fresh dates and steamed jasmine rice for you in the office. Go. Eat."

He scooped up the bucket and made his way to the store room, leaving Samantha to debate whether her exhaustion would win out over her protesting stomach. It wasn't much of a contest.

Each date was a juicy burst of sweetness in her mouth. She couldn't recall the last time she had enjoyed one right out of the bowl. They had always been cooked into a dish or tossed into a salad at a fancy restaurant. She was so enamored with the fresh fruit that it was hard to pay attention to the what man was saying as he entered the office.

"...looks satisfactory, thank you."

"Happy to help," she said around another pulpy date, assuming he was referring to her back-breaking job on the prayer hall floor. "So this was the first step in saving the world? Scrubbing motherfu...scrubbing floors?"

He perused the bookshelves as she spoke, hands clasped behind his back as his eyes traveled across the tomes. The one he tipped from the shelf was monstrous, its spine approaching the width of a brick. The weight of it hitting the table made her teacup skitter across the saucer.

"Yes," he said. "And this is step two. Commit this book to memory as best you can."

She was afraid to look at the title, but gave in to curiosity. It was worse than she expected.

Fundamentals of Simple Machines: A Reference Guide.

Samantha looked up at him then back to the title, hoping it had somehow changed. It hadn't.

Fuck me.

"I hate to be repetitive, but...really?"

"Mornings will be spent with industrious tasks, afternoons in study."

Samantha studied his face, daring him to break the facade and burst into laughter. He didn't.

"How in God's name or Allah's name or whoever's name do you expect me to memorize this beast?"

Her palm came down on the hardcover, upsetting her tea again and popping a gelatinous blister that had formed on the heel of her hand. She winced.

"I hate to be repetitive, but...as best you can."

"Shit. Nice one. Touché, I guess."

"Language."

Samantha shook her head as she sipped at her tea.

"You may retire to your quarters when you have finished your lunch," said the man. "Take the book with you."

He turned to leave.

"Wait a sec. What do I even call you? 'Master' isn't going to happen, just so you know, and 'Papa' would be a bit weird."

"You may call me Imam while we are within these walls. It is proper."

"And when will we be outside of these walls?"

"When you are ready."

The silence that followed was palpable.

"Fair enough, Imam," said Samantha. "Thanks for lunch."

She picked up another date and squeezed it between thumb and forefinger to test its tenderness.

"Hey Imam. What's to stop Ana from blowing up the world while I'm in here growing blisters and being bored to death by huge books?"

He was already through the door, but his answer reached her with clarity.

"I'm monitoring the situation. We have the time we need."

His statement did little to allay her worries, the two words that followed even less so.

"For now."

Chapter Eight

OKAY. $V_F/V_W = 2R/(r_2 - r_1)$. I know this one.

Samantha closed her eyes and tilted her face to the ceiling.

The ratio of the force—no. The ratio of the velocity at which force is applied to the chain to the velocity of...wait, no. Yes, that's it. You had it. The ratio of the velocity at which force is applied to the chain to the velocity at which the larger object is raised is equal to twice the radius of the large object divided by the difference in the radii of the smaller objects and oh my god kill me now.

She rubbed her eyes and returned them to the book balanced in her lap.

Depending on friction, of course.

And that, boys and girls, is the wheel and axle.

She turned the page. The bold-faced heading of the next chapter dared her to continue.

The Screw

Her thoughts took a sharp left turn.

David. What did he think when I freaked out and turned on the National Guard? I wonder where he is, what he's doing right now.

Certain words such as thrust and torque and Archimedes stood out to her as she perused the chapter's introductory paragraph, but the concepts didn't register.

He's probably hatching some misguided plan to take on a thirty-thousand year-old telepathic monster bent on becoming the queen of a broken world. And I bet Marissa is helping his sweet, overconfident ass.

More details from recent events had become clearer to her over the past several days, where previously they had been nocturnal insects buzzing about in the darkness as she lay in bed, just out of reach. Many hours of busy work had centered her frenetic mind, restored her ability to concentrate for long periods of time. She was now able to reach out and snatch an insect here and there, careful not to grasp it too hard lest she crush the life out of it.

She had been mopping the angular tiles of the foyer when one flitted within arm's reach, and she added it to her jar of recovered recollections and scrutinized it with fascination. The memory took the shape of a manila envelope or, more specifically, the contents of that envelope stacked onto her kitchen table. Mal had been stalking her chicken noodle soup. Ana was recovering in Samantha's bed upstairs. The photographs depicted Ana throughout the decades, dating back to the mid-19th century, unblemished and eternally youthful. The postmark on the parcel revealed that it had been sent from New York. The sloppy stamp imprint was as clear to her then as it had been on that day in her kitchen before...

...before my insane life became even more fucked up.

Samantha closed the large instructional tome and rolled to her knees to place it on the bench at the foot of the bed, then rose to shut off the overhead light. Her slumber was restless, hounded by a swarm of memory bugs hovering just outside the light of her waking consciousness.

It was the seventh day. Samantha was sure of it. The seventh day since she awoke in this foreign place, disoriented and alone. She rolled out of bed and started her routine, which had become familiar, comforting. Rise, wash, dress, breakfast, manual labor, lunch, study, dinner, study, sleep. Rinse. Repeat. She had finished *Fundamentals of Simple Machines: A Reference Guide* the night before, only to be presented with *The Physics of Complex Machines* the following day. Samantha had accepted it with stoicism, but not without a sarcastic quip about her anticipation of diving into the page turner with alacrity. The blisters on her fingers and palms were beginning to give way to hard calluses. The aches in her arms, back and legs— the result of constant bending, squatting, crawling and lifting—had dissolved, leaving her feeling strong and able. She had grown used to the hijāb and niqāb as well. Wearing the nebulous headgear meant she had a secret.

The only secret she had left.

Samantha's morning tasks were given to her by Isra seconds before she bounded away in one agile gymnastics stunt or another, almost late for school as usual. Samantha hadn't had time to clarify her orders to clean the lower levels before the little girl had exited the janitorial closet that morning, leaving her standing bewildered among the buckets, brushes, brooms, dusters and mops.

The lower levels? Wow, okay. This is unexpected.

Samantha started in the recovery room—or *her* room, as she now called it—first changing the bed linens and wiping down the bench before fetching the bucket which was overflowing with suds. She dropped to her knees and began the familiar, circular motions with the saddle brush, anticipating the arrival of the meditative state that she had become accustomed to during her morning tasks.

The repetitive sound of the bristles moving across tile or linoleum or cement had become a mantra, lulling Samantha into a contemplative state where her mind was free to roam.

Swish swish swish...

She would repeat formulas and reiterate definitions from the reference guides she had been assigned, often checking them against the text later that evening to confirm that she had a solid grasp on the principles. Sometimes she discovered missing pieces to the puzzle of her recent past. The depressing part was that she had lost the puzzle box and had no idea what the finished product should look like. She knew that a gigantic piece fit in the center, a single piece that dwarfed all others. This piece always loomed just out of range, no matter how meditative her state of mind. It had to do with David, that much she knew, but also with Ana. It was something Ana had told her—shown her?—in those last moments before...

Before Kinetic Star died.

Swish swish swish...

Samantha leaned back on her heels and twisted around to survey her work. She had covered the entire floor in a soapy sheen without realizing it.

Yay, busy work.

She removed her slippers and tip-toed to the exit, careful not to slip and break a hip or a wrist. It was a dance that felt unnatural, one she hadn't had to perform when her abilities were intact.

But you're normal now, sister. So don't be stupid.

It wasn't long before she had changed out the grey, tepid water for a clean, steaming refill. More suds slopped over the rim of the bucket as she paused at the top of the spiral staircase. The yawning chasm of the Lair, as Samantha had come to call it, loomed at the bottom of the stairs, inviting her into its maw. The lights had been left on for her, but were dimmed considerably as if to warn her to keep her eyes on the job and not on the myriad of interesting things that begged to be explored. Not the least of which was the computer console on the raised platform in the center of the room. A flashbulb went off in Samantha's mind, conjuring a snapshot of the computer's desktop screen that she had glimpsed an instant before the Imam had shut it down.

Regenesis. What does that mean?

She banished it from her thoughts and went to work.

Swish swish swish...

Despite her best efforts, her mind wouldn't calm itself. Meditation wouldn't come. She had been at it for two hours, and had barely covered a third of the massive floor.

Looks like I'm skipping lunch today.

She dipped the brush into the bucket and set it to the cement floor.

Swish swish swish...

Another hour was spent in restlessness. Her attention was constantly drawn to the dark corners of the chamber, unknown places to be probed, searched. Places she hadn't paid attention to the last time she was down here, overwhelmed by the revelations that the Imam had thrust upon her.

Swish swish swish...

The spacious projection area loomed over her, impotent and lifeless.

Regenesis...Regenesis...

Her efforts brought her close to the large, black, vessel-like thing in the middle of the room. She stood and ran damp fingers over the surface, leaving tiny droplets as she traced the strange symbol. Her eyes darted to the staircase. When she found it unoccupied, she rapped her knuckles against the side of the vessel. Metallic taps echoed back at her, quickly fading into silence.

"Hello in there," she sang. "Can you hear me? If so, what the fuck are you?"

She abandoned the uncooperative vessel and continued scrubbing until the brush bumped against the bottom of the access ramp.

I'm sure he wants the platform scrubbed, too. Of course he does.

She went to work, cleaning her way up the incline.

Swishswishswishswishswish...

The console was close now. She pushed the desk chair out of the way and continued scrubbing. Her eyes moved to the spiral staircase. No one was there.

No, Sammy. It's invasion of privacy. This guy saved my ass and now he's feeding me and giving me honest work. I shouldn't pry.

She submerged the brush in the bucket and withdrew it, shaking off the excess water before pressing it to the floor. Again, she found herself checking the stairs.

Swishswishswishswishswish...

But he had those surveillance videos from the National Mall. He knew all along that I had been tricked. What else is on that computer? What else is he hiding?

The brush fell into the bucket, displacing a dollop of soapy water that lapped over the side in protest. Samantha placed her palms on the floor and arched her back into a catlike stretch. She got to her feet and interlocked her fingers overhead, moving her arms back and forth as another stretch overtook her.

That feels good. Gonna take a quick break.

Her hand rose to brush a phantom lock of hair over her ear as her eyes fell over the computer keyboard.

Alright, let's be honest. He has information about me in there. And I'm entitled to know what it is.

The bucket caught her attention, a reminder of why she was in the Lair in the first place. The brush floated on the surface in a silent accusation of neglect. There was a lot more floor to cover, and there was no time to go poking around where she didn't belong.

Yeah I really shouldn't—

"Just a quick peek," she whispered.

It took a full three minutes to find the button that activated the overhead projector. She passed the time by convincing herself that she would be able to handle whatever she found among those files and folders, that the information was owed to her. The machine stirred, the exhaust fan waking up as white light spread across the wall. Samantha tapped the knuckle of her thumb against the keyboard's spacebar, rousing the computer from its sleep. The projection darkened, then flickered. An image replaced the flickering, a strange symbol that matched the one on the vessel looming behind her. She felt her pulse quicken. She rubbed her fingertips against her palms.

A password screen appeared. Her heart sank.

Oh, but of course. Wonderful. Fuck.

Her fingertips hovered over the keyboard, dancing and flicking without touching a key. The cursor flashed in a steady rhythm against the white field, waiting.

Okay, let's see.

K-I-N-E-T-I-C-S-T-A-R

Her pinky found the Enter key.

The cursor blinked out of existence, replaced by a ring that chased its own tail.

Password incorrect. Two attempts remaining.

Motherfucking... That was just stupid. Stupid. Not everything is about you, Sammy.

She pressed her hands together in prayer fashion and rubbed them together.

Okay. What have we got? Isra, mosque, Imam, Allah, Quran, New York, Harlem... I don't freaking know. Pick one, but make it look like a password.

!-S-R-@

She hit Enter.

Password incorrect. One attempt remaining.

Fuck fuck fuck.

Samantha pictured her last attempt failing miserably. Red lights and sirens would erupt around her, strobing maniacally as a robotic voice shouted "INTRUDER!" over and over again.

Mosque, Imam, Allah, Quran, New York, Harlem, Batman, Lair, Regenesis, mosque, Calm Redemption, Allah, Imam—wait a minute.

R-3-D-3-M-P-T-!-O-N

Her index finger was poised over the Enter key. A bead of sweat trickled down the back of her neck. She closed her eyes and drew in a deep, steady inhale.

Swish swish swish.

She held her breath and tapped the key. The display went dark. Samantha felt her toes curling inside the slippers. A pleasant chime banished the anxiety in an instant. She issued her exhale through puckered lips as the screen filled with dozens of icons. The cursor appeared as if to say "At your service, madam."

Her hand fell over the mouse. It was cool in her hot, calloused palm. She directed the pointer to the Regenesis folder but paused when she spotted a juicier target among a cluster of folders in the lower right portion of the screen. They had been grouped that way on purpose. Her vision sharpened on the titles.

Subject Zero: Archive

and

Subject Sixty-Seven

and

Subject Zero: Test Results

and

Subject Sixty-Three

Samantha moved the cursor over the folders, unsure where to start. She double-clicked Subject Zero: Archive and blinked several times as the folder expanded into view.

Hundreds of new icons appeared, both files and folders. Samantha scrolled through them, trying to decrypt the nonsensical, numerical titles into some semblance of meaning and order. She finally clicked one titled **Scans** at random. Another subfolder opened, this one filled with image files. Samantha clicked the first icon in the set, which brought up an image viewer. Her eyes narrowed in familiarity.

There she was in full color, dancing at Woodstock with a joint clutched between index and ring finger. There she was in black and white, smudged face and head covered in a bandana as she worked in the factory during World War II. There Ana was, in sepia, wearing her wedding dress and a stoic facade beside her Civil War-era groom. All of the photos were there, digital versions of those that had been printed and sent to Samantha.

It was *him. He wanted me to know. He wanted me to find him.*

She swallowed hard as she reviewed the photos on the giant screen. *He was trying to warn me.*

But there were more scans. A painting of her mother from the Renaissance era. A rough sketch in charcoal that also bore Ana's likeness. Samantha stole a glance at the spiral staircase before continuing her clandestine activities.

Still unoccupied.

She clicked back to the main folder and selected files in rapid fashion, opening one only long enough to comprehend each new piece of information before closing it. She found a census from 1794 France with Ana's name highlighted by some sort of modern graphics program.

She had used the last name Flambert. There was a passenger list from the Dutch East India Company dating back to 1631. Her name had been Ana Beckmann then. A passenger list from another voyage was dated 1587. This one had been bound for the Roanoke colony in the New World. Ramsey, Ana's fictitious last name, had been scratched out and replaced with Claybrook. What had life been like for Ana during those years?

Well I guess I don't have to worry about living forever now that I'm just a regular ole girl.

Samantha closed the folder and returned to the desktop. Her next target was **Subject Zero: Test Results.**

The folder swelled into a host of video files with text documents sprinkled throughout. Samantha summoned the first video in the top row. There was no sound, only an angled, overhead view from what appeared to be a surveillance camera mounted in the corner of the small room. The subject was a cluster of men in medical scrubs surrounding a hospital bed not unlike the one in Samantha's room. The men buzzed about the bed like diligent bees around a summer perennial, adjusting settings on blinking and flashing machines that formed the perimeter of the bed. They checked digital gauges and unfurled coils of tubing and wiring, moving among each other with practiced agility and allowing only brief glimpses of the bed's occupant. Samantha shook her head and closed the video, moving to the next video file in the row.

Her hands left the mouse and keyboard when the visual leapt onto the screen. She took a step back from the console, eyes locked onto the projection. There were only two scrub-clad men now, conferring in close proximity with arms crossed over their chests as they observed their subject. The patient was dressed in a white hospital gown. Her eyes were taped shut and a hair net covered her head. The tubes and wires from the previous video now connected the patient to the machines. Samantha recognized the room now. She had been in it. A medical bay in a bunker hidden deep underground, beneath the snowy slopes of the Arctic Circle.

Why would the Imam have this?

She reviewed more videos, pushing the progress slider along to skim through the footage. Each video showed more of the same. Surveillance of the patient. Surveillance of Ana prior to her liberation at the hands of her hopeful-yet-foolish daughter. There were hundreds of these videos.

How long was Ana imprisoned there?

Samantha moved on to the text documents. Most of them were very technical in nature, readouts from the monitoring machines or daily dosage logs of the chemicals they were pumping into her. A few of the pharmaceuticals stood out to Samantha, psilocybin and dimethyltryptamine in particular, and she wondered if she'd come across those names while browsing social media or listening to a podcast. Perhaps she remembered them from a college text book, yes, from that anthropology class on ancient South American culture. She recalled that the drugs were hallucinogenic.

She was preparing to move on to another folder when a file titled **Subject Zero: Results Overview** captured her attention. She double-clicked it.

...while basic brain function remains nominal, spikes in the cerebral cortex and thalamus remain steady at unprecedented levels when compared to case studies in both historical and modern medical journals. Subject Zero is very much aware...

Samantha scrolled further down the document.

...electroencephalogram results are problematic. Three EEG machines have failed due to overload from an unknown

surge. Data analyzed prior to these failures remains inconclusive...

Samantha skipped to a heading labeled **Findings**.

Attempts to isolate and identify source energies continue to yield ambiguous results. Doctor Frankel's hypothesis that Subject Zero's 'abilities' have conferred a means to self-extend beyond the confines of this installation remains falsifiable and therefore scientifically unproven. However, it is the opinion of this researcher that Subject Zero will suffer neurological trauma if these tests continue. Prognosis: degradation of the frontal lobe resulting in the deterioration of reason and judgment. Efforts to emphasize the gravity of these revelations to superiors have been met with resistance thus far, but this researcher will continue to...

Samantha couldn't close the file fast enough. She ran her hands over her face, pressing her fingertips into her eyes and rubbing them. She looked back at the desktop screen covered in its crowded field of colorful icons, but the display was a nebulous background to a specific string of words that floated there in a crisp afterimage.

... deterioration of reason and judgment...

Reason and judgment. Ana isn't evil. She's mentally ill. Delusional.

Samantha backed away from the console, stumbling to the center of the platform and pivoting in a circle as another memory unfurled itself from a dark corner in her subconscious. It was one of the last things Ana had said to her.

"You still don't understand, my sweet child. There is no such thing as good and evil. There are only our choices and our actions."

Samantha tented her fingers against her chin and raised her eyes to the shadowy crevices of the rough-hewn ceiling.

"And your choices and actions are informed by a malfunctioning brain," she whispered.

She's not rational. Maybe I can still save her.

She strode to the console.

But first things first. Why the hell does the Imam have all of this stuff? And how did he get it?

The mouse pointer danced across the icons, circling in indecision until coming to a rest on **Subject Sixty-Seven**.

Four subfolders leapt out at her without hesitation.

Ohio

Illinois

Virginia

Washington, D.C.

Samantha sifted through their contents one by one, unsurprised that she had been subjected to surveillance as well. She found snapshots of her past, taken incognito through a telescopic lens. Images of her youth in Centerville, her college days at Northwestern. Comings and goings to and from her apartment in Clarendon, her first day on the job at the Bibbing Plot in the city.

Holy shit. 'Stalker' doesn't quite cover it. This is...this is...psychopathic.

She tried to ward off the sickening feeling that grew in her stomach like a sponge soaking up her sense of security and clicked back to the main folder. She spied a folder that had escaped her notice during the first pass.

Emergence

Well, I've come this far. Can't wait to find the nudes.

She opened the folder and found more covert photography within. The image files seemed to be arranged in loose chronological order, beginning with a series labeled **Adams-Morgan** and ending with one called **National Mall**. The first several photos showed Samantha clad in a loose, off-the-shoulder tee shirt and gauzy black skirt. She was entering a cab in the foreground of the shot, the colorful neon sign of a club named The Lizard Queen visible in the background.

The night I learned I could fly.

Samantha advanced to the next photo.

She was in the same outfit, standing in line at a food truck with a large decal of a slice of pizza plastered to the side.

Samantha advanced to the next photo.

She stood just outside of her apartment door in Clarendon, her hands shoved into the pockets of her skirt, a look of consternation on her flushed face.

Wait, no one was in the hallway with me that night. Were they?

She scrutinized the photo further. The photographer must have been standing at the top of the staircase.

You were lit, Sammy. Deep, deep in the Bibbing Plot. Focused on finding your damn keys. There could have been a huge chimp bashing cymbals together in that hallway and you wouldn't have noticed.

She advanced to the next photo, the first in a sequence of drone surveillance images using night vision technology. A large swath of grassy field was depicted.

That night out in Manassas County. Evan.

She kept going, transfixed by the secretive documentation of her emerging powers while at the same time fully aware of her growing anxiety at the implications. Each image brought her back to that central question.

Who the hell is my gracious host, really?

But none of the photos provided an answer. There she was, at the Occidental with David, grabbing a napkin to cover her face. There she was, at the top of a building in Rosslyn, convincing a grieving mother not to end her life. There she was, with Marissa in the shopping mall, a new dress shirt in hand to replace the one she had splattered with hair dye after her mission to the Mexican border.

Wait, I saw him that day.

Marissa had drawn her attention to a strong-chinned man looking down at her from the balcony.

"Someone's checking you out, lady," Marissa had teased.

Samantha tried to summon a smile at the memory but it wouldn't come. She missed her friend.

It had to have been him. He's been following me for that long. Even longer. All of my life, maybe.

The sponge in her stomach constricted, now secreting a burning anger that filled her capillaries. Her fists curled into tight balls.

And he knew my secret the entire time. Knew it before I did.

She shook out her hands and closed the folder, unable to continue. She had seen quite enough.

He's going to answer my questions. Explain this to me. I don't care if he's with a parishioner or whatever they're called. I don't give a shit if he's busy with—

Regenesis

The icon lodged itself into her peripheral vision and held fast.

No, I can't take any more of this. I'm tired of being everyone's puppet, tired of being in the dark about my own goddamned life. He'll tell me what I want to know, or I'll... Or I'll...

Regenesis

The title sharpened, tiny pixels becoming crisp and clear while the rest of the desktop icons blurred into insignificance.

Just a peek. Then I'm hunting him down.

Only seven files made up the contents of this folder. They were all videos, the filenames titled chronologically from **nov-17.mp4** to **nov-23.mp4** .

What day is it now? I missed Thanksgiving.

Samantha opened the video from November seventeenth and expanded it to full screen. She clicked the play icon and watched as the projection burst into motion.

She saw the room with the hospital bed. Her room. The camera in the ceiling corner provided a full view of it. The medical machines weren't surrounding the bed, but instead were lined up in a neat row against the wall and covered in clear, plastic dust covers. The entry door slammed open and a dark form rushed in. Something large and oblong was slung over one shoulder and wrapped in a white sheet.

The Imam. Has to be.

He wore an outfit very similar to the one he had been wearing when she had first men him in the prayer hall; a black, form-fitting suit covered in circular, glowing nodules. But the strange devices were now dark and lifeless. The body suit was ruined, hanging from his shoulders and back in tatters. He deposited his burden onto the hospital bed and tugged at the edges of the sheet until it fell away.

Samantha's toes and fingertips were suddenly encased in ice. Her breath stuck in her throat. Her jaw loosened and her eyelids fluttered.

A woman lay lifeless atop the white sheet, which Samantha now noticed was stained with blood and littered with ashy specks. The entire left side of the woman's body was a mass of cooked skin over charred flesh. What was left of her hair sprouted from the right side of her skull in patchy, reddish-gold clumps. The remains of her cashmere sweater and denim blue jeans were burnt and singed into uselessness. It was impossible to tell where the decimated garments ended and her cauterized skin began.

The Imam pressed two fingers to the woman's neck, then ripped the mask from his head. Thick, raven hair clung to his scalp in matted, sweaty curls. He leaned over to place his ear over the woman's nose and mouth, then straightened and exited the room in a sprint. Samantha was left staring at a nightmare reflection of herself laying near the brink of death on a strange hospital bed in a strange, subterranean room below a strange holy place.

She wasn't sure how much time had passed before the Imam returned, clad in scrubs and wearing a surgical mask, gloves and head covering. She hadn't been able to capture a good look at his face before he had left the room, and none would be afforded to her now. He pushed a wheeled table before him. Medical instruments flashed in the overhead lamplight as the table met the side of the bed with urgency, jostling the tools across the table's surface. The Imam went to work without hesitation.

He picked up a pair of large, stainless steel shears and cut away the remains of her clothing, down to the sooty and singed Chuck Taylor All-Stars that were once a bright red. He traded the shears for a pair of forceps and set about the gruesome task of picking away tiny, scorched bits of cotton and wool that had melded with her parched skin. Samantha couldn't bear to watch. She seized the mouse with shaky fingers to scrub the video forward. The time index progressed passed an hour, then two. The Imam was indefatigable, not slowing as a third hour went by. After five hours of intense extractive work, he plunked the forceps onto the table and stepped away from his patient. He pressed his knuckles into his lower back and twisted from side to side.

Samantha let the video play in normal time when the Imam approached the bed again. His hands extended to cover her seared forehead and blackened belly. His eyes closed and his chin fell against his chest. He stood in that position for several minutes. The video was silent, yet Samantha thought she could make out moving lips behind the surgical mask.

He prayed for me.

The screen went dark. Samantha opened the next video as fast as she could.

November eighteenth. The machines now surrounded the bed, dust covers removed and monitor displays alive and busy. A respirator had been fitted over Samantha's face, the thick tube that extended from it being one of many tubes and wires that now tethered her to the machines. The Imam was there, dabbing at her burns with a white cloth soaked in an unknown pinkish substance. A dozen more swatches of cloth lay on the wheeled table next to him, stained with blood and pus and decorated with pieces of sloughed skin.

November nineteenth. The patchy remains of her hair had been shaven off. Her body was draped in a light, thin coverlet of powder blue. Most of the left side of the covering was stained with brownish splotches. The Imam entered the room and checked the monitors. A quick glance at his patient turned into a startled double take. He turned to the bed and lifted the coverlet. Samantha could clearly see his dark eyes widen above the face mask. He slowly pulled back the covering until she was exposed to view and inspected her with a renewed interest. The coverlet came off with a quick yank. The Imam's eyes found the camera in the ceiling corner and moved from it back to his patient. What had been a field of scorched, ruined skin was now a massive, angry rash of pink and yellow blisters.

November twentieth. Patient Samantha twitched. Hands rose under the coverlet, disturbing the wires that protruded from beneath. Her entire body spasmed. Her head lolled from side to side in slow, weak motions, closed eyelids tightening then relaxing. The left side of her face and scalp was covered in scabs where the blisters had been. Patient Samantha rose from the bed, levitating under the coverlet like an assistant in a Las Vegas magic show. The wheeled table shot across the room to slam into the opposite wall. A frenzied flashing erupted across one of the monitors. The Imam rushed into the room and went to Patient Samantha, guiding her back down to the stained bed.

November twenty-first. The Imam pulled aside the light coverlet. Most of the scabbed tissue was gone, replaced by large swaths of new, pale skin untouched by time or the elements. The respirator was gone as well. He shook the folds from a hospital gown that matched the bright hue of the coverlet and dressed her, then stood over her and bowed his head in prayer, his hand spread over the ginger stubble that had sprouted across her shiny pate.

November twenty-second. The door cracked opened. Tiny fingers wrapped around the jamb. Isra entered and stood watching Patient Samantha from the other side of the room. It took some time to gain the courage, but the girl shuffled closer to the bed. A little finger reached out and pressed into Patient Samantha's nose. The door widened to admit the Imam. The scrubs and protective medical gear were gone, replaced by civilian clothes. He ushered the girl from the room with a scowl and a rigid, extended finger.

November twenty-third. Isra was back, this time standing near the door and wearing a pensive expression. Patient Samantha sat up and took in her surroundings, rubbing her eyes with the heels of her hands before opening her eyes again for a second opinion. Her stare was vacant and distant. She placed her hands over her lower stomach and blinked several times. Her mouth opened in a silent scream. Isra tensed and clutched at the door handle. Patient Samantha began tearing at the tubes and wires, extricating them with violent necessity. She threw her legs over the edge of the bed and pushed herself up, but she had missed one of the tubes during her frantic untethering. She doubled over and fell to the floor. Isra's mouth opened to echo the silent scream as she bolted from the room.

Samantha closed the video and shut down the projector. She braced herself against the console as her legs became gelatinous and unsupportive. The blank wall taunted her with ghostly images of a floating, sheet-laden woman. Of a table carting itself across the room.

Of third-degree burns healing within a week. Her breakfast roiled in her stomach. The feeling was familiar. She had felt it when she first discovered her powers.

" وتعويض الشر هو عقاب مثله."

Samantha almost leapt through the ceiling. She spun about, her hands still clutching at the console to take her weight. Her voice was just above a whisper.

"Those words..."

They were the last thing I heard before I died.

The Imam was there, standing at the bottom of the platform ramp with his hands clasped behind his back.

"It is Arabic. A passage from the Holy Book," he said. "The English translation is 'And the recompense of evil is punishment like it'."

Samantha stared at him open mouthed.

The Imam offered his hand.

"Come. It is time to put down the scrub brush and pick up the sword."

Chapter Nine

RAGE SUFFUSED HER BEING. Samantha welcomed it with a snarl.

"You knew."

The words exited her mouth in an accusatory growl. She pushed herself from the console as her muscles filled with adrenaline, refueled with naked ire.

"You *knew*," she said. "You knew about me all along! Followed me!"

She tore the hijāb from her head and cast it at the Imam. It struck his chest and fluttered to the floor, limp and lifeless.

"That video showed me floating! You led me to believe that my powers were gone, had me on my hands and knees scrubbing your precious floors!"

She advanced on him without realizing it. The Imam attempted to reply, his face calm and his posture still as stone.

"You need to understand—"

"I'm not *DONE!*"

The final syllable boomed throughout the massive chamber like a thunderclap. Emerald eyes flashed.

"You let me believe that I was..."

Her slippered toe found the wash bucket. She looked down as if in a dream, her tone softening.

"...normal again."

But you'll never be normal, Sammy.

She reached out with her will, attempting to levitate the bucket from the floor. Nothing happened.

But I was floating. I forced the table across the room.

The Imam's expression remained impassive.

"I protected you, Samantha McAllister," he said.

"Protected me from what?" she said. "You know what I'm capable of!"

"From yourself. If you had run off to exact your revenge without knowing the facts, without knowing the full story, all would be lost. And I wouldn't be there to pull you from the dragon's mouth this time."

He paused to let his words penetrate her emotion.

"Ana fooled you, Samantha. She pitted you against the military and condemned you to a fiery death. Not me."

Samantha felt her muscles relax. She was suddenly very tired. The draining vessel of anger was refilled with confusion and an unexpected clarity.

He knew I'd go through his computer. He wanted me to find it. All of it. Wanted me to know.

"Ana is no longer the woman you knew as a child, Samantha. She has become something dark and terrible."

Samantha walked to the edge of the platform and sat down, head bowed and fingertips pressed to her throbbing temples. Images of the Imam picking bits of fabric from her blackened skin revisited her, along with the persistent reminder that she had healed so quickly, that she had levitated herself from the bed while unconscious.

This is too much. Too much to sort out.

She held out her left hand, fingers spread wide, and rotated her wrist. There was no sign that she had been burnt alive, aside from the missing freckles on the back of her hand that had not returned with the new layer of skin.

My powers. I still have them. Why can't I use them? Why can't I feel them?

Her fingers curled into her palm then relaxed.

"Who are you, Imam?" she said without looking up, her voice just above a whisper. "Tell me the truth."

She sensed him moving closer. An extended hand entered her field of vision.

"Come. I'll put on some tea."

"No," she said, ignoring his hand. "No tea. I want answers."

The Imam let his hand drop to his side. He took a seat next to her.

"Very well," he said with a sigh. "In short, I am the last of a brotherhood once called the Sharuri. The term is a rough translation from ancient Sumerian meaning 'Hunters'."

Samantha turned her head to regard him.

"No, really. Who are you?" she said with a quiet chuckle.

His right eyebrow arched in indignation.

"It is true. The Sharuri date back to Mesopotamia, fourth millennium B.C., or so we were taught."

Maybe I shouldn't be so quick to judge, given how I used to fly around in a mask. I'll play along for now.

"Mesopotamia. Isn't that now Iraq?"

The Imam nodded.

"Indeed it is. I am a direct descendant of the founder of the Sharuri."

"You said you are the last of the Shar...Sharu..."

"Sharuri," he finished for her, "although our organization ceased to exist in its original form millennia ago. There was war and famine and migration. And there was progress. The world changed and we changed with it. But our mission was undeterred."

Samantha settled into a more comfortable position on the edge of the platform and waited.

"We were created to hunt the spawn of Mammi," he said, turning to meet her eyes. "The Mother of the Gods."

Samantha leaned away from him as the implication landed. The Imam waited.

Ana.

"Oh, please. No fucking way," she said.

"Language."

"This is...this is just—"

"You must realize that my ancestors were sworn by oath to destroy your ancestors. And we did. For many thousands of years your mother walked the earth leaving abominations in her wake. Some were strong. Others were cunning. All were gifted, thanks to your mother's genes. The Sharuri were always there to make sure they never gained the upper hand, never had a chance to use their abilities to control humankind. Life was savage back then, Samantha, and your ancient brothers had a decided advantage against normal folk. Kings and peasants alike."

I thought Roger was the only one. But there were so many. There had to have been so damn many.

Samantha felt a chill on her neck beneath the black silk.

"You put them down like stray dogs," she said.

The Imam's head dipped in an almost imperceptible motion. His eyes dropped to the freshly-scrubbed cement floor.

"It is so. Your mother possessed an innate—even unnatural, one might say—talent for eluding us. She was always our primary target, and always one step ahead. She never stayed in one settlement for very long. Of course, there were times when my forebears crossed her path.

The Mitutu, they were called. The Dead Ones. We found them slobbering and soiled, their minds obliterated by the horrific phantasms she had visited upon them."

Samantha caught the sudden feeling of satisfaction that arose out of nowhere and quickly suppressed it.

No. That's terrible. Even if they were hunting my mother. Jesus, Sammy.

"We learned to resist her powers by training our minds and bodies, and by embracing the true God. His presence protected us."

"Can you teach me? Just the first part, though. I'm all good with the God thing."

The Imam's brow arched again, this time accompanied by the slightest hint of a wry smile.

"I have been doing just that."

Samantha's face screwed up at that. He continued before she could protest his cryptic answer.

"We developed new tactics to fight her offspring as the centuries passed, handing them down to our descendants over many, many generations. They improved and modernized them to fit the times. Our sworn enemies had supernatural powers, but we had human ingenuity, unwavering discipline and perseverance."

He leaned over to pick a piece of lint from his dark, suede shoe.

"And that is who I am, Samantha McAllister, the last of the true Sharuri. My name is Jibril Wasem."

"Quite a tale," she said. "I'd say it is nice to finally meet you, Jibril Wasem, but it sounds like our people are ancient enemies."

"If I wanted you dead I could have murdered you as a child."

That hit Samantha with a jolt, but she stood her ground. Her retort was immediate.

"Then why didn't you?"

"Let me put it another way," he said. "If I still followed their ideology, I *would* have murdered you as a child. I am a descendant of the Sharuri, yes, but I utilize their lessons and training for other means. They have become something unrecognizable. There is no honor in what they do."

...for other means.

A memory bubbled up from the fog of her trauma. Samantha sat with Marissa watching breaking news unfold on a tiny smartphone screen.

The video. That's right.

"'Other means'? Such as running around New York busting up opioid rings?" she said. "Evading the cops on rooftops?"

Jibril's expression was a blank slate.

"You asked me who I am. I am telling you," he said.

Oh well. Worth a try.

"You said you are the last of the Sharuri as if they no longer exist, but then said that they have become something else," she said. "Which is it?"

"It is both. The order was much the same until recent history, but it realized that it would need to adapt as civilization evolved. It was either that or perish, particularly as agrarian culture began to centralize into cities, then into governments. Ancient Athens, for example. As governments grew and became more sophisticated they became almost indistinguishable from one another. My point is that the order gradually became the very thing it had spent thousands of years trying to protect humanity from."

"A single, unopposed power," Samantha said.

Jibril raised his chin to look at Samantha with approval.

"Very astute," he said. "But they never lost their interest in Ana and her children. Even while forming and toppling world governments from behind the scenes, the Sharuri—by this time dispersed and folded

126

into a smattering of global intelligence agencies—assigned an agent from each generation to keep track of her. But they no longer had an interest in the traditional, barbaric directive of removing her children from this earth; no, they were looking for ways to harness her children's power to dominate this earth. What was once a unified order of noble hunters had split into geopolitical factions separated by imaginary lines drawn on a map."

"It's you," Samantha said. "You're this generation's agent. You were assigned to track Ana."

Jibril rose and took several steps away from the platform, hands clasping behind his back once more.

"I was, once upon a time. Yes."

Samantha waited for more, noting the change in his body language. "And?"

He roamed the immediate area of the platform, brushing his fingers over a railing and inspecting the tips for dust.

"That ended over twenty years ago," he said.

"What changed?"

Her eyes followed his pacing. It reminded her of David when he was deep in thought. Or when he was anxious.

"She had you," he said. "Her first female child. Ever."

Oh...

"I followed her for years. I watched her fall in love with your father, saw the way she looked at him. It was authentic. Every agent is required to study the tomes of reports compiled over millennia of following Ana, and every mate she chose was for a single purpose: to further her line. But not this time. I knew something had changed when you came along. It was the subtle shift in her disposition, in her expressions. It was the love in her eyes for you and for Alan. I was there that day on the bridge, Samantha."

Samantha was glad he wasn't looking at her. His form became blurry as her eyes welled up.

"I knew that she would settle, that she had stopped running. So I was there on the bridge that day, following at a safe distance and waiting for my chance to bring her in. I watched you blow bubbles from the car window. One of them even popped on my windshield. Your little hands reached for them. Then, just like that, Alan's car veered out of control."

Samantha bowed her head. A tear found its way down the bridge of her nose and dropped onto her slipper.

"I was out of my car and descending the river embankment just as you and your mother disappeared below the surface, still trapped inside the vehicle. Alan lay in a tangle of reeds near the bridge stanchions, ejected from the impact. Ana surfaced, flailing her arms and gasping for air, then submerged again. Twice more she did this, Samantha. The third time she surfaced she wasn't alone. She dragged you to safety before collapsing into the mud, exhausted and unconscious."

Samantha sniffled and drew the black sleeve of her robe across her eyes as she processed his narrative. She projected the timeline forward, filling in the missing pieces with recent events.

I know what happened next.

"You took her to those people!" she said. "You delivered her to those men that kept her strapped to a bed for twenty years, filled her with drugs that twisted her mind!"

Jibril spun to face her for the first time since beginning his tale.

"The Sharuri's great hunt was over at long last."

The callous reply left Samantha gaping at him, red eyed and open mouthed.

"But so was my time as a member of an order that had become misguided and self-serving," he added. "My theory about Ana's change of heart was confirmed when she was willing to give up her freedom—and maybe even her life—to save you."

"I don't...I don't understand."

"I sensed her presence in my mind. She knew I was there, knew I was watching. Samantha, your mother knew who I was and what I would do and chose to save your life anyway."

"Why didn't you hand me over, too?"

"Because my mission changed that day. And so did my allegiance. I told my superiors that your gifts hadn't manifested, and crafted a false theory that Ana's genetic abnormalities didn't pass to female offspring. My expertise on Ana gave credibility to my claim, and they appeared to believe me. What was more important was that they had their grand prize: the most powerful being to ever walk the face of the earth. They were satisfied. Nevertheless, I watched over you in case they became greedy and tried to snatch up the daughter as well. I divided my time between here and wherever you happened to be; Ohio, Illinois, Virginia. To my surprise, my flimsy hypothesis turned out to be partly true. Your emotional trauma from the accident suppressed your abilities."

"Until it didn't."

"Until it didn't," the Imam confirmed.

And when my abilities revealed themselves, they got greedy.

"So you've been following me all this time. How come I've never seen you? No one is that good."

"I am," he said. "And you have seen me. Many times."

Samantha watched his hand go to his opposite wrist. The thick-browed, chisel-cheeked face she had become accustomed to shimmered and flashed, then disappeared. In its place was the black, form-fitting mask and the strange bodysuit. A poised finger dropped onto a small screen strapped to his wrist. The alien nodes on the suit pulsed with a purplish glow. His entire visage skewed and flashed again.

Samantha leapt to her feet.

It was a hazy memory, dampened by whiskey and the euphoria that had accompanied the revelation that she could fly, but the oval-shaped patch sewn onto the breast of the blue work shirt solidified the details of the recollection, down to the gold band encircling his finger.

"Rich?" she blurted.

"The fact that the name is right here on my chest notwithstanding, yes, that is correct," said Jibril. "Your first flight was exhilarating, I'm sure, but the fact that you left your keys in the lobby was sloppy. Might I suggest you lay off the alcohol?"

Samantha's head swiveled from side to side in mute disbelief as she backed away from the illusion.

"It is how I monitored you undetected."

He touched the wrist device again. His image shifted to a new persona. This one of the strong-chinned man with his upper face hidden in the shadows of a baseball cap.

Marissa told me to look up at him on the mall balcony. I looked right the fuck at him!

His appearance changed again. An older man now, with bushy eyebrows the shade of fresh snow almost touching the wide brim of his cowboy hat.

"It's how I watched you make mistakes and grow."

He sat next to me at a roulette table in Vegas. I even let him win a couple of times.

More memories of her ill-fated trip to Sin City came to the fore.

Please don't change into Noah.

Jibril did change, but not into the young man from her adrenalin-fueled one-night stand.

"It's how I got you out of Washington without being caught."

A young man wearing the uniform of the National Guard stared back at her. A medic patch was displayed on his shoulder.

"Okay! Stop! Please..."

Jesus Christ, that is creepy.

The dark bodysuit returned with a tap of the wrist. Samantha moved closer to study the strange nodes.

"Holographic emitters," he said, as if that explained everything.

Samantha nodded, but her expression was skeptical.

"Right," she said. "And suddenly I'm in a *Mission: Impossible* movie."

"I told you that the Sharuri developed tactics to counter the abilities of your ancestors. They stopped their research when they became consumed with gaining political power. I didn't."

Samantha's head tilted to the side as she regarded his expressionless, masked face with narrowed eyes.

"And now you use your technology and training to fight crime," she said.

The conservative, wise facade of the Imam returned.

"I use it to protect you. And there have been times when I failed at that."

"You mean like when Roger beat me senseless and almost unmasked me at the Capitol?"

"Roger Harkins is a spoiled man-child. But he is not a real threat and never has been."

"It didn't feel like that at the time. His puppets knew how to throw a punch."

Jibril issued a sound that was somewhere between a *hmph* and an *ah*.

"'Allah looks at you when you are in the state of hardship and despair, and laughs, knowing that your relief is close.'"

Samantha blinked.

"What?" she said.

"Your friends give you more power than your natural gifts ever will."

Good point. Marissa did show up out of nowhere to pepper spray the shit out of Roger.

But Samantha wasn't ready to let him off the hook that easy.

"And what about Braithwaite? Did you know that part of his torture was to make me watch the 9/11 attacks and everything that came afterwards in a continuous loop? That he actually had me wondering if all Muslims really are fanatical terrorists? That he actually had me thinking about teaming up with him to wipe your people from the planet?"

Jibril averted his eyes and released a slow exhale before answering. Samantha noted a change in posture, a slight droop in his shoulders.

"I lost track of you for a time," he said. "And for that I will never forgive myself."

Calm down, Sammy. You're acting like an asshole.

"My wife, Isra's mother, was dying. I was needed here."

Way to go, jerk. I deserved that.

"Oh my god. I'm so sorry. I didn't—"

"You came into your own after that incident. You didn't run and hide, didn't fly off to feel sorry for yourself. You immediately rushed off to save lives during the worst hurricane in recent memory, possibly in recorded history. All after enduring this torture you so poignantly reviewed for me. I made the correct choice in watching over you, even though I have failed to do so at times. You are the first of Ana's children to deserve the title of hero. And rightfully so."

Now it was Samantha who averted her eyes.

"My people have been judged by our worst element for generations," said Jibril. "More so since the attacks on the towers and the Pentagon. But I choose to judge people on their individual merit. So I ask you to judge me now."

With that, he tapped the wrist device. The Imam shimmered and faded, replaced again by the mask and bodysuit. He reached behind his neck. Samantha heard several soft, metallic clicks. The mask slipped over his head.

Her hands flew to her mouth before she could stop them.

My god...

Samantha estimated that at least two weeks had passed since her encounter with the rocket-propelled grenades and, while her wounds had been grievous, they had healed in less than half that time. Jibril Wasem wasn't blessed with regenerative healing abilities, however. He spun around to reveal oozing, puckered burns along the back of his head that disappeared into the neckline of the black suit. His right ear was covered in a bandage that once was white, but was now stained a brownish yellow. The shape of the bandage left little doubt that most of the appendage was gone. She got her first look at his face—his real face—when he completed the spin, and found bright, cinnamon eyes regarding her. One of them was slightly askew, pulled taut by the damaged skin on that side of his face.

"The previous suit provided protection against extreme temperatures, but grenade blasts are another matter. We are fortunate the illusion technology still functioned long enough to get you to safety before it failed. Not to worry, though. I've made some upgrades."

Samantha barely heard the words. Her bottom lip trembled.

He almost died. He fought through incredible pain for hours, for days, after the attack. He probably still hurts.

"I...I, um," she attempted. "Does Isra know?"

Jibril shook his head and replaced the mask. He was the Imam a moment later.

"I will wait until she is older. If she lives that long."

The implication struck Samantha like a wrecking ball. An unwanted, horrible image filled her mind. A charred, tiny skeleton lay smoking in the ruins of a mosque destroyed by a nuclear blast.

She approached Jibril and touched him for the first time, placing a firm hand on each shoulder and squaring her body to his.

"What do you want me to do?"

"Simple," he said. "Bring Kinetic Star back from the dead."

Chapter Ten

SAMANTHA MET THE IMAM in the expansive subterranean chamber as she had for seven days in a row following her unsanctioned exploration of his digital records. This section of the room had been blocked off by portable dividers during her initial exploration, but now served as a classroom of sorts. Jibril Wasem was the instructor, and the subject was meditation. The student was trying her best to get the hang of it.

Samantha's morning cleaning duties had been replaced by hours of breathing techniques and stillness. She found herself missing the energetic Isra, missed the girl's hurried issuance of Samantha's daily tasks before rushing off to school. The morning after the revelations of Jibril's origins, however, she was informed that Isra had been sent to stay with her *ja-ad* and *ja-ada*. Samantha hadn't asked what those terms meant, but assumed they had something to do with family. Maternal relatives, she surmised. Samantha felt a pang of regret at the news. She hadn't had a chance to say goodbye, and wondered if she would ever see her little Watcher again.

Evenings were spent reading more exciting and suspenseful treatises on the intricacies of simple and complex machinery. She was on the fourth volume now, and found that the previous texts had provided the fundamentals needed to understand principles and inner workings of machines as small as a mechanical watch or as large as a construction crane. The latter lesson had summoned an unwanted memory of Evan, one among a multitude of remembrances that continued to resurface as a result of her increased calm and mental focus. Jibril told her it was to be expected, a side effect of her meditation training. Nevertheless, that major, elusive memory still hid in the shadows of her consciousness. It had teased her, just out of reach, since she had awoken in the hospitable bed weeks earlier.

"Relax your facial muscles. Relax all of your muscles."

Samantha opened her eyes at the sound of the Imam's voice. Seven days wasn't a long time to master a practice that took most practitioners a lifetime to perfect, but Samantha was making progress. She had let her mind wander again and Jibril detected it right away.

He sat cross-legged on the prayer rug opposite Samantha with his palms resting on his knees. His eyes closed and he initiated a long inhale. She waited for his eventual exhale and the inevitable query that would follow.

"What is your question for today?"

It was a tactic he had suggested to help put her mind at ease before they began the daily lesson. Rather than bombard Jibril with the myriad of questions that had arisen from his story, he permitted her to ask only one of them before they began the morning meditation. Samantha reasoned that eventually her investigation would exhaust itself, but began to doubt that theory when every answered question spawned new ones.

Wednesday's question had been:

"If your suit projects holograms, how am I able to see your facial expressions?"

To which Jibril had answered:

"Microscopic sensors inside my mask pick up muscle movements in my face which are sent to the emitters in real time, thus creating a realistic recreation of my expressions."

The answer had led to Thursday's inquiry.

"How did you get the technology to make the suit? It's more advanced than anything in the world, or at least anything I've ever heard of."

He had replied with:

"You would be surprised by what goes on behind the closed doors of secret labs with bottomless funding. And as I said, I continued the Shururi's research and development long after they lost interest."

She had changed the topic for yesterday's question.

"What was Isra's mother like?"

The tiny sensors in the mask detected a narrowing of the eyes and a tightening of the lips. They passed the information to the emitters in real time. The Imam's eyes held Samantha's, but she didn't withdraw the question. His voice took on a tone she hadn't heard from him before. Quiet reverence. Love.

"She was kind and patient. Beautiful and intelligent. Impassioned. Pious. Fierce."

For a moment it seemed like he would go on, that he wanted to go on, but his stoic veneer returned.

"Keep your questions on mission, Samantha. Now let's begin."

Samantha let the tension ebb from her face and shoulders, allowing the release to find its way throughout the rest of her body as she had been taught. The rhythmic breathing technique felt more familiar now, though she knew it would be a long time before it became second nature.

What is my question for today? Good...um...question. So many to choose from. Even if I decide to stay on mission.

She breathed, aware that he was watching her even though her eyes were closed. She inhaled, pulling a question from the ether at random. It bubbled up from the depths and presented itself. Samantha exhaled and opened her eyes.

"What is that?"

She inclined her head toward the shiny black vessel with the strange marking. The Imam's eyes followed her indication.

"That, Samantha McAllister, is today's lesson."

"What? But—"

"Come with me."

He rose and left Samantha sitting on the intricately embroidered prayer rug, speaking over his shoulder as he made his way to the center of the chamber. She rose and hastened her steps to hear him.

"For most it is a tool for meditation, a way to remove the burdens of the physical while enhancing the metaphysical."

Jibril ran his fingers along the glossy contour of the large container, pausing to press his palm over the rune etched across the top.

"Right," Samantha said as she joined him there. "But what is it really? Layman's terms."

"An isolation tank," he said. "A sensory-deprivation chamber. Call it what you will. For you, I suspect it will be something much more dynamic."

"And the symbol? What is that?"

Jibril removed his hand and turned to a tall, wrought-iron table beside the tank. His thumbs flipped open twin latches set into the lid of a small, flat, wooden box, its oak slats faded with age.

"It is a pictograph."

Samantha waited, watching as he manipulated something within the box.

"And?" she said.

His head turned slightly as his hands stopped moving, as if perturbed by her persistence. Samantha heard a soft sigh.

"It means Qareen," said Jibril. "An Islamic myth. Nothing more."

Samantha circled around him for a better look at the contents of the box. Several envelopes of brittle, yellowed parchment had been unfolded to reveal pockets filled with dried herbs. It became apparent that Jibril had been crushing the herbs, mixing them together on a silver disc. Her attention didn't linger there, however. A genie's lamp of tarnished brass with a blue, stained-glass base rested beside the box. A sinuous hose sprouted from the stem, coiled neatly on the table like a compliant serpent.

Wait. That's not a genie's lamp. That's a fucking hookah.

Jibril seized a robust pinch of the dried herb mixture between thumb and forefinger and pushed it into the small, conical receptacle that protruded from the stem of the device.

"So...what's that for?" Samantha said.

I guess we're getting baked?

"It is your vehicle for the journey ahead."

Jibril clapped the herbal residue from his hands and turned to the isolation tank. He opened a panel just below the seam of the egg-shaped vessel and flipped a switch. A hiss erupted from somewhere within, followed by the electronic hum of hidden motors.

Samantha watched with a mix of anxiety and fascination as the seam widened, the top rising on hinges like a futuristic, alien mollusk. She half-expected to find a miniature orchestra playing the Imperial March within the strange vessel. What she found instead was pinkish-purple light illuminating an oddly-shaped bathtub, complete with balance-assist bars bolted to the sides. The light danced across the water's surface in curious patterns. Jibril consulted a digital gauge on the control panel before turning to her.

"The water will be at temperature soon," said Jibril, moving the hookah closer to Samantha. "Remove your clothing."

Samantha blinked, wondering if she had misheard. The order was issued in such an offhand, casual manner that he might as well have said, "Hand me that socket wrench."

"Um, do what now?"

He retrieved a jet lighter from the wooden box and tested it with a flick of his thumb. Concentrated flame of icy blue was born and died in an instant.

"You need true submersion. There should be nothing between you and the water," he said. "Strip down."

She noted that he didn't bother to turn his back.

Got it. Well I guess it's too late for proper modesty with this guy. I mean after all, he does know his way around a catheter.

Samantha did as she was told, and became very aware of the draft that moved throughout the large room. She suddenly wasn't sure what to do with her hands.

Jibril already had the lighter poised at the conical fixture, and offered the tip of the hose to Samantha. She took it between thumb and forefinger and put it to her lips.

Okay, looks like I'm doing this.

"Breathe in, Samantha. Slowly."

Fire leapt from the lighter, igniting the nest of packed herbs as she inhaled. The smoke dried her mouth and flowed down her windpipe like black silk in the summer sun, hot but not in the least bit harsh or agitating. She reclined her head as she exhaled, expecting to cough but feeling no urge to do so. A plume of gray smoke was caught by the draft and dispersed to the four corners of the chamber. The aftertaste was peculiar.

Is that lemon?

Jibril nodded to her with approval.

"Again."

His thumb snapped the lighter into action. Samantha's second pull was just as smooth as the first. This time she exhaled through her nose, imagining she was a great dragon lounging atop her mountain of treasure. She grinned at the absurdity.

"Very good," said Jibril, taking the hose from her and replacing it next to the hookah.

His eyes consulted the gauge on the side of the tank again.

"It's ready," he said. "Get in. We don't have long."

Samantha climbed onto the lip of the tub and tested the water with an exploratory toe. It was as though the water wasn't even there. Jibril read her confusion.

"The water is set to your body temperature and diluted with epsom salts to provide buoyancy. Now get in, Samantha. Quickly, before the herbs take effect."

She knelt in the water and flipped to her back with tentative movements, then stretched out and let her limbs go limp.

"Okay, what now?"

Her head and upper torso rose from the bottom of the tank, just breaking the surface of the water. Now she couldn't feel anything. The electronic hum sounded again as the lid began to close. Waves vibrated through the water into her submerged ears. Jibril's voice was muffled as he replied, barely audible. She thought she heard:

"Float and breathe, Samantha. That's all. Float and breathe."

The lid had almost completed its descent now. The pinkish-purple light flickered out of existence, leaving Samantha's world lit only by the fading light outside of the tank. She again thought she heard Jibril say something just before her world was lost to impenetrable blackness.

"Float and breathe. Journey and learn."

Samantha floated but nothing happened. She breathed, too, but still nothing. Her eyes were open, but there was nothing to see. Her submerged ears muted all sound. One thing did exist, however. A tenacious, unrelenting itch at the tip of her nose. The week of meditation training helped her to ignore it or, better yet, to isolate and study it rather than reach up and relieve herself of the madding sensation, but a week of practice wasn't long enough to prevent her from remedying the situation. The itch returned mere seconds after she scratched it away. Or was it minutes? It was hard to tell.

She decided that the isolation tank was flawed when she heard the voice. It carried through the water in waves, diluted and disjointed yet familiar.

Ana's alive. Oh my god. Oh my god.

Daddy?

Samantha felt the urge to leap out of the tank and embrace her father, who had somehow found his way to her in the bowels of a Harlem mosque, but her rational mind dismissed the outlandish idea.

It's that weed—or whatever it was—that Jibril gave you, Sammy. Daddy's not here.

Then what did I hear?

Nothing. Your ears are underwater.

She closed her eyes to concentrate on her weightless sensory deprivation experience, though it made little difference in the lightless interior of the tank. She reached up and scratched at her nose again. This time the tip of her finger stuck to the tip of the protruding organ and stayed there as though an invisible gremlin had coated her digit in superglue before scurrying away in silent laughter. She attempted to break the bond by doing the only thing she could. She pulled. Her nose followed the fingertip away from her face, extending and elongating in impossible, comical fashion. Samantha couldn't see it happening— couldn't feel it either, for that matter—but she knew it was happening.

Pinocchio. What in the holy hell?

She flexed the fingers of her hand, which was somewhere off to the left of her. She could tell by the disturbance in the water.

If my hand is over there, then I never touched my nose.

Then she did, just to make sure her nose was the normal size. It was.

I heard him. I heard Daddy's voice. I'm sure of it. But how?

Rational Samantha answered for her.

You know how.

Her consciousness splintered, separating and exploring like branching fingers of lightning seeking all avenues of conduction.

Samantha did indeed know how.

Icy manacles froze her numbed wrists. Starvation. Electrocution. Galina just outside the rusted iron door, her thoughts broadcast directly into Samantha's mind like a psychic Bluetooth connection.

Good. She's back with us. Time to give it another go.

I can hear you, bitch.

Is she too far gone to understand me?

No, I can hear your thoughts from over a year ago. By the way, I'm coming to visit when this is all over.

That's it. Do you get it now?

Yes, Rational Me. I get it now. Telepathy. We've always had it. You're a hot, strong lady, by the way. Even with the buzz cut.

Hey thanks. You too. Now check this out:

I want you to come with me and join your brothers. We will rebuild the world together and—

Mother?

Hold on. There's more.

Samantha said no. You killed her for it.

Wait, that's a man's voice. Who is that? Roger?

Rational Samantha said nothing.

What's this about "brothers"? She said "brothers", plural.

Her only answer was blind, immutable silence.

Ana is with Roger? Oh god no. If she's trying to coerce him into...
Samantha sat up, bumping her forehead into the lid of the tank.
Have to go. Have to get out of here.
How? You don't even know how to use your powers anymore.
Shut up, Rational Me. I have to try.

She commanded the vessel to part at the seam, not caring about the ruined hydraulics or the warped opening mechanisms. Its audible protests reminded her of the titanium-lined cell in which Sharp and Braithwaite had imprisoned her. It made the same sounds when she had exerted her will over it, albeit on a much grander scale. A blinding light greeted her as the mouth yawned open.

Samantha emerged from the water and stepped from the tank.

Chapter Eleven

SAMANTHA'S CHEEK ITCHED just to the left of her nose. It was the exact spot where the cowl had always given her trouble. There was an errant stitch in the seam that protruded with aggravating tenacity, but she could never find it upon examination. Her fingertip came up of its own volition to scratch away the annoyance, but bumped against something that was decidedly not her skin. The world came into view through amber lenses. She could now feel the tightness of the cowl gripping her skull, could smell the leather.

Wait a sec... Where was I just a second ago?

She felt the weight of the motorcycle jacket hanging from her slim shoulders. The leather creaked at the elbow as she let her arm drop to her side. She took in her appearance. The red-striped cowl and jacket were accompanied by the red-striped motorcycle pants and thick-soled boots to complete the outfit.

It felt comfortable. It felt right.

Okay, wasn't I just in... I can't remember. This is...

Tall buildings surrounded her, once familiar but now dilapidated and abandoned. Some portions of the buildings were demolished and showed sooty burn marks, others were rebuilt in haphazard fashion. Her curious gaze dropped to find thick weeds and grasses pushing through gaps and crevices in the varying shades of marble as nature reclaimed its ownership of the land. Samantha could make out a grid design as the cracked stone stretched away from her.

Is this Freedom Plaza?

She spun about, head swiveling with frantic motion. Pennsylvania Avenue was still and silent, as was 13th Street and 14th Street which served as bookends for the plaza. No pedestrians were to be found, not a single soul was in sight. No cars, busses, or bicycles occupied the quiet streets. A flock of birds chirped overhead, dark specks outlined against a sky the hue of a rotting orange. The sun was obscured by thick, ashy clouds, illuminating them from behind in an alien backlight unlike anything she had seen before. Lightning moved in horizontal webs among the clouds here and there, as silent as the city around her. All was still. Too still. Not even the slightest breeze to rustle the golden topknot that sprouted from the back of her cowl. But a chill washed over her nonetheless. She felt her skin prickle into goose bumps beneath her leathers.

"Pretty freaky, huh?"

Samantha thought the voice belonged to Ana at first, a hypothesis that was solidified when her attention was wrenched upward to find a woman hovering above her with bright green eyes and long red hair hanging in a motionless curtain about her shoulders. The theory crumbled to dust when subtle traits that didn't belong to Ana became apparent. The hair was more of a reddish-blonde than true red, a trick of the ambient light from the unnatural sky. The nose was slightly upturned and smaller than Ana's, the bridge decorated with freckles where Ana had none. Samantha felt her legs give out when her brain finally registered the true identity of the newcomer. Her rear end hit the marble with more creaks of leather.

"All of this space and no one to occupy it," said the stranger, motioning with a coffee cup to the emptiness around the plaza. "Well, they made their choice."

Samantha sat dumbfounded as the figure descended to the cracked marble. An unbelted, plush robe the color of rose wine flared open to reveal a white tank top stained with coffee droplets and navy pajama bottoms patterned in bright yellow sunflowers. The fluffy slippers matched the robe. She was heavier than Samantha, fuller around the neck, bosom and hips, but was otherwise a perfect doppleganger.

"Let me guess," she said, peering down at Samantha with squinted eyes and puckered lips. "You just dropped Marissa off at the Basilica of the National Shrine of the Immaculate Conception and were about to go investigate a fire at the Arboretum. Am I right?"

She was close enough for Samantha to smell her breath in the still air, and decided that whatever was in that cup was much stronger than coffee.

"I..." stammered Samantha, "I...uh..."

"No? Well you're not banged up and bleeding all to hell, so it couldn't be after that. Maybe... Hm, let's see. Oh! You were about to fly to Rosslyn to save that jumper. What was her name..."

Samantha noted the Cheetos dust that covered the lap area of the pajama bottoms and that the stranger had neglected to put on a bra. Her hair was oily and unwashed.

"You were about to fly up north to rescue David?" said the stranger. "No? Come on, help a girl out. I'm really trying to tiptoe around the spoilers here."

She sat on the ground across from Samantha, who was still too stunned to get back to her feet. The coffee mug extended toward her.

"You want a snort? Macallan."

Samantha found the wherewithal to close her mouth, which had been gaping like a flytrap. She shook her head.

"Y-y-you're...you're me," she managed.

"Y-y-yep," said the stranger. "And I was y-y-you once upon a time. It's the when that I'm trying to figure out."

Apparently I'm a smartass bitch in the future.

Future Samantha grinned.

No, we were always smartasses. Always will be. You don't become a bitch til later.

Wait a minute. I can't read thoughts.

Are you sure about that?

"So tell me, *me*," said Future Samantha, "What's the last thing you remember?"

Samantha rolled to her feet and backed away, head spinning from the absurdity of the situation.

"I was...wow, um...I think I was in some sort of what do you call it..."

Her mirror image rose and took a sip of whisky, waiting.

"Like a...tank thing. It's all very cloudy. Hard to recall," said Samantha.

The cup lowered from Future Samantha's lips. All playfulness disappeared from her expression.

"Oh," she said, averting her eyes and repeating the syllable in a lower register. "Oh."

"What?" Samantha said, leaning to the side in an attempt to regain eye contact. "What is it?"

"Can't tell you," said Future Samantha. "But I will say this. You'd better buckle up, lassie."

"What does that mean? What's going to happen?"

Future Samantha turned her back and raised her hand into the air. She stood in that position, saying nothing further.

Samantha spread her hands and shook her head.

What in the hell?

Just a sec, Sammy.

An oblong object rounded the corner of 13th Street and approached them at a frightening speed. Samantha tensed.

SLAP!

Future Samantha's extended hand now grasped a bottle of Macallan whisky, which she promptly uncapped and tilted over her cup. Samantha could smell the barrel-aged spirits from where she stood. Future Samantha spun to face Samantha with the cup at her lips. Her other hand offered the bottle to Samantha as she swallowed.

"You should probably drink right now."

Samantha accepted the bottle and sniffed it, her eyes never leaving her counterpart.

"Come on," said Future Samantha, pivoting on a furry heel towards the west.

Samantha upended the bottle and swallowed, anticipating the burn as her nostrils came alive with the oaky aroma. She followed her supposed future self onto 14th street as a familiar euphoria spread from her warmed stomach.

"What the hell is going on, Samantha?" said Samantha.

"So formal," said Future Samantha. "I'm a Sammy too, you know. Or just Sam. Whatever."

Samantha raised the bottle to her mouth again as they walked, letting the liquid courage kick in.

"Okay then, Sam," she said. "You obviously know more about me than I do, so what year is this? Where is everyone? And most importantly, what happened to you? I mean, us? I mean, uh, me?"

This is so confusing.

"Let's see," said Future Samantha. "This is about..."

Her voice quieted as she whispered a series of numbers to herself.

"...65 years into your future. Give or take," she said.

"Holy shit," said Samantha. "We look great. I mean, we could eat a few more salads, but other than that we haven't aged a day."

"Ouch," said Future Samantha, stopping to hold out her cup. "You try being alone for decades with a drinking problem and an insatiable craving for snack food."

Samantha filled the coffee cup. They continued on.

"What else did you ask me? Oh yeah. Well, Washington D.C. is a city of politicians, so when I took over the country they weren't needed anymore. They left the city, and everyone else followed suit. There were no more jobs, so no more commerce. Economics, am I right? I stayed because all of the toys are controlled from here. Plus the cherry blossoms. I made sure those withstood the—"

Future Samantha made it seven steps before she realized Samantha was no longer keeping pace with her.

Samantha watched her counterpart's shoulders drop as she turned to face her.

"Okay, let's have it. What's making that leather seam ride up your ass?" she said.

Samantha was once again wide-eyed and speechless. The bottle hung at her side with numbed fingers.

"Yeah. I took over the country," said Future Samantha. "I had no choice. That vision we had a while back? The one where you obliterated an international coalition of armed forces? That happened. Well, sort of. It wasn't exactly like that. I mean, we can't see the future, as far as I know. But there was a horrible battle, and there was a nuke. We managed to throw up a force shield just before it hit."

Samantha's brows furrowed, her head shaking left and right in an increasing motion of denial and disbelief.

"The impact blasted us a mile into the Earth's crust. It took two days to dig out. We went into hiding to recover. After that, it was on. All out war."

"No..." Samantha said.

"Yep," said Future Samantha, her eyes peering up at the eerie sky. "They tried more nukes, appealing to allies to help them fight us. Some even tried EMP weapons, thinking that would disrupt our powers. The atmosphere still hasn't fully healed itself."

"I can't believe it," said Samantha. "I won't."

Future Samantha shrugged.

"Up to you, Sammy. But remember that we tried to talk with them first. They backed us into a corner. And when they went after Daddy and Marissa, well...you get it."

Samantha's knuckles whitened around the whisky bottle.

"Stop saying 'we'! I had no part in this!"

"Not yet you haven't."

"I don't even have my powers anymore!" Samantha shouted, ripping away the cowl to reveal a face reddened with frustration. "How could I possibly defeat an army? How could I possibly defeat—"

"Mom?"

The interjection was timed to perfection. The shared thought patterns and memories allowed her doppleganger to follow her line of reasoning and complete the outburst before Samantha could finish it.

Samantha fell silent and lifted the bottle to her lips.

"About that," said Future Samantha. "Ana lied to us about a great many things. She loved to get into our head and knock around our synapses like a game of croquet, didn't she? She's still in there."

Future Samantha pressed two fingers against Samantha's forehead and pushed.

"Let's walk while you let this sink in. We're almost there."

What was left of the National Museum of African-American History came into view as they reached Constitution Avenue, and beyond it lay a sight that chilled Samantha to the core.

"What do you think?" said Future Samantha.

The Washington Monument, Samantha's favorite attraction in the entire city, the stone obelisk that served as a symbol of her heroism to the citizens of Washington D.C. after her extraordinary efforts to rescue people from its crumbling pinnacle during the worst hurricane in history, was gone.

Oh my god.

In its place stood a new monument, one taller than its predecessor, a female figure carved from white, veined marble. Her face was upturned to the heavens, gaze traveling along outstretched arms that ended in extended hands. One leg was hiked high against the other, completing the position and leaving no doubt that the figure was leaping into flight.

"Come on."

Samantha felt herself being lifted into the air by an unseen force. Future Samantha flew just ahead of her, carrying her past self with telekinetic ease. The details of the statue came into focus as they neared, and Samantha felt her stomach drop as her fears were confirmed.

The face was unmistakably her own, as was the long mane of hair that flared behind the sculpture like a rippling cape frozen in time.

Samantha was deposited on the statue's massive forehead with a light touch.

"How could you do this?" she said as her future self touched down next to her. "The monument was so old, so revered. It was a symbol of our—"

"It was destroyed in the war," said Future Samantha. "Leveled to dust. I tried to protect it but, as you well know, we can't be everywhere at once. Despite our incredible gifts."

"So you replaced it with a narcissistic monstrosity?"

Future Samantha arched an eyebrow. Fingers combed oily hair over an ear.

"I didn't build this. The people of the former United States did."

Heat flared in Samantha's cheeks, spreading to her ears.

"Yeah! I bet they had no fucking choice!"

Her counterpart shrugged and looked out over the mall.

"You weren't there, Sam," she said. "Times were...difficult. And I hope this future never comes to pass for you."

A period of silence followed, punctuated by a sudden wind in Samantha's ears.

"Where is Ana?" she said finally, her tone softening.

Future Samantha took the whisky bottle and upended it into her cup, waiting for the last drops to slow and cease. She tossed the empty bottle high into the air and shot her hand out after it, fingers in a pistol formation. Her thumb knuckle bent and she issued a quiet *kpow!* just as the bottle shattered.

"I killed her."

Samantha studied her strange counterpart's face, noting how her eyes tensed, how her jaw firmed up. The green eyes were far away, reliving the memory.

"It changed you, didn't it?" said Samantha. "It changed us."

Future Samantha sipped at the Macallan. Samantha continued.

"It's something I could never do. I won't. I mean, I can't even—"

"You can and you *will*," said Future Samantha

The final syllable dripped with venomous urgency. Identical pairs of emeralds locked in silent combat.

"I don't have my powers anymore. At least, I think they might be in there somewhere but I can't use them. So that's pretty much the same thing. There's something blocking them, something... I don't know."

A firm hand grasped Samantha's shoulders and turned her, squaring their bodies.

"Sam, do you remember that weird, sort of cracking feeling in your head when you were in the museum, just before the explosions?"

"Not really, I—"

"Well there was. It was Ana fucking around in your brain. It was her influence, her suggestion. Think about it. The explosions would have disintegrated you instead of causing mere burns. We're not immune to fiery explosions, but our telekinetic shields can certainly mitigate the damage. If your powers were truly gone, then you would have died in burning agony. Not all of our gifts are voluntary, you know."

"But something, some*one*, knocked me clear, I..."

Future Samantha waited for the stars to align in Samantha's rational mind.

"Oh my god!" said Samantha.

"Yep," said Future Samantha. "He intervened, but you still would have died if your reflexive powers hadn't kicked in. Jibril too, most likely."

Samantha crossed her arms over her chest and let her gaze sweep over the skyline of the city framed by the alien sky. Many more familiar buildings were blackened and crumbling. Others were simply gone. Dark craters now rested where the White House and the Capitol once stood, sinister divots in the torn earth.

"There is no escaping who we are," said her counterpart. "Your powers will return, and you will use them to kill our mother. If you don't—"

Her arm swept over the landscape that stretched away from them far below.

"—then this will look like a utopian paradise. You know I'm right, Samantha. You're not that scared girl tearing up her apartment bedroom in her sleep anymore. You've become what Evan wanted you to be. What you were afraid to be. And that means you've made some hard choices. Well, you need to make one more."

"I can't kill my own mother!" Samantha shouted, eyes burning with tears.

"Samantha, listen to me! She is pure evil. She is a psychopath! What can I do to convince you that she needs to be..."

Samantha watched as her counterpart trailed off with widening eyes and a blanched, peaked complexion. It was as though someone had pulled a plug and powered her down.

"What?" said Samantha. "What is it?"

Samantha could barely hear her future self's voice as she spoke again. She leaned in closer without realizing it.

"You don't remember. I get it now," said Future Samantha. "I forgot where you are in the timeline. Your physical and emotional trauma. Your brain threw up safeguards to protect itself, hiding certain memories."

"What memories?" whispered Samantha.

"That day on the mall. The last day."

"Yeah?"

"Our verbal confrontation with Ana. You don't remember, do you?"

Samantha searched her fragmented recollections of that conversation. There had been something about David, but the words had become faint and distorted, someone shouting in a snowstorm.

"Not...not really."

"She guided us, showed us how to turn our powers inward. Let us discover for ourselves what we had created with David."

Samantha felt the snowstorm abate in an instant. Her breath caught in her throat. The words returned, summoned from the past to linger in bold face against the stark white canvas of her mind.

Your beau played a small part, yes, but it appears that your fertility rivals my own. We are givers of life, Little Star.

"Oh no... Oh my god..."

"That's right," said Future Samantha. "That's it. Remember!"

Samantha was thankful that her future self still held her by the shoulder. She felt she might topple over.

"Her lies are endless," said Future Samantha. "Her intentions are self-serving. That's all she is now. A cruel husk of a person. Twisted and ruined by decades of torment by the government and being hunted for millennia before that."

Future Samantha raised the coffee cup and drained it, savoring the final drops. Her opposite hand still gripped Samantha's shoulder.

"Now, my dear, go fuck that bitch up. End her."

Samantha felt an overwhelming force blast into her shoulder. She spun a full rotation, limbs flailing like a marionette. Her booted feet left the marble. Her stomach leapt into her throat. Air rushed past her ears, deafening her. She tried to fly but couldn't.

End her.

Despite her impending and unavoidable appointment with the unyielding marble stones below, her attention was occupied by a singular tactile sensation.

That of Ana's throat collapsing in her hands.

Chapter Twelve

A SHARP, CRACKING SENSATION pierced every fiber of her being, echoing near and far and near again before it died away into utter silence. Samantha screamed in panic. She found herself in limbo, a prison devoid of sight or smell or sound or feeling.

Am I dead?

A motorized hum came to life, vibrating the water around her.

Water? Where am I? No, where was *I?*

Her answer was a sliver of piercing white light that grew into an all-encompassing field of blind nothingness.

She poured out of the isolation tank and curled into a wet, naked ball of misery as her eyes readjusted to the light. Somebody was there, gathering her in a soft, merino blanket.

"Who are you?"

She pushed the person away, squinting her eyes to aid her focus.

"Hush, Samantha. You're home."

Jibril?

She stood and leaned against the isolation tank, clutching the blanket to her neck.

"I was...I was...um..."

"Few remember the details of their journey under the effects of the herbs," said Jibril. "They will return in time, along with the rest of your memories. Relax and let your senses become reacquainted with the world outside of the pod."

"How am I supposed to learn something if I can't recall the lesson?"

"It is a safeguard I concocted as part of the treatment. The experience sometimes calls forth a madness that people have suppressed their entire lives. It is best not to bring that back with them."

Samantha's bare feet slapped against the floor as she began to pace.

"I don't understand. That means all of this was a waste of time," she said. "The meditation, the drugs, the tank. All of it."

"I disagree. You had an experience. I heard you talking to someone, though I couldn't make out the words. You even shouted once or twice."

She turned to the table next to the tank and ran her fingers over the smooth glass of the hookah.

"I don't know what to believe anymore, Jibril."

"Turn around. Look at me."

Samantha sighed and spun to face her mysterious mentor. The barrel of a semi-automatic handgun stared back at her.

"The world needs you to believe."

She froze. Her extremities went numb. The blanket slid from her shoulders. Her eyes widened in disbelief. Her lips moved to shape the sounds in her throat into words, but she was too late. His index finger moved. The slide retracted.

KRAK!

Samantha saw a flash of burnt orange light behind ashen clouds. She saw veined, white marble beneath her feet, then she was falling. There was a another sharp report, but this one an echo from only moments ago, from her awakening inside the tank.

Your powers will return, and you will use them to kill our mother.

It was her voice, yet the words hadn't been spoken by her.

Samantha felt the lightest tickle on the skin of her chest, like the fluttering contact of a tiny gnat on a summer's day. Her head tilted down to investigate.

There it was, .45 caliber probably, still spinning in place from its trip down the rifled barrel of Jibril's handgun. It hovered there as though waiting for her permission to pierce her skin, shatter her ribs, and destroy her heart. His aim had been impeccable.

She raised her eyes to his. Jibril's dark features were unreadable. Her hand shot out.

The gun was ripped from his grasp. It floated between them for a second, then simply disassembled into its component parts. The pieces flew to the table and dropped there in a pile, the barrel on top and still smoking.

The spinning slug dropped into Samantha's palm. She studied it as she spoke.

"You're not the first one to test me with a bullet."

Jibril's usual stoic expression transformed into one Samantha hadn't seen before. It was as though he were seeing her for the first time. His nod was solemn.

"I understand now," she said, dropping the spent round to the floor. "I understand what I need to do."

Samantha turned and reached for her clothing.

"No, wait," said Jibril. "If Kinetic Star is going into battle then she'll need armor that befits her station. Come. I have something for you."

159

PART THREE

SEND IN YOUR SKELETONS

WINDS OF WAR
The Horizon Is Darker Than Yesterday

By May Patsiavas, Metro Inquirer Opinion Columnist

The word *insidious* comes to mind. Stealthily treacherous. Proceeding down a seemingly harmless path right to the edge of a cliff. And then beyond.

Our country's leadership has failed us as a nation. President Dietrich has failed us through his hawkish policies and isolationist ideology.

But he wasn't always this way.

He was elected as a champion of the working class, an ally for unions and a creator of jobs. Dietrich's platform was based on global partnership and the notion that a rising tide lifts all boats. His inspirational speech at the primaries emboldened some members of the opposition to switch their party affiliation, a political feat not seen in decades. Dietrich was inclusive, forgiving. Dietrich was optimistic, a trait that resides on the endangered species list among the fear-based rhetoric of the modern politician. All of this is to say that something has changed. President Dietrich has changed.

Cable news pundits and conspiracy podcasters disguised as truthful, unbiased purveyors of fact speculate that Supreme Leader Quong was given classified information about Dietrich's past by Russian covert intelligence operatives, providing the leader with blackmail leverage. The details of this information seem to change from week to week, so I won't repeat them here, though I am tempted. I prefer provable facts over anecdotal evidence in my writing. Yet, if this is true, could it explain the sudden change in Dietrich?

We have weapons of mass destruction staged in strategic locations around the world. Our enemies have them as well, and the survival of our civilization rests on the sound judgment of human beings. Fallible, insecure human beings.

We may never know what has come over our president. Why his decisions performed an about face and put us on this precipice. Made us hold our breath and wait. Cooler heads have prevailed in the past. Let's hope they do so again.

***

I want to end with a goodbye and a heartfelt thank you to my readers. The word on the street is true; this will be my final column for the Metro Inquirer.

Without getting too inside baseball, our prestigious and respected publication has been purchased by an international media conglomerate who I will not name here. Our writing and editorial staff is united in our stance on freedom of the press and freedom of speech, and so we will pack up these beliefs with the rest of our belongings and look toward our next adventure.

At the risk of having this column stricken from the record and never seeing the light of day, I'd urge you, dear reader, to consume what is printed after our departure with a level head and a healthy dose of rational, independent thinking. Our new bosses find such approaches, shall we say, threatening. A reflection of the current administration and its iron-handed adversaries.

Insidious indeed.

Stay strong and be well, my friends. Until we meet again.

May Patsiavas

Chapter Thirteen

ANA TOSSED A CRACKED SHELL into the trash bin and retrieved a fresh egg from the carton. Her sharp thumbnail pierced the brittle outer layer as she upended the runny contents into the stainless steel mixing bowl where the dark orange yolk took its place among the others. These eggs were straight from the hen, purchased from the farmer's market that Adrian frequented now that he had left Los Angeles to join her in the nation's capital. They reminded her of how food used to be, before proper animal farming had been turned into an aberration by the corporate food industry. There had never been white eggs until recently, she mused. Her thoughts drifted to the sizzle of a lean, unmarbled elk steak over an open fire, the majestic animal felled and butchered only hours before by the hunters whom provided sustenance for the village. She cracked the last egg and took up the whisk. Fresh elk wasn't available at the moment, so omelets would have to do. Her boys were hungry and now she would provide the sustenance.

The upscale Georgetown penthouse was spacious and modern. The floor-to-ceiling windows provided a stunning view of the monuments that decorated the skyline in a topographical map of patriotism. Ana hated the view. She couldn't wait for those monuments to come toppling down. Nevertheless, she loved the penthouse's kitchen. The apartment had been owned by the CEO of a successful government contracting firm. She couldn't remember the name of it, nor the name of the domicile's previous owner, but she recalled that the man stank of capitalistic selfishness, of greed and power. Such a narrow, misguided point of view. His mind had revealed to her the manipulative, dishonest means by which he had attained his wealth. Ana had taken great pleasure in relieving him of his home, and the contents of his financial accounts as well. She was pretty sure the authorities had picked him up by now, a slobbering mute who had succumbed to the darkest terrors of his psyche made real before his eyes. That was after he had legally transferred his assets to Ana, of course. She grinned at the memory.

"Come and get it, lads!"

Ana took a moment to take in the aromatic fragrance of the long stem roses that served as the table's centerpiece before setting the serving platter next to the ceramic vase that held them. Talbot hadn't known of her fondness for roses when he had picked them up while shopping that morning. It was a pleasant surprise.

She insisted that they eat at the dining room table. It was only proper. If her sons had their druthers they would take their meals in front of the massive television screen, scarfing their food like a pack of wild dogs while watching a pointless contest between padded and helmeted men chasing each other across a field of fake grass. She wouldn't have it in her home.

Talbot's cavernous voice rumbled across the table as he sat down and laid into a vegetarian omelet that Ana had prepared especially for him.

"Chow time."

"How the hell did you get that big grazing like a cow?" Liev said without looking up from his phone. "Wasn't everything meat and potatoes way, way back when you were a kid?"

Talbot's deep facial creases formed a scowl.

"This old vegetarian can still snap you like a twig, son," he said.

Ana interjected without looking up from filling her tea cup.

"He is not your son, Talbot. And Liev, your brother is only sixty-five years old. If his advanced age amuses you so much, then I must have you in stitches."

"I'll have him in stitches if he doesn't shut up and eat," said Talbot between bites of broccoli.

Ana caught the roll of Liev's eyes through the corner of hers and leaned back in her chair as she sipped at the herbal brew. It was a touch light on the peppermint for her tastes.

Liev was her youngest boy after Adrian, and ten years older than Samantha. His father was a stockbroker in Chicago, and it was there that she and Talbot had found Liev and convinced him to reunite with his other family. His true family. Liev's gift had made it hard to locate him, but a string of police reports about bewildered citizens waking up in strange locations without their valuables provided a useful trail for Ana to follow. The foolish young man had tried his trick on her, a mistake which he wouldn't soon repeat.

"Listen to your sibling, Liev," she said. "Eat."

"Yes, mother."

Ana smiled at his quick acquiescence. He knew his place. The young man would be quite useful in the coming days. She squeezed his forearm with a smile, wondering if he had an inkling about what was about happen.

She regarded Marcos, who hadn't yet spoken. He looked much younger than his fifty-seven years as he used his fork to pry open his omelet, curious to find out what Ana had cooked into the gooey cheese. She had been in South America at the time, her command of the Portuguese language sharp enough to get by without drawing too much attention, despite her archaic verb conjugation and outdated use of formality. Centuries had passed since she had spoken the Romance language, yet romance blossomed when her peculiar dialect caught the ear of Marcos's father, a gorgeous, olive-skinned shipping magnate from Porto Alegre. She had taught him the true meaning of a passionate love affair, and absconded with his child before he knew she was pregnant.

"Is the dish not to your liking?"

Marcos's dark eyes rose from his plate to settle on the teacup in Ana's hand.

"It's fine," he said. "Thank you...*mother*."

Silence filled the room, expanding to every corner of the penthouse. Liev broke it.

"It speaks! I'll be damned."

Ana ignored the quip.

We've been through this, Marcos.

Marcos flinched as her words registered in his mind. Ana maintained the telepathic link and used it as a conduit to force images of his adult children into his surface thoughts. Francisca was showing now. Lucas was clad in cap and gown, having just graduated medical school.

My assurances stand. Your children will be safe. My great-grandchild will be safe.

She knew that the implication was not lost on Marcos. His initial resistance to her overtures had rivaled Roger's, but Ana knew her way around the human mind. Roger had nothing to lose by refusing her offer. He was stubborn and impertinent, and would pay the price for it. Marcos, on the other hand, had become quite agreeable once the proper motivation had been made clear.

"More juice?" she said, rising from the table and making her way to the refrigerator.

The stainless steel door reflected Marcos rising as well. Talbot straightened his broad back and looked to her for direction.

Let him go.

A door closed in the distance. Ana returned to the table and filled her sons' glasses with fresh-squeezed orange juice before taking her seat.

"Look at this," Liev said, eyes rooted to his phone screen. "President Dietrich is going to address the nation from the Lincoln Memorial later this week."

"Abow whuh?" said Talbot, his cheeks stuffed with his third omelet.

"Don't speak with your mouth full, dear," Ana said. "Go on, Liev. Regale us with your fascinating piece of modern journalism."

Liev cleared his throat and slid his thumb to the top of the phone screen.

"A press release issued from the White House this morning announced that the President will address the nation in a live, televised rally from the steps of the Lincoln Memorial on Saturday. The issue of faltering relations with our allies amid calls for war with Russia, China, and newly-formed factions in the Middle East is expected to be among the topics covered in the address, but sources inside the White House tell us that a bombshell announcement is forthcoming as well."

Liev paused to bring his juice glass to his lips. He took his time, enjoying the spotlight by smacking his lips and swallowing before he continued.

"Political and military experts believe the President, in coordination with the Joint Chiefs of Staff, has enacted a plan to place an appropriations bill before Congress requesting an emergency increase in military spending. We'll know more when Dietrich takes the podium on—blah blah blah it just rambles on from there."

Liev tossed the phone to the table and shrugged.

"Who the hell does he plan on invading, anyway?" he said. "That Quong idiot in North Korea? One of those tiny countries that end in 'stan'?"

Talbot snorted. Ana rested her slim elbows on the table and tented her fingers over her plate.

"You think small, my dear boy," she said.

"You know what he's going to announce, don't you?" said Talbot.

Ana took up Talbot's empty plate and went to the sink. Her hand rested on the tap lever, but she paused before opening the spigot.

"Of course I do."

Hot water spilled from the faucet with a twitch of her wrist, rinsing away the remains of her son's meal. She imagined the shared look of surprise that had no doubt made its way across the table by now.

"Isn't it funny the inspiration that comes to us when we lay awake in the dark hours before dawn? It's almost as though it appears from the ether."

She opened the dishwasher and set the plate into the rack, then spun to lean against the sink while taking up a dish towel to dry her hands. Her sons watched her, waiting for more.

"The appropriations have already been approved," she said. "The announcement to the American people is but a formality. Preparations have been made for months. New tools of war have been produced. But not for invading uncooperative countries. No, my lads, they have had that technology for a long time."

Her pause was intentional. She used it to read the expressions on her sons' faces. Liev was impatient for her to finish the thought, but Talbot was already working it out.

"They're going to use them as a safeguard against people like us."

"Very good, Talbot," Ana said.

She pushed away from the sink and planted her hands on the back of her chair, leaning over the table to bring her head closer to theirs.

"Your sister, rest her soul, put all of us in jeopardy by placing herself in the public eye. The world changed in that instant. National security had to be re-evaluated. Measures had to be put in place. Other countries will follow. This is why our time is now."

Liev plucked the napkin from his lap and tossed it onto the table, shaking his head.

"She put us in danger," he said. "All of us. Marcos's family, too."

"And attacking the National Guard didn't help matters," Talbot said. "She went through them like a hot knife through butter. They didn't have a chance."

"Until they disintegrated her, you mean," Liev said with a smirk. "Serves her right, the stupid little—"

The table chair in Ana's hands slammed against the floor with a voluminous echo.

"Liev! If you finish that sentence I'll have you drooling in a padded cell for the rest of your pitiful life!"

Liev's gaze dropped to the napkin before him, his fingers pulling at a loose thread with sudden interest.

"That's why you brought us together, isn't it?"

All eyes found Marcos leaning against the back of the sofa across the room, arms crossed over his chest.

"We're your junior varsity team," he said, "called up when your star player was out of the playoff picture."

Ana straightened and turned to face him, cursing his gift. How long had he been standing there?

"That sound about right?" he said. "This 'Kinetic Star'—our *sister*, for Christ's sake—risks her life across the city for months, saving suicide jumpers and pulling victims from wrecked memorials and burning busses, and then all of a sudden she freaks out and gives the U.S. military a bloody nose for no reason?"

Ana took a step toward her son.

Mind your words, Marcos.

"Tell me, Ana, how long did it take you to decide to punish her when she refused to take your side? Minutes? Seconds? Yeah, I know what you did to the owner of this penthouse. I'm well aware of your 'gifts' as you like to call them. "

Talbot and Liev were on their feet now. Ana raised a hand to stay them.

"You forget your place, boy."

"I'm sorry, is this a dysfunctional family or a dictatorship?" Marcos said. "At least you can speak freely in a dysfunctional family. I guess this is the latter."

"Your sister made the wrong choice and paid the price," Ana said. "She would have done everything in her considerable power to prevent my utopia from taking shape. And yes, she was the first choice to be at my side when the new dawn rose over the world. Our world. I loved her with all of my being. Then she crossed me."

The air was sucked from the room. Ana let her words simmer in the distance between her and her sons.

"Be grateful that I took you in, Marcos. You and your brothers will fill the void she left in her insubordination. You will all be wealthy and powerful beyond measure once the dust settles. What was hers will be yours."

She let her features soften before continuing, her eyes panning across her sons' faces.

"You are my blood and I would not have let you perish in the coming darkness, whether or not your sister were at my side. Your family will be safe, Marcos, as I promised. Just be patient. I need you. All of you. Each of you joined me for your own unique reason, and I will repay that decision a thousand fold. Let us see this through together. We are almost at the end."

Marcos shifted his weight and turned his head to peer at the sprawling skyline. Talbot's posture relaxed. Liev retrieved his phone from the kitchen table.

"You each have a part to play in this, which will be revealed to you in the coming days," said Ana. "Until that time, I ask for your patience and cooperation."

She scanned Marcos's surface thoughts and detected hesitant compliance. An image flashed through his consciousness, clear and crisp in her mind. Marcos was on his knees, weeping over the bodies of his children while beyond them the world burned. Ana resisted the urge to smile.

Liev's voice drew her back into the penthouse apartment.

"Where's Adrian?"

Ana moved back to the table and continued to clear it.

"Adrian is already playing his part. He'll rejoin us soon. Now come. Help your mother clean this up."

Chapter Fourteen

DAVID COULDN'T DECIDE IF MARISSA WAS SERIOUS. He pressed forward anyway, sidestepping her typical quirkiness in an attempt to decipher her intent.

"So you'd like...what? Carry a Taser or something?"

Marissa kicked off her sandals and put her bare feet on the dash, curling her toes for a better grip.

"Why not?" she said. "A Taser could come in handy. You could teach me to fight like you did with Sam. And I'm pretty sure her uniform and cowl would fit me fine. Well, I mean, it might be a bit tight around the hips, but that can't be helped. She was built like a beanpole."

David banished the image of Samantha's body from his mind before it could manifest. The grief returned, resurfacing as it had with all whom had known and loved her, as evidenced by the ensuing silence in the SUV. A month hadn't been long enough to dull that ache. The edges were still keen, and cut into everyone.

Brie's voice emerged from behind them, still groggy from her nap.

"Not a Taser. You should use pepper spray."

David noted that she had been awake long enough to ingest the most recent portion of their amusing conversation, but preferred that she keep her opinions to herself. Marissa didn't need any encouragement.

"Maybe," Marissa said. "But that might give away my secret identity. A lot of people saw me use pepper spray on that jerkoff at the Capitol."

Harkins. David couldn't help but wonder if Marissa's misguided aspiration to pick up where Samantha had left off wasn't a subconscious effort to deter David from his plan. Every mile drew them closer toward what could be a monumental—and potentially deadly—mistake, and memories of the battle on the Capitol plaza were no doubt being rehashed in Marissa's mind with growing clarity. David readjusted his position in the driver's seat, remonstrating himself for playing armchair psychologist. It was going to be fine. He loosened his grip on the steering wheel, unaware that he had been clutching it like a vise.

"What would your codename be?" Brie said. "Kinetic Sidekick?"

Marissa swiveled around to regard her paramour, throwing an elbow onto the headrest to support her weight. It was an impressive display of flexibility considering that her feet remained on the dash.

"You'd have to figure out the sidekick's name, Brie, since you'd be the sidekick. I'll let the members of the fan club decide my codename."

David and Brie's surprise was blurted in unison.

"Fan club?"

"Yep," said Marissa, uncoiling her torso to face forward again. "You made one for Sam. Why not me?"

"Hm. I don't know about that," Brie said. "David, do sidekicks get fan clubs?"

David shrugged. Marissa scoffed.

"*I* wouldn't be the sidekick!" she said.

David couldn't help but pile on.

"Well I don't know a lot of superheroes who use Tasers or pepper spray. I think you need a superpower for that. Or a tragic, interesting back story at the very least. Without those, maybe you're a sidekick."

Brie's giggle was muffled by her neck pillow.

Marissa issued a "Pth!" and buried her nose in her phone.

David checked the rear view mirror before flicking the blinker lever and guiding the vehicle into the passing lane. A sign for Lake Salvador loomed ahead, which meant the Gulf lay just beyond. It wouldn't be long now.

He wondered if Elyse had ever been to the Gulf coast. In all the years he had known her, he'd never thought to ask. Or maybe he'd been too self-absorbed or preoccupied to listen to her story about a family trip to Clearwater or Pensacola from her youth. Maybe she had taken Duncan there in the past several years. He pictured her in a wide-brimmed straw sunhat and a wider smile as she introduced their son to the ocean for the first time. He saw her lounging in a beach chair while Duncan struggled to complete his architectural masterpiece made of sand before the tide washed it away. That second image persisted and came to life in his mind. Elyse became distracted from her son and sat up, searching for something. Or someone. David was right there, the hot sand insinuating itself between his toes, the alkaline breeze permeating his nostrils. Why couldn't she see him? A stranger came into view, shirtless with the body of a swimmer. He paused to plant a light kiss on Elyse's sunblock-laden shoulder before kneeling in the sand next to Duncan and scooping up a bright yellow bucket to aid in the boy's construction efforts.

"I think you missed your exit."

Marissa's casual observation returned him to the rental SUV. She had claimed the shotgun seat, which meant she had been assigned the position of navigator. David relaxed his grip on the steering wheel again.

"There will be another one," he said. "Nothing in front of us now but ocean."

And uncertainty, but David decided to leave the secondary observation unspoken.

The lane to 1808 Cypress Shore Drive was blocked by gates of solid iron carved with exquisite scrollwork that would have taken the most skilled craftsman many months to complete. Half of an embossed capital H was sculpted in flowing calligraphy into the left gate, the letter fully forming when the gates were closed. But the H was broken, leaving an opening just large enough to admit a person.

"This must be the place," Marissa said. "Brie, Goddess of the Ones and Zeroes, retains her title as Queen of the Hackers."

Brie imitated a royal curtsy as best she could from the back seat.

"Have my handmaiden sent to my drawing room with a spot of tea and a fresh pair of knickers," she said in her best English accent.

David was glad that Marissa had patched things up with Brie, aside from the obvious reason that he wanted Marissa to be happy. Brie's extraordinary talent at digital infiltration had come in quite handy when he needed to locate an address for someone who didn't particularly want people darkening his door. Their relationship could easily have gone another way. Samantha's mother had implanted horrific images into Brie's mind that had made her piss herself—quite literally. Visions taken from her own past, of her abusive father transformed into a hideous, threatening creature. Marissa had told David that she didn't blame Brie for running after the incident. The traumatized young woman needed time to heal from the madness that had been inflicted upon her. But Marissa had told him she was beyond elated that Brie was back in her life. In their life, he had corrected.

David supported Marissa's praise of her partner with a nod, but kept his eyes on the crease in the gate. The SUV's brake pedal pushed against his foot, urging him to release it and move closer, but David held fast. People sometimes left their gate open if they were running a quick errand, but this space was in no way wide enough for a vehicle to pass through and there was nothing within walking distance but water. He thrust the shifter into park and opened the SUV door.

"Stay here."

The door closed behind him before any protests could reach his ears. He slipped through the gates and paused to get his bearings before making his way onto the property.

The cement drive was marked with sporadic imprints of sea shell designs and was flanked by rows of landscape lighting that stretched away atop short, iron posts. Beyond, palm sentinels loomed overhead like silent guardians. The drive resolved into a broad roundabout that surrounded a towering, multi-tiered fountain. Its merry bubbling grew louder as David neared the mansion, which was a modern architect's dream project—a sprawling, sharp-angled structure of glass and steel with a style all its own.

David stopped at the fountain to take in the massive garage to the west. The five garage doors were closed but, just like the entry gates, the arched double doors of the mansion were ajar.

A familiar sensation returned. The slight quickening of his breath. The persistent prickling of his nape hairs. A primal alarm system hardwired through millions of years of evolution. A genetic missive handed down from early man that reads: "The fire follows the thunder" or "The forest is too quiet." David's hand went to the small of his back, but found no weapon there. They had flown into New Orleans instead of making the fifteen-hour drive, a time-saving tactic that had prevented David from carrying a weapon. The trade off had seemed reasonable at the time, but now he found himself cursing the decision.

He approached the entrance and planted his fingertips against the open door, widening the gap with gentle force. Cool air washed over him from the foyer, carrying with it a familiar, coppery scent. David felt his bowels clench. He barreled through the doors, ready to face whatever lay beyond, but stopped short as his eyes were drawn to the floor.

The close curls that covered the man's scalp were bleached with age where they weren't matted with coagulating crimson. The starched white collar around his neck was stretched and misshapen, and drenched with so much blood that it rivaled the shade of his maroon formal coat. He lay on his stomach, a white-gloved left hand extending toward a cell phone near the front doors that he would never reach. David looked down to find the glass screen smashed into uselessness. Perhaps this poor soul had been trying to call for help. Maybe he was trying to call Harkins.

David knelt and eased the victim onto his back, trying his best to ignore the lifeless flopping of limbs. Pale eyes stared into nothingness through filmy cataracts. David dismissed the notion of checking for vitals. The man's throat now lay outside of his neck and clung there by a single tendon that had been spared. Blood still dripped from the macabre mass of ruined tissue.

David's eyes narrowed. He leaned in.

The wound was in no way clean nor surgical in any fashion. The weapon hadn't been a razor blade or even a finely-honed knife. There were no straight lines. It was the product of a gruesome tear, like that inflicted by a bear or a great cat. This man's life had been ripped from him in a very literal sense. Perhaps it was a hook of some sort? David couldn't be sure. He closed the man's eyes with thumb and forefinger. The poor soul probably didn't even see it coming.

Yet he had lived long enough to crawl toward his phone, which his murderer may have stomped as a parting gesture on his way out. Had this man been holding his phone when he was attacked? Or did he pull it from the pocket of his impeccable formal coat, threatening to call the authorities when the encounter took a dangerous turn? David shifted his weight to inspect the device. It was beyond use now, which was a shame. It could have provided useful information such as the whereabouts of Harkins.

Or maybe Harkins was still at home.

David rose and turned toward the interior of the house. Shouting for Harkins might alert the killer to his presence if he—or she—was also in the house. Searching for Harkins's body would waste precious minutes, but David had no other choice. He had to know if Harkins also lay in a pool of his own blood somewhere in the mansion. At the very least, David might find some hint as to where Harkins was if he hadn't been home during the murder. And the killer might have found it too.

He raced into the great room, an enormous chamber with a vaulted ceiling and rear walls of immaculate glass that overlooked a terrace and the sprawling pool area beyond. The horizon drew an unbroken line in the distance, clear sky above and the calm waters of the Gulf below. A single engine aircraft towed a rippling banner in the distance, too far away for David to read. The decor of the room was spartan, almost nonexistent, much like his own modest dwelling in DuPont Circle.

Sweeping the rest of the mansion took longer than David would have liked, and the time spent searching every room that held neither Harkins nor any information on his location put more distance between him and his quarry. He ended his hunt in the spacious kitchen, staring through another window that looked out onto a manicured lawn bordered by a tall, trimmed hedge line. His eyes lingered on a round aluminum frame that rested in the middle of the yard like a strange lawn ornament. It was angled like a satellite dish, and black netting sagged beneath the rim in a wrinkled web of vinyl weave. A bright yellow target had been affixed to the center of the netting.

David cocked his head and stepped closer to the window.

Small chunks of sod were missing in a semi-circular array at varying distances from the contraption. David stepped away from the window and pivoted, his hand digging into his pocket.

That was no lawn ornament.

His phone came alive with Marissa's voice several seconds later.

"*How did it go in th—*"

"I'm coming to you," David said as he exited the kitchen in a sprint. "He's a golfer. I want you to search for country clubs in the area."

"*Well of course he is,*" said Marissa. "*Rich guy...huge mansion...nothing else to do on a Saturday morning but waste time hitting a tiny ball with a metal stick... Kind of makes sense.*"

David paused in the foyer as Marissa rambled, his attention drawn to the ghastly wound at the corpse's neck. He grimaced and scooped up the ruined phone on his way out.

"Just find out where Harkins went."

He ended the call and raced past the fountain, but stutter stepped to a halt when a thought struck him. He twisted at the waist and looked back at the front doors, which he hadn't bothered to close, and summoned a mental image of the kitchen he had just left. Yes, there it was. On the countertop next to the refrigerator. A block of varnished wood sprouting silver and black handles.

Marissa was working her magic before David returned to the rental SUV, calling one country club after another in methodical fashion. David caught the tail end of the final call as he slid the key into the ignition.

"Oh thank you so much," Marissa said, greeting David with a nod and a finger pointing to the phone at her ear. "He ran out of the house without his medication again."

"Ask them what hole he might be on," David mouthed in a half whisper.

Marissa showed him her palm and nodded again, this time in confirmation.

"I think his tee time was around eight fifteen, but we might have gotten our wires crossed."

David could hear consonants and vowels through her phone's earpiece, but they made no sense to him.

"Eight thirty-five. No, that's right. That's what he told me," she said. "No, you're correct. Any idea where that might put him by now?"

More unintelligible chatter. David tapped several buttons in the dash display to bring up the GPS and left his finger hovering over the panel as he swiveled his neck to face Brie in the backseat. She looked up from her laptop screen.

"Twelve forty-nine Green Meadow Lane," she said. "Two point seven miles."

David punched the address into the touch screen then shifted his attention to Marissa.

"Twelfth or thirteenth hole. Got it," Marissa said into the phone. "Thank you again. He always skips breakfast on the weekends and will get hangry if he doesn't have his meds."

She ended the call to find David wearing a smirk.

"What?"

"You just had to add that little detail at the end," he said.

"Hey, it's the pink bow on the pile of crap that makes it pop."

The parking lot of the Vert Prairie Country Club overflowed with vacant vehicles abandoned by their owners in favor of battery-powered, open-cabin two seaters that fit much better on the narrows pathways that meandered throughout the sprawling golf course. David didn't bother to search for an empty space, opting instead to park the rental behind a monstrous white pickup truck near the first hole. He unbuckled his seat belt and drew in a breath to speak.

"Yeah, we know," said Brie from behind him.

"Stay here," said Marissa.

"Yep," he said, opening the door.

He felt Marissa's hand clamp over his upper arm as he slid from the driver's seat. He expected a firm yet unnecessary word of caution, but Marissa wasn't quite the meek assistant that she used to be.

"He's probably on the fourteenth or fifteenth hole by now. Go get 'em. boss"

David nodded.

"And here I thought you were going to tell me to be careful."

The corner of her mouth arched with her eyebrow.

"You don't pay me enough for that."

David produced his phone, ignoring the comment.

"Keep an open line. Put it on speaker so we can maintain comm—"

A shriek erupted somewhere in the expanse of rolling fairways and manicured greens. A flock of sparrows burst from the towering oaks that lined the parking lot.

David leaned into a sprint and leapt into one of the three golf carts queued up at the first hole. His heel smashed into the accelerator, causing the cart to lurch forward. Golf clubs protested with metallic rattles in their bags behind him, drowning out the shouts from their owners who stood angry and bewildered in the tee box.

The trees proved to be an immediate danger as he maneuvered the cart with maximum speed across hole after hole. A bone-crushing collision with a thick bole was without a doubt one of the risks he had accepted, but that wasn't what made his palms sweaty as he ramped the cart over a drainage ditch, narrowly missing a low-hanging elm branch. No, it was the fact that Roger Harkins had no control over organic material. The old, hulking trees that crowded this country club course wouldn't obey the whims of his strange ability. Harkins was likely defenseless against an assassin in this environment, and unaware that he was being stalked. And from the number of golfers fleeing the scene of whatever lay ahead, it was apparent that the stalker had found its victim.

David burst from a copse of young oaks onto a flat stretch of green fairway. He had no idea which hole he had intruded upon, but it didn't matter. His mad dash was at its end. David got his first look at the killer as the man advanced on a stunned and bleeding Roger Harkins.

He was young, perhaps a handful of years older than Samantha, with a lean frame and well-proportioned limbs that lent credence to his astounding athleticism. The assassin gripped a sharp, gleaming claw in his right hand—a karambit, David now noticed, quite capable of ripping the throat from a man—and weaved his body around what had once been the metal framework of a golf cart, now an automaton protector for Harkins. Samantha's half-brother stood several paces away, clutching a nine iron and directing his construct to save his life with sharp jerks of his free hand. Harkins's golfing partner lay nearby, his entrails ripped from his belly to lay steaming on the bloodied grass beside him. Perhaps he had tried to intercede, had gotten between the hunter and his prey. David didn't have time to reconstruct the sequence of events. The murders were still in progress, and David was about to be an active participant at the scene of the crime. He kept the accelerator pedal pinned to the floor and pointed the nose of the cart at the young assassin. He reached behind him, his fingers extended toward anything useful, and felt a soft rubber grip press into his palm. David pulled.

Ahead of him, the killer evaded and countered the construct's lumbering strikes with preternatural swiftness and skill, the curved knife in his grip bringing sparks to life with each perfect parry. David couldn't decide if Harkins's construct was sluggish or if this young man possessed some sort of enhanced ability. David had pored through the video footage of Samantha's battle with these mindless creatures a thousand times. He had even seen one up close and personal. Harkins's creations were not to be trifled with, yet this young man made the golf cart-turned-monster look like a marionette with twisted strings. It didn't matter, however. All the assassin had to do was get past it, not stop it. And that was going to happen any second now.

Almost there.

David jammed the head of the golf club—a broad-faced putter, it turned out—against the pedal and thrust the other end into the seat back before clutching at the roof of the vehicle and swinging his body from the cart. He kept his hand on the steering wheel until the last moment, hoping Harkins's wide eyed stare wouldn't reveal the sneak attack. But Harkins didn't give away David's oncoming attack. His construct did. It was almost comical how the faceless automaton shifted its "head" to look with nonexistent eyes past the assassin at the speeding golf cart with a stranger hanging onto its side. The motion synchronized perfectly with the look of surprise on Harkins's face. It was all the warning the killer needed. The assassin crouched and sprung in an instant, executing a perfect back flip that would have shamed a gold-medal Olympian. His body arched over the cart-turned-battering ram, which in turn smashed into the construct with devastating result.

David, having leapt free at the last moment, felt the impact of the collision through the earth beneath him, heard the crunch of the fiberglass body and the high-pitched protest of spinning wheels that no longer touched the ground. He gathered himself and lurched to his feet, forcing his body into motion. Golf clubs, tees, and dimpled white balls rained from the sky around him, accompanied by bits of fiberglass shell and random cart parts. The killer had landed on his feet with perfect balance, the karambit still in his possession and held at the ready. David met his calm stare as he closed the distance between them.

Harkins stood transfixed by the stunt that had just been performed in front of him. David sucked in a breath and shouted.

"Get out of here!"

He was barely able to get the Santoku chef's knife he had stolen from Harkins's kitchen into play before the assassin was upon him. The attacks were furious, the angles unorthodox and executed with frightening speed. David was forced to back away to avoid having his throat or belly ripped from him, despite the fact that the eight-inch blade of the Santoku gave him the reach advantage. The crescent-shaped weapon in his opponent's fist was most often held in the reverse grip which limited the range, yet this murderer used the steel ring in the pommel to flip the dangerous claw into distracting slashes when not jabbing or thrusting. David used the spacious fairway to keep his distance, but this man moved like a panther and struck like a cobra. David hadn't seen anything like it. Every exploratory jab or feint from David was either dodged or ignored. It was almost if this young man could sense David's counter attacks just as his muscles twitched to deliver them.

A knot formed in David's stomach. He had been here before. On a deserted, dusty street just outside of a dive cantina in Mexico. A knife fight he knew he was going to lose. Braithwaite's skills couldn't begin to compare with those of this dangerous stranger. And there would be no guardian angel to save David this time.

David's shoulder exploded in pain, a line of fire drawn across his deltoid. The slash had been aimed at his carotid artery, but his combat reflexes forced his body into a defensive shoulder roll before he knew what he was doing. The move saved his life. Somewhere, David heard the eerie screech of bending metal. He ignored it, keeping his focus on his opponent. Harkins stood in David's peripheral vision, and his expression had turned from shock to determination. David realized he had to decide whether or not he would give his life to save Samantha's brother. It was now obvious that the idiot wasn't planning to retreat as David had ordered. But he needed this idiot. The country—perhaps the world—needed this idiot. Samantha was gone, and only Harkins had the power to stop whatever was to come.

The killer moved and David evaded. He moved again, and David blocked the karambit only to take a fist to the chin. The man was simply too quick. David fell for a feint and found himself victim to a spinning rear leg sweep that had him on his flat on back and staring at a turkey buzzard riding the air currents against the blue sky high above. He wondered if the scavenger would be picking at his bones in the near future. He rolled away from a follow-up heel stomp that would have crushed his larynx. He wasn't sure if he could regain his footing before the killer dropped onto him with all of his weight behind the wicked, curved blade but, fortunately for David, the spider was there.

David blinked.

The spider?

Roger Harkins insisted on only the best gear for his Saturday morning hobby, and the latest edition of the top-of-the-line Ping Ultra Loft 3000 golf club set ensured that the shafts were made from the best titanium. Trees, grass and shrubbery were useless to Harkins, but titanium....

The thing was nightmarish and haphazard in its hastily-assembled form, and no larger than a Labrador. Yet from its central bulk of fused club heads sprouted eight shiny, titanium legs of varying lengths which undulated in eerie fashion and made its gait unwieldy and skittish. The assassin halted his killing blow and turned away from David just as the arachnid construct finished its metamorphosis and joined the fray. David didn't miss the fact that this young man was aware of the new danger before it had fully formed.

David got to his feet and delivered a series of long-ranged thrusts to the killer's back. Again, the assassin dodged at the last possible moment, spinning away from the spider's wicked, pointed limbs at the same time.

"Eyes in the back of his goddammed head," David muttered as he sought to align his offense with that of the weird titanium creature.

"Go for his legs!" he shouted to Harkins with a wink. "I'll disarm him!"

There was no point in trying to veil their strategy.

The killer had a sixth sense, which was why David went against his own orders and dove for the killer's knees. The assassin's vertical was impressive, at least six feet from a standing position. David's arms wrapped around empty air as his chest skidded across the turf. Harkins diverted his automaton lest it collide with David instead of its intended target. David was pretty sure he could see Harkins shake his head in annoyance. The idiot had apparently misconstrued David's true intent.

The assassin attacked as he landed, planting the karambit blade into the central mass of the construct and using his descending momentum to roll and fling the thing away from him. It tucked its legs and rolled like a strange, creepy child's toy until a thick tree trunk stopped its inertia. The legs unfurled and took its weight as Harkins directed it back towards the assassin. But now there was nothing between Harkins and the harbinger of death that had come for him. Neither David nor the automaton would reach him in time. David knew he had failed, and there was nothing he could do about it.

"Hey batter batter!"

A flash of movement stole David's attention away from Harkins's impending death. The electric hum of a speeding golf cart approached and was gone. David froze in horrified shock as Brie leaned out of the passenger seat, a sand wedge clutched in her fists. She swung just as her battle cry was completed. The sound of steel on flesh was sickening. The crunch of bone was worse. The assassin's knees wobbled, then buckled. The karambit dropped to the fairway. His limp body followed in short order.

"I'd have shouted 'Fore!' but whatever."

David was not at all surprised by Marissa's criticism as she calmly brought the cart around and engaged the emergency brake.

"It was the first thing that came to mind," said Brie, shaking her arms to lessen the numbness that had been born there upon impact.

David found Harkins staring at him, an incredulous look painted across his face. David shrugged and nodded toward the couple.

"You get used to it."

Chapter Fifteen

THE WAIL OF SIRENS SPURRED THEM into motion before Marissa could fully process the scene she and Brie had burst upon with foolish bravado. David and Harkins stood on the back of the stolen golf cart, clutching at the frame for stability as Marissa navigated the vehicle with as much haste as the battery-powered accelerator would permit. Her thoughts were on the abandoned SUV rental parked near the first hole. The police would trace it to one Derek Mendelbaum, yet another of David's aliases that he would have to burn. A positive was that Brie had grabbed her laptop and stuffed it into her backpack before they left the SUV. It wouldn't do to leave incriminating evidence at the scene.

"Veer right," Harkins shouted. "Head for that utility tower."

They ditched the golf cart at the edge of the country club property and crossed a two-lane highway before emerging from the roadside foliage onto a stretch of sandy beach. The Gulf of Mexico lapped at the shore, stretching to the horizon in a still sheet beneath a brilliant morning sky. Marissa kicked off her flat-soled, red sneakers and let the gritty sand slip between her toes. The fact that she had just been party to felonious assault and fled a murder scene wouldn't stop her from enjoying her time at the beach, however brief it may be.

"This way," said Harkins, leading them north toward a reedy inlet.

Marissa checked Brie's expression as they fell in beside David, who had placed himself between them and Harkins. Brie's eyes darted about, always returning to the direction in which they had come. The sirens were distant now, quiet and impotent. The prevailing thought, although unspoken, was that the authorities would find the abandoned cart at the edge of the property and assume that a getaway vehicle had been waiting for the suspects on the side of the highway. They would set up checkpoints and launch a helicopter or two to canvass the area.

Marissa knew that David was already putting together an escape plan. He was good about such things. An "extraction strategy" as he liked to say. Still, she couldn't help but lift her eyes to the blue expanse above her, strain her ears for the rhythmic beating of rotors. Whatever extraction strategy he was concocting, it had better be quick.

They rounded a bend in the beachhead and plodded through ankle-deep brackish water before reaching the inlet Harkins had indicated. An array of large stones created a natural sitting area at the water's edge.

"I used to fish here," Harkins said as he plopped down on one of the stones. "Naturally secluded. And the perch are pretty gullible if you have the right bait."

Marissa wrinkled her nose. She had never seen the point in forcing barbed hooks into the flesh of living things for the sake of sport, or any other reason for that matter. She glanced at David who was staring out into the Gulf, and noticed the angry red slash on his shoulder for the first time.

"Jesus, David, you're hurt!" she said, shuffling through the sand and reaching toward the bloody, frayed rip in the sleeve of his button-down shirt.

He didn't respond until her fingers made contact, and flinched away from her as if she had woken him from an unpleasant daydream.

"What? Oh, it's just a scratch."

"Bullshit," Marissa said, peeling back the fabric to reveal a deep laceration. "You need stitches."

She expected a curt remonstration of David's nonchalance from Brie, or at least a comical reinforcement of Marissa's assessment, but her girlfriend stood apart from her companions with arms crossed and attention focused on her feet. Had she caught a glimpse of Harkins's disemboweled golf partner? Maybe she was just skittish around Harkins. Marissa couldn't blame her. After the stories Brie had been told about the man, coupled with the psychological horrors visited upon her by this man's mother, she had every right to be apprehensive.

"He's not answering," Harkins said, lowering his phone from his ear. "Damn it. Do your fucking job."

"Who's not answering?" Marissa said.

A quick glance from David silenced any further inquiry.

"I'm trying to get us a ride out of here," said Harkins, looking at his phone screen. "He always answers. Night or day. I don't—"

"Your butler is dead," David said. "The assassin was looking for you. Found him instead."

Marissa's impression of Roger Harkins was that of a spoiled, rich, entitled man with a bad attitude and an apathetic world view. After all, his words and actions up to this point in time had illustrated these traits. He had tried to kill her best friend. Had been unrepentant when he was forgiven and saved from prosecution after terrorizing the nation's capital. Marissa remembered the ecstatic look on his face when he had finally defeated Samantha and was about to humiliate her in front of the world. Marissa had erased that expression with a dose of pepper spray, but it had been replaced by rage. She was sure that Harkins's emotional toolbox consisted only of smug self-righteousness and childish anger, but the series of expressions that traveled over his face after David's revelation set Marissa back on her heels.

Harkins stood tight-lipped, his eyebrows raised and trembling, his dark eyes wide and glassy. His lips warped and fluttered, trying to form words that escaped him. His eyes were locked onto David with a stare that demanded more.

"I found him in your foyer. Throat slit ear to ear by the same weapon that did this."

David motioned to his wounded shoulder.

Marissa stepped closer to him and lowered her voice.

"Christ, David. Really?"

Harkins took a step back from them, stumbling over a stone before righting himself. He looked at his phone as though his manservant was going to return his calls at any second and prove David to be a liar. The phone didn't ring. Harkins raised it over his head as if to dash it upon the rocks, but let his arm drop. He walked in a tight circle, repeatedly consulting his silent phone before stopping to throw his head back.

"Fuck!"

"Harkins. We need to get out of this area. Now. Is there anyone else you can call?" said David. "Anyone that has a boat?"

Harkins hung his head, eyelids clamped tight against the emotions that had been thrust upon him. Marissa felt Brie's hand slip into hers, heard a whisper at her ear.

"Maybe he is a human being after all."

Marissa squeezed Brie's hand in silent reply. She almost felt sorry for Harkins when David closed the distance and seized him by the upper arm.

"Harkins! We can't stay here! A boat! Do you know anyone who has one?"

Harkins nodded.

"I have one," he said, wiping at his eyes with the back of his golf glove.

David pointed to the phone in Harkins's other hand.

"Good. Call someone to pick us up. Do it. Then smash your phone and throw it into the ocean before they start tracing our location."

He turned away from Harkins and shook his head while rotating his shoulder in its socket as though the motion would somehow ease the pain.

Marissa didn't need to say anything when their eyes met.

"Yes, that was necessary," David said. "We don't have time for this. He can grieve later."

She looked past David. Harkins had the phone to his ear once more. Marissa could hear the heaviness in his voice as he spoke into the device. David leaned into her field of vision.

"Let's keep our eye on the prize, okay?" he said.

Brie pressed her palm against Marissa's back and rubbed it several times before hanging her hand on Marissa's shoulder.

"He's right. We need him."

Marissa nodded as Harkins approached.

"He's on his way," he said.

Harkins's voice was stronger now, his stoic veneer back in place as though nothing had happened. But his red, puffy eyes told Marissa otherwise.

"Now," he said, turning to David. "What the fuck were you doing at my house?"

David winced as Brie smeared a gelatinous salve into his torn shoulder.

"Stop it," she said. "Hold still."

"It hurts like a motherfucker," he said.

"Weren't you like a green beret or something? Suck it up."

Marissa chuckled from the other side of the contents of the first aid kit that lay strewn across the table. Brie knew full well that David was once a Navy SEAL. She pushed a box of butterfly bandages toward Brie.

"Use these. I don't see a suture kit in here."

"That works," said Brie. "Not much of a seamstress anyway."

Marissa followed David's eyes to Harkins who stood at the window with his arms crossed, watching waves lap against the hull. She had expected a speedboat or maybe a broad, flat fishing craft to pick them up at the inlet, not a towering, one hundred-foot yacht with the name *Junesong* painted across the upper hull in playful script. She learned that the weathered, sun-kissed man who had piloted the boarding skiff to shore was also the captain of the *Junesong*, and was kept on standby at the marina. Marissa surmised that Harkins also owned a private jet, and probably kept a pilot at his beck and call as well. Affluence had its perks, after all.

"There. All better," Brie said as she gathered up the packaging from the bandages and stuffed them into the red and white first aid box. "The nurse will give you a lollipop on the way out."

David ignored Brie's whimsy and stood, unfurling the rolled sleeve of his blood-stained shirt and buttoning it at the wrist.

"All right, Harkins. Let's talk."

Harkins didn't move. Didn't respond at all. His back was to them, his face hidden.

Marissa caught David's attention. She mouthed two words and urged him on with a nod in Harkins's direction.

"Be nice."

David's nostrils flared as he took a deep breath. He exhaled with a shake of his head as he joined Harkins at the window. Marissa moved to the edge of the semi-circular leather seating that surrounded the table and concentrated on listening to their exchange. Her hand dropped to her lap, fingers tracing a raised, rectangular outline in her front pocket.

"Look, I know it's difficult," David said. "We've all lost people. Important people."

Harkins placed the heels of his hands on the window pane, straightening his arms and leaning against it.

"I feel a 'but' coming," he said.

"Do you think I want to be here?" David said. "Do you think I would have risked my life and those of my friends to save your neck if it wasn't absolutely necessary?"

Harkins didn't answer.

"You've been nothing but a pain in the ass since I first heard about you. Since you first started harassing—"

Marissa watched as David's expression locked up, his jaw clenching along with his fist. He didn't want to say her name. Not to Harkins.

Harkins turned his head an inch toward David.

"Then we have something in common."

Marissa was sure that David was going to punch him. They would be set adrift in the landing craft while Harkins enjoyed fresh lobster and chilled champagne as he watched them float away. But David didn't lash out. No, she knew that look. The gears were turning. His fist relaxed.

"We have more than that in common," he said. "We have a mutual interest. From what I understand, this woman Ana is your mother, too."

Harkins pushed away from the window pane and moved to the bar on the other side of the cabin. He retrieved a crystal decanter from a shelf and set it on the granite, leather-trimmed bar top followed by a single, shallow glass.

"She came to see me, you know."

The stopper left the decanter with a clink. Marissa and David locked eyes. Brie's spine straightened.

"Ana strolled right into my gallery like she owned the place," said Harkins. "Had this big guy with her. Giant motherfucker, if you want the truth. Referred to him as my brother. Said there were others."

"Holy shit!" Brie said.

Marissa seconded the exclamation with wide eyes. David's face was impassive.

"And?" said David.

Harkins took his time pouring a caramel-colored liquid into the glass. He didn't replace the stopper as he lifted the glass halfway to his lips.

"*And* she wanted me to join them. Join her. She killed my sister because she refused. I refused, too."

Their host took a drink as he let his words sink in. David closed the distance and flattened his hands on the bar with an audible smack.

"The assassin was an E.I.," he said.

"A what?" said Harkins, refilling his glass.

Marissa and Brie rose as one and joined them at the bar.

"How many are there?" Marissa said.

Harkins raised his eyebrows and shrugged.

"You guys want a drink? Least I could do."

Marissa marveled at his detachment, at the absence of urgency. His apathy was astounding. She knew in that moment that they had made the trip to Louisiana for nothing. Her fingers found the folded paper in her pocket again.

"No," David answered for all three of them. "This man was enhanced. Had to be. Just the way he moved, how he anticipated—"

"Suit yourselves," Harkins said, raising his glass again.

"That man was your brother! Sent by your own mother to kill you! How can you not care about that?" said Marissa.

"What did she say?" said David with a placating hand raised to Marissa. "When she came to your gallery. Specifics."

"I just told you."

"That's it?" said David.

Harkins nodded, his gaze falling over each of his guests one by one.

"You want me to come with you, help you take her down," he said.

David didn't miss a beat.

"That's right," he said. "I've never met the woman, but these two have. I've heard their stories, how she entered their minds and pushed them to the brink of insanity."

Marissa squeezed Brie's knee below the bar. It was trembling. Harkins poured his third glass before finally corking the decanter and pushing it away.

"I have to admit that I'm tempted. I really am," he said. "That bitch got in my head too, did some weird shit. Tried to coerce me into coming with her. A show of power, I guess. I haven't felt that much power since, well...heh...since Samantha."

Harkins's voice lost some its false bravado. His eyes found the bottom of his glass.

"Samantha can't help us now," David said. "But you can. You almost defeated your sister. You're a threat to Ana, and she knows it. Why else would she try to end you?"

Marissa felt Harkins's glance shift towards her. David's choice of words had no doubt rekindled the memory of his loss at the Capitol, of Marissa's sudden appearance there. She met his eyes and held them. She'd do it again in a heartbeat. His half smile said it all. Message received.

"...listen to me damn it," David was saying. "Did Ana say anything about what she's planning? Anything at all?"

Harkins planted his elbows on the bar and pressed his fingertips into his eyes, rubbing them in small circles.

"I don't know," he said with a deep exhale. "She... she made me conjure images in my mind. Flashes, really."

"Of what?" David said.

"Of recent news events. Of Samantha."

"And?"

"And what?"

"For fuck's sake, Harkins, this is like pulling teeth. What events?"

"The declaration of martial law. President Dietrich. War."

Marissa squinted with interest and leaned in, hanging on his words.

"What else?" David said.

"She said the world is broken, but she can make it better. For us."

"Us? Which us?" Brie said. "*You* us or *us* us?"

"For them, Brie, for them." said Marissa.

Harkins nodded before he spoke.

"Better for every one of us poor fucks she squeezed out of her—"

"Okay, I get it!" Brie said with a raised hand.

"She said it has to get worse before it gets better," Harkins said.

David stepped away from the bar and hung his hands on the back of his neck.

"Martial law," he said. "The president. She got in his head. War. World War Three..."

Marissa felt her toes grow cold. The icy sensation lanced into her chest and shot to her neck.

"She's been pulling the strings this entire time," Marissa said, her voice fading into a whisper.

"The headlines," David said, letting his arms drop to his sides. "The unhinged way world leaders have been acting. Our own president, too. Ana's been at this for years and years, setting up the dominoes from a hospital bed in a drug-induced coma. She was aware the entire time. She... Oh god, what has she done?"

Harkins nodded.

"All it would take is a single launch," he said. "We've seen it in so many movies. That one with Kevin Costner about the Cuban Missile Crisis comes to mind."

"Except the superpowers have had decades to improve and increase their nuclear arsenals since that crisis," said David. "This is far worse than I thought. This is the end of all things."

Marissa read his face again. He wouldn't say the words, so she did.

"I wish Sam was here."

This time all eyes fell on Marissa. She shifted her weight on the barstool.

"We'll have to do it ourselves," said David, seizing the decanter and pulling the stopper as an exclamation point.

Harkins set three more glasses on the bar and slid them toward David. Marissa let the liquid burn her throat and sit in her belly like an ember. A gravelly voice called down from cockpit.

"Marina off the bow!"

Harkins shouted a quick confirmation then addressed the others.

"I have a car waiting for you. It will take you wherever you want to go."

Marissa licked the taste of whiskey from her numbed lips.

"So that's it then?" she said. "You're just going to send us off on our own?"

"That's exactly it," said Harkins.

The crack of glass on granite jolted Marissa's already frayed nerves. David's fingers still clutched the vessel despite the webbed fractures that now adorned it. His face was flushed, his brows knit together.

"What?" Harkins said. "You going to beat me up? I'm not tied up in the middle of a forest this time. It may not go so well for you."

David's reply was a pair of daggers and a silent promise.

The leather seat of the Lincoln Town Car creaked as Brie situated herself next to David. Marissa stood inside the open door, one hand on its edge and the other inside her front pocket. Her bottom lip was clenched between her teeth as she watched Harkins. He stood beside a white Escalade idling behind them, speaking to the captain of his yacht. The corner of the folded paper was worn where her fingers had probed it for most of the remaining voyage to the marina.

"Marissa," David said from the car, "what are you doing?"

She watched Harkins nod at the captain and open the door to the large vehicle.

"He was pretty clear. He's not coming," said Brie.

"I know," said Marissa.

Harkins disappeared inside the Escalade.

"Marissa? Come on, let's—"

Brie's voice faded as Marissa ran to the Escalade, catching Harkins just as he was closing the door.

"What was his name?" she said, holding on to the door frame.

Harkins kept a hold on the interior door handle and raised his face to hers with a sigh.

"What now?"

"Your butler. What was his name?"

"My...what are you talking about?"

"The man David found murdered in your foyer," Marissa said. "What was his name?"

Storm clouds moved in Harkins's eyes.

"Woodley," he said. "Will you people leave me alone now?"

"No," she said. "What was his name?"

Harkins sighed again.

"Alistair Woodley. I forget his middle name but I can text it to you later, for fuck's—what's that?"

Marissa held out the folded paper pinched between her index and middle fingers.

"It's an address," she said, stuffing the note into the pocket of his striped polo golf shirt. "In D.C. You'll find something you lost there. Something that will help you even the score for what was done to Mister Alistair Woodley. That is, if you aren't too much of a chicken shit to do what's right for once in your miserable life."

Marissa returned to the Town Car before Harkins could respond. She couldn't know that she had rekindled a very specific memory in his mind as she left him with a baffled look on his face. A memory of a massive, heavy wooden crate being wrestled up a flight of stairs by an aging man too proud and devoted to his duty to ask for assistance.

Chapter Sixteen

THE DOWNDRAFT FROM THE ROTORS banished the morning frost from the manicured lawn, beating a perfect circle of bright green. Chesterfield "Chet" Dietrich returned the salute from the marine who stood rigid and alert just outside the door of the Sikorsky VH-60N, also known as a White Hawk or, as it would be called on this particular day, Marine One. The usual retinue of Secret Service agents flanked Dietrich, joining him inside the helicopter and securing the door behind them.

"Good morning, sir. We'll be departing momentarily."

Dietrich nodded to Agent Sapolski, a man in his late thirties who had been assigned to the President since his inauguration. Sapolski was the epitome of what Dietrich had always imagined an agent of the Secret Service to be; a nondescript, ex-military product of the cookie-cutter hiring pool from which the Secret Service seemed to hire more often than not. Dietrich sat down and reached inside his suit coat for his handkerchief, which was already soaked despite the brisk chill of the young day. He dabbed at his brow and upper lip before returning the embroidered swatch of cloth to his pocket. On second thought, he retrieved the handkerchief and draped it over his knee for easier access. Maybe it would even dry out a little before he needed it again.

He sensed Sapolski's eyes on the reinforced steel case on the seat beside the president. Dietrich knew the man was studying it through the dark lenses of his sunglasses, wondering what secrets lay inside. The chain that connected the case to Dietrich's wrist jingled as he balanced the container on his lap, a gentle, quiet sound that somehow became louder than the *WHUP! WHUP! WHUP!* of the helicopter blades overhead. The slight, almost imperceptible shift of the other agents' heads told the president that they, too, had become transfixed by the case's reflective, metallic surface.

The protocol in past administrations had been to assign a member of the Joint Chiefs of Staff to carry the president's burden, accompanying him wherever he went and standing ready to obey his command if the need to open the case arose. But Dietrich had insisted that he "bear the cross" as he had put it. When asked for a compelling reason why the protocol should be broken, he had simply reminded his would-be interrogators that he was the Commander-in-Chief. And that was that.

Except that wasn't that.

Chet Dietrich's life had changed after Inauguration Day in ways far more anomalous than he had imagined. Sure, he had felt the beginnings of the burden of office that had aged his predecessors with ruthless prematurity, and the appearance of Sapolski and his hand-picked security detail suddenly involved in every aspect of Dietrich's life had been most unsettling, but it was the change in his basic values and day-to-day decision making that alarmed him most. His wife had informed him of this moral shift in the weeks and months that followed his inspiring inaugural speech. Julia had become critical of the policies he drafted, accusing him of breaking his promises to the American people and warning him that he would lose his base—and with it his chances of re-election.

The pilot's voice lit up Dietrich's headphones.

"We have lift off. Please secure any loose items."

The sweat-slick case handle was hot in Dietrich's palm. It wasn't going anywhere.

"It's just a short hop over to the Mall, Mister President. We'll have you there in no time, sir."

The travel arrangements had been Sopalski's call. A motorcade was out of the question. The horde of both pro and anti-war protesters now choked the streets of Washington D.C., swelling with each new hawkish media broadcast. North Korea had always been a provocateur, but Supreme Leader Quong had inexplicably gained support from other powers in the region. It was unprecedented, as was the emergence of international power grabs among America's most trusted European allies. The continent had become a flimsy cardboard box filled with feral cats. Feral cats with weapons of mass destruction. There was no way to put a spin on it in the media, no way to conceal the message that civilization was on the brink of extinction. It was too late for that. The world had become a place where the accumulation of human knowledge, particularly current events and breaking news, could be accessed in real time by anyone from a device in their pocket. So Dietrich would let it be known that he would do whatever was necessary to protect the American people. Even if it meant taking everyone else down with him.

Even if it meant striking first.

It went against the platform he had run on, one of international cooperation and a mutual draw down of national defense initiatives. Supporters and detractors alike had called him "Peacenik Dietrich" on the campaign trail only three years ago. Now the fate of the planet was balanced on his knees next to a sweat-soaked handkerchief.

His stomach lurched as the horizon fell away outside of the cabin window. Dietrich suspected that the sensation wasn't solely caused by the sudden ascension of the helicopter.

His acceptance of the current state of affairs had evolved slowly over his time in office. The initial rumblings of political instability overseas had at first kept Dietrich awake at night. Sleep eluded him during the first year of his administration, but he would inevitably drift off only to wake with a new perspective on matters both foreign and domestic. Pieces on the global chess board became clearer to him as time went on, political strategies and overseas maneuvers that would reveal themselves to him with each new day as though he were recalling scenes from a memory or a dream. He remembered the quizzical look on Julia's face one night as they turned off their reading lamps. She said "Good night, dear" as she always did, and Dietrich answered with: "I'm off to visit my Muse."

It was his Muse that had suggested he give a speech at the Lincoln Memorial, one that would honor the spirit of the memorial's namesake and rival the one delivered there by King. The American people were waiting for their leader to address recent events, not only the looming crisis but also the period of martial law he had imposed on the nation's capital, and he didn't intend to disappoint them. What better way to distract a population from the horrifying prospect of a world war than with a more urgent, more immediate problem? What better way to push his agenda through so that—

Tak Tak Tak!

Dietrich's train of thought hit a warped rail and veered into a ditch. All heads swiveled to the starboard side of the aircraft as the entry door opened. A powerful wind filled the cabin, flailing ties and mussing hair. Dietrich's handkerchief fluttered from the aircraft like an escaping moth. Sopalski was on his feet before the president could react, shielding Dietrich's body with his own. The other two agents had their weapons in hand in the blink of an eye. The door closed—seemingly of its own volition—and the roar of the swirling air died away as quickly as it had begun. The sudden silence was broken by a feminine voice, strong and firm.

"Scooch."

Dietrich watched in mute fascination as the two pistol-wielding Secret Service agents across from him slid away from each other without moving a muscle of their own, creating an empty space in the seat between them. The cushions depressed as though they were taking weight, yet there were no other visible signs of an occupant.

The empty space shimmered like the still surface of a forest pond disturbed by tiny fauna, then she was simply there. All of the data he had read in domestic intelligence reports told him it was her. He didn't know of anyone else who could fly to a military helicopter and open the latched door with a thought. The reports had failed to mention invisibility, however.

Nevertheless, it was *her*.

She looked different than she had in the videos and surveillance photos. The suit was no longer red and black leather. It was more practical than the last one. No, not practical. Tactical. It was form fitting and flexible, made of an unknown material and fitted with twin vertical accessory straps that descended from shoulder to belt. There were no markings on the suit, no declarations of identity or affiliation, only small, disk-shaped nodules of alien design and mysterious function. The mask matched the smoky, charcoal tone of the suit, and covered her entire head like a balaclava. Slits were stacked vertically over the nose and mouth region, and twin lenses of indeterminate origin and hue covered her eyes. Their color appeared to play with the light, shifting from amber to violet to azure depending on the angle of her head. Those lenses remained pointed at Dietrich, even when the muzzles of his protectors' weapons were placed at her temples. She was so tiny sitting between the two burly agents, yet their firearms shook in their grasp.

It only took a second for Dietrich to take in the details of the intruder before his line of sight was blocked by Sapolski's body.

"Okay gentleman, relax," she said.

"On the floor! Do it! Now!"

Sapolski's order was punctuated by his men attempting to seize the woman by her upper arms and force her compliance. They never got close. The agents were repelled from her like a pair of powerful magnets attempting to occupy the same space. Pistols tumbled to the floor of the helicopter cabin as their faces met its chassis. Safety harnesses slithered from their couplings and found the agents' wrists and mouths, binding and gagging them in a serpentine dance.

"Okay gentlemen, relax," she said.

The discarded firearms rose from the floor and found their homes in the agents' shoulder holsters. Sapolski stood his ground, extending his weapon toward her and stabilizing it with his free hand.

"You need to sit down now," she said. "If I wanted the president dead, I would have imploded this thing like a papier-mâché submarine at the bottom of the Mariana Trench. Believe me, I've crushed choppers before."

Dietrich placed his hand on Sapolski's shoulder and gently applied pressure.

"At ease, agent."

Sapolski didn't ease up, however. He brought his wrist to his mouth.

"Command, we have a bogey on board Marine One, the package is in—"

The tiny communications device left his wrist and hovered before his face for a split second before it snapped apart and fell onto Sapolski's polished shoe.

"It's alright, son," Dietrich said, guiding his protector back to his seat. "The lady's right. If she wanted me dead, we wouldn't have been graced by this polite intrusion. We'd just be dead. Plain and simple."

Sapolski relented, but kept his firearm in hand.

"I wish your guy hadn't done that," she said, the strange lenses focusing on Sapolski. "They're probably scrambling jets right now. Can't let your man purse fall into the wrong hands, right?"

A grey, gloved finger uncurled toward the steel case in Dietrich's lap.

"They're not scrambling jets yet," said Sapolski. "But they are changing the codes. The case is useless to you now."

The eerie lenses shifted to Dietrich.

"I'm here to speak with you, Mister President, but I'd be happy to make sure your man has securely fastened his seatbelt for the remainder of the flight if he insists on pointing that weapon at me. It won't hurt me, but the ricochet might hurt you or one of your men."

Dietrich's eyes returned to the two agents on either side of her, lashed and immobile. He raised a hand to Sapolski.

"Let me handle this, son."

He sensed Sapolski's hesitation.

"That's a direct order, Sapolski."

The agent fell silent, lowering his firearm but keeping it in his trembling hand.

"I see you've changed your appearance," said Dietrich. "You look much more serious now. More like a threat than a motorcycle enthusiast."

"Oh, this old thing?" she said, brushing imaginary dust from a gloved forearm. "Present from a friend of mine. A graduation gift, I suppose."

"The world thinks you're dead, young lady," Dietrich said. "My boys lit you up like a fourth-of-July firework."

The woman shifted in her seat and crossed her legs, presenting the thick toe of her sturdy, charcoal boot. The motion would have been very ladylike if she hadn't been wearing what appeared to be something out of a science fiction film.

"Yeah, that stung quite a bit," she said. "But thanks for bringing it up. That's part of why I'm here."

Dietrich sat up straight and waited, forcing himself to breathe through his nose in an attempt to slow his heart rate. She turned her masked head left and right, then looked at Dietrich again.

"That can't be comfortable," she said. "If I let them go, will they promise to keep their hands to themselves?"

Dietrich watched as the agents' eyes fell on him.

"They will do as I tell them," he said. "Isn't that right?"

They nodded in unison. The harnesses uncoiled from their bodies and resumed their normal, inanimate positions. The pair of agents gasped for breath and began an urgent regimen of massaging their wrists. Dietrich straightened his tie and leaned back in his seat.

"You have my attention," he said. "Although I'm hesitant to parley with a domestic terrorist who attacked the brave men and women of the National Guard, not to mention violated protected air space over—"

"A parley suggests that we're enemies conducting an informal discussion to come to terms," she said. "And while this discussion is indeed informal, we're not enemies."

She unfolded her legs and leaned forward, elbows resting on her knees.

"We're victims."

Dietrich scoffed. She continued.

"It's true. Tell me something, Mister President. How many of us do you think are out there? And when I say us, I mean *us*."

She jerked a thumb at herself. Dietrich sucked in a breath to answer, but she didn't let him.

"You know about me and the one at the Capitol, but—"

"Yes, you mean the one that you carried off into the night when he should have been put behind bars for endangering the lives of American citizens and law enforcement? For millions of dollars in damage to the city?"

"I didn't let anyone die and you know it, Mister President," she said. "He was misguided and foolish, and I made sure he won't be hurting anyone again."

"Now *you* tell *me* something, Miss—I don't even know what to call you. How about you take off that mask and tell me your name? Speak to me like a human being. Person to person."

"And waste all of those taxpayer dollars you've already spent trying to find out who's behind this mask? Where's the fun in that?"

Sapolski moved in Dietrich's peripheral vision. Dietrich tried to raise an arm to stay him, but it was too late.

"You're a wanted criminal who—*augh!*"

The lead agent of the President's Secret Service detail was silenced by writhing, grasping safety harnesses. He made a strange sound when his body hit the cabin wall and hung suspended there in a splayed position.

"The man from the Capitol and I, we're not the only ones," she said. "You missed one, Mister President."

Dietrich tore his eyes from the struggling Sapolski and returned them to his uninvited guest.

"Who?"

"The most powerful and most dangerous of *us*. Unlike me, she doesn't give a shit about the American people. Or the people of the world, for that matter. Unlike me, she doesn't feel the need to protect those who can't protect themselves."

The masked woman leaned back and recrossed her legs.

"And unlike me, she wants to tear apart this planet and reshape it in her image. She believes she is an omnipotent mother figure who will give birth to a new era of humanity."

"I can't possibly believe this," said Dietrich. "This is insane!"

"That's what I said. Pretty much word for word. But it's true."

The woman cleared her throat and folded her arms over her chest, but not before bringing a gloved hand to her left ear to smooth back a lock of hair that wasn't there. Dietrich's gaze followed the motion, suspending his demand for proof for the moment.

"Mister President, this woman is ancient. Aged far beyond all comprehension of a human life span. She's seen empires rise and fall. She knows human society better than we do. Better than anyone. And that's what scares me. She isn't wrong about us."

"You're referring to the human race," Dietrich said.

A moment of silence followed, ending when Sopalski grunted in his reinforced nylon bonds.

"I'm referring to the self-obsessed, avaricious society we've built," she said. "A world where the patriarchy makes the rules and reaps the benefits, rapes the earth for its resources while keeping a boot firmly planted on the necks of those who would try to bring about real change. And all because that's how it's always been. Long before you or me. Long before there was an America."

Her hands spread out before her.

"As I said, she has a point."

Dietrich shifted his weight as he replied.

"Speaking of points, get to yours. Then get off my 'copter. We'll be at the mall any second."

"No we won't," she said. "We haven't moved since I came on board."

The masked woman turned to look through the cabin window.

"I think we're hovering somewhere over Independence."

Dietrich felt his heart rate increase again. He could feel the perspiration soaking through the armpits of his dress shirt.

"Abducting the U.S. President is a crime punishable by—URK!"

The Secret Service agent to her left ended up back in the restraints, stifling his interruption. She turned to the agent on her right, who suddenly decided that his cuticles needed a thorough inspection.

"So yeah, this woman is bad," said the masked intruder. "She's done a number on both of us. Imagine what you could do, Mister President, if you could read minds. If you could take over someone's senses and make them see what you want them to see? What you want them to hear and smell and touch and taste? What if you could implant subtle suggestions over time, from anywhere on earth, quietly turning the tide of world events? What if you could hold someone's mind in your hand like a lump of clay and mold it into whatever you liked? What would you do?"

"I...I uh..." stammered Dietrich. "I don't—"

"Nevermind. Those questions were rhetorical," she said. "And you don't believe me anyway. So let me ask you a few more. Ones that aren't so rhetorical. Why would a woman who one day woke up with extraordinary gifts and used those gifts to rescue people and to stand up to a misguided, super-powered buffoon tear-assing through downtown D.C., why would such a person suddenly attack the United States military for no reason?"

Dietrich's brows knit together.

"I bet you're going to tell me."

"I am," she said. "Maybe she confronted this madwoman. Maybe she refused to become part of an insane scheme pulled from the pages of a comic book and stood her ground. And maybe that resulted in her perception being twisted by said madwoman because the madwoman didn't get what she wanted and descended into a tantrum. Maybe the National Guard appeared to be shooting at civilians, cutting down men, women and children, forcing the victim's hand. Now take away all the maybes and there you have it."

"Do you really expect me to—"

"I'm not done. Now imagine that, prior to this, the madwoman spent twenty years in a secret, underground U.S. Government facility being pumped with psychotropic drugs and who knows what else, becoming a test subject for who knows what purpose, and all the while you and your predecessors were unaware of it. Then imagine that she was supposed to be in an induced coma to control her, but that her mind never actually rested. Envision that. Trapped in a nightmare, unable to move for two decades. A person relegated to a lab rat, except a lab rat with the ability to read and project thoughts. Reach out and touch someone, if you get my meaning. Who do you think this rat might try to contact? Who do you think this unwilling guest of the government might try to control?"

She motioned to Sopalski, then to the agents on her left and right.

"Not these guys. And not me. So—"

Dietrich patted the air in front of him.

"Yes, yes. I get it!"

"But not just you, sir. Not just the leader of the U.S. Foreign leaders, too. The UK and France. North Korea. Probably Russia and China as well. I can't be sure. But she quoted something to me in those minutes before she took over my senses. I think her words were: 'What is government itself but the greatest of all reflections on human nature? If men were angels, no government would be necessary.'"

"Madison," Dietrich muttered.

The masked head cocked to the side.

"James Madison," Dietrich said. "The fourth president."

"Oh," she said. "I didn't know that. Well, she also called you all frightened children."

Dietrich stared at his reflection in the surface of the case in his lap. The man who stared back appeared older than he should be.

"I'm sure I don't have to tell you that using that case will end everything," said the masked woman. "A single launch will be detected and retaliated against."

"Of course it will," said the reflection in the steel case.

"I may have pretty cool powers, but I can't chase down every single missile in the world. This isn't a superhero movie, Mister President. I can't save America. But you can."

Dietrich once again found those odd, polychromatic lenses, and once again his reflection stared back at him.

"You came here to warn me," he said. "After everything I did to try to bring you to justice."

The woman paused a beat before replying.

"As I said, I'm not your enemy. I'm not a threat to you, sir. I want the same things you do. I'm sure you met a lot of people during your campaign travels who asked you to change things for the better, American citizens who want to live in safety. I'm one of them. I'll do everything I can to keep people safe, even if that means breaking into Marine One and forcing the president to have a conversation. But understand something. Me, and others like me, are here to stay. I don't know how many there are and I don't know their motives, but I will do everything in my power to keep them in line. Starting with the woman who made us victims."

Another pause. Dietrich could feel eyes boring into him from behind the lenses.

"But I need your help," she said. "I'm pleading for your help. You have quite a crowd down there waiting for you to help them make sense of things. I'm going to let you go give your speech now, but I hope it's one that comes from the duly-elected President of the United States and not the disembodied voice that has led him astray for years.

We need hope right now, not the parroted words of a deranged madwoman."

Dietrich's eyes flickered to the cabin door then back to the masked woman.

"What? You expect me to thank you?" he said.

"No. I expect you to do what you were elected to do. Protect your country. Even if that means taking the ultimate risk. And if the shit hits the fan, I'll be there for you."

She rose and took hold of the access door latch. Sapolski and his agents slackened in their bonds, released from her telekinetic hold.

"Wait!" Dietrich said. "Who are you? Really."

"The people—*our* people—call me Kinetic Star. Let's stick with that for now."

The door opened to admit another strong gust. She stepped outside as though she were embarking on a relaxing afternoon stroll instead of stepping into an empty void. The door closed and latched behind her. She turned to place a gloved hand on the window. The masked head dipped once toward the President of the United States. Then she was gone.

Chapter Seventeen

THE CROWD SPREAD OVER THE NATIONAL MALL in an endless human blanket, from the edges of the cordoned areas at the steps of the Lincoln Memorial to the World War II Memorial and beyond, parted only by the still waters of the Reflecting Pool that were a calm contrast to the bustling confluence of both Dietrich's protesters and his supporters. The groups had drawn a line in the sand—or water, in this case—down the center of the pool, sign carriers on both sides pumping their poster board proclamations to the rhythm of their rehearsed chants. Samantha had never seen a gathering of this size, but it made sense. The stakes had never been higher. The world was on the brink of collapse and, for all of her power, she was unable to stop it. But she had to try.

You might get your wish, mother. You just might get it.

No one could see her standing atop the Lincoln Memorial. It was one of the useful perks Jibril had built into the suit, a re-engineering of the holographic emitter technology in his own suit that he used to mask his appearance. Like Jibril's, this suit bent light around it, allowing Samantha to come and go unseen. She could be spotted if anyone looked directly at her long and hard enough, but the people below were too embroiled in their battle of ideologies to look for an invisible woman high above them, and the authorities present were too busy watching the people.

She had resisted wearing the full head mask at first, arguing that her old cowl (as ugly as it was) exposed her nose and mouth, which was less intimidating. It expressed her humanity to those she sought to help. But Jibril had poignantly rejected the notion, informing her that her nose, mouth, cheekbones and chin made up at least half of the data points required for facial recognition technology, and that he was amazed she had been able to keep her identity concealed for so long.

He'd had a point.

In addition, the radar cloaking "feature", as Jibril had called it, had been useful as well. Samantha doubted she would have been able to access Marine One as easily as she had without it. Restricted airspace was only restricted if you could be detected, as far as she was concerned.

Samantha liked the suit overall. It was missing the sharp, angular flair of the red trim on her motorcycle outfit, along with the satisfying creak of leather when she moved, but the tricks Jibril had built into this suit far outweighed the nostalgia of her old one. The motorcycle leathers didn't have self-contained, internal heating elements to keep her warm at high altitudes, for example. Still, David had worked hard to upgrade her old cowl to include audio and video communication. Samantha remembered Marissa trying out the new capabilities and making all of them laugh.

Maybe I'll go back to that suit when this is all over. Maybe not.

She stepped from the top of the Lincoln Memorial and rose into the air. President Dietrich had arrived some time ago, and was no doubt undergoing final preparations for his historic speech. He would be taking the podium any minute now. She decided she had time for one last sweep of the crowd.

Jibril had assured her that Ana would be in attendance. Samantha had her doubts, but she hadn't been the one to shadow Ana for years on end. He no doubt knew her mother better than she did. Besides, she had trusted Jibril's instincts this far, so why stop now? Samantha would much rather be laughing with Marissa or snuggling up to David at the moment, but she couldn't risk contacting them. As much as it pained her to admit it, Jibril had been right about that as well. The world needed to believe she was dead, and that included those closest to her. There was no other way. Everyone had to play their part if this was going to work, even those whom weren't aware that they were playing a role. The president was the key. Samantha hoped she had gotten through to him. She was counting on it.

She floated above protesters and impartial citizens alike, an invisible guardian angel drifting over an oblivious congregation. She searched for a familiar flash of crimson that would stand out in the crowd below, but instead found herself singling out tall, lean men with dark hair.

I don't even know where you are David. I don't know if you're okay. I guess that's what I get for—

Samantha's heart skipped a beat. Her concentration faltered and she almost plummeted from the sky before catching herself. It was her attachment to the man that singled him out among the press of the crowd, a mental search engine in the brain that automatically cycles through every face it has ever perceived until it scores a familiar hit. And this was the most familiar face in the world to Samantha. It existed in her earliest memories.

There he was, clad in the khaki overcoat she had bought him for Christmas two years ago, his navy blue woolen scarf tucked into the collar, salt and pepper hair blowing in the late autumn breeze.

Daddy?

Samantha flew closer for a better look at her father.

Dark channels now underscored his eyes. New lines had been etched into the gauntness of his face. His skin was almost as pale as the steam that escaped his nose with every exhale.

She hovered there, fighting the intense urge to go to him.

No one will see. I'll stay concealed. I'll just whisper to him that it's me and that I'm okay.

Alan withdrew his phone from the inside of his overcoat and consulted the screen.

No. I can't. Not yet.

Her father looked around, then tapped his thumbs across the screen before returning the phone to his pocket. Samantha scanned the crowd, attempting to follow his gaze to whomever he was looking for. She instead detected motion at the podium. A gentle thump crackled through the massive speakers of the public address system as Dietrich adjusted the microphone.

Samantha filed away Alan's location, then returned to her position atop the Lincoln Memorial.

"My fellow Americans..."

The president's voice overtook those of the heated protesters, echoing with authority across the smooth surface of the Reflecting Pool.

"...I come to you today in a time of unprecedented uncertainty. Our nation is under threat, and that is something I do not take lightly. At my inauguration I swore to uphold..."

The majority of protesters from both sides fell silent as the president began his address. Samantha used the sudden stillness of the crowd to continue her search, wishing Jibril had integrated some sort of telescoping capability into the cowl's lenses.

"*...and that's why I'm here today. To do just that.*"

Dietrich paused. Samantha found her attention drawn back to the president. He stared at the teleprompter then took a deep breath as his eyes fell to the podium where his speech was laid out in print before him.

Do it, Dietrich.

"*I...I uh...my prepared remarks are...I don't know if I...*"

Samantha caught herself holding her breath and exhaled slowly.

Come on.

"*My apologies, folks. It's been a long couple of weeks. A long year, actually. What I'm trying to say is that the security of our country is in dire jeopardy. And not just from nefarious regimes thousands of miles away.*"

He was reading from the teleprompter again.

Fuck.

Samantha resisted the urge to rip the microphone from the podium.

"*A power—a* superpower—*walks among us, in the very streets and neighborhoods where you raise your children. Where you live and care for your loved ones. An existential threat is right here on our shores. I would be derelict in my duty if I didn't...didn't...*"

Again the president faltered and fell silent. His fingers traced the edges of the leather portfolio resting on the podium, his eyes moving over his speech. Advisors and federal agents standing just offstage exchanged glances of uncertainty. A murmur spread throughout the onlookers, steady and constant like a bubbling brook feeding into a great river. Dietrich raised his face to the cold, gray sky as though seeking guidance from above.

Last chance, Dietrich. Did I get through to you?

President Dietrich flattened his hands on the podium and regarded his speech once more. He closed the portfolio with resolute swiftness and raised his eyes to the assembled crowd. A wail of feedback screeched from the speakers then was gone.

"You know, folks, I had an unexpected visitor today. A very interesting person dropped by to give me an earful."

I'll be damned.

Dietrich chuckled.

"To be honest, she sort of reminded me of my dear Julia that time I forgot our anniversary. All fire and brimstone without the sermon."

Samantha's eyes flicked to the south side of the Reflecting Pool. Something had drawn her attention there.

"I don't know if I believe what I was told, but as Commander-in-Chief I'd be a fool to not to consider it."

There it was. A bustle among the onlookers. Someone parting the crowd, moving closer to the president.

"My plan today was to come before you and share a two-pronged solution for our problems, both at home and abroad. But now, as I stand here in the moment, I'm not so sure my decision is sound."

Samantha followed the commotion near the pool and flew over the throng of people for a better vantage point. Her gaze locked onto its source.

Whoa.

He was massive. A giant of a man with cinder block shoulders and a tree trunk neck. His head was uncovered despite the chill in the air, clean shaven and reflecting the drab light that filtered through the clouds overhead. Thick arms parted people like a horse-drawn plough through packed soil as his gargantuan frame moved him closer to the memorial steps.

Samantha was so stricken by the man's appearance that she almost missed the two smaller forms that followed close behind him; a slight man wearing a black, puffy jacket and a petite woman in a long winter coat of hunter green. Both wore knit caps and scarves. Large, cat-eye sunglasses rested on the woman's nose despite the dreary day, masking her appearance. A strange sensation formed in Samantha's stomach, twisting and hardening into a knot. She flew closer.

"...and then I was quoted the great James Madison: 'What is government itself but the greatest of all reflections on human nature...'"

The woman tapped the giant on the back, bringing their procession to a halt. Cat-eye lenses angled towards the sky. She adjusted her cap. A lock of hair escaped with the motion, resting on the uppermost fold of her scarf.

Samantha froze, hovering above them in absolute stillness.

Red. Like blood.

A presence revealed itself at the edges of Samantha's consciousness, a familiar stir like a gentle breeze threatening a precarious dandelion seedling clinging to its seed head. It was searching, probing.

Not this time, mother.

Samantha closed her eyes and inhaled slowly through her nose.

The ratio of the velocity at which force is applied to the chain to the velocity at which the larger object is raised is equal to twice the radius of the large object divided by the difference in the radii of the smaller objects.

She exhaled through her mouth.

Swish swish swish...

The presence grew, creeping along the borders of her mind. She wanted to withdraw, to put more distance between them, but she dare not move.

$V_F/V_W = 2R/(r_2 - r_1)$. *The ratio of the velocity at which force is applied to the chain to the velocity at which the larger object is raised is equal to twice the radius of the large object divided by the* *difference in the radii of the smaller objects. $/V_W = 2R/(r_2 - r_1)$. The ratio of the velocity at which force is applied to the chain to the velocity at which the larger object...*

The president's voice cut into her concentration.

"...and so I'm hesitant to deliver the message of my original address. I appreciate that you all came out on this cold, overcast day to hear..."

The presence dissipated, simply faded away as though it had never existed. Samantha opened her eyes to find Ana speaking to the small man. The giant turned around to join the private conversation. The towering man nodded and turned his attention to the people close by, looking over his shoulders at them in both directions. The motion reminded Samantha of the time she had taught her brother Cole how to swipe a candy bar from the local drug store. The giant put his back to the smaller man and drew himself upright in a wide stance, partially obscuring his companions from view.

Dietrich continued to address the crowd, his voice growing from a droning tone in the background of Samantha's attention to a clear presence at the forefront of her mind.

"I...I'm sorry, I..."

Samantha looked to the podium in alarm. President Dietrich's aides were there, supporting him with hands hooked into his armpits. Agent Sopalski was there too, placing himself between the president and the crowd, his eyes appearing to dart everywhere at once. Samantha swiveled back to Ana and flew in a semi-circle to find an angle that would let her see past the hulking man. The smaller man was now kneeling, head bowed and fingers planted on the ground like a sprinter waiting for the starting gun. Ana's fingers spread over the man's cap as though guiding him in prayer before his race. Samantha turned back to the president, who was now shrugging off his concerned aides.

What is this?

Dietrich readjusted the microphone and straightened his suit coat.

"My apologies once again, ladies and gentlemen. It's been one hell of a day. Now where was I?"

His tone was stronger, more self-assured. His expression was now one of confidence.

Once more, Samantha's focus ricocheted from the president to Ana's group and back again. He was re-opening his speech portfolio. An electrical impulse shot through her nervous system. An unmistakable warning.

"Ah yes. As I was saying. It is in this nation's best interest that we show no weakness in the face of these aggressors. After careful consideration and numerous consultations with the Joint Chiefs of the Armed Forces, I have ordered our military to stand at DEFCON one. Our missiles are armed and ready to launch at the first sign of provocation from our enemies. Furthermore—"

The entirety of the crowd erupted, drowning out their president. Cheers rang out from one side of the Reflecting Pool, as ear splitting as the disapproving jeers from the opposite side. Samantha felt her heart go numb, stunned by the rabid divisiveness among the citizens of the same country. This was it. The first step towards annihilation. Ana was keeping her promise.

I have to do something.

Samantha angled her body toward Ana.

"No. We wait."

The calm, familiar voice sounded in her ear. Of course Jibril had a way to see her. It was his tech, after all. He had been monitoring her this entire time. She spoke into her mask's communications system with a harsh whisper.

"We can't! She has people with her. I think one of them is somehow influencing Dietrich. We can't let this—"

"We discussed this."

"He was doing it. I got through to him. He was going off script. Rethinking his—"

"It is too late for that. Do not veer from the backup plan."

Samantha turned back to the president.

"And in regards to this 'Kinetic Star' and the monster who attacked our Capitol, our most sacred symbol of democracy, we have no choice but to call them what they are. Domestic terrorists. We will stop at nothing to ensure the safety of the American people..."

No no no no no...

"...so I have worked with Congress to draft legislation that will ensure that these terrorists and all like them are brought to justice for their crimes. This funding will allow us to develop new measures, new weapons to bring them to..."

How can I just stand by and watch this happen?

Samantha's bottom lip disappeared between her teeth. Her fists clenched. A fuse lit in her amygdala, burning through her hypothalamus and carrying with it the anger she had suppressed for so long.

Ana stood just below. Right there. Unaware.

President Dietrich stood at the podium. Right there. Unprotected.

Her eyes volleyed between them in indecision.

She let the fuse burn to the quick, felt her body radiate with adrenalin.

Fuck it.

She dove from the sky like a raptor.

Chapter Eighteen

CONCENTRATE, MY SON. His will is strong, but no match for yours.

Ana knew that he couldn't reply, even through his thoughts. Liev's entire being was locked onto his task. She kept her gloved hand on his head, steadying him as the tremors began. His power was considerable, but a mixed blessing. A gift that exacted a toll.

Center yourself. Use my voice as a guide.

Ana had waited until Liev completed kindergarten before leaving. He would come home from school clutching an aluminum lunchbox adorned with imagery from one of those silly space opera movies that were popular among the children at the time, his tiny hands as pale as his face, dark strings of damp hair painting his forehead. There was always a new story to tell, a new excuse to sell.

Tommy O'Bannon wouldn't share the new crayons with him. Loretta Cruz said he smelled like boogers. Ana would later hear from the neighborhood mothers how Tommy inexplicably punched Loretta in the mouth then jumped from the top of the slide and broke his ankle.

The teachers were worried about Liev. They said he would sit and shiver, eyes transfixed and distant. They never connected the dots, never pieced together that Liev's "episodes", as they called them, always occurred prior to the injury of a student that had wronged him. It didn't matter to Liev if the wrongs were valid or if they lived only in his perception. He was too young to know the difference.

At first, Ana thought he might have powers that mirrored her own. But no, Liev's abilities were external, a trait shared by all of the children she had brought into the world. All except one.

She was relieved when the time came for her to depart. There was no shame involved. She had become proficient in compartmentalizing the guilt associated with abandoning her children centuries ago, and had perfected the discipline long before the early 1980s. What she didn't expect was that Liev's father had followed her example two years later, sending Liev into the inept foster care system and setting him on a course for failure as an adult.

No matter. She was with him now, reunited under a common cause. Her cause.

That's it. You're doing fine, Liev. Now underscore the urgency of Dietrich's anti-superhuman resolution one more time.

She listened to the president's voice echo her wishes as she widened the scope of her perception across the vicinity, searching for the familiar connections.

There.

Marcos. Report in.

Ana counted three breaths before he responded.

I'm here, right where you told me to be. These protesters are pretty riled. Are we almost done? It's cold.

Ana looked down to the kneeling Liev and slid her hand from his head to his shoulder and gave him a gentle squeeze. His body shivered against her hand.

Almost done, yes.

She shifted her attention to other matters.

Adrian, my son.

I'm here.

I trust your failure in Louisiana hasn't rattled your senses. What do you see?

You try walking away from being punted by a speeding golf cart. And I see the same thing as the last time you checked in. A bunch of sheep, No wolves.

That is because we *are the wolves. Keep watching.*

Ana decided to have a private chat with Adrian. His attitude needed a realignment. While his healing abilities had allowed him to escape the authorities after his failed mission, she had a talent for inflicting other kinds of pain. Marcos needed to be set straight as well. She couldn't accomplish her ultimate goal if discord was being sown among her leadership. That would simply not do. Each of her sons had inherited her unfavorable temperament, and that could lead to ruin, especially when separated by expansive land masses and vast oceans.

She hadn't yet decided where she would assign each of her sons. The Americas would be her domain, of course, but what of Australia, Asia, Africa and Europe? They would also need a strong hand to guide them into the new world once the dust settled. Talbot didn't have the finesse to steer the squabbling countries of Europe to success. A blunt instrument was the wrong tool for such delicate political surgery. That continent might be better served under the cunning auspices of Liev. Yes, Liev would thrive there. And Adrian in Australia. Perfect. Talbot's imposing strength in Africa. But Marcos in the ancient, traditional Asia? His brooding, independent nature might not be suitable for the task. No matter. She had time to make her choices.

Ana smiled at the notion of letting them fight it out.

The musing was interrupted when the ghost of her original plan materialized in her mind's eye, now fragmented and fading. She had been so happy to wake up to her daughter's face after her decades-long nightmare. Her Samantha. Her Little Star. The one who would have shepherded the entire planet into paradise. It had all come together for Ana in that moment, when her slumber had finally abated and her eyes opened to find the perfect instrument for the symphony of domination she had been composing for so long. There should have been no need for her sons, no need to bandy about where they might best serve her. Ana would have passed the torch to Samantha. Let her engineer a better world while Ana stepped back and enjoyed the fruits of her long, painful labors. But it didn't matter now. Her only daughter had refused to accept her destiny.

Attitude realignment indeed.

Samantha had nonetheless played a role in her own way. Her popularity among the commoners—if not among the ruling class— would pave the way for the acceptance of Ana and her sons. The people would look to them to proffer the light when the darkness lifted. They would realize that their leaders had failed them, and would revere Ana and her sons as ancient civilizations once worshipped their omnipotent pantheons. It seemed that her Little Star had been useful after all.

Okay, Liev. Bring it to a close.

It would soon be over. All of it. World events would take on a life of their own once Dietrich's involuntary speech was complete. This new fate would become an unstoppable momentum, a victim of its own inertia. The pieces she had maneuvered during her interminable sleep were now in place. Checkmate was imminent. The old world would change in a flash, and a new one would be ushered in.

A new world. *Her* world.

Dietrich's final words would be a subtle declaration of war, inferred as such by his enemies. The panicked retractions once Liev released his hold wouldn't matter. Her son just had to speak those words through the mouth of the president. It wouldn't be long now. Ana wasn't sure which side would strike first. That had never been part of the equation because it was inconsequential. All it would take was one launch. The first domino to fall.

Finish it, Liev.

Ana closed her eyes, preparing to savor every final word. The end of the long road was finally in sight.

"And so, my fellow Americans, it is with a heavy heart yet firm resolve that I announce a military operation that will ensure—"

SCREEEE! KRNNNCH!

A wave of surprise rippled through the crowd as Dietrich's sullen announcement became a cacophonous, ear-splitting squall. Ana's eyes snapped to the podium—or what remained of it—and watched the possessed president stumble backwards with arms raised in protective reflex. Sparks flew from the monstrous P.A. speakers on either side of him as they imploded, the hardwood cabinets crumpling as though constructed from dead leaves.

"Mother!"

The voice penetrated Ana from her booted toes to the top of her knit cap. It permeated her entire being and lingered with cruel persistence in her chest, clamping onto her heart with a vise-like grip. It took forever for her line of sight to shift from the ruins of the president's speech to the person standing behind her. Her surroundings passed in a Doppler effect as her head swiveled with agonizing slowness, as her body pivoted on her heel to face the owner of that voice. Her knees weakened when her unblinking eyes finally found their target.

Samantha was just as Ana remembered her in those final, peaceful moments before her daughter had chosen betrayal over obedience. Except now a silly, bug-eyed cowl covered her pretty face, reminding Ana of her daughter's foolishness.

"Oh shit!" someone shouted nearby. "It's Kinetic Star! Look!"

"She's alive?"

"Oh my god!"

"Dude! Look!"

Ana took note of the commotion, of the attention now focused in her direction. Her mouth tightened as the sudden scrutiny grew with exponential interest.

"The madness ends here, Ana."

Ana felt her muscles relax as the initial surprise receded. Tension melted from her and was replaced by calm purpose, a skill she had honed over thousands of years of being put in dire peril. She established a telepathic link.

My sweet Little Star. I am beyond relieved to see you.

Talbot was helping an exhausted Liev to his feet in her peripheral vision, her younger son's hold on Dietrich now broken as the Secret Service ushered the president to safety.

So you say, yet it was through your machinations that my life was threatened.

Ana's eyes narrowed to slits as the unspoken reply reached her. Something nagged at her, miniscule but important.

You had a simple decision to make, my dear. You just chose poorly.

I made the correct choice. The only choice. Your treatment at the hands of the government has addled your judgment. Warped your very nature. Your plan has failed, Ana. Now come. Let me help you.

The nagging feeling grew until it couldn't be ignored. It was the subtlety that gave it away. The choice of words. The unfamiliar body language spoken in her stance.

Who are you, imposter?

The masked person in front of her paused a beat before speaking aloud.

"You know who I am, Ana. I've followed you for half of my life. I pulled you from a watery grave. I watched over your daughter while you were plugged into machines, your mind slowly corrupted by chemicals and deprivation. So listen to me now, as I will say this only once: 'And the recompense of evil is punishment like it; but whoever forgives and amends, he shall have his reward from Allah; surely He does not love the unjust.' "

A gloved hand extended toward her.

"Take my hand, Ana. Come with me."

Ana couldn't stop the laughter that bubbled from her gut to erupt from her lips.

"Foolish child! You should have taken the advantage when my back was turned!"

The image of Samantha shifted and flickered like a television with a loose cable connection. What replaced Ana's only daughter was a tall, lithe man in a tight-fitting bodysuit of foreign design. His expression was unreadable behind a full face mask of matte black, yet his voice, now deep and masculine, reached her with clarity. The offered hand dropped to his side.

"But your back *is* turned."

His head cocked slightly to the side.

A disturbance in the air alerted Ana to a new presence, one immediately behind her.

Ana, the most powerful being to walk the earth, was still human. And humans relied on their senses just as Ana was the master of twisting them to her will. She might have created a false reality for the newcomer, might have introduced horrors beyond imagination had she been afforded the time to perceive and assess the new threat. But Ana had fallen for the misdirection, a snare no doubt planned long before she had set foot on the grounds of the Lincoln Memorial. The voice that sounded in her head was quite authentic this time, as real as the love she had felt the first time she looked upon her newborn daughter's face.

You lose, mother.

The sides of her neck compressed just below her ears, seized and held by an unstoppable, invisible force. Dark spots moved in her vision, which narrowed with frightening speed, a door closing to trap her in unfeeling nothingness. Ana resisted with everything she had, trying desperately to locate and penetrate her attacker's mind before it was too late. But she was out of time, her brain thirsted for oxygenated blood.

Somewhere nearby, she heard the coarse rumble of Talbot's panicked voice. It focused her, centered her long enough to issue one final command to her sons before she succumbed.

Kill them! Kill them all!

PART FOUR

A RED SO BLOODY

A SAFER WORLD WITH DIETRICH
President to Deliver Remarks on the National Mall

By Thad Pritchard-Spencer, Opinion Columnist for The New Metro Inquirer

It will be a bright, glorious day at the Lincoln Memorial tomorrow, despite the gloomy weather forecast.

Our esteemed president will deliver his highly-anticipated speech at the foot of the memorial, among the people he so deeply respects and protects. President Dietrich is slated to be joined not only by his cabinet and Pentagon officials, but also by you and I. By our families. Our people. Our countrymen.

While the details of his address remain shrouded in secrecy, contacts inside our parent conglomerate, NationTel Media, have let slip that President Dietrich will unveil his new policy on Enhanced Individuals and the grave national security issues inherent in their existence. We can be sure that he'll take a direct and forthright stance on the issue, one we can all get behind.

In addition, some of the water cooler talk at NationTel Media headquarters revolves around an even bigger announcement. One that will affect every American, as well as the foreign dictators and fascist regimes that threaten our safety across the world.

The New Metro Inquirer encourages you to dress warmly for the most inspiring occasion in recent memory, a speech to rival that of Abraham Lincoln himself.

So grab your scarf and gloves. It's going to be a day none of us will ever forget.

Chapter Nineteen

IT WASN'T CHANCE that put Marissa in close proximity to the chaos that erupted at the Lincoln Memorial. She learned long ago that working for David Daniels had a tendency to place one in harm's way.

David had deduced that President Dietrich's event would provide the perfect opportunity for Samantha's mother to enact whatever plan she had been devising behind the scenes and, as usual, his instincts were correct. Marissa was barely settled back in D.C. after their failed mission in New Orleans before her phone lit up with David's urgent text message.

Meet me on the southeast side of the Pool. We'll walk to the Memorial from there.

The question arose as to whether or not to include Brie in whatever plan David had in mind. Marissa had decided against it, despite the fact that excluding her partner may put pressure on their relationship. They had been through so much already, endured more strain than most couples. Their problems transcended cheating or money or whose turn it was to take out the trash. And that was just it. Brie had experienced enough excitement, enough risk. It was better that she be oblivious to Marissa's foolish rush into possible danger. Better that Brie be safe than dead.

Marissa included herself in that sentiment. She had been through enough peril for ten lifetimes. Her fingers went to a spot just below her right collar bone and scratched at the scar through her layers of clothes even though there was no itch to be addressed, an unconscious habit she had picked up. She couldn't let David do this alone. Besides, there was a chance—albeit a small one—that a seed she had planted would bear fruit.

She had listened to the beginning of the President's speech through an application on her phone during the cab ride downtown, and was confused by the mixed messages Dietrich had sent. His lack of concentration was out of character, and his convictions seemed to contradict each other. It was as though two people had spoken with the same voice. The speech continued as Marissa worked her way into the crowd, pulling her smartphone from her coat pocket as she moved. Fingerless knit gloves allowed her to text David that she had arrived.

Hey I'm here. Where are—

SCREEEE! KRNNNCH!

Marissa never completed the message. The President's speech morphed into a piercing eruption from the P.A. speakers that ended in a twisted, mechanical crunch as the speakers were reduced to kindling. As horrible as those sounds were, the declaration that followed froze Marissa's heart.

"Oh shit! It's Kinetic Star! Look!"

The words were distant and distorted, and Marissa wondered if she had mistaken them, if her subconscious had substituted the words with an exclamation she wanted to hear. But the follow up was closer and reached Marissa's ears with sharper clarity.

"She's alive?"

Marissa forced her legs to move, shoving her phone into her pocket and clambering up the side of a small outbuilding. The uneven stones allowed her boots to find purchase, and she pulled herself onto the roof in the span of a few heartbeats. She rose to her full height and turned back to the source of the enigmatic shouts.

"Oh my god," she heard herself whisper, though the words seemed to drift in and out of her awareness, their chill rivaled by the November wind.

The crowd parted to form a circle around a woman clad in black leather with red trim. A matching cowl covered her head, dark as pitch except for the burst of gold that flowed from its top in a swaying braid. She faced off against a giant of a man, hulking and bald, and a slight woman in large sunglasses with a wisp of crimson hair dangling from the rim of a knit cap. A second man was there as well, kneeling next to the capped woman. The woman's arm left the kneeling man's shoulder as she turned to confront...

Could it be?

Marissa wasn't certain it was Samantha. Not yet. Her heart wouldn't let her. The mere notion was unnatural. The pain was still fresh. The motorcycle leathers were convincing, as was the cowl, but there was something off, something that she couldn't quite put her finger on. It was as though Marissa was looking at a perfect digital facsimile of her departed friend rather than the real person. There was an uncanny valley that even the most powerful computer graphics engine couldn't traverse with infallible accuracy. The crowd seemed to be one hundred percent on board with the sudden appearance of their resurrected hero, but they hadn't been best friends with her. They didn't know Kinetic Star like Marissa did.

It occurred to Marissa that the standoff unfolding before her wasn't between this Samantha figure and the giant, an honest mistake considering that the eye was drawn directly to his imposing figure.

243

Rather, the conflict seemed to be centered around Possible Samantha and the woman in the knit cap. They stood before each other trading words that Marissa couldn't hear. For some reason, Marissa's eyes were glued to the scarlet lock of hair that danced below the cap, disturbed by the breeze. Her mental gears churned in the span of a few microseconds, seeking the proper configuration to make everything fit together. There it was, the reason she was there in the first place.

Recognition slammed into Marissa like a charging bull.

A shrill ring beckoned to her from her coat. Marissa's eyes never left that lock of hair as she retrieved her phone and brought it to her ear.

"*I'm close. Coming in from the east. The streets are so packed I can't—*"

"David," Marissa said. "Y-you need to hurry."

"*What? Are you okay? Your voice is shaking.*"

"David? You're not going to believe—oh my god!"

The image of Kinetic Star blurred and shifted. Marissa's friend was once again lost to her in the span of a surprised gasp, now replaced by a taller form, broad of shoulder and narrow of hip. The masculine shape was covered in a black bodysuit of strange design.

"*Marissa?*"

But Marissa's arm had dropped to her side of its own volition. David's voice became tiny and distant as it crackled through the device.

"*Marissa?!*"

A figure materialized out of nothingness, hovering above the impossible scene unfolding near the steps of the memorial. The newcomer wore a dark bodysuit as well, but the similarities ended there. This was a woman. A flying woman.

Marissa's lower lip trembled.

A new wave of surprise pulsated through the crowd as people backed away from the conflict, giving Marissa a better view of the interaction that followed. More words were exchanged. Ana—Marissa was sure of it now—dropped to her knees with gloved hands clasped to her throat. The giant man turned to the fallen woman, pained concern painted across his broad features. The smaller man knelt beside her. She clutched at his arm, lips parting to speak to him, though Marissa was still too far away to understand the words. She didn't have time to try to comprehend them anyway. Her attention was stolen by a sudden, nightmarish scene playing out mere inches away from Samantha's mother.

The transformation happened in the span of a deep breath, though Marissa would replay it in slow motion for the rest of her days, usually slicked in a cold sweat in the middle of the night. The giant man threw back his head and roared at the sky, arms extended wide and hands clenched into massive balls of muscle, blood and bone. He doubled over and fell to a knee as his body convulsed and swelled. Joints popped in sharp, sickening snaps. Bones reconfigured and thickened, those that were visible sliding and pushing against his skin like sinuous eels struggling against an elastic, pale sack too small to contain them. Sinew stretched and expanded. Seams and stitches were overtaxed and split apart to reveal a new, preposterous girth. Fleshy cysts of dark purple and blood red erupted across his naked scalp and torso. His jaw expanded and thickened, sprouting dark, wiry hairs. The giant man became even more gargantuan as he rose, towering over the stunned onlookers that now appeared to have the stature of children. Frightened children who shrank away from him like tall grass in a tornado. His leap was impossible, as was the size of the hand that encircled the flying figure's slim waist as he snatched her from the air and bore her to the concrete in his descent.

The impact reverberated into Marissa through her boots, ending her awestruck paralysis and challenging her balance. The people closest to them scattered, most of them knocked from their feet.

The ensuing scene was obscured by a plume of grey dust and falling chunks of pavement. Horrible sounds erupted from within the powdery gloom. Marissa was reminded of a movie night she and Brie had enjoyed before their lives had been upended. Brie had control of the remote that evening, and her indecisive clicking had culminated into the opening credits of Rocky. It was a favorite of her uncle's, who was old enough to have watched it in the theaters, but it was new to the young couple. The training scene came to the forefront of Marissa's mind, in which Rocky pummeled hanging slabs of meat with his fists; not the visual of an aspiring boxer practicing his craft in a meat locker, but rather the sound of bone on meat. Those deep, smacking thuds escaped the obfuscating cloud born from the impact of the monster's attack. Her knees threatened to buckle.

The breeze began to dissipate the cloud, revealing motion within. A small, gloved hand rose into the air, palm up and fingers curled toward the sky as though cradling an imaginary skull in an impromptu Shakespearean soliloquy. Marissa's dear friend was attached to that hand, her body ascending from the impact site with a swift, vertical thrust that scattered the remnants of the plume in its wake. Somewhere, Marissa heard David's voice screaming at her from the tiny speaker in her phone, but she was too entranced by the events unfolding before her to register its urgency.

The massive creature followed Samantha into the air, towed behind her like baggage. Mammoth legs kicked and flailed, scrambling to find purchase where it didn't exist. The gnarled fingers of one hand clutched at its throat, while the other groped for Samantha who hovered just out of reach. Grotesque, bloodshot eyes were wide with alarm as oxygen became an endangered resource. The tremendous, pock-marked jaw unhinged and closed in a series of desperate gasps, both hands now clawing at its neck as though the motion would somehow alleviate the invisible choke hold.

Marissa issued a deep exhale, unaware she had been holding her breath. Her friend had evened the playing field, had stolen the monstrosity's leverage.

"Talbot!"

The shout came from below the levitating combatants. Marissa detected a sudden motion. The slight man in the puffy jacket had thrown something into the air, and it wasn't until the object was caught by the struggling behemoth that Marissa could discern its nature. A piece of rebar, twisted and ruined and no doubt scavenged from the devastation created from the monster's initial attack on Samantha. The steel rod was caught and redirected in one smooth motion, its inertia coming to an end when it found Samantha's cowled forehead.

Marissa was certain that the impromptu missile would have decimated anyone else's skull, but Samantha's head simply snapped back as though a lucky jab had connected there. It was enough to break her concentration. The creature dropped, crouched, and thrust its substantial bulk back into the air, catching a stunned Samantha's ankle. It became an anchor many times the size and weight of the sinking ship that was Samantha.

"NO!"

The scream had come from Marissa's own mouth, but its origin seemed far away.

The monster planted its feet on the bottom of the Reflecting Pool, regaining its precious leverage. It twisted its torso and flexed its sinewy back muscles, uncoiling its body into a powerful throw. Samantha tumbled head over heels like a rag doll, not stopping until one of the fluted Doric columns of the Lincoln Memorial completed her involuntary flight. It buckled and cracked, chips of marble exploding forth as the human projectile found its mark. The monster reached the site of impact in two quick bounds, scattering people before it and leaving them injured in its wake. It wrenched a ruined piece of marble column from its mooring and brought it to bear above its head. The marble shattered as it came down, and Marissa clearly heard a cry of agony.

Marissa's throat tightened. Her fists clenched and relaxed as she stood atop the stone building. She knew she had to do something. She refused to lose her friend again so soon after her unexpected rise from the grave. She had to try. After that, she would tear Samantha a new asshole for not letting her know that she was alive. But for now her eyes darted left and right for something, anything, that could help. They came to a rest on the man in the puffy jacket. The one who had given that beast the tool to escape Samantha's hold. Her fists tightened again.

Maybe she couldn't take on an enormous, ugly troll-thing from a child's nightmare, but she sure as hell could make his sidekick pay.

He was kneeling over Ana by the time Marissa had descended from the roof and emerged onto the walkway beside the Reflecting Pool. Her hands were shoved into her coat pockets, the fingers of her right hand pressing against the metallic cylinder she had safely deposited there. The man was shaking Ana by the shoulders and shouting to her. The knit cap came off, releasing a waterfall of crimson tresses. The woman's arms came up, warding the man away as she rose to a sitting position.

Marissa increased her pace, careful to steer clear of the protesters whom, for some reason, still milled about like sheep in a pen with no boundary fences. She sidestepped a pair of these lost souls, losing sight of her quarry for a moment. Marissa stopped in her tracks when she reacquired her target. To his left, Samantha's mother stood tall with eyes closed and face tilted to the sky. Her arms were spread wide, elbows slightly bent and hands out with fingers spread as though gesturing to a grand feast that she had prepared.

Or a grand horror.

Marissa nape hairs prickled. She pivoted on her heel and ran.

Perhaps it was just instinct, or maybe it was her past experience as an unwitting victim of Ana's power, but Marissa stopped her desperate flight a dozen steps after it had begun and went into defensive mode. She ducked behind a hedge and sat with her back to the evergreen twigs, eyes closed tight and fingers pressing the pliable cartilage of her tragi against her auditory canals. The chaos surrounding her funneled into a near silence. Stomping feet and shouts of alarm and anger narrowed to the pounding of her pulse and the churning of blood through her head. She attempted to concentrate on the rhythm of her heart, to diminish her world to that sound.

A wave washed over her, cold and sinister. It crept along the edges of her consciousness, pushing and probing. It was familiar. She had felt it before. An image of Samantha's townhouse bedroom played against the red light coming through her eyelids. Marissa had survived Ana's mental attack and was now attempting to comfort a hysterical Brie, who was still held in its terrible grip.

"Brie," she whispered.

The presence prodded Marissa's concentration again, testing her resolve.

"Yes, focus on Brie."

Marissa was sitting in her desk chair reading the first flurry of correspondence through the dating website's chat window. Brie was funny. She liked that. David was on the phone in his office ten feet away, arguing with someone behind the closed door. Marissa wouldn't let the bad vibes ruin what she was feeling.

A pressure was born in her skull, growing more intense by the second.

"Focus, lady," she whispered to herself. "Focus on Brie."

Brie wrote that she worked with computers, and that she had started a fan club for the world's first superhero. She talked about

Kinetic Star a lot. Marissa smiled at the memory of Samantha walking downstairs in her full red and black leather regalia, sans mask, only to find a stunned Brie staring at her with her jaw at her knees.

The pressure let up, but the presence remained.

Marissa's fingers clacked into the keyboard.

Maybe we could talk about superheroes and fan clubs over coffee?

Brie's reply:

Coffee doesn't go well with pizza, but I'm free tonight. D'Antonio's has a special on their supreme.

Their first kiss tasted like salty pepperoni and spicy tomato sauce. Marissa's smiled broadened.

A vise closed over Marissa's upper arm, wrenching her finger from her ear and hauling her to her feet. A man was there, eyes wide and veiny red. He screamed something unintelligible at her while shaking her roughly in his tight grip. His other arm came up. There was a metallic flash. Marissa didn't think, didn't hesitate. Her free hand cupped the back of his neck as she planted her feet. His screaming stopped with an abrupt yelp when she pulled his face into the top of her capped head with all of the force she could muster. The yelp became a porcine squeal when her follow up placed her bony knee into his genitals with equal force.

Marissa wrenched her arm free and fled for her life.

Her flight was short-lived, however, when the mass insanity revealed itself. The attendees of Dietrich's landmark speech at the Lincoln Memorial had lost their minds. She stumbled to a stop and stood astonished at the scene surrounding her. From the steps of the Lincoln Memorial to the World War Two Memorial and beyond, people assaulted each other with fists, feet, rocks, branches, shoes, phones— anything they could get their hands on. And not just the antagonistic protesters whom had come looking for a fight, but placid tourists and families as well. Marissa had never seen such unfettered chaos. Bodies littered the Mall, some rolling around in agony, others laying still in unconsciousness or death.

Shots rang out near the Lincoln Memorial, accompanied by shuddering booms that shook the ground. She glanced about, searching for the stone outbuilding which might provide a temporary respite at best, a hiding place if she was lucky. A burst of motion in her peripheral vision became a man thrown headlong to the concrete at her feet. His attackers advanced on him—and on Marissa by association— with wild glints in their eyes and mouths twisted into threatening sneers. She stepped over their prone victim and raced into the trees.

The report from another gunshot cracked through the air, this one much closer. Marissa paused with her back to a tree, listening for a second shot which would help her decipher the shooter's position. The last thing she wanted to do was run headlong into a firefight. The stone outbuilding was too far away now. She'd try for Constitution Avenue. It was right there. So close. Only a hundred yards of grass and sidewalk lay between her and the city, where she hoped to find refuge from this madness. A football field. She could sprint the length of a football field. The problem was that dozens of regular-people-turned-crazed-maniacs barred her way.

How had it come to this? Was Samantha's mother so powerful that she could transform thousands of people into mindless creatures of violence? Better yet, *would* she? But Marissa had now twice felt the brush against her mind, the eager probing for control. Once in Samantha's townhouse and a second time less than a minute ago. It was hard to believe that her kind, compassionate friend had come from this terrible woman.

Crack!

There was the second shot. Marissa peered around the thick bole at her back and spied a tall man in a maroon workman's jacket and bright

orange hat training a revolver on a smaller, older man hiding behind a
trash can of solid black metal.

"I'll kill you! I'll fucking kill you!"

The gun waved wildly overhead, punctuating his threats.

The tip of a navy blue scarf peeked out from behind the trash can,
ensnared by a fresh breeze.

"I'm going to crush the life from you when you run out of bullets!"
said Orange Hat's quarry from behind the metal receptacle.

Marissa looked toward Constitution Avenue and the writhing,
frenzied mass of people locked in combat between her and her
destination. Escape was so close. A hole had just opened up. She might
be able to slip through unmolested. Her eyes found Orange Hat and his
helpless, soon-to-be victim. The man raised the gun again.

Crack!

Marissa started at the gunshot even though she fully expected it.
She watched the bullet penetrate the metal side of the trash bin. What
could she possibly do against a lunatic with a gun? It would be suicide.

What would Samantha do?

Marissa sighed in defeat.

"You had to ask yourself that, didn't you?" she whispered.

Her hand slipped back into her coat pocket as she pushed away
from the relative safety of the tree. Her lips moved as she drew close,
issuing a silent string of expletives that synchronized with each hurried,
uncertain step.

"Fuck fuck fuck fuck fuck fuck fuck..."

Orange Hat was unaware of the newcomer as his thumb pulled back
the hammer of his revolver.

"...fuck fuck fuck fuck fuck fuck—HEY FUCKFACE!"

She ripped the cylinder from her pocket as Orange Hat wheeled
about. The trash can bowled into Orange Hat as the figure behind it
burst into motion. Her arm came up in time with Orange Hat's

handgun. Her finger curled over the top of the tiny cylinder and she pressed down with everything she had. The liquid hiss was drowned out by a thunderclap.

Something stung her left ear. She flinched and turned away, disoriented by the sudden, high-pitched note that rang in her head. By the time she corrected her senses she found Orange Hat's victim looming over his former assailant, raining fists into the man's face and neck while Orange Hat clawed at his eyes in a desperate attempt to alleviate the excruciating burn of Marissa's pepper spray. The revolver lay beside the overturned trash can, just out of reach of its former owner. It wasn't long before Orange Hat's arms fell to the sidewalk, limp and lifeless. The man on top of him didn't relent.

"That's enough! You're killing him!" she said.

Orange Hat's victim straightened and shook out his hands. She retreated a step, unsure if his fury would be redirected at her. He stood and turned to face her.

Marissa's eyes widened.

She had been with Samantha the day her friend had purchased the khaki overcoat for her father. It had been Marissa that suggested Samantha also buy the navy scarf to go with it.

Samantha's father's face screwed into a fiery rage, his kind eyes now wild and unrecognizable. He descended upon Marissa before she could react, before she could bring the pepper spray to bear.

"Alan! No!"

They clinched up, his larger mass driving her back as she resisted with every ounce of her strength. But she knew it would be over soon. Alan would probably strangle her to death. It was eerie how silent he was, how he didn't even seem to breathe heavily as he overpowered her smaller frame.

Marissa reacted without thinking. The trauma of being attacked by combat choppers, of being shot by a sniper, of taking on a super-powered maniac by herself, of ramming an assassin with a golf cart, all of it had rewired her fight-or-flight response. She was no longer the mousy, meek assistant. Marissa would have to process the fear and anxiety later, but in that moment she just reacted.

Her muscles initiated a desperate reflex conjured from the recesses of her memory. A tactic stolen from one of the times she had watched David train Samantha in hand-to-hand combat. Marissa had no idea she'd even retained the memory of the move until she was executing it in real time.

She removed her right hand from Alan's arm and took hold of his left bicep in both hands, keeping her weight against his until the last moment when she pivoted and tucked her shoulder into his sternum. At that point she reversed her energy, pulling instead of pushing while shoving her hip into his center of gravity.

"Take away the leverage," she recalled David saying to Samantha.

Alan flew headlong over her shoulder and landed hard on his back. Breath exploded from his lungs, leaving him gasping. Marissa leapt on top of him before he could recover and pointed the pepper spray canister at his face, hoping she wouldn't have to use it.

"Alan! It's me! It's Marissa!"

Strong hands came up to grip her shoulders. He growled and bucked his hips to be rid of her. His eyes were frantic and dangerous. Her finger tightened against the top of the spray canister.

"Alan! Look at me!"

He continued to struggle. She held fast to his coat with her free hand and tightened her knees against his torso, refusing to give him room to escape. Her voice swelled into a scream as she dropped the pepper spray and smacked him hard across the cheeks several times in quick succession.

"FUCKING STOP!"

Alan blinked. She felt his body relax beneath her as though someone had deflated his rage like air from an old tire.

"Alan?" Marissa said. "You in there?"

He blinked again. His eyes focused as they looked her up and down. "Marissa?"

She helped him to his feet and they embraced without another word. Alan held Marissa at arm's length as though reaffirming that this was indeed his daughter's friend. His friend.

"You're bleeding," Alan said, unwrapping his scarf and bringing it to Marissa's ear. "Here. Use this until we can get you to a hospital."

Marissa felt the sting with more urgency now, though she suspected it would get worse once her adrenalin spike had run its course. She accepted the garment and pressed it to her wound.

"Thanks," she said.

"We need to get out of here," said Alan. "Is David with you?"

Marissa pulled the scarf away from her ear to inspect the severity of the wound. The dark fabric made it difficult to discern.

"We were supposed to meet near the Lincoln Memorial before everything went to hell. He's here somewhere. Probably looking for me."

"Well," said Alan, "if anyone can take care of himself, it's that man."

There was a powerful boom from the direction of the memorial. They felt the resulting shockwave vibrate into their knees. Marissa kept her gaze on Alan's face as his attention was drawn toward the memorial. She swallowed hard.

"Alan," she said, "there's something I need to tell you."

"What is it? Can it wait?"

"No," she said.

Samantha's father listened with patience as Marissa recounted the series of events since her arrival. It took massive self-control not to interrupt with the multitude of questions that surfaced with each new development, but he kept silent. His eyes were glassy with tears when Marissa finished her tale. Neither of them spoke after that. There was only the sound of violence and suffering, both near and far away, as Ana's influence continued to rob people of their sanity.

Alan pointed toward Constitution Avenue.

"Go find help. I'm right behind you."

Marissa nodded and ran toward safety. She didn't see Alan's hesitation as his eyes became fixed in the direction of the memorial.

She didn't see a bloody-knuckled hand close around the grip of a discarded revolver.

Chapter Twenty

THE JOINT DISCONNECTED, hyper-extended until cartilage cracked apart and tendons snapped. The kid's scream was quick and urgent before he passed out from the pain, his right leg splayed beside him at an unnatural angle. He wasn't a kid per se, probably in his early twenties. That was a kid to David. A kid assaulting a woman twice his age.

"Ma'am, you'll be fine," David said, extending his hand to the disheveled, would-be victim. "He can't hurt you—"

She was almost to her feet when she lashed out at her savior. Her wail was inhuman, her eyes wild and shot with tiny, vascular bolts of red lightning. Just like the kid's had been. David tried to sidestep her long, painted nails as they raked at his eyes, but he was off balance from pulling her upright. The best he could do was to snap his neck to the side. Four bloody weals appeared on his left cheek. He grunted against the sudden sting and flexed his obliques, twisting his torso to bring the bony point of his elbow into her chin with a swift, upward motion. The crazed woman's winter cap flew from her mop of bleached hair as the blow lifted her to her toes, chin pointed to the sky. David was already moving by the time she joined her former assailant on the pavement.

He pulled a black leather glove from his hand and pressed his fingertips to his face. They came away wet.

"What in the *fucking* hell..." he murmured to himself.

It had become a mantra since he arrived on the National Mall that day.

His light jog had become a mad dash after losing contact with Marissa, and it wasn't long before he found himself in a hellscape of savage violence. He tried to stop and intervene where he could, but there were too many people to help. It was a war zone. He couldn't save the family far off to his right from being gunned down by a trio of police officers whom had afterwards turned their firearms on each other. He couldn't save the elderly man far off to his left from being bludgeoned by a pair of young women wielding wooden planks, pieces of protest-laden poster board flying free with each blow. He couldn't save the teacher far behind him from being drowned in the fountain of the World War Two Memorial by a mob of his own students. The kid and the lady just happened to be in his way. Maybe he'd saved her from death. Maybe not. He couldn't shake the sound of the woman's skull hitting the pavement. It was an exclamation mark on the insanity taking place everywhere he looked.

So why hadn't he turned into a stark raving madman? Why wasn't he attacking everyone in sight like every lunatic he passed?

David thanked the dense traffic of downtown Washington D.C. for the first time in his life. It was the only solution he could conjure. The pandemonium party had already been in full swing by the time he arrived. That, of course, wasn't to say that he wouldn't succumb to whatever influence had overcome these people the closer he got to its source, but the unknown kept him moving. He didn't know where

Marissa was. Didn't know if she was safe amidst this chaos. And he had asked her to meet him there. If anything had happened to her it was his fault.

David ignored the burn in his quads and pumped his legs faster. He could see the top of the Lincoln Memorial now. His redoubled efforts faltered as a shockwave emanated from the Reflecting Pool just ahead. The boom was deafening, and David had to plant a palm in the grass to keep his balance. He wasn't able to discern what had caused his stumble until he cleared a copse of trees and emerged onto the expansive concrete walkway that encircled the pool. He stopped short, chest heaving and heart thundering in his ears. His eyes couldn't make sense of what lay before him, no matter how many times his open-mouthed blinks tried to reset the scene.

Most of the people had evacuated the area, or maybe their homicidal urges had carried their viciousness to the edges of the National Mall and beyond to find new victims. Some lingered in the tree line to either side of the pool, shouting and fighting and bleeding and dying, but these pockets of brutality couldn't hold David's attention in that moment. Nor could the dozens of lifeless and bloodied human forms that lay strewn about the area like a mass grave that had regurgitated its macabre treasures back into the world.

No, David's focus was centered on the enormous, impossible goliath of a man-beast locked in pitched battle with—

David's breath seized in his throat. His stomach clenched and his spine was lanced with ice. His vision tapered to a single point, blocking out everything and everyone else from his awareness.

Everyone but her.

She stood toe to toe with a monster twice her height and at least ten times her mass, trading blows, taking punishment. The gray, form-fitting bodysuit was lacerated and tattered in places. The full head cowl was torn, revealing a freckled cheek, a swollen eye. She sidestepped a

tree trunk arm that swatted at her with surprising speed for someone—
some*thing*—so massive, weaving her body around the blow and
countering with a slick right uppercut.

David recognized the move.

The counter strike was bolstered by the power of flight, reinforced
by a telekinetic power David still didn't understand and never would,
and punctuated by a guttural exhale. The monstrous, half-human thing
staggered backward, almost tripping on the stone lip of the Reflecting
Pool, but managed to maintain balance. It wiped its tusked mouth with
the back of a brutish forearm. Bloodied, worm-like lips split into what
might have been construed as a grin.

The woman arched her back shook out her hands before placing
them on her knees in a half squat. Her chest rose and fell in rapid
intervals. Her eyes never left her opponent.

"Christ, man!" she said between breaths. "Go down for fuck's sake!"

Yes, this was definitely Samantha. Potty mouth and all. But how?

David parted his lips to call out to her, but stopped himself. At first
he thought it was due to the tactical disadvantage he would be forcing
on her by diverting her attention from combat, but it wasn't that. It was
an unnatural feeling, a primal sense that was triggered in that split
second.

Someone was watching him.

David wrested his eyes from the battle before him and scanned the
remnants of the once-pristine surroundings that bordered the pool and
the approach to the Lincoln Memorial. To the north, a young man in a
red fleece vest warded away a family of four with an uprooted signpost.
To the south, close to the Korean War Veterans Memorial, a group of
men circled each other with similar makeshift weapons held out before
them. Looking back the way he had come, a dozen people engaged and
broke apart, those not falling to the ground re-engaging with new
targets like some depraved perversion of a square dance. It was

madness. But to the west, against the columned backdrop of the memorial, he spied a trio standing still amongst the cement stanchions that blocked the road in front of the memorial steps. They were an island of calm in a sea of ferocity. A slight man in a puffy jacket glanced about with quick jerks of his capped head. Next to him was a taller man with a curly shock of graying hair framing the almond skin of his face. And in between them stood a smaller figure, slighter of height and build. A knit cap was clutched in her gloved hands. The wind whipped her long hair in a scarlet banner. She was quite some distance from David, but he could feel her eyes on him. He didn't know how, but he was sure of it.

David took a step in the direction of the unmoving threesome, fighting the urge to rush to Samantha's aid. Her battle continued in the splashing waters of the Reflecting Pool close by, but David knew he couldn't help her. He didn't know who or what she fought, but the thing was beyond David's abilities. He had no clue as to how she was alive, or what events had led to this devastation. Marissa was nowhere to be found and he had no time to search for her among the bodies that surrounded him. After several moments of indecision he settled on doing what he did best. Finding answers.

He set off toward the trio.

You must be the love interest in this thrilling little tale.

David had closed half the distance between them before he stopped cold and whirled about, searching for the woman who had spoken to him. He found only a sea of prone, unmoving bodies.

I'm sure you are beyond elated to find your belle alive and well. I was too.

Again David spun, and again found no one.

I wish she had come to me, let me know. Surely you feel the same, no?

"Who are you?"

He twisted in the opposite direction until his eyes rested on the red-haired woman. She seemed familiar now that he was closer. The shape of her face. The green glint below her thin eyebrows.

You know me. You helped my daughter rescue me. What a pleasure to properly make your acquaintance, Mister Daniels.

He locked onto her gaze and held it, saying nothing as he stepped forward.

Oh dear, what a menacing expression. Are you going to hurt me? The way you hurt all those people in Iraq and Afghanistan? The way you chopped your Navy friend into tiny pieces before visiting his mother? Wally, was it?

David quickened his pace, trying his best to clear his mind of all thought and memory. It was impossible. An unbidden emotion reared its ugly head.

Ah, yes. There it is. The sweet spot. The guilt. What would my Little Star think if she knew you betrayed her to your government spies?

David felt his jaw lock tight. His fists curled into balls. He leaned into a flat out charge.

Maybe I'll share this juicy detail with her right before you die.

It was a clear shot to Ana. He was almost there. Close enough to match her facial features with the woman from the medical bay.

Yes, I think that is how we will do it. I want you to see the pain in her eyes.

David's sudden stop was through no decision of his own.

All forward momentum he had built was stolen when a heavy weight crashed into him from the side. Air evacuated David's lungs when the concrete rose to meet him. He rolled several times then lay gasping, his field of vision filled with dancing, black spots and the gray November sky. A male voice spoke nearby.

"Yes, mother. I'll take my time."

A young man's face appeared over David's.

"Remember me?"

Harkins's would-be assassin. David's mind raced.

"Yeah, I remember," David said between quick gasps. "Another asshole brother, right? I'll be with you in a sec."

"I'm in no hurry."

David sucked in a breath and rolled away from the man, jumping to his feet with legs slightly bent and hands held loosely at chin level.

"Pretty sure you had multiple fractures from a sixty-degree Taylormade wedge to the floating ribs," he said, circling to the right.

The young man cracked his neck and rolled his shoulders. His only answer was a fleeting glance at Samantha's mother and the pair of men with her.

David filed that away. Harkins had mentioned only a large man with Ana when she came to visit his studio. If these people were indeed Ana's sons then it would stand to reason that they too had inherited some form of her strange abilities. Point in fact: the behemoth locked in combat with Samantha somewhere nearby. Not to mention how this one moved while evading Harkins's constructs at the golf club. What about the other two?

The man sent a series of exploratory jabs David's way, followed by a spinning back fist delivered so fast that David could only roll up his shoulder to deflect it. His freshly-stitched deltoid exploded in pain, a sensation so abrupt and intense that David almost missed the rear leg sweep that followed the follow up. He spun away from the low attack that would have put him back on the pavement and countered with an overhand left combined with a right hook. But his opponent wasn't there, having danced away with casual, mocking nonchalance.

They circled again.

David double jabbed with his left, feinted with his right, and sent an oblique kick to the young man's closest kneecap. It wouldn't drop him, but it might slow him down. Again, the strikes missed their mark. David swallowed his frustration. The oblique kick shouldn't have missed. Every combat veteran SEAL he had sparred with had fallen for it. Every single one.

It was time to get inventive.

David lunged forward with another jab—this one open handed to block the man's eyes—and planted his trailing leg. He bent and uncoiled the leg, snapping his back taut as he angled his entire body into a dive. His arms extended, hands outspread to catch the back of the young man's knees and secure them as his forward momentum bore the man to the ground in a double-leg takedown. David lost sight of his opponent. A line of fire ignited down David's back. His palms scraped concrete. His torso followed suit.

Had the assassin flipped? Had the man really performed a forward somersault over David from a close-quarter standing position? There was no other explanation.

David rolled to his feet again, spinning to meet the flash of a curved blade. The pieces fell into place. Not only had the young man executed a very difficult acrobatic feat, he had also deployed his karambit and slashed David while in midair. David didn't have time to ponder it further. He barely had time to slip and slap away the blade that flicked out at him like a serpent's tongue. He missed one parry and was rewarded with another fiery slash. His brown jacket sleeve darkened just below the cuff.

David backed away, blinking.

"What's your gimmick, kid?" he said, eyes flicking left and right for a makeshift weapon that might even the new odds. "Are you supposed to be a super ninja or something?"

The young man wiped the curved blade against his thigh, painting a thin abstract in David's blood.

"Something," he said, the corner of his lip curling upward.

That was all the confirmation David needed. This was an E.I. like Samantha and her mother. Like Harkins. Like whatever the hell Samantha was fighting. Probably like the two men with Ana. He re-evaluated the situation. There was nothing nearby he could use to fend off his attacker. No weapon, nor any implement he could employ as one. It wouldn't matter anyway. This man had fought off one of Harkins's animated killing machines with just a knife.

David took off his jacket and wrapped it around his injured forearm. He kept his distance as the man advanced. If he was going to die, it would be doing what he was trained to do.

Inflict pain.

They re-engaged in a discordant symphony of bone on muscle punctuated by quick, forceful breaths through pursed lips and accompanied by soles shuffling on pavement. Cracks and booms reverberated underfoot as Samantha's titanic struggle continued across the immediate area. David caught glimpses of her but pushed them out of his mind. It was all he could do to focus on keeping this enhanced assassin at bay, to keep his vital organs protected. He knew he was being toyed with and that Samantha's mother watched the lethal contest with amusement, waiting for the perfect moment to drive Samantha's attention to his death. He had no doubt that she was in telepathic communication with her son, reminding him to draw out their encounter until she issued the order. He had no doubt because he was certain he would already be dead if his assumptions were false. So the young man played with his quarry, the curved blade nicking here and slashing there with superficial cuts that served only to distract David and disrupt his concentration.

It worked.

This foe was beyond him. It was only a matter of time.

David found himself thinking of Elyse and Duncan, of their life together had David stayed with her years ago. Vignettes found their way into the forefront of David's consciousness. David teaching his son to hunt and fish and shoot. Dry red wine with Elyse by a glowing fire after she had tucked Duncan in for the night. Relaxing on the porch after a long day of planting in the garden outside of their cottage in—

"HNGH!"

David's exclamation erupted from his gut. The hooked blade had found its mark. The extent of the damage wasn't clear, but he felt the steel inside of him. The karambit had pierced deep, and took a piece of him when it was retracted. David's jacket-wrapped hand went to the wound of its own volition, his training taking over and applying pressure without any deliberate action on his part. He broke away from the young man and let the first wave of agony wash over him.

The karambit was dark with David's blood as it hovered close to its wielder's sternum, poised for the final strike. The assassin's voice was distant.

"Mom says it's time to wrap this up, mister."

David nodded, turning his head to spit a glob of blood to the concrete before replying through the coppery taste.

"Your mom's a cunt."

David's abdomen was filled with molten lava. He felt his heart beating in his belly. Another wave of agony washed over him, this one tinged with an icy aftereffect that lingered in his toes and fingertips.

So this was it. The end. David found it strange that he didn't feel self pity, didn't feel the expected guilt that had plagued him for so long. He didn't find himself retracing the missteps of his life or regretting having done this or not having done that. Weren't those feelings common at the end of all things? For most, maybe, but not for David. He had served his country with honor. He had even helped to save it through his mentorship of Samantha.

Samantha.

She was still in the fight. He could still hear her thunderous blows, feel them through the pavement. She wouldn't give up until her mother was taken down. The problem was that she could never end her mother's life. David knew that, even if Samantha didn't. The dark sentiment was punctuated with a lighter one: Samantha's family was royally fucked up.

Family. Elyse and Duncan.

David did find one regret in that split second of introspection before the end. It wasn't that he'd never see Elyse or his son again, nor was it that he hadn't been able to tell them that he loved them. It was that he hadn't had a chance to tell Samantha to watch over them. Maybe she would anyway. Maybe. Somehow.

The karambit flickered out. David attempted a parry-and-slip combination that he knew would never work. It would be too slow. Too late to save him.

David's world faded from view.

KNCH!

It happened so fast. He didn't even feel the killing blow. And that sound?

KNKT! SKRIT!

How was he hearing those sounds? Better yet, why was he even thinking? He was supposed to be dead. Dead people didn't have thoughts, didn't wonder about sounds.

He felt himself floating, heard a dull thud and faint grating like stone dragged across stone. His vision returned to find ropy tendrils composed of a black mineral substance flowing away from him, melting from his body and flowing toward—

"I'll be damned," David said aloud to no one in particular.

Roger Harkins smirked at David as the mineral oozed over him from foot to neck, forming a second skin. He must have read the look on David's face.

"What?" he shrugged. "I had a pedicure appointment downtown."

The substance covered his head as he turned his attention to Samantha's—and Harkins's, David reasoned—murderous, knife-wielding brother.

The young man backed away after testing his blade against the mineral skin with several exploratory jabs that had no effect. David heard Harkins's voice through the black coating as he advanced on David's former attacker.

"Don't just stand there with your dick in your hand, Daniels. Go get Ana."

David had to tear his attention away from Harkins as thin coils of the mineral shot from his body toward the retreating young man, who sheathed his weapon and leapt into a series of dodges and handsprings to avoid the attack. Another explosion sounded close by, driving David's gaze to the trees lining the Reflecting Pool.

An old oak fell across the pool and the surrounding walkway, barring David's path to Samantha's demented mother. Samantha emerged from the trees in full flight and stopped to hover above the fallen timber. The tusked beast rose from the other side of the bole dazed and unsteady on its massive feet, and David wondered if Samantha had used her opponent's impressive mass as an implement of tree removal. She gestured to the thick trunk. It exploded into thousands of pieces, ranging in size from splinter to spike to spear, all of which gathered into a massive, arrow-shaped configuration that begged to be fired at Samantha's command.

That was when her half-cowled head swiveled toward David. Her lone, visible eye blinked in sudden recognition and held his gaze The unspoken communication that followed was fleeting but tangible. Then the moment was stolen.

The creature sprang into the air, barreling into Samantha and carrying her to the opposite side of the pool. Their impact ripped concrete and soil for a dozen yards as though a spiteful god had reached down to unzip the earth. Samantha lay beneath the behemoth at the end of the terrestrial laceration, arms held over her head and upper torso as the monster rained devastating blows down on her. The impacts scattered debris in a circular wave away from them. Several powered through her defenses and connected with punishing effect.

The storm cloud of wooden shards sputtered out and dropped to the ground. A spear-sized fragment of the oak bounced several times before clattering into the toe of David's boot. He swooned from the agony in his stomach as he knelt. His hand closed over the rough-hewn shaft and tightened until his knuckles turned white.

David turned back to Samantha, whose arms had fallen to her sides, her visible eye at half mast as the monster's devastating strikes continued to rise and fall. He leaned on the impromptu weapon for support and took a step toward what would no doubt be his death.

David managed a weak chuckle. He was on borrowed time anyway.

Strong fingers closed over his upper arm.

"No, not that way."

The voice was deep, and tinged with a familiar accent. David had heard it thousands of times while overseas. He twisted around, breaking the newcomer's grip and bringing the point of his spear to bear.

The man wore a black suit that resembled Samantha's charcoal toned garb. It was in no better condition than hers. The expressionless, full-faced cowl was torn in places, revealing tufts of black curls here, a dark, stubbled chin there. Small, round devices covered the suit, many of them shattered to expose ruined micro-circuitry. The masked man bled from a dozen small wounds, and David had no doubt that the alien uniform hid even more bruises. The absurdity of asking a masked man who he was wasn't lost on David, so he changed the question.

"The Arabic symbol on the card. The photos of Ana. That was you?"

JASON ANDREWS

The cowled head dipped in acknowledgement.

"Miss McAllister has been in my care," said the man, "convalescing after the unfortun—"

"Well thanks for saving her then, but I have to save her now," David said.

He turned back to Samantha, who now lay unmoving as the punishment continued. The man blocked his path and gestured toward the combatants.

"Talbot Sharp, son of Ana. Converts energy drawn from others into physical mass to increase skin, muscle and bone size and density. Impervious to mundane weaponry."

David looked past him to the towering creature that now rose to its full height, holding a limp Samantha at arm's length in one monstrous hand. David got the picture. He already knew this "Talbot" was beyond him. He just didn't care. No wonder Samantha hadn't overpowered him. He was stealing her energy.

The newcomer bowed his cowled head to their left. David followed the motion to where the assassin danced around the mineral-encased Harkins and his weaving tentacles. He was too fast for Harkins to snare, yet unable to penetrate the black armor with his knife.

"Adrian Bryant. Son of Ana," said the man. "Hyperkinetic. Perfect aim, perfect reflexes. Olympic-level athlete. Weapons expert. Assassin."

David nodded.

"Yeah, I got that last part. And Harkins and I are already acquainted," he said.

"Yes, I heard," said the man. "Samantha and Roger are on their own. We have other concerns. Two more sons guard Ana."

David's suspicions about Samantha's ever-growing family were confirmed.

"I bet those two also won Ana's genetic lottery, didn't they?"

"A body thief and a light bender, yes. Samantha will have a clear path to Ana once they are removed from the chess board. We each have our objective, and ours requires stealth and cunning."

David caught motion from the corner of his eye. Talbot had thrown Samantha upon the steps of the Lincoln Memorial and was lumbering toward her, taking his time before finishing his grisly task. A hand fell over David's shoulder.

"She will rally. She is mighty in the eyes of Allah," said the masked man. "Come."

David gathered what strength he had left and followed the man into the trees, wishing his own confidence matched that of this stranger.

Chapter Twenty-One

THERE ARE MANY CONSTANTS IN THE WORLD. Gravity, the mass of an electron, the speed of light in a vacuum, et cetera. But there are other, less scientific constants that also unveil themselves with inevitable certainty.

Samantha's constant was pain.

She thought she knew pain at the hands of Roger's violent, animated constructs at the Capitol. She thought she knew pain at the hands of Galina, as her former torturer sent electric currents into Samantha's body with masochistic glee. Bloody, split lips creased into a weak smile behind the tattered cowl as her body was battered into the steps of the Lincoln Memorial.

No, this *is pain.*

The creature was relentless, untiring. Their battle had raged from the Lincoln Memorial to Arlington National Cemetery to Foggy Bottom and back again. Their struggle had caused a pile up on Interstate 395, had damaged the Theodore Roosevelt Bridge that spans the Potomac. Samantha thought flight would give her the advantage, would keep her out of range of its massive, punishing fists while she caught her breath, but its tree trunk legs afforded it a leaping ability that may as well have been flight. She could have fled, could have soared into the cloud cover and cowered there, waiting for the nightmare to end, but that wasn't an option. There were too many people to protect, too many targets for the beast's wrath. She was forced to split her efforts to save lives while choosing her moments to attack and defend.

The monstrosity gave as good as it got—and then some. Samantha had uprooted highway signposts and used them as giant, makeshift clubs. She had ripped up sedan-sized chunks of concrete and rough-hewn stone and pulverized the creature with all the telekinetic force she could muster. They had stood inches from each other, trading savage blows fueled by fury and desperation. Samantha's much smaller frame had become a liability despite her considerable power. She was, more often than not, knocked from her feet or swept aside by the thing's overwhelming leverage. It was simple physics.

Her foe was another constant.

Their contest had fallen into a rhythm of pain, a brutal dance of punishment with no end in sight. That rhythm was broken when she saw David.

She had thousands of sharp projectiles, the remnants of a great oak, loaded and ready to fire at the beast. She knew they wouldn't stop the creature—nothing had up to that point—but she had to slow it down to give herself time to think. Ana was still in the area, and Samantha needed to end this fight and move on to the next one.

But a familiar shape had insinuated itself in her peripheral vision, one of only a few people that still stood upright in the general vicinity. He stood bloodied and battered, hunched in pain. His collared jacket was rolled over his forearm and pressed to his abdomen. Samantha could see the blood dripping from it, leaving a grim trail behind him. Their eyes met and widened in mutual recognition. Her heart swelled and dropped into her stomach. Then he was stolen from her, replaced by a vision of wrecking-ball fists scheduled for the immediate demolition of her face.

David... Oh no...

KRAK!

She had blacked out for a moment, her world reduced to a single vibrato note that wailed in her ears. Her senses returned in time to find herself hurtling through the air. The steps of the memorial stopped her momentum in an explosion of dust and debris. An enormous shape materialized through the detritus, ending its leap to smash her further into the stone. Her lungs contracted, expelling her breath and forcing her diaphragm to spasm. Blood flew from her mouth to decorate the shins of her giant tormentor.

Spots were born in the darkening edges of her vision and wriggled about like amoeba under a microscope. Jackhammer fists pummeled her about the face, neck, shoulder and chest, driving her even deeper into the stone ruins. She sucked in a desperate breath but her mouth was filled with powdered stone. Her arms were pinned. She couldn't defend herself. The strikes were coming too fast and hard to mentally thrust the beast away from her.

Can't focus... Can't breathe... David...

Give up, Little Star. Slide into the darkness. Rest.

Samantha's eyelids fluttered, somehow heavier than the brute on top of her.

No.

Your brother has bested you. Go to sleep now.

No!

The weight was lifted. She stared up at the creature looming over her, its gnarled lips curling into a gloating grin. A meaty hand encircled her torso and reared back, lifting her above its head. She was airborne again, tossed up the steps and through the Doric columns like a despondent child hurling a doll into the sandbox because it was time to wash up for dinner. Samantha managed to halt her inertia just before slamming into the marble pedestal upon which sat the serene likeness of the sixteenth president of the United States. But the sheer effort of applying the telepathic brakes took its toll. She dropped to her hands and knees, gasping for breath.

I can't beat it. I can't do it.

She heard gunshots and sirens accompanied by the chopping thrum of helicopter rotors. The National Park police, the National Guard, the United States military; they would stand no chance.

I have to get up. Have to do something. Anything.

Samantha rose into a kneeling position. Pain lanced through her ribs, her shoulders, her neck, her skull. Something shifted in her chest, bringing new waves of agony. She found herself back on her hands, head hung low, staring at bloody spittle that dripped from her swollen lips to pool on the floor.

Ana's telepathic exultation echoed in her mind.

Your brother has bested you.

Samantha coughed up more blood.

No, can't give up.

Mild tremors vibrated her gloved palms through the stone as the behemoth approached with measured steps. She could hear its labored breathing. It was wounded too, just not enough. She kept her head low, waiting until she could smell the sweat and musk.

Almost.

An eager, deep-chested growl reached her ears, like that of a famished grizzly after a long hibernation closing in on a weakened faun. It's scent was caustic and foul. A shadow fell over her.

Now.

Samantha reached deep inside of herself to muster whatever fight she had left. She snapped her body taut. Her fists came together and swung upward in a mighty arc as her feet left the ground.

"NGAH!"

KROOM!

Columns shook. Girders shimmied overhead. Lincoln rocked on his perch. The creature's head snapped back, dark blood forming a liquid tracer that followed the path of the sturdy chin. The beast lumbered backward on its heels, almost losing its balance and falling to its broad back.

Almost.

Well, fuck.

Samantha landed on one knee, fingertips pressed to the floor to support herself and wondering if she had enough energy for another uppercut.

Or enough energy to stand up, for that matter.

Her question was answered for her when the beast righted itself and lunged, plucking her from the floor to gather her in a bear hug. Anaconda arms closed around her lower back and tightened. The creature's broad chest and stomach were iron against her torso. Its fetid breath was hot on the exposed part of her face.

Your brother has bested you.

Her arms flailed uselessly. She heard something crack in her spine.

Your brother...

Samantha acted without thinking. Survival took over.

She reached up to rip away her cowl, dropping it as her gloved hands gripped the back of the massive, gnarled head in front of her.

...brother...

She pulled with all her might, extending her neck as best she could. Their foreheads drew together. Skin touched skin.

The world shimmied and vanished.

A sheet metal road sign embossed and painted with **Route 66** hung against nicotine-stained, floral wallpaper, its edges burnished with time. A jukebox stood in the corner, dark and silent, the glass dome opaque with dusty neglect. Round stools sat empty around a Formica bar trimmed in chrome, as did the dun-colored booth benches that flanked unadorned tables nested around the room's perimeter. A small, boxy television set rested on the corner of the bar, its curved screen flickering from signal interference.

Samantha narrowed her eyes at the black-and-white image being broadcast. A star field with a large celestial object at its center.

A nebula.

Of course it is.

She turned her attention to the thick-shouldered man on the other side of the booth table. She hadn't gotten a good look at him upon arriving on the mall. She had been focused on the bait and switch she and Jibril had perpetrated on Ana.

The plan was working. I should have killed her right then and there. Wasn't planning on this...whatever the hell this hulking pain in the ass is.

He appeared to be in his mid-to-late sixties, as evidenced by the deep wrinkles around his cold, gray eyes and the faint promise of liver spots on his bald scalp. Sculpted muscles protested against the tight-fitting black T-shirt. A faded tattoo of indiscernible design disappeared into the right sleeve. He fixed Samantha with a granite stare, face impassive. His voice was a gravelly baritone.

"What is this?"

Samantha pushed a long lock of golden hair from her left eye and smoothed it over her ear.

My hair. Really do miss my hair.

Her eyes moved down to her grey, fleece sweatshirt, **Northwestern** embroidered across the chest in bold purple. She noted that she had given Ana this very sweatshirt to wear after her rescue.

I should have ended her when I had the chance.

She looked up to meet the stare.

"I don't know," she said. "But I've been here before."

She glanced behind him at the mid-twentieth century decor and added:

"Sort of."

The image of the nebula was visible from the corner of her eye.

Oh you've been here alright.

"Talbot, right?" she said. "I heard Ana call you that."

He didn't answer. His jaw tightened, his eyes never straying from hers.

"Don't worry," said Samantha, "these visions never last long."

Meat-hook hands grasped the edge of the table. His gravel-timbre lowered to grating stone.

"Why did you bring me here?"

Samantha closed her eyes and tilted her head back, enjoying a moment free from agony and conflict. She inhaled the musty air of the old diner and took her time releasing it from her lungs.

Daddy, I don't want to go to school today.

An image of Alan was projected against the nothingness behind her eyelids.

"Okay, sounds good," he said. "I need help cleaning out the garage anyway."

The covers were warm against her chin.

Just a few more minutes?

"You're going to be late, kid."

Her eyes snapped open when the table was ripped from the floor and tossed aside.

"WHY?" Talbot thundered.

Samantha looked up at her brother who now towered over her.

"Because," she said. "I had to get creative or you were going to kill me."

Misery slammed into Samantha as the world returned. She lay on her back, marveling at the intricate laurel and oak ornamentation on the bronze girders overhead. Every fiber of her being ached, every nerve flared with pain. She lurched to her feet with an unsteady sway and located Talbot who knelt just a few feet away. He shook his head and blinked in the aftereffects of the strange vision. Gone were the monstrous facial features, the incredible size and mass. He appeared as he had in the vision, a normal—albeit seven-foot tall and heavily-muscled—man.

Better make this quick before he turns again.

Samantha applied telekinetic pressure to Talbot's neck, a tactic she'd tried several times without success during their titanic battle. As with Roger, this brother's abilities countered her own. But Talbot succumbed in his unaltered form, the interrupted blood flow in his carotid arteries putting him to sleep as though an expert grappler had secured him in a choke hold. He slumped to his stomach, his widening eyes reversing their course and closing in slumber. Her unyielding, invulnerable opponent now lay before her, a line of spittle issuing from his parted lips to pool on the cracked stone.

The brief respite in the imaginary diner had given Samantha a chance to breathe and recover, and she used that replenished energy to launch herself into the air with an unconscious Talbot in tow. She retrieved her torn cowl as an afterthought, summoning it from the floor of the Lincoln Monument and pulling it back over her head.

Samantha touched the communication device built into the cowl to activate it. White noise and crackling fuzz erupted in her ear.

"Jibril, are you there?"

The reply was sporadic and broken, barely audible over the static created by the damaged communications component. Samantha wasn't surprised after the punishment her cowl had taken.

"*I copy.* "

"I'm taking Talbot to the GW hospital with strict instructions to keep him restrained and sedated. Very restrained. Very sedated."

"*Understood. Make it fast. We're not done here. Your final task is at hand.*"

"Will do," Samantha said. "Jibril, David is down there somewhere. He's hurt. Bad, I think. Can you look for—"

"*Daniels is with me.*"

"How is he? Can you tell if—"

"*Hurry back, Samantha. Over and out.*"

The static went silent as the connection was severed. Samantha tightened her telepathic grip on Talbot and concentrated, propelling herself through the air with renewed urgency.

Chapter Twenty-Two

SHEER WILL KEPT DAVID MOVING. Will and a discipline burned into his psyche years ago. He had been in this position before, on the sandy beaches of California. In the cold, pre-dawn waters of the Pacific. They called it Hell Week, that special stretch of time during Basic Underwater Demolition/SEAL training when exhaustion and physical duress stripped away your identity and forged you into something new. Something stronger. Your mind played games, your body wouldn't obey your commands. David was sure he could smell the salt water, feel the gritty sand sticking to his skin.

He moved through a morass of images and sounds that sharpened into hyper-realistic focus then faded again. He was cold, then hot, then cold again. His pulse was constantly in his ears, the vibrations permeating his body. He put one foot in front of the other, following the stranger in the black bodysuit and mask for reasons he had yet to decide. Perhaps it was because he was a friendly in a sea of enemies.

Another concussive report burst from the interior of the Lincoln Memorial.

"Give him hell, Sam," David muttered.

David had seen her perform amazing feats, crushing Apache combat choppers with her bare hands for example, yet the ferocity of this creature, this Talbot, seemed to be more than she could handle. David's strange new companion had chalked it up to stealing Samantha's power and using it against her, but David couldn't wrap his head around that. She was the strongest person he knew, yet she had been tossed inside the memorial building like a crash test dummy ejected from a prototype sports car. It was David's last glimpse of her.

He hoped he'd get to see her again before the end.

David had trouble keeping pace with the masked man, who moved with the grace of a jungle cat through the pockets of violence that persisted in the immediate area. He fought like one too, always dropping back to protect David from random attackers with the speed and precision of a natural-born fighter. David tried to help but he could barely keep himself upright.

"Come, Daniels," said the man who hadn't yet given his name. "We're almost there."

The frenetic discharge of firearms was close now, hundreds of snapping cracks and deep barks from what David knew to be pistols and shotguns. Standard issue defense tools for local police. He might have been able to identify the makes and models of the weapons if his head wasn't drifting in and out of clarity.

They emerged from the tree line close to Lincoln Memorial Circle Northwest, the avenue that formed a ring around the memorial grounds. Dozens of police cars were jammed up, bullet-ridden doors flung open to serve as shields against gunfire from other officers. Several of the cruisers had burst into flame. Shouts and cries of pain provided a tumultuous counterpoint to the continuous firing.

David winced as his companion pulled him into a squatting position beside The Three Soldiers monument, which gave them a direct line of sight to the firefight just ahead. He had trouble keeping his attention on the nearby battle, had trouble focusing on anything in particular. His eyes drifted upward to the sculpted trio wrought from bronze, replete with their Vietnam-era uniforms and weapons, frozen forever as they looked upon the names engraved into the Vietnam War Memorial. David could swear he knew them, had served with them. Yes, there was Wally. The resemblance was uncanny. Was this some sort of trick? More mental subterfuge from Samantha's mother? And that one was Braithwaite. David was sure of it. He even had a healthy pinch of tobacco in his lip. The three heads bowed to look down at David, who crouched beside the decorative shrubbery and solemn tributes laid in remembrance at feet of the statues.

The third face was his.

"Daniels."

Someone was shaking him. Had he passed out?

"Daniels!"

It was his new, mysterious partner.

"Ana and her sons are just across the roadway. The problem is that there are two dozen raving mad police officers between us and—"

David roused himself and struggled to his feet. He wasn't sure why the masked man had stopped in mid-sentence until he realized that the reflective lenses set into the cowl were no longer pointed down at him. David's head swiveled to follow their line of sight.

Harkins had driven Adrian from the Reflecting Pool into Constitution Gardens where David and his companion were strategizing their route to Ana. A threesome of human-sized golems had been summoned from marble and sandstone, and Harkins now directed them in coordinated attacks on his adversary. Watching the young assassin fight made David's head spin even worse. Each move was precise, anticipatory of his immediate opponent's action as though he possessed a form of precognition. And perhaps he did, David mused. It wouldn't be at all surprising considering Adrian's lineage.

The agile man wielded a post of black iron, one of the hundreds used throughout the National Mall to link and support chains along walkways and section off prohibited areas. This post had a chunk of earth-encrusted concrete still attached to one end, and Adrian swung it like a sledge into Harkins's puppets, breaking off an arm here or a leg there before dancing away unharmed. Thin tentacles erupted from Harkins's mineral armor like striking serpents, but these, too, missed their spry target. It was obvious to David that there would be no victor in this contest. Adrian didn't seem to tire, and Harkins, despite his incredible abilities, couldn't match Adrian's speed and combat prowess. Something needed to change.

It appeared that David's cowled companion concurred. The man sprinted into the fray, weaving through Harkins's embattled constructs with a physical finesse rivaling that of Adrian. He dropped his weight in full stride, skidding beneath a wild swing from Adrian's makeshift club, then rolled to his feet and dodged his way through the obsidian tentacles. David thought he heard him shout something, but it was difficult to discern what was said amidst the gunpowder-fueled cacophony that continued on the nearby road. Everything that David was compelled him to join the fight, despite the fact that he knew he would be useless. He gathered himself and took a step forward, then another.

The fight ended before he got to his third step.

The masked man reached into a pouch at his belt and threw something at Adrian in the time it took David to blink. David couldn't make out what it was until Adrian caught it with preternatural dexterity. A tiny, chrome sphere glinted in the light from the grey sky above, clutched in Adrian's palm for a heartbeat before it exploded.

Adrian's self-congratulatory, taunting smile disappeared as quickly as it had formed. David heard his companion's voice with clarity this time.

"Now!"

Harkins thrust his arms forward, hands flattened and palms down. The black mineral substance sloughed away from him with lightning speed, starting at his feet and flowing from his pointed fingertips. It smashed into Adrian, still recovering from the unexpected consequences of catching a concussion grenade, and oozed over him like sentient, onyx mercury. His scream was cut short when the mineral engulfed his head. It was as though Harkins had tapped the mute button on Adrian's terror. A new monument now stood on the National Mall, black, rigid and motionless.

David made his way to the pair of men who now squared off across from each other.

"...thought of that. Would have saved a lot of time," Harkins was saying as David reached them. "Who the fuck are you, anyway?"

The masked man greeted David with a nod before addressing the question.

"You may call me Qareen, Mister Harkins."

"Kareem? Like the basketball player?" Roger said.

"No, Kah-*reen*," said David. "Like the mythical spirit of evil used to scare unruly children into good behavior."

The reflective lenses settled onto David.

"We were ordered to study Arabic history before shipping out for our first tour," David said. "Islamic folklore wasn't really required, but hey, I had a lot of downtime in those days. Glad you could join us, Harkins."

Harkins's eyes fell over David pallid face.

"You don't look so..."

His voice trailed off as his gaze dropped to David's abdomen.

"We don't have time for this," said Qareen, stepping between them to break Roger's line of sight. "Let's go."

He strode back toward the Three Soldiers statue, motioning for David and Roger to follow.

"Harkins, your mother is busy causing pandemonium among the authorities who don't seem to realize that the more people they send, the more toys she has to play with," said Qareen, pointing to the scene he had shown David just minutes ago. "Liev Garrison and Marcos Souva are with her, guarding her."

"And am I supposed to know who the hell they are?"

Qareen turned and nodded to the immobile Adrian.

"Like him, they are your brothers. And like him, they are dangerous. Daniels and I will take them out. You stay here and create a path for us through the gunfire. The range of your powers should allow for that. We just need to buy time for Samantha."

Harkins huffed.

"You expect me to hang back after my own mother sent an assassin after me? Are you fucking cra—"

"You *will* do as I say," Qareen said. "Ana belongs to your sister. It is the only way."

Again, Roger sucked in a breath to speak. David put his hand on Roger's shoulder and shook his head.

"There is a guy over there who can control other people's bodies," David said. "If he gets to you, it's all over."

Roger sighed.

"Fine, I'll do it. But if you two get into trouble..."

David managed a weak smile.

"Ah, now see? You do care. I'm touched."

Qareen signaled for David to follow him and left the cover of the statue, calling to Roger over his shoulder as he skulked away.

"When I give the signal, Mister Harkins."

"You take care of yourself, Roger," David added. "And maybe try to be more friendly to your sister?"

He though he heard a scoff from behind him as he trailed Qareen through the trees.

Their quarry lay seventy yards away, and now David could see Ana and her sons under the tree cover at the northwest corner of the Lincoln Memorial building. One of the sons was a small man whose eyes twitched about with anxiety. Was that Liev? The other one, possibly Marcos Souva, stood with his eyes closed and head bowed. The thrum of helicopter rotors drawing near from different directions roused David from his reconnaissance.

"Oh shit," he muttered. "This is going to get ugly."

Qareen's unreadable face turned toward the sky.

"Ugli*er*," David amended.

Qareen pulled David behind a tree. The sudden shift in his weight made David woozy. His vision narrowed again, then pulsed outward from its focal point. He noticed that his breath was coming in shallow gasps.

"This might work in our favor," said Qareen. "Watch Souva."

As if on cue, the sky suddenly darkened. A heavy blanket of shadow formed, replacing the dreary November sky. There was no form to it, no roiling motion like an angry thunderhead. It was as though someone had simply pulled the blinds down over the sky. Flipped the light switch. The ambient light was eerie, creeping in from far away to cover the Mall in a deep dusk. David heard proximity alarms screaming over the beating helicopter blades. They even drowned out the constant barrage of gunfire less than twenty yards from where he stood. Another sound grated in David's ears, foreboding and horrific.

TANGTANGTANGTANGTANG—CHOOM!

The helicopters came down in tandem, their rotors interlocked like embattled elk antlers during mating season. David surmised that one of the pilots had managed to direct their emergency descent away from the Lincoln Memorial, but that put their new landing zone on top of the chaotic expanse of stationary law enforcement vehicles. David wondered if the officers had even seen the twin helicopters dropping, so engulfed were they in their mindless firefight.

A great gout of flames bellowed into the sky, the orange flare beating back the unnatural darkness that shrouded the scene. Men and women screamed and burned and died. The darkness dissipated, readmitting the grey November day.

Qareen cursed in his native tongue, then spun around and shouted. "Harkins!"

If the carnage David had just witnessed wasn't enough to send any sane person scurrying for cover, the destruction of Lincoln Memorial Circle Northwest should have sealed the deal. The ground rumbled beneath David's feet as asphalt and concrete rippled and separated ahead of him. The road buckled and rose, splitting apart like a rubber band stretched beyond its structural integrity. It peeled away from the earth in two new sections, curling away from the center seam in a twisted, industrial homage to the parting of the Red Sea. Service lines snapped, vomiting their contents into the air; water and sewage and natural gas. The burnt husks of patrol cars and helicopters were flung about like ruined, tiny plastic models of themselves, rolling and tumbling and falling as gravity took hold. But a clear pathway now presented itself despite this horrendous destruction.

"Now, Daniels!"

Qareen seized a distracted David by his collar and propelled him forward. David's legs had grown numb from loss of blood. He stumbled and would have fallen if not for Qareen's iron grip.

"Stay with me, Daniels," Qareen said as he ushered David through the concrete canyon Harkins had created for them. "Remember, Liev Garrison is your target. The puffy jacket."

Qareen's hand dipped into a compartment on his belt then flicked outward in the direction they were heading. A trio of marble-sized polyhedrons met the ripped sidewalk at the far end of the canyon and detonated. A dense cloud of black smoke materialized, obscuring their egress from Harkins's handiwork. Qareen disappeared into the dark, swirling morass.

David's ears picked up Qareen's voice again, this time more distant. David couldn't tell if he had fallen behind or if oblivion had finally begun to swallow him.

"Complete your mission, soldier," Qareen said. "No matter the cost."

The ominous words tumbled through David's head as he lurched from the disorienting smoke screen back onto the National Mall. He spotted Garrison and Souva flanking Ana just as they had been during the brief reconnaissance at the Three Soldiers. Liev Garrison's beady eyes continued to dance about, and he flinched periodically in response to the nearby violence. Marcos Souva was older than his brother Liev, taller and more solid in stature. He scanned the area with a solemn vigilance. It appeared that Qareen was right. They had been tasked with guarding Ana while she had her fun. David saw no visible weapons, and no indications that any were concealed, but he knew that if they were truly relatives of Ana—of Adrian and Talbot, of Samantha and Roger—then they didn't need conventional weapons. They were weapons. Qareen's words echoed again in David's mind. He mouthed them in silence.

"No matter the cost."

He knelt and planted his palms in the brown, pre-winter grass and let the coolness wash into him, closing his eyes and dropping his chin to his chest. His breathing was ragged. The molten agony in his belly had turned to ice. His head throbbed. The world tilted. It would be so easy to roll onto the grassy slope and go to sleep. Just a quick nap, then he would complete the mission. Just a few minutes. That's all he needed.

A new commotion came to life close by, snapping David out of his reverie. David lifted his head to see Qareen lunging from the cover of a burnt-out police cruiser that had been blasted a touch too close to the Lincoln Memorial for comfort. Souva spotted him first, being closest to the sudden movement, but was too surprised to mount a defense against the ambush. Qareen leapt at him, hands extended and fingers outstretched, but passed through Souva to crash into a tangle of shrubs that lined the memorial's retaining wall behind his quarry. Souva shimmered and rippled, along with Ana and Garrison, as though the three were fading mirages under bright sunlight.

"What the fuck?" David heard himself whisper.

He grunted in pain as he put his feet under him and rose, eyes darting around the immediate area. A flash of red caught his attention high and to his left, an errant lock of hair flowing in the breeze just over the top edge of the retaining wall. Qareen had spotted it as well, and scrambled up the stones with such fluid agility that David could have sworn he was watching some weird, masked, primate-arachnid hybrid. He forced himself to move, rounding the corner of the wall to mount the final tier of stairs that led to a grassy terrace bordering the columned memorial building.

Another outlandish scene presented itself when David crested the top of the stairs and turned toward the lawn terrace. Dozens upon dozens of Anas, Garrisons and Souvas stood in trios across the grass, a battalion of brothers standing guard over their mothers who in turn were locked in deep concentration. David blinked in astonishment. He wasn't sure what Qareen had meant when he described Souva as a light bender, and now he had his answer. The darkness. The duplicates. Adrian's inexplicable and sudden appearance right next to David at the Reflecting Pool. Adrian had been there all along, stalking his prey under the cloak of Souva's power. David shook his head, cursing the existence of enhanced individuals. All of them but one.

He spotted Qareen standing on the edge of the wall, masked head swiveling to and fro in an attempt to locate the real trio among the mirror images. All of the Souvas were smiling with smug satisfaction at the bewildered Qareen.

All of the Garrisons turned their attention to David.

David was too weak to run and too depleted to charge. If he'd had a gun, he knew he could never hold his arm steady enough to hit his target. He commanded his body to move forward, willed himself into action as he had done since Adrian's blade had found his belly.

He didn't get far.

Spectral fingers curled around the edges of his consciousness, splitting and widening it like double doors made of gossamer. A presence stepped through, letting the doors close behind it. David couldn't see or hear or smell it, but it was as real as the cool air entering his lungs in shallow gasps. As real as the numbness in his arms and legs. As real as the lifeblood draining from his abdomen.

David's vision clouded and refocused. He now stared at Garrison staring at himself staring at Garrison in some twisted, funhouse-mirror hallucination. The visual echoes continued, reflections of perception that deepened into infinity. David lost all sense of being.

"Am I dead?" he tried to say.

But he no longer had a mouth, tongue, or larynx. Or at least none that he could control.

He watched his body move from afar, but he wasn't behind the steering wheel. The engine sputtered when it tried to lunge at Qareen, whose strange goggle lenses had turned a shade of violet, the masked head moving with deliberation as those lenses scanned the crowd of duplicates. David's divergent awareness saw Garrison's face blanch as all color drained from his cheeks. He watched from afar as his own hands fell over his ruined stomach. David's body fell to its knees, bloody hands held out before it. Realization crept over both of their faces at once. The same realization.

A voice resonated in David's mind.

"No matter the cost."

The reflective white hue of the pristine dress uniform did little to relieve the oppressive heat. The band of David's cap sealed the perspiration to his forehead, but allowed moisture to escape in occasional rivulets that gathered at his brow. He knew he wouldn't move if it dripped into his eye. He'd take the sting and remain at attention as he had been commanded to do by his superior officer, whose voice boomed from the public address system.

"And now, I present to you the newest group of the United States Navy's Sea, Air and Land graduates. At ease, gentlemen, and congratulations."

A roaring cheer rose from the stands, accompanied by eager applause. David felt a clap on the shoulder and turned to find Wally Pritchett's gleaming smile.

"You did it, brother!"

David returned the grin.

"We did it, Wally. We did it."

Their brief embrace was a welcome reward after all that they had been through together. Wally left the stage to find the arms of his proud mother along with the rest of the class whose family waited with beaming pride.

David loosened the brass button at his neck and slipped away. There was a bottle of scotch waiting for him in a bar somewhere.

In lieu of real, physical arms and hands, David visualized a pair of phantom limbs and reached out with them, intangible fingers extending into the void.

Elyse held the blouse up to her chest, the white price tag fluttering about the yellow and orange floral print like a hungry butterfly.

"What about this one?" she said.

David shifted his weight in the fitting room chair. His left cheek had gone numb. It was time to switch back to the right.

"It really brings out your eyes," he said.

"That's what you said about the last one!"

David shrugged.

"They both do. What's the big deal anyway? I'm the one who should be nervous."

Elyse turned to the mirror, smoothing the garment over her torso.

"My parents will love you," she said. "This is about looking presentable to my dad. He can be...judgy about my appearance. And about everything else in my life. Just prepare yourself for questions about marriage. And children, of course."

David wasn't sure what it was, but everything he knew, everything he had left in him, sensed it. His logical mind struggled to put a name to it, to label it so that he could analyze it and make sense of it. Yes, there it was. That was it. The word he was looking for. Intruder. His spectral fingers curled into claws and latched onto it.

The pressure cooker in his chest was about to blow. No one would find him until the hurricane had passed, a bloated body floating in the Tidal Basin. Another victim of the cruel storm. But they would find only one body if David had any say in the matter. He dove deeper.

His pinky finger snagged a strand of seaweed. No, not seaweed. Not here. Hair.

Her.

The skin was slippery, and he almost lost her to the choppy waters again before he pulled her into the fierce winds and pelting rain of the embankment. Long, thick locks pleated her pale face in soggy strands. He pushed them out of the way to search for signs of life, to administer emergency CPR if needed. It was his first good look at the woman.

The woman who could perform miracles.

And she was beautiful.

The intruder resisted. It panicked. David held on with every fiber of his fading presence in this world.

"No matter the cost."

The boy had David's eyes. The conclusion couldn't be contested.

"I heard you like superheroes," David said, forcing his mouth into a tired smile.

Duncan returned the smile, his bashful gaze dropping to the floor. He accepted a shallow cup from his mother and brought it to his lips with both hands. David's own eyes stared back at him from over the rim.

"Me too," said David, giving the boy's fine hair a soft rustle.

"I have to go now, Duncan. You be good for your mother, okay?"

Duncan lowered the cup and nodded.

"Okay."

Letting go and holding on. Two opposing actions never meant to be performed at the same time. But nothing made sense in those final moments. Nothing except sheer, unflinching determination. David clung to that. He sensed the intruder thrashing in his grasp, desperate to break free. David held fast.

He sensed something behind him. Something unknowable yet intimate. Something inevitable. It loomed over him. He felt its touch. David kept his grip on the intruder as finality flowed over him, flowed through him, gathering him up and taking away the pain and fatigue.

David held onto Liev Garrison.

Lazy waves lapped against the grassy shore, carrying a cooling breeze from the expanse of water that stretched to the horizon. The surface was a rippling reflection of the perfect sunny afternoon. David's head rested on her soft lap as they watched the day grow old, her nails carving rows in his hair with gentle strokes.

"I wish we could stay here forever," she said.

David drew in a lungful of crisp air and let it out with a contented smile. He almost looked up at her, but didn't. He was too comfortable. It didn't matter anyway.

"We can, my love. We can."

Chapter Twenty-Three

"DO NOT, UNDER ANY CIRCUMSTANCES, let this man wake up."

Samantha almost felt sorry for the stunned medical staff. They had gathered around her without delay, a bloody and bruised woman who had burst into the emergency room carrying a seven-foot tall, bald, naked and unconscious man. It was a strange reversal of the domestic violence cases that typically came through their doors. She became aware of her own appearance as the nurses and orderlies gathered around her. The hi-tech suit, an immensely expensive parting gift from Jibril, now hung from her frame in a tattered patchwork, the full face mask destroyed to the point that it barely hid her identity. Perhaps they thought she had rushed in from a local science fiction convention wearing a costume carefully distressed to pay homage to a particular movie scene that only hardcore fans would recognize. They were quite unaware that the large man had transformed into a towering beast and shredded her across marble and stone and cement like a block of Asiago against a grater.

"Put him in a damn coma or something. Just do *not* let him wake up!"

They just stared at her in disbelief.

Fuck.

One of the gawkers wore a white lab coat. Round spectacles framed her brown eyes and a stethoscope hung from her neck.

She'll do.

Samantha gathered the lab coat's lapels in telekinetic fists and pulled her to within an inch of Samantha's half-exposed face. White rubber soles squealed against the linoleum floor as she covered the distance between them in the blink of an eye.

"Do you understand me?" Samantha said through clenched teeth. "This man is responsible for what happened on the Mall. What is still happening right now. Get a gurney. Get a syringe. Get some fucking elephant tranquilizer, for all I care. Just keep him under or everyone in this building could die. And that will be on you."

She punctuated the final word with a poke to the doctor's chest. The woman nodded. Samantha released her and turned away, parting the crowd that had gathered with a casual wave of her hand. She was through the doors and airborne before they knew she had left.

Okay. One monster down...

She couldn't help but picture David's expression when she had burst from the tree cover. The scene played over and over in her mind, a broken projector stuck on a short series frames that restarted as soon as it ended. She knew Jibril could take care of himself, and was probably devising a way to get close to Ana and her sons undetected. But David...

I hope you didn't do anything stupid.

Things had gone according to plan, for the most part. She had gotten through to Dietrich as she and Jibril hoped she would. But the president had surprised her by changing his intention again mid-speech, as though he had been swayed by an external influence to put him back on track with his original intentions. She could still hear the piercing screech of the microphones when the P.A. system was obliterated with a thought. It had been a nice touch. Her split and bleeding lips erupted in pain when the smile came.

But who could have influenced Dietrich on the fly like that? Ana? No, she is quite capable at cunning deception, but can't make puppets out of people. At least not as far as I know.

Ana had called the monstrosity her brother—a fact that had revealed his single weakness—so maybe the other two men with Ana had powers as well? Which would mean they, too, were her brothers.

What if one of them controlled the president? What if he can control me?

The thought made her shudder.

More importantly, does Jibril know? Of course he does. But why did he keep it from me? Does he think I was too soft on Roger?

Samantha made a mental note to have a little talk with Jibril when this was over.

If we live through this, that is.

The chaos and violence Ana had caused made Samantha's battle with the National Guard all those weeks ago look like a minor altercation. This time she had exerted her will over an incredible number of people, twisting their senses with such malice that their darkest, most primal hatred had taken over. Peaceful protesters. Innocent families spending time with their loved ones. Teachers and students on field trips, excited to be out of the classroom. They were all victims of Ana's malicious control. They were all helpless against her will.

Well I'm not. Not anymore.

She swooped low over the eastern bank of the Potomac and angled south towards the Lincoln Memorial. Hundreds of tiny, distant pops grew into gunpowder-fueled mini-explosions as she closed in on Ana's handiwork. She had noticed the impromptu war between the local authorities, first responders and government law enforcement on her way to deliver her oversized patient to the hospital, but decided not to intervene. Time had been of the essence.

What a clusterfuck.

A bullet buzzed her left ear. Another one tapped against her chin and ricocheted away.

Jesus. The collateral damage alone...

Samantha dove into the crossfire, focusing on the center of the battle. Lincoln Memorial Circle Northwest crumbled under the weight of her thunderous descent. She threw her arms out wide and lowered her head to concentrate, drawing in a sharp breath before raising her face to the sky and expelling it with a word.

"ENOUGH!"

A shield of impenetrable, invisible force materialized around her body and burst outward in a wedged ring. It hurled people and vehicles before it, plowing them away from Samantha in an ever-widening circle. She dissolved the construct and rose into the air to survey the results of her efforts.

An angry shout sounded from somewhere within the wreckage, followed by another. A single gunshot erupted, then a second and third. Those whom had lost their firearms engaged new foes with extendable batons or random parts from the ruined vehicles—even their bare hands— while those still armed resumed firing upon each other.

Dammit. No time to disarm and restrain them all. Have to stop this at the source.

She crouched and shot into the sky, pausing to scan the area close to the memorial where she had last seen Ana. Pockets of violence still dotted the Mall, but they paled in comparison to Ana's first instigation of the mass psychosis. Again, Samantha couldn't help but marvel at the extent and duration of Ana's influence.

It must be taking a toll on her. She hasn't been out of that drug-fueled coma for very long. No wonder she recruited her sons to help. No wonder she needed my help.

Samantha singled out a teen boy who brandished a broken piece of stone and was about to brain a random young man. She sent a telepathic flick to his temple, dropping him before he could execute his victim. The would-be victim picked up the stone without hesitation and raised it overhead with both hands, standing over his former attacker.

Oh, for fuck's sake...

Samantha dropped him in similar fashion and continued her reconnaissance.

"Samantha. Northwest corner of the Lincoln. Atop the retaining wall."

Jibril's voice crackling into her earpiece was a welcome sound. She twisted around to find him weaving through a field of mirror images of Ana and her two remaining sons, moving and striking and moving again in search of a solid target.

How the hell?

Jibril must have found what he was searching for when one of his exploratory attacks connected with the chin of Ana's taller, curly-haired son. His concentration interrupted, the duplicates faded away to reveal two figures lying in the grass.

"Take her out now! Do not hesitate for one second!"

One of the prone men was Ana's son, the one in the puffy jacket that her mother had protected during Dietrich's speech. The other one looked like—

"NO!"

Samantha plummeted from the sky to the earth in a heartbeat, not bothering to land in any sort of balanced fashion. Instead, she crumpled over the second figure and gathered it into her arms before rocking back and forth, holding tight.

"No. No! Nonononono..."

David face peered over her shoulder, eyes open but unseeing, his cheek icy against hers. She laid him back down and smoothed his hair over his forehead, his still features obscured by the blurry screen of her tears. She blinked them away and looked him over, hands cupping his peaked jawline. His stomach was ruined, a cruel gash the source of the blanket of dark crimson that saturated his shirt and trousers. She threw her head back and wailed.

Somewhere someone was shouting into her ear.

"She's coming, Samantha! Do it now! Do it right n—"

Sorrow and rage engaged in a pitched battle for control over her. She buried her face into David's motionless chest. Her fists clenched into tight balls as she screamed.

"ANA!"

Her world fell silent.

Then, the musical, mechanical chime of a metal comb over a studded drum.

Mothballs and old cardboard. Aged cedar and dust. The gentle, tinkling notes of a music box built into a child's mobile.

Samantha whirled around to confirm her suspicion.

The attic in Centerville.

"Welcome home, Little Star."

The glow of the setting sun filtered through the lone window set into the wall just below the peak of the A-frame ceiling, illuminating a sheet of translucent construction plastic that hung from an angled column. A figure of similar height and build to Samantha loomed just beyond the sheet. The head was bowed, the hands holding something at chest level.

Samantha batted the plastic aside. Ana stood just beyond, cradling a small piece of paper as though she had gathered up a wounded baby bird that had fallen from its nest. Samantha's eyes darted to the paper. She didn't need to scrutinize it. Her instincts told her all she needed to know.

Faded ink against yellowed newsprint.

FAMILY PLUNGES INTO LAKE
Woman Missing, Feared Dead

Ana let it go. The clipping wafted to the dusty floorboards like the last leaf from a dormant maple tree.

"And so here we are," Ana said, locking onto Samantha's gaze. "At the end."

Samantha's heart churned in her ears. Fingernails bit into her palms. A red film tinted her vision as raw fury seeped from her every pore. Her accusation was growled through a clenched jaw.

"All of those people. You made them kill each other. You killed..."

Ana said nothing. Her expression was stone.

"You killed...*him*."

Samantha's voice cracked on the final syllable.

"'Him'?" Ana said. "You mean your special friend?"

Samantha's eyes were smoldering coals of bright green.

"You mean the one who betrayed you? The one who gave you up to his government colleagues in an effort to save some woman from his past and their snot-nosed whelp? That one?"

The coals sputtered out, smothered by Ana's assertion. Samantha felt her pulse skip a beat.

"Yes, dear. I peeked into his traumatized, scattershot brain."

"You're lying," said Samantha. "He wouldn't...he would never—"

"It's a shame, really. That means that everything he went through to protect you meant nothing. Your friend—Marissa, was it?—getting shot, his Navy associates dying during my daring rescue, all of it was for nothing."

Samantha's mind raced.

Oh David.

She took a breath and girded her resolve. There would be time to grieve later. Right now, people still needed her help.

"He died protecting innocent people from you and your sons. He was a warrior and he died like one," said Samantha.

Ana nodded, one eyebrow arching high on her brow.

"That is also true," she said. "My troublesome little Liev overestimated his own power and was pulled into the great mystery by your doomed paramour. An unexpected strategy, but admirable nonetheless. I'm quite sure none of Liev's victims have ever tried that before. My poor, lost boy didn't know what to do. May he rest in peace."

Samantha took a step toward her mother.

"It's over, Ana. The president didn't blow up the world. Your sons are out of the fight," Samantha said, moving closer. "There will be no reshaping of a broken, post-apocalyptic world in your image. Its fine the way it is. Face it. You lost."

"Hmph," said Ana.

Ana shouldered past her into the larger attic area. She pushed a stack of boxes from the top of a wide cedar chest and opened the lid with a soft creak of old hinges. Samantha pivoted to watch her mother rifle through the contents of the chest, wondering how to escape this forced memory realm that Ana had created.

Will my powers even work here? Am I at her mercy?

"Oh look," Ana said. "Senior prom?"

The waning sunlight fell over powder blue satin as Ana stood and held a dress out before her.

Samantha answered, fatigue and grief diverting her from urgency. "Yes."

Ana wrapped her arms under the garment's midriff and let gravity fold it over her forearms. Her amused expression melted into nostalgic remorse.

"I'm so sorry I wasn't there, my dear. I never got to see you on one of the most exhilarating, exciting nights of a young woman's life."

"Ana, end this. Now," said Samantha.

"Will you put it on for me? Just for a minute?"

Ana offered the dress at arm's length.

"What? No! You need to stop this—"

Samantha had no recollection of how the full-length mirror got there, nor did she recall acquiescing to Ana's wishes, yet the reflection revealed a young woman almost a decade too old to be wearing a high school prom dress. The shoulders and bust were a touch too snug, but the rest of the satin fell over her waist and hips as it had on that chilly spring night. Her thick hair was piled atop her head, falling in golden ringlets at her temples and neck. A beaded band around her wrist flaunted a pink rose surrounded in baby's breath.

There wasn't a corsage in her cedar chest. It had been lost in the alcohol-infused adventures that had followed the dance that night. The flower hadn't been a rose anyway. Tyler LaBrie had presented her with a gorgeous and rare blue orchid.

"It still fits!" Ana said, hands clasping over her sternum. "Oh, and that beautiful rose! Just look at you, my dear."

Oh my god. She's further gone than I thought. Way further.

Samantha whirled on Ana, eyes flaring dangerously. Samantha ripped the corsage from her wrist and tossed it aside.

"Ana, listen to me," she said. "You were abducted and held against your will for twenty years. You were filled with drugs that entire time, pharmaceuticals that messed with your brain, warped your reality. You need to come back to us. You need to atone for what you have done."

Ana's hands slid from her chest to fall at her side.

"No one comes out of that unscathed," said Samantha. "No one. Not even you, Ana."

Ana's wistful expression melted away, replaced with an imperiousness that set Samantha on her heels.

"You think I'm insane."

It wasn't a question.

"Ana, you set innocent people against each other, twisting their minds and turning them into psychotic, raging murderers! Hundreds have died because of you. You used your sons in an attempt to coerce a sitting president to start a war that would end in the mutually-assured destruction of all civilization on this planet! You...you even tricked your only daughter, the one you said you've waited thousands of year for, into attacking the military! You took away my powers and left me for dead, mother!"

"Oh no, my Little Star," said Ana. "No, my dear. You suppressed your powers on your own. I only made a suggestion, gave you a nudge in the right direction "

Samantha shook her head in disbelief.

I lay out a list of atrocities straight from the bucket list of a despotic dictator and she focuses on that part?

Wait...

"Wh-what?" Samantha said, her jaw slackening.

"You've always had the ability to dampen your gifts if you so desired, to be boring and useless. To be like *them*."

She punctuated the last word with a sneer.

"You just had no one to show you how."

305

Samantha spun away to find her own stunned countenance staring back at her. She searched the mirror for anything that might expose Ana's words as a lie. Ana appeared at her right shoulder.

"And I can show you so much more, daughter. It's not too late."

I can control it. I can be normal.

A recent conversation that never was, never will be, replayed in her thoughts. The memories were spotty but an image slipped through, that of her future self speaking to her atop a colossal abomination where the Washington Monument once stood.

"It was Ana fucking around in your brain. It was her influence, her suggestion. Think about it."

A normal life. With my family.

Yes! Our family! Let me guide you.

Samantha's eyes traveled over her reflection, from the mountain of wavy gold on her head to the powder blue bodice of the dress. She found it ridiculous that she was wearing the thing, yet Ana had truly been touched by the sight of it. That moment had been real.

Maybe... Maybe it isn't too late for her. Is it?

Of course not, my Little Star. Think it through.

Her eyes dropped further, noting how the dress clung to her flat abdomen.

What else can I learn from her? What else can I do that I haven't discovered yet?

Her gaze lingered on her stomach. Something itched at the back of her head. Itched from inside her brain.

My family...

Her hands shot up to cover her belly. The memory that had eluded her since waking up confused and alone in Jibril's medical bay broadsided her with devastating force, completing it's journey through the past to slingshot into her present with a mental thunderclap.

The Mall. We were near the Washington Monument.

Let me guide you.

Samantha felt the mental intrusion. Ana was there, nudging her forward with a gentle push, a mother prompting a toddler to take her first steps. She sensed her power taking on a new form. It folded in upon itself faster than she could comprehend until her entire being was contained in a single atom. It traveled through her skin and muscles, narrowing to a pinpoint then growing even smaller. It infused her entire body like a sixth sense, laying everything bare, magnified for intense scrutiny. Her cells became visible in her mind's eye, trillions upon trillions floating in her perception.

She found it clinging to her uterus, a cluster of cells. They were similar but different. A part of her, yet separate. They belonged to something else. Some*one* else.

Yes, that's it. Do you see?

Samantha lurched forward and caught herself on the mirror's solid wooden frame. She clung to it as she retched, expelling bile onto her satin gown. She gasped and coughed, swiping her forearm across her lips as she let go and turned to face Ana, eyes burning with tears, heart aching with betrayal.

"Yes, Ana. I see. I see now."

A calm confidence came over Ana's face, yet she backed up a step as Samantha advanced on her.

"Every word that leaves your cruel mouth is a lie. Every intention a selfish deception."

"I needed you!"

"You made me think I was pregnant!"

Their noses were separated by millimeters, their raised voices rattled the pane of the lone window that had grown dim in the early twilight.

"I would have done anything, used every last mote of power I possess to persuade you that my cause is the right one! That your place is at my side!"

"Anything? Even kill me?"

Ana's retort caught in her throat. Her mouth opened to reply in rhythm with their exchange but no words were uttered.

"We're just tools to you," Samantha said. "Me. My brothers. I bet you even tried to recruit Roger, didn't you?"

Ana's expression confirmed it.

"End this illusion, Ana. It's time to face the consequences of your actions."

"To what end, Sammy?"

"Don't ever call me that."

"Do you think they'll let me live after this? Do you think there will be a fair trial before my peers? I have no peers!"

Ana threw up her hands as she continued.

"Or maybe they'll take me back into their tender care, keep me sedated for the rest of their lives, passing me down through generations of government-funded cretins until one day, far in the future, someone makes a mistake and I wake up again."

Samantha hadn't considered that.

She's not wrong.

"Then I'll stop you again."

"No, my dear," said Ana. "I think not."

"I'm not going to let you walk away from this. Not after what you've done. I can't. I won't."

Ana nodded and moved to a large cardboard box that rested on a card table. She reached inside and withdrew the mobile, holding it high with one hand and twisting the large white knob with the other. The planets and moons began their dance as the mechanical song restarted. Samantha couldn't help but hear the words.

Twinkle twinkle, Little Star...

Ana's head swiveled to regard Samantha with languid, deliberate motion.

"And how, exactly, do you intend to stop me?"

David's voice came unbidden to Samantha, a memory imprint from a past training session.

"The hook is one of the best tools in your toolbox. If you connect to the jaw right here..."

Samantha still felt his warm, calloused hand on her jaw line.

"...it will cause the head to move in a horizontal plane. The neck muscles won't be able to compensate, and the brain gets knocked against the skull like a pinball. Lights out."

Samantha reached out with her mind. A quick, forceful tap on the side of Ana's mandible should do it. But as her telekinetic strike took shape, she realized there was nothing in front of her. There was simply no jaw to punch, no Ana at all. Samantha changed tactics and thrust her palm forward, launching a blast of force that would knock Ana from her feet.

That should give me a moment to think.

But the blast didn't so much as ruffle Ana's hair. The tables and boxes and other mementos were also unaffected.

Ana's lips spread into a grin.

"You are in my world, daughter. And here, I make the rules."

Samantha's perception shifted. A great heat washed up from below her, burning her feet and lower legs. She clung to an outcropping of obsidian rock with one hand. The crag seared the skin of her fingertips, but she dare not let go. A vast sea of churning orange lay far below her, pockets of hot magma exploding into the super-heated air. Ana's head appear over the lip of the precipice above her.

"All you have to do is let go, my dear," she said. "Give up and become a mindless shell of who you once were."

"This isn't real!"

Yet she could smell the singed skin of her blistering fingertips, hear them sizzle and pop. She reached up with her other hand but there was no purchase to be found.

Yet it feels quite real, doesn't it?

Her vision shifted again. Samantha found herself underwater. There was no way to tell which way was up. Her lungs burned for air. Massive shapes swirled about her, sharp fins buffeted her. Dead, black eyes evaluated her helplessness.

Or maybe you'd prefer something a touch more personal.

The water blasted into Samantha, pummeling her and filling the plexiglass enclosure at her feet. The manacles were cold against her wrists. She knew what was coming next. She screamed as the electricity coursed through her body.

"Stop!"

She was on the plaza at the East Front of the Capitol building. Dozens of stone automatons battered her to her knees. She couldn't lift her arms, couldn't bring her powers to bear to repel and destroy them. They piled on top of her and rained down a storm of agony.

"Stop this!"

She coughed the dust from her throat and rose to her feet on unsteady legs. The toothy maw of a Tyrannosaurus Rex greeted her. Nearby, a gaping hole yawned in the wall of the Natural History Museum. A contingent of National Guard soldiers had taken position just outside. Several of them raised rocket-propelled grenade launchers to their shoulders.

"*Mother! Stop!*"

Samantha crumpled to the attic floor soaked, scorched and aching. She tasted blood in her mouth. Her ribs flared in pain with each breath. Her hands and feet were numb.

Not real. Have to...

Ana loomed over her.

"Pitiful girl," she said.

Have to figure a way out of this.

"There is no way out of this unless I say there is."

Despite the terrors Ana had visited upon her, despite the traumatic memories Ana had forced her to relive, Samantha found herself retracing her steps under Jibril's tutelage. The strict adherence to routine he had forced on her. The study and the chores. The equations she had memorized. They had worked to mask her presence from Ana during the execution of their initial plan, but it was too late now. She was already in Ana's mental grip. She forced herself to concentrate, to recall.

The isolation tank. My reawakening. My power.

Ana was gloating over her in another verbal attempt to tear her daughter down, but Samantha's attention was elsewhere.

Open your mind, Sammy. Let it in. It's right there. It's not out of reach. Think!

She rolled to her stomach and planted her palms on the dark floorboards, hoisting herself to her knees with supreme effort. She felt Ana's fist in her hair. There was a sudden pain in her scalp as her face was jerked upward.

"...listening to me, girl? You have one final chance. One last—"

Samantha tuned her out. She concentrated on the memory of nothingness, of floating without perception. She unfettered her thoughts, let her mind overwhelm her physical being and shrink it down until it was a single pinpoint in the corner of her awareness. She inhaled through her nose, long and smooth. There was no pain in her body because there was no body. Not anymore.

She pictured the floorboards below her. She couldn't feel them because she had no hands, no palms, no skin. No nervous system to interpret physical sensory input. The floor flickered and faded, then returned as a spectral echo of itself. Another memory resurfaced from the past, crawling from the depths of her consciousness to reinforce a lesson taught to her not so long ago, even though it felt like eons.

The junkyard. Her first steps toward understanding who she was. What she was capable of. A spray of dirt and gravel on the invisible bubble of force she was struggling to maintain. It was a Herculean task in those days.

The sphere became visible, if only for a moment.

Evan Douglas winked at her.

"Just a tip in case you ever have to fight invisible enemies."

Samantha focused harder and reached out, releasing a single sense back into her world. It wasn't one of the five common senses, nor was it the inexplicable, metaphysical sixth sense that lived in conjecture. It was an exploratory knowing, a primal perception fed by Samantha's power. It radiated from her and pushed outward, flowing from her to slide undetected beneath Ana's illusory universe. The floorboards were there but became intangible. The attic walls and ceiling shimmered and lost their opacity. They were there, yes, but so were the trees. So was the carpet of grass and the soft earth beneath it, chilled by the crisp November day. David was there, limp and lifeless in Samantha's arms. More intangible, human forms lay beyond. Was that Jibril holding up Ana's son by his coat, pounding him into oblivion? They were mere images cast onto the backdrop of the attic of Samantha's childhood home. Another form lay nearby. The son David had killed with his final breath. Liev, Ana had called him. And there was Ana herself, her physical self, directing her energies to keep her daughter locked in a mental prison.

But there was someone else, too. An ethereal silhouette creeping up behind Ana.

Who is that?

Samantha was wrenched back into the attic, reeled into Ana's reality with whip-neck speed. She gasped as the pain returned and looked into Ana's eyes.

"There will be none of that, my dear," said Ana. "No tricks. No back doors to slip through."

Samantha hung her head. There would be no defeating this monster. She couldn't win. It was too late.

I love you, David. I love you, Daddy.

"See?" Ana said. "You just expanded your power array all on your own. Very impressive. I'm so proud of you! And it almost worked. Now think of what you could do under my—"

CHOK!

The terse bark came from outside of the illusory attic, from far away yet very close. Samantha's eyes swiveled upward in slow motion, filling with dread as they traced Ana from toe to torso to face.

Ana's mouth was still open, frozen in her final offer to Samantha. A green bud appeared in the center of her chest, popping from her breastbone like an early perennial conquering the last snows of late winter to begin its annual journey into spring. Leaves grew and unfurled, revealing a crimson that rivaled the locks framing Ana's shocked expression. The crimson bud separated and matured into petals, flourishing until a single red rose sprouted there.

Emerald eyes dropped to inspect the inexplicable flower that had just grown from her body. Ana's lips parted into a smile. Her voice was weak, fragile. It chilled Samantha to the bone.

"I've always...loved...roses."

A single drop of blood traced the imperfections of one of the petals and found its tip, gathering there in preparation for its descent to the attic floor.

Everything was still and silent except for Samantha's quiet, trembling inhale.

The attic shattered into trillions of pieces around her before she could expel the breath. She curled into a ball, arms wrapped over her head for protection, but no shards or splinters or debris fell over her. Instead, she was bathed in a cold, brisk wind. She relaxed her arms and lifted her head.

Ana stood on the grassy lawn not far away, facing Samantha with hands clutched to her chest. Her eyes were wide, mouth agape and dripping blood as she fell from Samantha's line of sight to reveal a figure standing behind her.

A smoking revolver stuttered in his shaking hand, and beyond it a stricken look was plastered over a very familiar face.

Samantha blinked several times in disbelief.

"Daddy?"

Chapter Twenty-Four

PATCHES OF FROST LINGERED in the shadows of the solemn birch trees, seeking refuge from the encroaching morning sun. The attendees welcomed the sunshine, their black attire soaking up its warmth to ward off the frigid air of early December. A percussionist beat out a solemn tattoo on his shoulder-mounted snare as the flag ceremony began. David would no doubt have thought the fanfare excessive and unnecessary.

Samantha felt her father's arm slide around her shoulder. She reached up to cover his wrist with a gloved hand. Her other hand was firmly clasped in Marissa's, and through it she felt the tremors of her friend's silent sobs. She squeezed tighter.

I'm here for you.

It was well over a week ago, a day after the horrifying events that led to the deaths of Ana and David, that Samantha had shown up battered, bruised and exhausted at Marissa's apartment door. Samantha watched Marissa's expression transform from hope to devastation after a single glance at Samantha's face. Marissa melted into her arms. Their anticipated reunion would have to wait. Grief would come first.

The sailors folded the flag with precise, practiced movements, wrapping it over and under itself until a perfect triangle was formed. It was handed to a high-ranking officer who held the flag before her and pivoted one hundred and eighty degrees to face a young boy who looked like a tiny Dickensian gentleman in his little black suit and tie.

Duncan.

Samantha stood in David's kitchen, her fingertips tracing the smooth surface of the granite countertop as a passionate memory punched through her veil of heartache before dissipating into the past.

"What about this one?"

Marissa appeared in the doorway of David's bedroom with a grey Armani suit held out before her. David had been wearing that same suit the day he introduced himself at Federal Triangle station. The day he had prevented her from falling on the escalator.

Paperboy.

"Why are you smiling?" Marissa said, her brows furrowing.

"Just thinking about when David and I met."

"Oh."

The suit lowered, its hem brushing the hallway floor.

"It was very formal," said Samantha. "He shook my hand and everything."

Marissa glanced over her shoulder, then her gaze dropped to the floor. Samantha leaned against the counter and crossed her arms over her chest.

"His dress uniform should be in the closet somewhere," Samantha said. "That would be more appropriate."

"Right, yeah," said Marissa. "Also, I found this with his cufflinks."

Marissa extended her hand with a tiny, white orb pinched between thumb and forefinger.

Samantha pushed herself from the counter, squinting at the object and taking a few tentative steps towards her friend. She held out her hand, fingers relaxed and palm up. The ball floated across the room to hover an inch from her skin and rotated there like a tiny, pale planet. Her solemn face was reflected in its glossy surface, revealing memories with each rotation.

Vegas. Violence. Visions of a future I hope will never come to pass.

"My lucky roulette ball," Samantha said, hooking a thumb in her jeans pocket to pull it open.

He must have taken it from my nightstand after I disappeared.

The marble dropped from sight, tucked away inside the denim.

"I didn't know he had it," she said. "Do you remember...?"

She trailed off when she realized Marissa was no longer paying attention her. She was looking at the front door, which now stood wide open.

"Can I help you?" said Marissa.

Samantha turned to find a dark-haired woman in a navy blue sweatshirt and light winter jacket standing in the doorway. A boy of no more than six peered out from behind her, a frayed ball of yarn perched atop his knit winter cap.

Those eyes...

Samantha's heart sank before the first words were spoken.

"Yes," said the woman. "You can tell me who you are and what you're doing here."

"We're friends of David's," said Marissa. "I mean...were. Sorry, I..."

Samantha rescued her dear friend.

"Good friends," she said. "I'm Samantha McAllister. And you are?"

"Elyse Moore," said the woman as she stepped inside. "And this is Duncan, David's son. His next of kin."

Samantha approached the pair and knelt before Duncan as Marissa introduced herself. The boy grabbed his mother's hand and backed away a step as Samantha studied his face.

The resemblance is stunning.

"Your father was a brave man," Samantha said. "A great man. You're going to be okay, Duncan. I promise."

Duncan accepted the folded flag and looked up at Elyse, unsure of what to do next. She placed a hand on his head and gave him a comforting smile. The officer took a step backward and issued a terse order. All uniformed men and women faced the flag and stood at attention. Another order had their hands at their brows in salute. Samantha noticed that Lange and Gonzales, David's surviving brothers-in-arms, had joined in as well. A nondescript man on the other side of the casket caught Samantha's eye and offered her the slightest of nods.

Thanks for coming, Jibril.

The first few melancholy notes of *Taps* rang out from a bugler who stood near the casket. Seven riflemen fired off the first shot, jolting Samantha with the sudden burst even though she knew it was coming. Her hand dug into her pocket and found the white marble. She tucked it into her palm and held tight as the second and third shots rang into the clear, crisp morning.

Samantha tucked her chin to her chest and let the tears come.

"I'm pretty sure he'll get ousted from the party before the next election cycle," said Samantha, scooting the last few spaghetti noodles around on her plate. "I feel bad. It wasn't his fault. He should get the Nobel for averting a world war, not punishment from his national committee."

Alan watched his daughter manipulate the tines of her fork to form S's with her spaghetti.

"No. You should be getting a medal. Not him. You intervened. You thwarted your mother. Broke her hold over him."

He crunched into a slice of garlic bread and raised his wine glass in preparation for a follow up swallow. Her eyes darted up at him, then drifted back down to her serpentine pasta art.

"I just distracted her before getting pummeled like a punching bag by a huge dick of a brother."

Alan shook his head.

"How many people did you save by taking that beating? How many people were you protecting the entire time you were fighting that monster?"

Samantha shrugged, eyes still on her plate.

"If your concentration hadn't been divided, if you hadn't been focusing on intervening in a hundred different altercations, that brute would have had his own ass handed to him by my little girl."

Samantha didn't acknowledge his comment. Didn't look up. Alan filled the ensuing silence with another swig of Merlot before setting the glass down and tapping his finger on the rim.

"They'll keep him under," Alan said. "There were enough witnesses, enough news coverage for the authorities to know that they can't let him wake up. He'll be locked away for the rest of his life. The other brothers as well."

"I guess the government finally got their super-powered guinea pigs to study after all," she said. "Their 'enhanced individuals', as David used to say."

"Better them than you."

They are my brothers.

"Really? What if one of them had been Cole?"

Alan's lips parted for a retort, but he paused to rethink it before replying.

"If Madelyn-—if *Ana*—had given birth to Cole, if he had been gifted with miraculous powers, you can be sure he would have been standing shoulder to shoulder with his sister from the get go."

Samantha nodded.

Wow. He said her name. Her real *name. Finally.*

"I know," she said.

Another pause, this one filled with the tinkle of Samantha's fork on her plate.

"You've done that since you were a child, you know," Alan said.

"What?"

Alan pointed to her plate.

"That. What are all the S's for?" said Alan. "Sad superhero sulking?"

"Spaghetti, silly," said Samantha. "So shush."

It was the first time she had seen her father smile in a long time.

They shared a piece of key lime pie for dessert, then recounted the events of the tragedy at the Lincoln Memorial for what seemed like the hundredth time as they cleaned the dishes. Certain parts were left out, as they had been ninety-nine times before, such as the climactic gunshot that had saved many lives while taking one. They instead discussed the repercussions of that terrible day; how the government was spinning it in the media, how the survivors were being lied to about what had happened to them, and other steps the government was taking to cover it up.

It wasn't until Alan pulled on his coat and stood in the doorway of Samantha's townhouse that he broached one of those unspoken topics.

"What did you do with her?" he said, eyes fixed on his hand as he pulled a thin leather glove over it. "Her body."

The final two words were barely above a whisper.

That's what a Batman is for.

Samantha reached up to tuck her father's scarf inside the collar of his coat with tender care.

"My friend, my *new* friend, took care of that. No one will ever know what happened."

Alan's eyebrows rose as he inclined his head. Samantha knew that look.

"Don't worry," she said, "he treated her with respect. Those religious types usually do."

Alan nodded and turned to leave.

"Is he your friend, though?" he said over his shoulder.

Good question.

"You know," she said, "I'm not really sure. Let's call him an ally. For now."

Alan moved past the cryptic answer and made his way down the front walk.

"I love you, Samantha."

"I love you too, Daddy."

Chapter Twenty-Five

ISRA SHUFFLED ACROSS THE POLISHED FLOOR of the mosque, her reflection mimicking the never-ending battle of good versus evil. Her arms pumped before her, fists tight as they lashed out in a series of lefts and rights. Samantha watched the heroic display from behind a cup of herbal tea.

"This is new."

Jibril nodded.

"Indeed," he said.

"Who is she? Batgirl?"

"No. Keep watching."

As if on cue, the girl flattened her hands and extended her arms like wings, angling her body side to side as her sneakers squeaked across the floor.

"Supergirl?" said Samantha, raising her cup.

"Wait for it," said Jibril.

Isra stopped, looking down as if hovering high above the ground. Her fingertips pressed against her temples and her eyes narrowed, her gaze moving upwards as it followed an imaginary object moving under her control.

"Oh!" said Samantha, the cup stopping just below her lips.

"Yes," said Jibril, taking a sip of his own tea. "She wants to be Kinetic Star when she grows up."

"Does she know that...?"

"No, and we'll keep it that way. One less person who knows your secret is one less person whose life is in danger."

Isra stopped her charade to look at her father and Samantha for approval.

"Samantha, guess who I am!" she said.

"You're the coolest little girl in the whole city. That's who you are," Samantha called back.

"Time for homework, Isra," Jibril said, turning away from his daughter before she could protest.

He motioned for Samantha to follow him into his office. She sat in the same chair where she had been fed dates and rice after that first long morning of scrubbing floors. She made a mental note to pick up some fresh dates at the grocery, but promptly forgot when her attention wandered to the faint outline of the secret door on the nearby wall.

Kinetic Star was reborn on the other side of that door.

Jibril seated himself behind his desk and interlocked his fingers, palms resting against his belly. Neither of them spoke for a time. Samantha's eyes roved the bookshelves, lingering on the dry, boring textbooks that had focused her mind, had allowed her to resist Ana's telepathic intrusions for as long as she had.

"I was wondering when you'd finally reach out," she said.

Jibril held her gaze, not blinking.

"I am truly sorry about David Daniels. Had he been a believer, his soul would rest with Allah."

Well that was comforting.

Samantha tried to keep the thought away from her expression.

"Thank you? I never know what to say to—"

"I knew him only for a short time, but he was a born warrior. He persevered to the end when most would have succumbed to their wounds. To their own mortality. His bravery is to be celebrated. Honored. Remembered."

Samantha looked down at her thumbs, which were rubbing over each other in her lap.

He should have called out to me. Should have let me know he was there. I could have protected him.

The thoughts were not new to her. They returned every time she closed her eyes at night, unwanted visitors that held restful sleep as a hostage.

"There is nothing you could have done, Samantha," said Jibril.

I hate when he does that.

"Thank you," she said again. "But I disagree."

"Do you remember the phrase I uttered as I pulled you from the burning museum?"

"How could I forget?" she said. "'And the recompense of evil is punishment like it.'"

Jibril nodded.

"But whoever forgives and amends, he shall have his reward from Allah," he finished for her.

He let that hang there, let it fill the space between them before speaking again.

"You must forgive yourself. You are quite powerful, but you can't save everyone."

She shifted in the wooden chair.

"Did you know, Jibril? Did you know that my powers never truly left me?"

"I had my suspicions, yes," he said. "Ana's control over the mind was near absolute. But the mind controls absolutely."

Sometimes he sounds like a fortune cookie.

"Now I suspect that you have the ability to control your powers, to shut them down if you want or need to."

Samantha's nod confirmed it.

"That's all I ever wanted."

"Your mother's parting gift to you."

"I suppose so," Samantha said, her lips curling into a half smile. "But she was still a royal bitch, you know."

Jibril's thick eyebrows rose at the remark. Samantha remembered where she was.

"Sorry."

Jibril's head bowed in forgiveness.

"I haven't told anyone this, not even my father, but..."

She paused to swallow, her fingers brushing the beginnings of a lock of hair over her ear.

"Please, go on."

Samantha heard her voice crack as the words spilled from her mouth.

"Ana, she...right before the attacks, before the museum, she made me think...she tricked me into believing I was, well, pregnant. I know she was a psychotic maniac and all, but I just...I mean—"

"And the recompense of evil..." Jibril said, propping his fingers into a tent. "I ran a full medical diagnostic on you several times while you were in my care. There was not a trace of pregnancy. Nothing of the sort. There was no child to lose in the trauma you sustained. It was a tactic. A way of appealing to your devotion and loyalty to family, which she manipulated from the moment she woke up in your bedroom until the bullet pierced her twisted heart."

"A tactic? It was a mindfu—"

This time only a single bushy eyebrow rose.

"Sorry," Samantha said. "Again."

"Yet you sit in my office now, healthy and hale, reborn from fire and despair. Grieve for her, yes, but don't let her become an albatross around your neck. Don't let her drag you into those depths. What's done is done, and your best years are ahead of you."

"Right. Maybe thousands of them."

Samantha locked eyes with Jibril, hoping that he'd shake his head in disagreement, wave off her comment like flicking a piece of lint from his shoulder. Instead, he squinted and leaned forward, elbows resting on his desk.

"Perhaps," he said. "That is indeed a possibility."

Watching everyone I love grow old and die over and over again. No thank you.

Samantha decided it was time to change the subject.

"Speaking of the future, what will you do now? Your mission is complete. Ana's gone and I'm safe."

Jibril rose and went to the teapot. He held it out to Samantha, who declined with a polite shake of her head, then took his time refilling his cup.

"I will continue teaching those who seek to know Allah," he said. "I will raise my child to be the best person she can be. Then I will rest."

Samantha crossed her legs and tapped her chin with her forefinger.

"So no more, um, extra-curricular activities?"

She detected the slightest curl at the corner of his mouth.

"We'll see," he said.

So he can smile. I'll be damned.

"Which reminds me of why I asked you here," he said.

"Oh, right," said Samantha.

And here I thought he just wanted to shoot the breeze over herbal tea.

Jibril went to a large chest of aged mahogany and flipped open the burnished brass latch. Old hinges creaked as the lid rose. The object he withdrew was the antithesis of the venerable wooden chest. It was the size of a large briefcase and constructed of black and red leather with shiny metal latticework overlays. He set it at her feet and stepped away to lean against the edge of his desk.

"It seems that a piece of my property was ruined by one Talbot Sharp while in your care. That is unforgivable. I prefer that my equipment remain in pristine condition at all times if it can be helped, especially when it is under loan. However, I'll overlook the destruction of my property this time since you bested Sharp in mortal combat."

Samantha's eyes fell to the futuristic case.

A new suit?

"Try not to let it happen again, Miss McAllister," Jibril said.

Yep. A new suit.

Her hand reached down to pick it up, to explore the technical wizardry he had no doubt integrated into the uniform, but she recalled an early lesson from him and thought better of it.

Never upstairs. Never in the mosque.

"I'm humbled," she said. "Thank you, Jibril. Truly."

He sipped his tea, peering at her over the rim.

"Samantha," he said, his voice softening, "Every hero has an origin, the first chapter in a tale that spans their lifetime, that explores great deeds and terrifying ordeals. Many believe that if a hero lives long enough, they become the villain. The good become evil through the best of intentions. The need for control and order replaces reason and goodwill. It begins innocently enough. A rule is broken, making it easier to cross that line the next time they are faced with an impossible choice. This continues until they can't remember who they were or why they became a hero in the first place.

So go change the world, but go with caution. With mindfulness. Never forget the trials you've faced. The trials you've overcome."

Like that's ever going to happen. Any of it.

Jibril continued, oblivious to her silent retort.

"Ana was born so that you could exist. You are her counterweight on the scales of Allah. You will bring a brilliant dawn to her smothering twilight. Samantha, your origin story is at an end, but your tale is just beginning."

Samantha stood and went to him, engulfing him in a tight hug—whether he wanted it or not. She felt an awkward pat on her back. Her voice was quiet next to his ear.

"Not quite yet," she said. "There's one more thing I need to do."

The sounds were the same as last time. Distant, hacking coughs. Doors opening and closing. The squeak of a gurney wheel whining for repair. The smells hadn't changed either. Bleach and body odor. Pungent soup simmering in a kitchen on another floor, its aroma carried through the ventilation ducts. Even the orderly that walked beside her was the same, along with his stained uniform and thick accent. He was saying something to her, but the assault on Samantha's senses caused her to miss the first part.

"...hemorrhaging in the arteries. They said she won't make it to Christmas. You'll probably want to say your goodbyes."

They stopped before the nondescript door. Samantha's eyes were focused on the faded brush strokes in the plain white paint as the orderly slipped a key into the lock.

"I plan to," she said as the man turned to leave.

Samantha listened to his footsteps until they grew faint, her eyes never leaving the door in front of her. She lifted a hand and held it between her chest and the door, noting its steadiness. Her stomach was calm, her breathing regular. For all of the similarities to her previous visit to this dreadful place, one thing was different.

I'm different.

She opened the door and entered the room.

The wheelchair was squared up facing the entrance, cradling the withered form of a woman once proud and stout. The ruined face met her head on, a lone, beady eye greeting her as she stepped inside. The side of her gaunt countenance that still functioned remained expressionless.

"Hello, Galina."

Galina remained still, staring straight at Samantha. She might as well have been carved from marble.

"I told you I'd be back," said Samantha, turning to close the door behind her.

She stayed where she was, her eyes flickering about the room in quick reconnaissance. The iron-framed bed. The broken ceiling light. The chest of drawers with the array of pill bottles covering the dusty surface. Nothing had changed. Even the postcard Samantha had brought last time was still tucked in the corner of the mirror above the chest of drawers.

Samantha released the doorknob and let her hands fall to her sides. Her attention returned to Galina.

"I'll spare you the self-righteous monologue this time," she said.

Galina's lone eye didn't move, didn't even blink. Her chest rose and fell in shallow swells beneath the filthy gown, the only evidence that the wilted woman was alive. Samantha moved forward and dropped into a crouch, balancing on the balls of her feet mere inches from Galina. The ruined face followed her, the dark eye never breaking contact with Samantha.

"I've come to say goodbye," said Samantha, her voice dropping into a murmur.

She reached out to place a hand on Galina's knee. The woman didn't flinch away as Samantha expected, didn't recoil in horror.

"And that...and that..."

Just say it.

"I forgive you."

Samantha sucked in a deep breath. When she released it she let go of the horror, the pain, the torture that this woman had visited upon her. She let go of the remorse and guilt of what she had done to Galina in return.

She let go of the vengeance.

"I forgive you, Galina," she said.

There was no reaction from Galina whatsoever. The sculptor had become the stone.

Samantha rose and turned to leave without another word. The door closed behind her in a swift, purposeful motion. Her Chuck Taylor All-stars pattered against the linoleum floor of the hallway as she made her way to the elevator. Her mind reached out behind her as she walked, retracing her steps.

The blood passed though the muscular tubes in weak, broken rhythm.

Pum pum...pum pum...pum pum....

Samantha re-entered the lobby and nodded at the receptionist with a smile.

Invisible clamps materialized beneath layers of skin, settling over smooth tissue.

Pum pum...pum pum...

Samantha took up the pen and pressed the tip to the sign-in sheet, making sure to note the time before scribbling it into the column labeled **OUT**.

Samantha squeezed.

Pum... ...pum pum.... pum... ...pum... ....

330

"Have a nice day," said the receptionist.

Pum... ... pum...

"You too," said Samantha.

Several floors above, a ruined mouth twisted into a satisfied smile.

... ... pum... ...

Samantha exited the hospital and raised her face to the sunny December morning.

I forgive you.

....

Chapter Twenty-Six

THE SNIPER LAY FLAT atop the crumbling building to reduce his profile against the skyline. His quarry had just darted into an alcove far below, and there was only one other way out. The reticle filled his vision, the scope enlarging the field of battle and bringing the alternate exit into sharp focus. An anxious finger tapped the trigger, waiting for the precise moment. Gunfire erupted nearby. He wasn't sure whether it was an enemy or an ally, but he wouldn't give up this hunt. Even if it meant dying.

Any second now.

One shot. One kill.

TING!

His phone chimed beside him, demanding his attention, but he refused to take his eye off the prize.

TING!

"Goddammit. Not now!"

Taptaptaptaptap Taptap

The knocking sound came from behind him.

"Fuck!"

He risked a glance at his phone just in time to comprehend the text message before the small screen went back into sleep mode.

Front door

"How in holy hell...?"

Roger stood and tossed the game controller onto the black leather sofa. Rifle shots blasted through the speakers of his top-of-the-line home theater system. One of the four massive television screens that covered his wall darkened with an ominous dirge. Computer-generated blood dripped from the top of the screen to slide over a single word.

DEFEAT!

The other three screens continued their news broadcasts, unaware of the macabre display on the fourth. Roger muttered under his breath and made his way into the foyer, wondering why he'd spent a small fortune on security cameras and a gate guard if anyone could just waltz up to his front door. An assassin had done just that, as a matter of fact.

His agitated tirade was already in progress as he opened the door.

"How the fuck did you get past my secur—"

Large, green eyes peered up at him, perched over a small, freckled nose and below that white teeth were bared in a wide smile.

"Oh," he said. "You."

It made sense now. She didn't need permission to get through a gate. Any gate. Anywhere.

"Hey bro!" she said.

She held up a flat, square cardboard box with an offensive caricature of an Italian chef splayed across the top.

"Brought you pizza," she said. "It's getting cold."

"I'm busy," said Roger.

She cocked her head, her expression quizzical.

"Oh yeah? Whatcha doin'?"

"Playing a video game."

"Can I watch?"

Roger looked over his shoulder then back to his uninvited guest.

"It's getting cold," she reminded him, raising the box a bit higher in case he hadn't seen it.

Roger sighed and pivoted on his heel, leaving the door open behind him.

"It's not like I could really stop you. Right, Samantha?"

He heard the door close behind him followed by the light slaps of rubber soles on tile.

"Probably not," she said.

He pointed to the broad slab of butcher block that made up the surface of the kitchen island.

"What are you drinking? I have beer and...beer," he said, opening the heavy door of his industrial-sized refrigerator.

Samantha plopped the box onto the countertop and opened the lid. The aroma of melted cheese and spicy tomato sauce wafted into the air between them.

"Beer it is," she said.

He set an opened bottle in front of her, then pressed the church key to his own. They stared at each other across the pizza box as they drank at the same time. Roger examined the pizza. It was party cut, with the peppers and onions and mushrooms chopped into tiny bits to accommodate each piece. He hated party cut. He liked wide, greasy slices with large toppings that he could fold and eat like a taco. Nevertheless, he popped an edge piece into his mouth and crunched down.

"Well?" he said, watching Samantha peel a cheesy coin of pepperoni from the cardboard lid and pop it into her mouth.

"Well," she said. "Family is hard to come by these days, and mine seems to be shrinking. Can't a sister drop by and visit her brother?"

Roger washed the pizza down with another swig, his eyes searching the delicious grid for his next victim.

"With proper notice, I guess," he said.

"A brother would have to answer his texts for proper notice to be given."

Roger shrugged.

"I suppose so."

They each took another piece, not speaking until they had chewed, swallowed and drank.

"Thank you, Roger. Thank you for coming to the Mall and joining the fight. Thank you for saving David."

"Did I, though?" Roger said.

Her chewing stopped. Pain flashed over her face, lingering in her eyes before disappearing as if it had never been. Roger averted his eyes to stare past her at the rightmost television screen, which he had dedicated to broadcasts from the BBC.

"You kept him in the fight," Samantha said. "You gave him time to complete his mission. In a way, we won because of you."

Roger shrugged again.

"You're, uh, welcome or whatever."

He didn't miss Samantha's smile as she brought the beer bottle to her lips.

The box was almost empty before they spoke again. Samantha relayed the events surrounding the aftermath of that day. Roger already knew much of it from cable news channels and social media, but he wasn't aware of the truth. The real truth. There was no reaction from him when he learned that their newly discovered half-brothers— the three that had survived—had disappeared, and were now most likely in the hands of the government. Roger knew that he was free and clear, having spent most of the fight in the trees which blocked the views of the cameras placed around the Lincoln Memorial. It turned out that most of those cameras had been destroyed by Samantha's conflict with Talbot before Roger had even arrived. She told him that their mother was dead, but didn't go into details. His complete lack of emotion at this revelation gave her pause.

Apparently Roger Harkins felt nothing and was fine with it.

"So what now?" said Samantha. "Back to good ole Roger Harkins? Yachts and jets and strippers and all that?"

"Yep," said Roger, but his attention had been hijacked from the conversation.

Three of the four television screens in the great room were now showing breaking news, while the fourth continued to remind Roger of his interrupted sniper mission. Three different networks had interrupted their normal broadcasts to present a makeup-laden talking head above a colorful chyron in the bottom third. Large, bold-faced letters summarized the alert.

London Police in Pursuit of Powered Individual

And on the second screen:

England: Authorities Under Attack Near The Thames

And finally:

BBC Reports PM Considering Lockdown In London

Samantha stood and turned, following his line of sight to televisions.

"Did you know about this?" Roger said. "Is that why you came here?"

Samantha didn't answer at first, still processing the information that was being presented in the other room. She shook her head, eyes glued to the broadcasts.

"No. No, I didn't," she said. "I had no idea. How is this possible?"

Roger upended his bottle and drained it. Samantha spun to face him. "Well?" she said.

His empty bottle thumped against the butcher block.

"Well?" he said, painting an expression of confusion on his face that was far from sincere. "What?"

He didn't miss the twinkle in those bright green eyes. He'd seen it before. Roger groaned.

"You gonna go get your super suit?" she said.

Roger pressed his palms into his eyes and rubbed until he saw stars.

"Are you fucking serious?"

"Where's your super suit, huh?" she said. "Where's your weird, rocky, black super suit thingy?"

David Daniels's final words to Roger spilled over the edge of the overflowing, imaginary box labeled **Leave Me Alone** that Roger kept on an easily accessible shelf in his personality.

"You take care of yourself, Roger," David had said. *"And maybe try to be more friendly to your sister?"*

Samantha watched his inner struggle with glee.

"Well, where is it?"

Roger's defeated sigh came from the tips of his camel-colored moccasin slippers.

"It's in the garage."

"See? That wasn't so hard, was it?"

Samantha came around the edge of the kitchen island with her arms spread wide.

"Now c'mere and give your sister a hug."

Roger recoiled from her.

"Don't push it."

Samantha's laugh echoed into the foyer.

ABOUT THE AUTHOR

Jason Andrews is a mild-mannered website editor by day and vigilante writer by night. His passion for a good story can be traced back to the spinning comics rack in the local drug store, where he discovered modern mythological heroes in four-color newsprint.

Jason received his Bachelor's degree in English and began his career as a technical writer for a computer company. His interests have led him into drawing, music, and filmmaking over the years, but he always finds his way back to the keyboard.

His novel Kinetic Star is the first in a series that explores a unique take on the superhero genre.

CONNECT

Website

www.jasonandrewsauthor.com

Facebook

www.facebook.com/JasonAndrewsAuthor

Twitter

@writerandrews

Instagram

@andrewsauthor

Samantha McAllister will return

www.ingramcontent.com/pod-product-compliance
Lightning Source LLC
Chambersburg PA
CBHW051330250626
47155CB00007B/2541